DREAM DANCER

Witch-girl on a backwater Earth. Unwilling heir to the vast Kerrion Empire. Rebel at the deep end of space . . . Shebat Alexandra Kerrion had lived a dozen lifetimes and now she meant to change the future of a dozen universes!

"Combining the rational wonder of SF with the extravagance of the best fantasy!"
—ISAAC ASIMOV'S
SCIENCE FICTION MAGAZINE

"Fascinating and lyrical, told with great invention and all the wit anyone needs!"
—PETER STRAUB, bestselling
author of SHADOWLAND

DREAM DANCER

JANET MORRIS

BERKLEY BOOKS, NEW YORK

This Berkley book contains the complete
text of the original hardcover edition.
It has been completely reset in a type face
designed for easy reading, and was printed
from new film.

DREAM DANCER

A Berkley Book / published by arrangement with
the author

PRINTING HISTORY
Berkley-Putnam edition March 1981
Berkley edition / February 1982

ISBN: 0-425-05232-X

A BERKLEY BOOK ® TM 757,375

PRINTED IN THE UNITED STATES OF AMERICA

For Chris, as they are all for Chris

Author's Note

This is a tale that has not happened yet, unless you believe that time's passage is a mirage, and everything is truly happening all at once. But let us not quibble, so early on. The tale has not yet taken place, as most men reckon time. It begins on Earth and returns to Earth but it is not about Earth at all, except in that cautionary fashion implied by word "yet." It has not happened yet, that man has gone out from Earth to live in habitations of his own creation under distant, variously colored stars. It has not happened that planets have become merely depositories of material, only anchors to swing man-created worlds around. It has not happened that these things have occurred in the now. But I do not mean to imply that they will *not* occur. After all, I have seen it. You take a look on your own, and tell me what you see.

Chapter One

A.D. 2248: On the day after the killer frost took a ready harvest, a trio of cloaked enchanters came riding into Bolen's town, New York, on froth-dappled black horses whose brasses shone like the sun.

There were plenty of folk to remark on the sight, lounging around on board sidewalks and split-rail fences with dour faces and bellies bloated from too much beer and too little food, as folk will when tragedy herds them together, and suddenly there is nothing left to do.

The three horses kicked up dust from one end of the single street in sere Bolen's town to the other. The dust tickled the noses of the townfolk above their kerchiefs; the awkward seats and unfamiliar scarlet eagles blazoned on the black cloaks of the riders tickled their curiosity. And the fact that the dust did not seem to settle on the shiny black boots of the riders kicked up suspicion in one man's mind that these must be the enchanters who had caused the demon frost to strike down their crops.

The suspicion, once voiced, spread through the ragged crowd like dust on the wind, touching one, touching all, uniting them in a heady rebirth of purpose.

These were the culprits who had brought the ill fortune, all agreed.

In a mass of nearly thirty, the people of the town advanced down its single street to Bolen's inn, the ramshackle way station around which the town had grown up and its most imposing building, being possessed of not only a cellar, but an upper floor.

1

The three horses snorted and skittered as the rumbling crowd approached, but their riders had entered the inn, and their reins held them fast to the porch rail.

Inside the inn one of the enchanters, who was tall and well made yet somehow lissome in skin-hugging ebony coveralls relieved with scarlet, pulled back a curtained window. He said something that lilted through his black beard in a language neither fat Bolen nor the uncombed, pinch-faced girlchild waiting sullenly upon the strange ones' table understood. The second man, whose presence it was that made the first seem delicate by the force of his impact and the width of his neck, answered and left the enchantress with whom he had been sitting to disappear through the door.

The enchantress furrowed her creamy brow, brushed an auburn wisp from it, and smoothed her coveralls down over her hips. Then she gave an unmistakable order to the lissome, slighter man, who looked displeased and scratched in his beard, but seemed to obey. At least, he approached the bar.

The barefoot serving girl, watching the first man cross the floor to where Bolen fastidiously wiped tankards behind the bar, tugged at her patched shift and straightened her shoulders in emulation of the regal woman with the shining, chestnut coif. She tried to imagine her black tangles magically straightened, shining like brass. She failed; she sighed.

"Is there another way out of here?" asked the bearded one of Bolen in a clipped, oddly accented voice as from without the rumble of the crowd grew louder.

"My pardon, gentle sir, but there is not," said Bolen carefully, all his chins bobbing in agreement. Everyone knew the dangers of deceiving enchanters. But the crowd wanted this lot. Should Bolen deny them, this would be Bolen's town no more and Bolen himself would be stoned alongside the strangers when they were caught. He was trying to figure out a way to claim their horses when the rumble turned to thunder and the windows shattered in a rain of stones and the door came bursting inward, all the town behind.

The lithe man at the bar whirled around, seemed to arch back like a mountain cat. But even as he did the woman went down clutching her bleeding head, and he hesitated, stunned disbelief giving him a moronic, slack-jawed mien. Then the ragged girl was pulling at him, babbling too fast in a tongue he had superficially learned, dragging him toward the kitchen whence she had first emerged.

A rock caught him as he ducked beneath the curtain, numbing his arm. Then her strong little fingers grabbed at his beard, pulling it violently, and he realized he had not been deciphering her words, only hearing another compendium of unintelligible sounds.

"Get down. Through here. Crawl. Oh, go on!"

"You first," he said grimly, pushing her ahead of him.

He pushed too hard, so that she tumbled down, and he recollected the frail, knobby backbone he had felt through the shift, and the gray, maelstrom eyes pleading, even as he picked up a stained kitchen knife and prepared to take a few of them with him.

But as a toil-roughened hand clutched the curtain from beyond, another clutched his ankle, jerking desperately. Off balance, he went to his knees. The waif's heart-shaped face gleamed out at him from the dim passage. "Please, please, or they will kill me too."

Thrusting the knife through his belt, he crouched low. Wedging himself into the waist-high passage, he pulled shut the door.

Then there was nothing left but to follow the scuttling sounds ahead of him in darkness. Suddenly, there was a crack of light.

"Your horses," the girl's husky voice announced with obvious pride, "are yet waiting. Will you take me with you?"

"I cannot."

"You cannot leave me to their mercy!" Full lower lip grew fuller as determination turned pout to accusation.

"They are your people," he fended her off, fidgeting now that escape was so close. A ridiculous vision of this tangled, odorous primitive garbed in Kerrion flight satins made his grin flash in the semidark.

"Then I will make a diversion for you," she offered dully. "Take which direction you choose and I will take another."

From such selfless courage, Marada Seleucus Kerrion could not turn away.

He rubbed his elbow, flexing his arm which was no longer complaining quite so bitterly, and wondered whether he might not be still dreaming off last night's revel and all this the wages of incontinence. "No," he sighed. "Come on then, small person, and if we reach the horses we will head them both the same way."

"Aieeee," crowed the girl in triumph, lunging through the half-door into the dusty street.

Later, he thanked the clouds that on this benighted world never lessened, and the cover it threw over the racing sprite, all knees and elbows, who by the time he reached her had two pairs of reins free and was trying with no success to mount the tall, dancing horse.

He boosted her up and scrambled atop a second quivering snorter, while from Bolen's inn came howls and crashings and one man's tortured scream rose above the rest.

"Bolen," the girl gasped, full lips blue with terror.

"Too bad," said the man bleakly, for his eyes had seen his broken companion all askew on the steps. "That way," he said pointing, and slapped his horse's rump.

There followed a nightmarish interval of leaves slapping him and branches raking him and pine needles seeking to blind him as the horse plunged wildly through the thicket behind Bolen's inn. By the time he had gained control, Bolen's town was far behind. The thicket became a copse, the copse gave way to forest. It was not until then he looked around to see if the rat-haired waif yet followed.

She did. She rode badly, though perhaps not as badly as he, and when they had been awhile in the lofty, dank trees he called a halt more for her than for the horses.

So there he was, walking a sweating horse in an alien glen with a more alien child whose disposition was easily as much a problem as his own would be to his superiors when all this came to light.

He scraped foam off the horse's neck and tightened the girth, watching her. She was painfully thin, except for her belly. Malnutrition? Her shoulders were sharp, boyish, a distinct contrast to wise, woman's eyes that dominated a child's face. Was that why he had succumbed, brought her along? No, she was not that pretty, or that pathetic.

She was humming as she rubbed her horse with dead leaves.

"How old are you?" While he spoke he prodded a bracelet on his wrist. It sang briefly. He took his hand away.

"Seventeen." She spoke sharply in an impossibly low voice. A shift of the wind brought her pungent odor to him like a warning. But it was too late to heed it. He was committed. And she was lying.

"Truly," he demanded.

"Fifteen." She turned to regard him, letting the leaves fall from her hand. The horse snorted, nuzzling her. She patted its muzzle absently, looking up at him from under the ebon froth that framed her face. Grass and dust hung in its thicket. The eyes, below, said: "You can't blame me for trying."

"Was Bolen your father?"

"No," very softly. "My parents are dead."

"Where would you like to go? Do you have relations, perhaps in the city?" He made his play casually, hoping she would be content, would let him off, take the horse and some money . . .

"No relations. I want to go with you." The pale gray eyes had thick black lashes. They came together, and the man found he had been holding his breath while she looked at him as if he could hold his thoughts withal.

"No, you do not. You do not even know where it is I am going." How could he explain to her that in the Consortium he served, she would be an object of ridicule, an oddity at which people would wrinkle their noses and turn away. He wondered if the malodor was congenital, as the wind brought it to him again.

"I do not care. I have no place else to go," she shrugged. "I will serve you as I served Bolen. You will be pleased with me."

He did not want to think about how she might have been serving Bolen, or might think to serve him. "Time to ride," he said.

"I can do some small enchantments," she proclaimed.

"Then enchant yourself up on that horse."

He mounted and in doing so felt the jab of the kitchen

knife. He took it from his belt. It was low-quality iron, crudely smelted. He threw it down. It stuck, wavering point-deep in the sod.

His elbow, still tender, objected, and he tried to credit the evanescent pain with having caused the catch in his throat. But he knew it was something else, something composed of black iron and unceasing clouds and enchantments and little girls in rags who stunk. From *this,* the mighty Consortium which ruled the stars was sprung?

"What is your name?" he asked, turning the horse deeper into the forest at an easy walk.

"Shebat," she said hesitantly, giving up a great secret.

"Marada," he introduced himself, leaving out all the rest which she would not understand, which made no sense here in this forest of forgetfulness on the world of his private dreaming.

Marada had come home, across vast reaches of lucent space, despite the fair warnings and suddenly sensible restrictions that prohibited landfall on the planet Earth.

His older brother and his betrothed, Iltani, would never leave it. He remembered Iltani's arch challenge: "How bad can it be?" She had found out. But it was not her fault, rather it was his, his alone; his the obsession and his the price to pay.

"You *are* an enchanter," Shebat breathed in fearful delight when she saw the little opalescent reconnaissance ship, perched like a stalking mantis in a sorcerer's seared circle in the verdant meadow. "I was afraid you might not be, after all."

His horse's reaction was quite another matter. By the time he had it calmed and stripped and turned loose in the clearing, the moment had passed to deny sorcery. Watching the little girl kiss the horse on his slobbery muzzle, he wondered whether there might not be *something* for such a one to do in the far-flung empire of the Consortium he served.

"You are *sure* you would not rather go to the city, apprentice at some trade? I will give you money, secure you a position. You can grow up to be the Enchantress of all the Earth." He had to kneel down to see her face, for she would not look at him. He took her by the arms, but she only repeated that she had nowhere to go and wanted to be with him.

So he took her onto the ship and showed her how to strap in, and soon there was nothing left in the dim clearing but a patch of seared ground and harness for two horses, and the beginnings of a legend that the townfolk—peering through the bushes but afraid to face the mighty enchanter, whose fire-spouting chariot rose on a deafening roar almost straight into the heavens—would tell to their friends and relations and to their children and their children for generations to come.

Within the antiquated reconnaissance ship needling upward, the sanguine enchanter in black relieved with red plied his trade. His aquiline profile bowed to flickering crystals whose images were never still. His voice hissed out softly in incantation. From somewhere above her head the air itself gave answer. Shebat shivered and looked around the padded, inward curving, light-bestarred chamber. An enchanter's cave? She had not heard of mobile caves before. Nevertheless, this cramped enclosure with its soft sitting beds was both more numinous and more luxurious than anything she had ever experienced. Shebat told herself fiercely that this was the most important day of her life, every bit of which she should remember, especially the enchanter, who could call voices out of thin air and command the lights of many colors and cause the crystal windows to show him whatsoever he might choose. She stared very hard around her, committing what she saw to memory. Understanding would come later, she swore, as Marada fell silent and turned slowly toward her. Or rather, made the very chair-bed in which he sat turn slowly, but not so slowly that the two gold rings of chain dangling from his ears did not swing madly.

"Your staring is going to burn holes through my back," he reproved.

He was more handsome than she had previously realized, though in a refined way that made him seem more alien. His beard reaching cheekward, his black hair reaching his shoulders, could not roughen his aspect sufficiently to disguise the androgynous, heavy-lidded eyes under straight, brief brows. Char-brown, they settled wide flung between distant cheekbones. His lips were spare, unyielding, antithetical to the poet's eyes, as if a battle was underway between the aboves and belows of his face.

"No, I cannot do anything like that," she answered.

"What? Never mind. I want to make you understand something. I am not an enchanter. Nothing I do is done of sorcery. It is science, the ingenuity of man that I practice, and that makes possible all you see about you."

"Then, teach me this science," she demanded, unaware that her lower lip had edged out into a pout.

He laughed, more easily at the beginning than the end, which trailed off in a way that told her he was troubled.

Then he said, "If it can be, I will see to it. But it is up to you, whether you have the capacity to learn." Most of them did not, a result of years of inbreeding humanity's dregs. He saw the small heart-face whiten, the gray eyes measuring him with a wisdom too sharp for her years. When the rats were combed from her black hair and her swollen belly shrunken with good food and her legs and arms not so bony, she might, after all, be a pretty child. But whether she could be taught complex subjects at the age of fifteen with no previous education and a strong genetic disadvantage, he could not even venture to guess. Blowing out an exasperated breath, and the stench of her with it, he began to consider who among his acquaintances might be able to help him with that problem, and then reminded himself that Shebat would not be anyone's problem if he did not think of some way to qualify her for citizenship in the Consortium, however limited that citizenship might have to be. After long consideration he found only two cogent solutions: to make her his ward in full adoption, or to make her his wife. Since he was not ready to be disowned by his kin, he chose the former. Then he thumbed open the channel to the great-grandmother of all habitational spheres, which had been called the Stump so long that the reasons for its name were lost in antiquity. To the same operator who had taken his report on the loss of two lives, he commended the alteration of another. Assured that he would have no trouble debarking the girl without entry papers, he remembered that she had been sitting, silent and unmoving, since he had deferred the matter of whether she might be teachable.

The stony countenance that regarded him had a slight tilt to it that instructors and foes alike would come to respect highly. "I can learn," she challenged him as if no time had intervened.

The language assimilation program he had used to while away the trip to her gutted planet still lay in his ship's bank. "Let us see," he said, and began to set up the program in reverse. When it was ready, he handed her the headset.

She did not speak again until it was nearly time for him to ready the ship to enter the docking bay. "Marada," she said slowly, experimentally, "I am hungry." And then she burst out laughing, for she had spoken to him in Consulese, the lingua franca of the Consortium.

And he, seeing his ready-lights flashing, reached over and took up the small white hand and kissed it without looking away from his work. What he was piloting was a near-idiot reconnaissance craft, crude, rude and in chancy repair. The Stump's bay was the oldest in the whole of the Consortium's ten thousand platforms, and no ship's pilot had entered it on instruments in years. So it was that he was too busy to glimpse the beatific radiance of the girl Shebat, who held one hand cradled to her promissory breast while she listened to the chatter of clearance and attitude corrections with triumphant understanding of the words, if not the meaning.

That will come, it will come, she told herself fiercely and, very cautiously so that he would not detect her meager ability, cast a spell of twelve coils binding over Marada to protect him from all evils of the night.

"We are almost there," he said. The tip of his nose bobbled when he spoke. "This is your last opportunity to see back the way you have come. After this, you must look only forward, and forget from where you came." And he passed his hand over a light: once, twice.

Shebat screamed. She kept on screaming long after the starry night with the bilious, oversized moon was gone from before her. But she saw it, even behind the palms pressed to her eyes: dark, dark, all around, dark.

"Where did you think we were?" she heard him ask, but she could not answer. Black, black night full of evil dreaming filled her sight and heart and her mind. The

tales of enchanters' depravity in the dark night among the
stars were true: here she was, carried off ensorceled as
children always were. But to what purpose?

It was that bitter curiosity which made her take down
her palms from her eyes, saying: "I am not a virgin, you
know. Stump only eats virgins."

Marada had been darkening all his lights, one at a time
with a touch. He stopped, straightened and turned to her
very slowly, saying: "What did you say?"

"I said, I am not a virgin, and Stump only eats virgins,
everyone knows that. So your debt will have to be paid
another way."

"I see," said the enchanter, leaning back against the
console. "Well, why did I go to all the trouble of teaching
you Consulese if I was going to do that?"

"Perhaps you are not so great an enchanter as you
claim. Perhaps you did not know. Your two friends could
not even keep their lives from the crowd's wrath. And you
were looking around in the kitchen for a way out, not
trying to save them, or even avenge them."

"It is not for us to strike down the helpless. I have lived
that adage so long it never occurred to me that the
helpless might strike first. Now my betrothed is dead."
Marada sighed deeply, then without taking his eyes from
her reached behind him and slapped at something. There
was a hissing and a light of soft quality flooded the room.
"Shebat," said the man gently, "I should not have teased
you, even for a moment. The Stump is an old name for
this place like a little Earth, and there is nothing here in
the least malevolent, any more than magical. Those
objects that caused you to scream when you viewed them
were the very Earth, and its moon. Sometimes, long ago,
talented children would be taken up to the little world you
are about to see. Like you, they must have been frightened at first. But Shebat, none of those who went ever
came back down to tell your people where they had gone,
because they did not choose to. Because they had no
reason to come back. . . ."

"You mean, never?"

"I mean, I doubt if you will want to. If you ever do, just
call me, wherever I am, and I will come and take you
home. That is my word, given formally. You are my ward,

or will be, summarily. Will you accept it, formally?"

"Yes," she said, stifling her objections that in the case of the enchanters who held the people of Earth in mortal subservience, there was oft-demonstrated malevolence, and mighty spells of example and retribution. There had been the early frost, because a townsman had denied a whim to the Arbiter of Enchantments. . . .

But Marada came and leaned over her, unbuckling her harness, lifting her effortlessly, and she caught her breath and lay her head on his shoulder, moving not a muscle until he put her down before the open port. She saw a dazzle of struts and lights, a cavernous expanse along which a little buglike carriage rolled smoothly without horses. Deceptively slow seemed its approach, but soon she could see the man inside it. Then Marada was urging her down dizzying lattices of stepwork that rang every time his boots struck them. Under her bare feet, they were cold, treacherous. She concentrated on negotiating them.

"They accord us great honor," he told her under his breath. "The secretary to the proconsul himself drives that lorry." The partially assimilated lexicon in her mind equated proconsul with governor, but her heart told her this sour man in his sorcerous transport was one of the most vile enchanters who held her people in thrall. She reached out and insinuated her hand into Marada's. He smiled at her encouragingly, and kissed the top of her head. "Do not worry."

She clambered up into the magical yellow carriage driven by an auburn, spectral man who managed to glower while not looking at her, settling into the yielding seat with a thrill that made her fingertips and the ends of her toes tingle. It was not a thrill of fear, for the powerful blackbearded enchanter was beside her, his arm thrown casually across the seat behind her head. Craning her neck, she seemed to study the vaulted ceiling with its bright lights and great crossbeams, but in truth she sought the infinite delight of laying her head on his arm. The cart jolted, as if one of its many wheels had struck a rock, and picked up speed. Above, superstructures painted with designs gave way to a tunnel of curved metal, where segmented lights blurred into a steady stream as their conveyance picked up speed.

"As far as I am concerned, her people and ours are conspecific," Marada was saying deliberately. The word was not among those the talking earmuffs had taught her at the enchanter's bidding. The jolt of the carriage had caused him to shift closer; his thigh rested against her own. She thought her heart might burst from excitement, and from something else that made her turn her head to the right so that she could watch the way his lips moved in their fringe of hair.

"I am aware of the Consortium's official position, but you are a long way from civilization, Arbiter, and from the Kerrion platforms where your opinion is of some moment. However, here are your papers and its, er, hers. I still think you should let us test her," grumbled the spectral man as he handed a package, wrapped in fine paper that seemed never before to have been used, across her to Marada.

But Shebat was not impressed by the virgin paper as she might otherwise have been. *Arbiter?* Her flesh turned so cold that the arm beneath her head and the thigh meeting hers seemed to scald her. There was no need to consult her new vocabulary for the meaning of that word: every denizen of Bolen's town cowered before its speaking, so that she had known it from her earliest days.

Marada was saying: "—get those bodies up here, posthaste. Have your 'enchanters' retrieve them. By the way, is it really necessary to propagate a reign of terror over a people whose situation could hardly be more abject?"

"Sir, I have a feeling you are going to find your own answer to that question, sooner than you might choose." He looked meaningfully down at Shebat. "And in a manner more convincing than anything *I* could say. I will have the proconsul order the retrieval of the bodies of your brother and your betrothed. They will be at your ship by 2400. Until then, I offer you the hospitality of the consulate and the proconsul's sympathies."

The magical cart seemed about to crash into a blank wall as tall as her faraway forest's oldest trees. She tensed, reached out for Marada, then stayed her hand.

The arbiter was talking yet to the other man, unconcerned. Then the blank wall split in half, drawing apart:
Shebat gasped as the eye-teasing vista of the Stump
opened before her. Above her head the sky rippled, a
candent pewter pond. From glaucous downward-curving
hills around it shining villages like jasper berries seemed
to hang suspended. Before her, a serpentine construction
of shimmering glass and enchanted iron glimmering bright
as silver crouched above the cinereous roadway, which
seemed to disappear within it.

The man who controlled the cart caused it to pull up to
a tessellated path that led to trident-blazoned pavonine
doors, saying, "Sir, you are from very far away. I suggest
you consider yourself lucky. I must remind you that you
were granted landfall at your own risk, against our
objections; and that you have bent the rules about as far
as you can without breaking one, Kerrion or no, in case of
which I doubt whether even your esteemed kinship bond
group could help you. Keep your pet in sight, Arbiter, lest
something happen to it."

"Let's hope nothing does," drawled Marada, sliding
out of the lorry and lifting the girlchild out of her seat. He
did not understand why she was suddenly so stiff against
him, putting it down to awesome sights and the disorientation of a planetdweller first confronted with an inverted
horizon.

It was much later, inside a gaudily threadbare visitors'
suite done in chatoyant taupes that he drew from Shebat
her understanding of what an "Arbiter of Enchantments"
was and did.

Cracking his knuckles in consternation, he paced before
the deep sofa in which the ragged girl was sunk, curled in
its corner with her feet drawn up, watching him from
leaden, luminous eyes full of resignation.

His disclaimer of the "enchantment" part of the title
did not ease her.

Out of the oral tradition which was the only store of
lore she possessed, she replied, "Thus it has always
been," incontrovertibly fatalistic.

"Well, it is not like this, everywhere, between the
platforms and the planets. Some consular families, mine

included, even maintain planetary estates. Shebat, you must trust me, not only half the time, but all of the time, if I am to help you."

She merely looked askance at him, calmly waiting, her bony shoulders hunched up about her ears.

He found himself at the end of his patience. Doubts he had not had previously crowded in upon him. Had he done the right thing? His professional self said he had not had enough information to make a decision, that he had acted without clarity, out of some murky self-aggrandizement, and that he had better start making sure that when there was enough information by which to make a judgment, that then the judgment would be incontrovertibly in his favor.

By her shrinking away, he realized he was hulking over her, glaring, and he knelt down there, taking her hand. "Little one, I have many problems, of which you are the smallest, but not the least grave. When I was your age, I was taught that no opinion can be held before investigation and meditation on its results, that any opinion formed on conjecture is unworthy of consideration. To that end, on the journey you might study the history of the Consortium, which is your history as well as mine, and you will see better how things developed, and how they have come to be."

Shebat huddled mute.

"Or, I can still send you back, if you have changed your mind."

She is just a child, an innocent, he thought, when still she merely regarded him from under her tangled black hair. He would have to get her cleaned up, if indeed this undertaking was not to be more of a disaster than two deaths and an adoption had already made of it. And he must civilize her, somehow, in ten days' time. Something deep inside him said smugly that he was so concerning himself because he was unable to face his real problem, painful and perhaps insurmountable: Iltani, who had been his to wed from the day of her birth, was dead. His elder brother who would be as much of a loss to their father as the girl would be to him, whenever he felt it. When would that be? When would the bubble burst like a ruptured pressure suit and spill his guts into the vacuum?

He said to Shebat, holding lifeless, cold hands in his:

"Citizenship is a serious matter. Should you not want to be a productive member of the Consortium, I cannot, would not dare to force you. It is a thing men crave, that they strive for, and have been known to kill for. An accident of birth puts me in a position to offer it to you. Do you understand? My adopting you is a matter of influence and its wielding. My family is haughty and powerful and may not be more than superficially gracious. Should you not covet this advantage, my conferring it on you will go hard with me. You asked, or I would not have brought you. Since you are here and I am here, and you have heard what perhaps you should not have heard, and I have done what perhaps I should not have done, let us take this moment to become of one mind: say your choice, citizenship or no; go or stay and be bound by your word to perform whichever without regret or hesitation." In his beard, only the very corners of his mouth tried to smile. "Say, Shebat."

Never had anyone consulted her about anything, much less asked her to make a decision. And the arbiter was not just anyone. "Then I will not be your pet?"

"By the Cosmic Jest, you will not."

"I will stay."

"And no more talk of the past and its prejudices?"

"I promise."

"Then let's get out of here and buy you clothes. Or perhaps you should take a shower first. A clean body goes well in clean clothes."

"Shower?"

Marada turned his head away in soft laughter. "Come and I will show you the magic of the bath." But he cautioned himself, seeing something as she stretched out childish limbs gangly in a rush of growing toward womanhood, something he found in her accepting, hungry eyes.

And so Shebat of Bolen's town became Shebat of the consular house of Kerrion; ward of the consulate Kerrion and the consuls thereof under the aegis of Marada Seleucus Kerrion, second son of the consul general Parma Alexander Kerrion, whose line had not ceded that seat in an election for nearly two hundred years.

All this was learned by Parma Alexander Kerrion, in

far Draconis, administrative sphere of Kerrion space, even while Shebat Kerrion learned to make hot water jump from the taps with a touch of her hand.

Had Marada been intended to succeed his father by primogeniture, he would have been an Alexander; all consuls general sprung from the house of Kerrion had always been Whomsoever Alexander Kerrion by reason of their primacy and their founding sire's historical whimsy.

The news of the death of Marada's elder brother would put the capital cities of a dozen worlds and the whole of one thousand sixty Kerrion platforms into deep mourning that would be well under way when the second son returned home with his brother's corpse; the ruination of a capital merger of gargantuan proportions symbolized by the body of his slain bride-to-be; and a girl of undivulgable heritage and questionable humanity. That Marada had unilaterally entered a planetdweller into a family than whom no more elite existed among the habitational platforms of the stars was the final burden which caused the distraught father to seek drink wherewith to steady his buckling knees.

Drunk as a sorrowing man could manage to remain when so sorely beset with difficulties, Parma sent his bald secretary scurrying out with orders: to inform the other consuls general of the formal day of mourning ten days hence; to send consolation to the dead girl's kinship bond group and begin joint funeral arrangements, suggesting as a site the Kerrion's most inner sanctum, Lorelie; to arrange a meeting with the patriarch thereof, that the projected union of Kerrion and Labaya not be stymied and the creation of the greatest bloc in the entire Consortium aborted thereby. And there was a final order, one the glabrous, anile secretary was most pleased to send speeding toward the fringes of civiliation, one that called Marada Seleucus Kerrion to audience in Lorelie ten days hence.

The sly old man would have given an outrageous sum to be in Lorelie on the day young master Marada faced Parma's fabled justice. But in Lorelie, whose hills were said to glow like sapphires and whose winds sang all the day, not even hoary Jebediah, most trusted retainer, could venture foot. Only those of Kerrion blood, since its orbit was set about the ringed world that anchored it in the bright sky of Centralia, had ever touched down there. Even the servants were of the Kerrion kinship bond group, had always been. But in ten days that would change, for the Labaya bond would not refuse so grave and prestigious an invitation.

Or would they?

For a moment, wizened Jebediah hesitated at his desk. He had a child or two himself, though no brood like the Consortium masters raised. How would he feel if one of such well-known impetuosity as Marada wooed his daughter to her death? His fingers hesitated, moved to the toggle that would open his master's channel. It would not have been the first time he had joggled old Parma's fusty wits. But then, what did he owe the senescent tyrant, after all? His finger retreated, impulse unfulfilled.

Instead, he fed the curt messages into the processing slot, and began closing down his office for the night, though there was no night that truly came to the platforms, nor day either. Old ways persist, he thought, and went around to the consul general's eagle-blazoned doors when all else was done. He knocked softly, received no answer, caused the doors to draw back very slightly. Through the crack came the sound of the stricken father's broken sobs.

With infinite care, Jebediah closed the doors again and tiptoed through the darkened foyer. Let him weep: he had lost his Perseus, and rash Icarus stood next in line. No wonder Parma was a broken reed. Were Jebediah in his seat, he might have called for a dream dancer to ease his soul. He wheezed a chuckle, thinking about dream dancers. He was feeling a bit in need of consolation himself, and he was not Parma, so he did not need to be so careful. There are some things in life which are worth the risk, he well knew, having often savored the particular one that drew him inexorably down the flights to the lower levels, where the streets were, and such things as dream dancers could be bought.

Chapter Two

The ten days shipboard passed in a quick-drawn breath of excitement for Shebat, though so much had happened to her in such a brief span that her head spun when she considered it and her amazement spoke into that spinning that nothing more wondrous strange could happen than had already befallen her. But happen such things did, crowding in, jostling each other's dazzling raiment to be the next to astound her.

Previously, there had been the sable "flight satins" and the "shop" where Marada took her to choose them, which were finer than festival garb and more mystifying than even the sky rippling above her head like a puddle perpetually showered with pebbles. Her gaping prompted Marada to tease her about keeping her mouth closed, but despite her wariness each new thing weirder than the last would elicit its tithe of sighs, and when she would remember to check again, she would find her lips parted, the odorless dry air wafting at will between her teeth, and Marada's ingenuous grin sparkling out from his beard like her last sight of Earth gleaming out from its dark abode. Then she would close her mouth tightly. But the gilded shop and the smoky, soft undergarment called a mil-suit which fit her like a second skin; which covered her from toes to fingertips to neck in cloudy shimmer; which Marada slowly explained would keep her soul within her body (well, he did not say soul, but that was what Shebat thought he meant) and the cold without; which could

18

protect her from harm by any projectile made of metal, or any made of light (this she just accepted: *laser* was in her vocabulary but out of her experience); *but* could not—and here Marada's tone rasped dry and ragged—protect her from a common rock or wooded shaft or any organic attacker that was in the mil-suit's experience not unfriendly—

Here Shebat stopped him, disbelievingly asking: "But it is not alive, this suit of skin?" while plucking with smoky fingertips at the shadow-gilded back of her other hand.

"Most exactly, it is alive. The mil-suit is—" She saw, as she had seen too often, him searching an explanation simple enough for her to understand. "—alive, an organic, living being, although designed by man. Its name comes from a measurement of thickness, its purpose is one of enclosing whatever is within, impervious to attempts by foreign objects to penetrate it . . . like a cell wall." He stopped, seeing her eyes go sideward, as they did when she did not understand. "It is just exactly like your skin, but tougher. It was meant to keep a man's blood in his body should all the air be drawn out of the ship in an accident, and to protect him from the crushing pressures beneath planetary seas in olden times, and from excessive acceleration in these days—"

She was looking at her feet, newly imprisoned in obsidian enchanter's boots.

Despairingly, he gave up trying to make her comprehend. "As you have seen, a rock or two can defeat its protection, but none throw rocks who abide the platforms."

Head still bowed, she murmured: "Is it this that keeps the dust from settling on enchanters' boots?"

He laughed, and her head raised sharply, somber eyes resentful at being infinitely the butt of his joke. He apologized, and said that indeed such was the case, inasmuch as the boots themselves had a similar coating of mil.

Shebat resolved to learn all there was to know, so that none could laugh at her for not knowing.

She could not see herself, so she could not see the hot iron glowing in her glare like a dagger taking temper in a forge. But Marada saw it, and added that moment to the load of disquieting events he was carrying, that slowed his progress and made his feet sink searching purchase in quaggy ground at every step. He looked around for the salesperson, who folded and refolded a clear mil-suit nearby in shameless eavesdropping, and motioned the portly man near, saying he also needed a mil-hood. The man's hirsute eyebrows raised, that a child of this age had never taken the hooding or so early had worn it through, but a Kerrion was a Kerrion, and though the Stump was a protectorate of the Orrefors bond, it would not do to question. And the price, of course, demanded a particular courteousness. Quickly the jobber calculated what the hooding of a fifteen-year-old might be worth, and went humming off to prepare an order, which would have to be executed, he assured Marada Seleucus Arbiter Kerrion, after the midday meal.

Which suited Marada, who needed at least that long to prepare the girl for the moment of choking panic, of smothering in unyielding dark in a hum-filled coffin, while the hood was fitted to not only the outer face and form, but to the inner cavities of her body.

"We are only started," he assured her as her glance followed the bustle of the corpulent proprietor, "making you into a Lady of the Consortium. Now comes the part you will like the best, if you are anything at all like the other ladies of my acquaintance: shopping. Then we will go to the finest restaurant in the Stump and shall feast the feast we have well earned, and then come back here to make sure that your head, your eyes, mouth, throat and lungs will be as well protected as the rest of you is now."

Shebat smiled, not because she was pleased, but because she wanted to please Marada. So she made no sign that the one-piece flight satins bound her in the crotch and about the arms, but copied Marada, unsnapping them at the wrist and bending the cuffs back. About the bite of the beautiful boots, she said not one word, but stumbled along determinedly after him, as he led her hither and thither, collecting additional subtle tortures to be worn about the waist or at the throat, where the mil-suit's butterfly-delicate pressure ceased.

When she thought back, at the end of the ten-day journey, it was the moment of the fitting of the mil-hood that caused her the most regret: in that moment she had lost all resolution and behaved like the barbarian Marada was with quiet desperation coaching her no longer to be, screaming (though he could not hear), gagging (though he could not know), pounding and kicking at the close enclosure that sizzled with noises like swarming bees (though he could not see). By the time the sarcophaguslike enclosure was reopened, she was leaning back, unmoving, breathing regularly. But the stink of fearful sweat preceded her out of the body chamber and on the sterile air rode straight to their noses: the proprietor's wrinkled distastefully; even Marada's nostrils flickered, pulling together briefly. Though his words were free of any notice, Shebat knew instantly that there was no place in the Stump for the pungent harvest of fear to hide. That he knew her fear shamed her, that he took her with discreet haste to their quarters forthwith riled her belly; that she cared so much what opinion he held of her took all the pleasure from her high-glossed finery of Kerrion red and black: even her bossed boots such as an enchantress might wear no longer pleased her.

It was that same evening when in the dark which whined and crackled and spat she could not sleep, she snuck in an age-long procession of stealthy steps out of her bedroom and into his bed.

He did not wake. Or he pretended not to wake. If he did, she was sure as she stood over his bed and drew the covers back and up, he would shoo her back to her own pallet. So she worked a deeper sleep onto him with her utmost skill, one hand drawing arcane figures in the air over his tousled head while the other held the blankets high. And the trails her finger, writing in the air, left were etched in blue, hovering a short while after above his head, illuminating his face in a soft glow, so that she knew the spell was well cast and strong.

In beside the sleeping man she slid, greatly comforted, her skin cold against his heat, her hip and thigh touching his. Twelve coils binding, she had put upon him earlier, to keep him safe, thus she had no fear that something might come upon him during the night, though he slept the sleep from which no man might return unbidden.

So it was that he slept with her and did not know, slept

until she herself woke at a shamefully late hour, betook
herself to her own bedroom, less malevolent now that the
"day" was come, and from there recalled the soft cocoon
in which Marada snored far from the sounds and sights of
life.

He had never slept better, he said to her over a meal he
had sent to their suite, and he had not been sleeping well
of late. But he had slept so long that they must hurry: the
ship had been readied for departure long since, and his
sudden somnolence would be ill-received by those who
controlled traffic to and from the platforms.

As she chewed the exotic foodstuffs doggedly, she
listened to the apologies, to the cajolery, finally to the
sharp hiss of anger that draped Marada's threats as he
spoke to a series of noncorporeal voices and ranks. At last
he seemed to have prevailed against the disembodied
speakers: they had been granted a new hour at which to
depart.

There was a great hurrying, a stuffing of her new
clothing into an equally new container of shimmering mil-
like substance, and a porter come to carry all to the ship.

But the ship, when she saw it in its cradle of lights, was
not the little pearly, spiky mantis of a ship she had gotten
into on Earth and out of at this place of endless wonders.

This was a grand, deep-water fish, roughly scaled,
opaline, striolate, polychrome lights binding it round. By
a commodious port the crimson eagle blazed. Beneath it
numbers danced: beside the numbers was the word
"Hassid." The ship was of awesome size, Shebat thought,
though Marada called it small. It was possessed of salons
and three cabins more elegant than the fine suite that had
held them overnight in the consular house of Orrefors.
But each cabin held more than opulence: the personal
effects and tastes of three very different personalities
therein had their say: they whispered to Shebat louder
than the three padded couches in the control room of the
ship; they spoke more clearly than the two refrigerated
corpses in gilded coffins draped with hastily fabricated
Kerrion blazons in the cargo bay. They spoke to Marada,
and he spent a time alone in each cabin in turn, leaving
Shebat to her own devices, emerging at last with arms full
of items and eyes full of grief.

His mouth, that day, seemed empty of words, or of tongue to speak them. He contented himself with a gesture when giving her the soft, pearly room that had surely been his lady's. When at dinner she bantered briefly, his scowl quickly seared all her own words to ash.

During the taking of space by the craft, there came no voice speaking from the air, after a monosyllabic exchange with the disembodied dispatcher of the Stump. And there was no sensation to prove to her that the marvelous Leviathan was truly embarked, no blinking of lights or flipping of toggles, though lights abounded and toggles bristled the control room's waist like quills on a porcupine. Shebat sat in a soft, canted couch to Marada's right. Sometimes he reached over her and brought a panel into view, livened it with a touch, but no more.

When it occurred to her that were she the woman who had sat here previously—for the couch was smaller than that on his left and was doubtless the enchantress's own, as the cabin was her own and Marada, too, was hers seemingly as much in death as in life—that woman, were she in Shebat's place, would have known what to do, would have been, in fact was accustomed to, bringing quiescent panels into rainbow excitation: *flying the ship!* Shebat's excitement overcame her kindness, her envy drove her empathy away, and she demanded: "Teach me to fly it!"

"No!"

"But she flew it."

He sighed, leaned back, staring straight ahead. *"She* and I were betrothed, so the ship and she needed to make acquaintance. I have returned all sensitivity to the master panel: if something happened to me during our flight, it would do you no good to have your keyboard sensitized. It was not a practical matter, in any case, but Iltani's whim and my pleasure to please her. These ships, unlike the little bird who came at my call in the forest, are tuned to the minds of their operators; one ship, one mind, though the possibility of sharing the navigation does exist. In this case, if I should drop dead this moment, the *Hassid* would still bear you without incident to my family's welcoming arms." He said it with a pride like a parent's in an exceptional child: like such a parent, he was boasting.

Why this was so she did not understand, but neither did she doubt her assessment.

She remembered the moment on horseback when she had seen him touch a bracelet, heard it sing, then fall quiet. He had not worn it since they had arrived at the Stump, but she had thought nothing of that. Still, another thing concerned her more: "Die? Why would you die? Are you sick? No man dies of grief!"

"How old did you say you were?" he retorted, but she made no answer.

"Normally, passengers do not talk to a pilot while he is navigating. It is not so easy, being with the ship and with you, both at once. I have heard that in the olden days, men died from it, from losing themselves between the stars, from not concentrating on what they are doing."

"But you are not doing anything!" Shebat cried defensively.

Marada's laugh was not kind, and at last he looked at her. "Go to your cabin, if after this you cannot keep silent. You will learn about the sponge between the worlds of space, soon enough. The ship and I speak silently, there is no need to touch more than the alarm to wake her. All this—" He waved around at the panels. "—is for a passenger's safety, should the pilot be incapacitated; or for the pilot's safety, should the ship's brain be incapacitated. But if either were to happen, that safety is not, by any of this, assured. We travel awesome distances, the only temporal binder being the insistent chronology of the human mind. In accelerating to the speed at which punching through the fabric of space is practical, elapsed ship time and planetary, platform, or calendar time are at variance. In a sojourn behind the surface of temporality, human time readjusts this variance, biological time being adamant and unchanging. The amenable nature of sponge—this reality behind the curtain of space—reverses any loss, until when one emerges, the time that one thinks has passed is indeed the time that has passed for those in the worlds of spacetime. Without the human part of the circuit, such travel would be impractical if not impossible. Do you see?"

"I see that you have told me not to talk and yet give a lecture. No, I do not see, but I suppose when I have learned to become such a pilot then I will."

He regarded her evenly. "Do not settle on that as an occupation. It is a thing that women can seldom do."

"But Iltani did it."

It seemed then when he winced that she might also have shuddered; casting the bolt was as hard for her as for him receiving it. She had spoken the dead enchantress's name.

He cast her out from the room where the ship's mind lived, telling her to content herself with the pearly cabin like rose-touched marble, to whose walls she might speak to her heart's content.

And content for a time she was with that, with the purring voice that answered endless questions without ever tiring, or rebuking, or making light of what might be asked. So content did she become in the company of *Hassid*'s womanly speech and the quality of the enlightenment she was granted by its aegis, that soon she forgot her anger at Marada, forgot even that she had entered the room with head hanging and neck aprickle, as she had walked often to the dung house to sleep when Bolen sought to impress upon her dull wit this lesson or that. She forgot, in a fashion, that she spoke to a disembodiment, a magic, or—how to conceive it?—to the mind of the great metal hull. She remembered, instead, a mellifluous voice from a gently blurred face hovering over a comforting form robed like the old goddess's statue hidden between the rocks a half-day's walk from Bolen's inn. She would lie on that bed softer than the down of fifty geese with her arm crooked over her eyes, and speak endless questions. And *Hassid* would answer untiringly, with never a hint of impatience. When Marada would call Shebat out to dinner, his voice flying to her ear instead of *Hassid*'s murmur, or her own—then she was always surprised that the room was empty, but for herself and the decorative tastes of the dead enchantress—and irritable, like one rousted out of bed before the sun to serve a horde of hard-trekking nomads—and blinking, like a cat caught in sudden torchlight.

But on the morning of the tenth day of their journey, all her contentment was washed away. Marada sluiced it from her with a quiet reminder that this was the day of debarking, that she should pack her things. Even his offer to let her sit again in the couch to his right while he brought the *Hassid* into her cradle did not ease the shock rolling over Shebat like frigid water.

She got wordlessly up and went into the pearly cabin and gathered her things, blinking often and fiercely. But the water flooding her eyes would not be banished so easily. Should she speak tender farewells to her invisible tutor? Could she, without dissolving her courage under a cascade of salty tears? She muttered hallowed formulae in her own tongue, her diction rough and uneasy after so long speaking Consulese. When she was ready all but for her heart, she went to the door, whose obverse gave back a reflection of who stood there, examining herself as she had not since she had spent so long there the day she had discovered it, trying to catch some hint of the mil-hood's presence between skin and air.

But like the voice of *Hassid,* the mil-hood's comfort was as invisible as a summer breeze. Shebat ran fingers through jet, wavy hair that suffered no tangle or speck of dust to mar its sheen. This, at least, was an improvement that promised not to be temporary. Once around Shebat pirouetted slowly. The stranger in sable flight satins wore them familiarly, open at the throat, tucked into gleaming boots. Shebat shivered at the girl whose gaze met hers. Then, with a lilting song she had sung from babyhood to summon up courage and dam back the tide of fear, she took wordless leave of the opalescent cabin whose student she had most willingly become, pausing only once in her song's rhythm: to kiss softly the doorjamb before she crossed its portal.

"Goodbye, *Hassid.* I will not forget what you have taught me."

But the room was silent. Marada had called its attention elsewhere.

Crystalline Lorelie lay bedizened in the brilliant heavens of Centralia, a testimony to Kerrion wealth, Kerrion style and Kerrion largess. Taste, had said grizzled Selim Labaya sourly as he traversed this same route thirty-six hours before Marada, had been no part of Kerrion concern when the platform had been conceived.

And the leather-jowled Labaya had not been wrong:

Lorelie sat like the central jewel in a monarch's fillet, the ringed giant about which she spun regardless of the difficulties in such a placement only pointing up the excellence of Kerrion skill. The choice of such a turgid planet (made more extravagant by the wealth of frozen oxygen, ammonia, and hydrogen that ringed her, unplundered, a mere decoration for the Lorelien sky) whispered of pride beyond conscionable limits and discernment refined so as to approach amorality. With the ability to stabilize a geosynchronous orbit around such a world should have come not one monumental temple of a platform, but a man-made ring of mining docks, shipping platforms; the busy glint of cargo ships like happy workers around a sweet hive.

And a specially sweet hive was the anchor of Lorelie's midsummer dream vista, Alexandria.

Selim Labaya had shaken his head, pursed his mouth in which the spittle had suddenly turned chalybeate, and called his shipboard bondmates to his side to sketch them the outline of their consul general's plan to turn tragedy into comedy, loss to gain, mortification to satisfaction.

Those who knew the countenance of Selim Labaya of old were drawn like swords to ready by the welcoming smile that slithered across the old patriarch's visage like a hungry python toward a burrow of mice. Some who knew him better saw the Labayan device of undulant dragons rampant replacing the airborne eagle above a circle of seven stars which was etched into the rings of Lorelie's anchor-planet, Alexandria. One, who could not set foot on Lorelie, whose face would have begun a war had Parma Kerrion beheld it, whose gerontic back was bent, whose inveterate mind was the more deadly from all the years poison had been baking into its blade, laughed a laugh which sounded through the Labayan ship like rending metal squealing in complaint.

But when the delegation had made dock, departing with those sent to meet them, there was no sign of the bare-pated man, who was holed up content with a dream dancer secreted in the ship's bowels for just that purpose. Old Jebediah giggled over the proximity of himself and his pleasure to Parma and his displeasure, when he remembered it, which was not too often, for the dream dancer was most talented, and kept him ecstatically engaged.

To Marada, surveying Lorelie, no hint of Labayan presence showed. But he needed no doubt of their attendance nor insight into Labayan intentions to make him wary. He was twelve hours late to the audience his father had demanded, a function of the deep sleep come upon him so disadvantageously in the Orrefors' guest suite. He bore with him mute testimony to the folly of his willfulness. The effect of his transgressions on his father's temper could be no less far-reaching than the results he carried so cold in *Hassid*'s hold.

The beauteous Lorelie did not beguile him: he was immune to her outward glory, knowing full well the passions swirling within like rot eating away fruit beneath a perfect rind.

Shebat's awe at the sight—soft *oohs* and *aahs* cooed from wonder's own throat—temporarily lightened his load, then brought it back redoubled when he added her again to the sum of his difficulties and found the number a heretofore undreamed of prime too great to be contained within the universe he had known. All would change; *how,* he had no idea.

At best, he would sit in his older brother's chair, a fate beside which death would seem the kinder to one who shunned the machinations of commerce. At worst, he would resign his citizenship quietly, if it were demanded of him, accepting the attendant sterilization without complaint. This, too, was an alternative beside which death's dirge was a celebratory hymn. But death, the eye-for-eye, tooth-for-tooth death of primitive times, was no part of Consortium justice. Its gentler sister, suicide, had been exposed upon a winter hillock: the shame of suicide upon the entire bond group would lead to a rash of the same; no man committed suicide without committing murder. Hence, no Kerrion had ever stooped so low, since the Jesters' first smirk.

Marada, in his rat's maze, turned back from the blind alley of what might occur in the unknowable hours stretching out before him, matched velocities with the man-made moon Lorelie, and docked his ship. It was not so difficult as it would have been even a hundred years previously, before the Kerrion codicils of supergravity had obviated the necessity of dizzying spin and Kerrion crystalline chemistries had freed habitational designers from restricting considerations of size and stress. But it was not easy.

When it was done, he felt buoyed, cleansed by *Hassid*'s palliative communion. Perhaps, somehow, he could retain the ship. For the first time since he had begun the docking maneuver, he remembered the Earth waif, and constructed various contingency plans that shielded her from any backwash of Parma's wrath.

So he came to the time of reckoning, and found the most difficult of it to be the consigning of *Hassid*'s facile brain to what might be a permanent limbo. Once all was dark in the ship but standby lights and all quiet without but for the soft hiss and thud of the automated repressurizing of the bay, he was past the worst of it; his hands steadied. Like the ship, he was ready, holding all faculties in abeyance but those standard functions: his heart beat, saliva jetted, breath came and went.

Loud in the quiet came the soft tone that signaled a safe exit, then Shebat's muted cry of delight when the port drew back and Lorelie's fragrant air caressed her cheek.

There were none to meet them. Marada's scant brows drew down protectively over his eyes, and his voice came from deeper in his chest. In the miasmic Lorelian light, the chain rings in his ears were divested of their sparkle; in the stiffness of his carriage, they dared not swing, but hung quiescent.

Shebat took note, but she had put on him the spell of twelve coils binding, and feared not at all for the safety of the Arbiter Kerrion, who had delivered her from the abyss of ignorance and surely would not be decreased on that account.

Chapter Three

Parma Alexander Kerrion had sired seven sons, the other six of which combined had not garnered half the troubles to hearth as had the one he now watched slowly but without hesitation climbing the last teal hill of several between port and tower, lissome of stride but sure in bearing, though he walked in company of a travesty, female, garbed in Kerrion colors. And doubtless also in the company of his fear: Marada could not help but have appraised the situation. But of this, the sauntering youth who paused often to point this way or that or touch the swivel-headed creature he had brought gave no sign. In the privacy of his bath—the only privacy to be had on Lorelie these days—the consul general leaned with elbows on sill, jutting chin cradled in flat hands which propped up the folds of his face so that it seemed that the Parma of a quarter century past stared squint-eyed out at his son's approach.

Of the bone white hair on Parma's head, Marada was responsible for bleaching the better half. Twenty-five years less one month ago, Marada had been born of Persephone, slaying her in his pursuit of life, and Parma's hair had begun to turn. How many times he had wished he could trade back this accursed spawn of passion for the woman who inspired it! But such bargains could not be made; even Parma's influence held no sway in Fate's court. All the Kerrion bond's awesome biochemical abilities were useless in the face of death. Once lost, no person could be regained: cloning reproduced body but not soul. He had declined the opportunity to bring wife up as daughter, to see her grow away, go away, wed away to some youthful scion of a rival consulate. She had taken unto herself the only immortality worthy of the name: in Marada her genes rode, awaiting their dissemination.

Parma sighed. Any possible consequence, of whatever gravity, was superior in his sight to the one facing him by law: he was not about to see his own son neutered and cast out. Whatever the cost, he would prevent that. No matter how much he disliked—must one mince words with oneself? No? Then: *hated!*—the boy at times like these, he was his mother's son. How could what was consummately attractive in the mother be so infinitely destructive in the son? It was as if the old crone Chance sat drooling on his ledger, each drop that fell upon some entered credit blurring it away.

Well, Marada would not be blurred away, erased for his evildoing as his stepmother had counseled, as Selim Labaya had demanded, as Justice herself seemed to require. But one could dream of it: a world without the constant weight the boy was upon his sire, without the continual parade of offended parties and the contumacious whirlwind which was ever the wake of Marada's passage.

A knock on the door and a concerned murmur from without caused the beset patriarch to snarl violently: *Can a man have no peace even sitting on his own pot?* through his dromedary's lips, no longer drawn firm by upholding palms. Persephone, Marada's mother, had called Parma her shaggy camel. The comparison had grown only truer during the ensuing years, though Persephone, like the dromedary, was extinct, forgotten by all but Parma, who kept the likeness of both woman and *Camelus* by his bed.

The voice, unflagging, demanded entrance.

And since it was young Chaeron, third-born son, he who thought to make up for the black presence of Marada by the bright light of his own (who would, if scheming succeeded, once more pull design and dynasty out of harm's way!), Parma got up from his defecatory throne, unlocked the door, and admitted him.

Chaeron Ptolemy Kerrion: auburn-maned, beryl-eyed,

wide-browed. And, as ever, smiling oh so slightly, the perpetual jest of which he was always the brunt accepted, even anticipated in altruistic good humor. First-born of Parma's third wife, he had always known it would come to this: all things would devolve to him: the power, the primogeniture, the privilege. All things good had been his due from birth. He accepted them with gracious aplomb, never questioning his great fortune nor his right to command all he surveyed. His mother, Ashera, was fond of saying he had slipped from her womb with nary a kick nor a cry, had lain face down on her belly, laughing, and had not stopped chuckling since. On this particular day, his only shadow of concern was that the smile not break its restraint and beam too brightly, that his humor jump its traces and, braying loudly, spoil all things by crossing the finish line prematurely, without the chariot it was meant to draw, thus disqualifying him from the race.

"Marada and friend have docked safely. They approach. As per your order, no one met them, nor was a lorry available for their use," said Chaeron carefully, once the door had clicked shut behind his back, absently toying with the drape of his teal dress-cloak.

"And our guests? Are they still so flushed with calculated passion? Or has Selim decided the time is appropriate to display some disposition toward compromise?"

Chaeron rubbed a hand across his chuckle, then let its sparkle touch his sire with just the right amount of incredulity mixed in. "Sir? Were you listening then?"

"Come now, boy, this is no time to hide your intellect, such as it is. Come over here." Parma walked to the window. Below, Marada and his companion were just beginning to climb the hundred-stair flight of synthetic sapphire that led to the tower's gilded doors. "Look there, Chaeron, get a glimpse of the newest Kerrion."

The confident smile dissolved, a rare flicker of thoughtfulness replaced it on that countenance which seemed designed by a sculptor's skill to beautify Kerrion coinage. Treated abruptly to a glimpse of the youth's classical profile, Parma shook off irritation: the boy could not help it that he so favored his mother. Then Chaeron reset the mask of his smile and peered downward. "So you are telling me you are going to accept his wardship of the girl?"

"Guess again, son of Ashera. Surely the mother's wiles must have migrated along with her grace behind the oh, so unprepossessing front you yet present? I could do with a little more evidence of that incisive wit your mother proclaims but I can only suspect you possess. Honesty, too, is a perquisite of my successor; at least, within the family john."

"So, then," said Chaeron easily, throwing a leg up on the sill and a calculating long look at his father, "you will take the girl in as a full member of the family, so that you can throw Marada to old Labaya's wolves?"

Parma's laugh pealed around the little room, filling it, drawing from the son seeking to become heir a tentative harmony, as the father chortled: "Good, very good. The time for mincing words and seemly humility is indeed past. If old Selim does what he must, then I will do what I must." Parma was sober-faced, suddenly. "I must keep my bargain," he added mysteriously. Then: "The girl would likely be one burden too many for Marada, whose tribulations are only beginning."

"And if there is a vote on this, you would like to count mine?"

"I *will* count yours, and your mother's, and your brothers'. In fact, it is you I am charging with securing unanimity on this point."

If Marada were allowed to remain guardian of the girl, Selim Labaya could claim him unacceptable by reason of that fact for the compromise Parma had in mind, and demand another heir of Kerrion blood to replace him. This, Parma was not willing to risk. Most definitely, it must be the very same son who had brought about this state of affairs and damaged Labayan honor, who repaired the damage and salved the wound. Most definitely, Marada would be his gift to Labaya: let the juggernaut rage in Labayan space. Indeed, let Labaya do what he would with the youth. No amount of firepower, no commercial coup or biochemical pestilence could compare to the havoc Marada would wreak in the Labayan consulate once he was part of it.

He spoke so candidly of this to Chaeron that the youth

snorted softly in unfeigned admiration, and began to bate. Observing this, Parma was content to loose him among the Labayans to see what he could do: "All haste, my boy. Your success, most candidly, hangs on it. When I walk out there I want old Labaya ready to spring his 'trap' on me. And I, all unknowingly, will fall into it without even a moue of protest. What, after all, is a father to do?"

"Next to you, I am a poor pup. But I will do my best, father. And—" Hand on door, fingers tapping the silver knob, the young consul-to-be gave one more candid look to his sire. "—as for the wardship of the little barbarian, should any objection be made on account of your having used up all your allotment of offspring, then I will take her, in full citizenship, as my first and lawful child. After all, can a man do less for his brother than he would for his sire?" And to his father's approval, he bowed out the door, closing it firmly behind him.

Chaeron had offered a great deal for the vacant seat of the first-born, with its consular privilege, which had not yet been offered him in so many words. But it would be. *It would be.*

With a determined straightening of his shoulders, Chaeron set off down the ultramarine hall to the salon where the Labayan delegation of four men and two women was being entertained. This, finally, was the day he had long hoped for. Opportunity had come in the way he liked best: simple, with clear-cut rules, a task to perform that would earn him the desired result that had been his sole absorption since he was old enough to understand that the two other women's sons stood between him and the honors that were his due. All of Ashera's schemings and weblike machinations over the years since he had been old enough to be privy to her confidence had not ever had even the wildest chance of succeeding, and he was reverently happy that he had always brushed them aside (when he caught her early enough) or stymied them out of hand (when he had caught her too late to do better).

She stood, now, talking to the stormy-haired consul general of the Labayans, her figure not in the slightest motherly, though she had borne Parma five sons and a daughter. As always, every male eye in the room darted often to her; also as always, none dared stare too openly or approach too closely the woman whose profile might have launched a flotilla in ancient times.

He sailed easily up to her, putting his hand about her supple waist. She was sheathed in the blues of Lorelie, where Kerrions had no need for the somber blacks they wore when venturing among commoners. She wore the jewels of the house of Kerrion.

She wore a beauty so all-pervasive that she needed to wear nothing at all, that reduced jaquard and platinum to mere setting, functional necessities like a band that holds a jewel upon the finger. Her face, like her figure, was of evolution's surest strokes: brow, capacious; nose straight yet slightly uptilted; mouth a generous bow in a creamy oval of a face that made its perfection out of balance: a symphony of restraint. "Mother," he whispered as his lips grazed her cheek, "our brother arrives even as we speak, and I think you should be the one to greet him."

Their beryl eyes exchanged a truer message, the flecks of gold in hers moving outward as the pupils widened. As always, the near-telepathic bond between them made Chaeron uneasy, but he pushed the disquiet away. Later, when all else was accomplished, he would deal with her. Now here was the fierce-jowled pepper-haired freighter of a man whose brows made an unwavering single line above his eyes, as if all subtraction and addition above the line was registered in the pale blue windows beneath it.

"Where's Parma, still blubbering over his lost boy?" snapped Labaya with a cursory slide of his ice eyes over Chaeron's person that came back with their assessment unhidden: *dilettante*.

All the better, thought Chaeron, as the raspy voice demanded to be taken to his father.

"Sir, it is on his behalf that I have come to plead with you. My father is ill with grief. To lose one son and immediately face the loss of another! Then, sir, there will be only myself old enough to be of any use. . . . Consider, Consul General, how you might feel in his place. My brother arrives directly. I beg you—"

"You do? How original, not to say pleasing. I suppose old Parma did not send you, then, if you are going to beg. Beg on then, little do-gooder. Though it will do you little service, it will add spice to what is to come."

The smile stayed in place on Chaeron's lips; he had well trained them. But behind them, teeth clenched hard together. When the time came again for him to speak, he let his eyes stray first to one of the women who had accompanied the four Labayan dignitaries to Lorelie and sat now on a deep-pillowed russet settee with her short leg hidden under the folds of her long golden gown.

Still looking at her, he said to Selim Labaya: "Any mercy, most honored sir, that you could see fit to bestow on our grieving house in this the moment of our mutual mourning would not go unappreciated. Should both our houses suffer? Should the greatest commercial entity the stars have ever witnessed go unconsummated because of a quirk of fate?"

"Fate," Selim Labaya spat. "It's not fate did this, but that son of his, spoiled rotten and deserving of the same *fate* he meted out to my daughter! I—"

"Sir, forgive the interruption, but time grows short. If you could find it possible to seek less than your due in this matter, our whole house would be eternally in your debt." He looked soulfully, desperately into the old consul general's eyes, letting his own mist slightly. Dangerous game, here, and he played it with an expert. But the girls would not be present if there was no hope of a lesser demand. . . . What was this one's name? *Madel,* that was it. No, the old man was just enjoying the sight of the entire Kerrion bond tiptoeing around its own fortress, obsequious and servile to the last man of them. It rankled him—if it were the true nature of affairs, it would have been insupportable. As it was, he could feel the heat in his loins, the drawing up of his scrotum, the tightness in his throat. But he spoke all his lines as carefully and precisely as might have Parma himself, with the proper nuances of emotion, as if the sweat popping out on his brow was the sweat of fear and not fury. "Sir, if you could find a daughter of yours willing to make another match, Marada to whomsoever you might choose among your offspring, I can assure you we would gladly welcome your choice."

"Ah, you would, would you? Well, I will think about it. Right now, I am thirsty from too much idle talk. Run and get me a drink, boy. And none of that hydroponic swill, but your father's man-trodden grape, of which I have heard so much.''

Like a bodyservant, Chaeron dropped his eyes and scurried from the room, looking back only once at the Labayans among the Kerrions, where none but Kerrions had any right to be. This, and the final touch, hand wiping brow in the manner of a youth beset beyond his capacity, he made sure Selim Labaya saw. Then, whirling quickly lest his joy pierce the façade, he sprinted down the hall to catch his father before Marada was brought to audience.

To Shebat, Lorelie was the truth within its wrap of fables: the enchanted towers overlooking sapphire mountains were finer even than legend had portended or mind's eye created; she was enraptured, transported, enthralled. The absence of a welcoming committee did not trouble her, though she had seen Marada's frown. The long walk over cerulean, velvety paths did not tire her, though her companion's steps seemed to drag more slowly over each topped rise.

At the cobalt, hundred-staired dais that led from any side up to the majestic crenelated tower that presided over all lesser towers, she ceased her breathless chatter long enough to wonder at the hoods drawn close over Marada's sepia eyes. The first soft shiver of apprehension crawled up her hand from where he had enclosed it in his, to prod her heart.

Brazen doors, thrice her height, opened effortlessly of their own accord. Marada's encouraging smile ghast her as no words could have. The bold enchanter would not be so affrighted for little cause.

Shebat held back timorously, until his appeal moved her forward, across the threshold all shadowy and cold, into Lorelie's treasure vault.

The doors hissed softly shut, approving.

Long halls of opalescent flags, ashlar walls muraled and richly hung, open doors framing unimaginable tableaux of magical goings-on, made her stumble and gape.

When a door at the end of all doors hummed open to reveal a tiny elevator, she clutched harder at Marada's hand and he put an arm about her shoulders.

"Nothing," he said in a tone that told her he did not believe what he said, "can happen to you, now. You are a Kerrion in the embrace of all Kerrions, here. Whatever comes to pass will cause you no grief. Rather, you will find a place among us."

"It sounds otherwise," she said in clumsy Consulese, conscious of her slight stature here where everything was twice normal size.

"We trust each other," he reminded her, as the elevator door opened to reveal an encircling gallery full of folk in muted festivity. Pinwheel flights of lapis stairs like swirling water led up to it and down from it; and just below, where they stood, spawned an inner rotunda of doors, mirrors and windows that made her sense of perspective spin, likewise.

Men and women in knots laughed and murmured; others promenaded the stairs in measured stride; some hung over the gallery rail; some wore jet and carnelian; some cream and argent; laced through the uniforms were all the cyanic tones of Lorelie and stipples of damascene-hued ladies in long gowns. Somewhere a computer sang bravely in a melancholy, muted mode.

Before the elevator doors had more than closed, a youthful yet raffish figure, in Lorelien blues with a sorrel mane of curls swept back like a lion's, appeared from between two of the swirling staircases and hailed Marada by name.

A deep sigh escaped the enchanter, and he stepped a pace away from Shebat, saying: "And to you too, brother, greetings. I trust you have been caring for the woes of Lorelie in my stead?"

The two did not embrace, but stood apart. The teal-cloaked brother looked curiously at her, smiling just slightly. Shebat straightened, tossed her head.

Still looking at her, the mage (for so he must surely be; how else to explain artful, indolently cultivated beauty in a man?) said: "Parma wants to see you. He wanted to see you twelve hours ago. Why so late, now of all times?"

"I overslept."

That turned the ultramarine, discomforting stare away from her, to Marada, whose own eyes were deep in their hoods. "Chaeron, my half-brother, meet Shebat, your—"

"Do not think you are going to determine that particular relationship, oh fallen one. This time you have dug yourself a pit too deep to climb out of. Where is our most lamentably deceased sibling's corpse—and that of our guests' bondchild, by the bye?"

"In the *Hassid,* where they will stay until someone restores services at the dock. Whose idea was it to empty the crew out of there? What if there had been a problem?"

"Then you would be dead and there would *be* no problem."

"Labaya is here?"

"With his brood about him."

"And Parma?"

"Sharpens his claws. I believe you are the main course, and she—" he inclined his head slightly to where Shebat stood forgotten, "is merely dessert."

"You are enjoying this so much, Chaeron, it is almost worth it, to see you smile."

"You, too, will enjoy this moment," he whirled half-around, speaking to Shebat from a near-crouch, "once you learn enough to know what you are seeing." He peered down into her face. "Can she speak? Say something!" And he put out his hand to touch Shebat's cheek. "Speak, child."

Shebat forced herself not to step back, and gave a good Consulese greeting as Marada had coached her. The hand touching her cheek was withdrawn with no more ill effect than a slight tingle where Chaeron's flesh had touched her own.

"Nice," spoke Chaeron to Marada, straightening up and stretching widely, "but hardly worth all you will soon have paid. Shall we go, or do I need to convince you further?"

"Your very presence convinces me," said Marada with a flash of teeth. "Come, Shebat, and you will meet our father."

"I do not think so," said Chaeron, putting out a hand.

"Then think again," advised Marada, brushing it aside.

She found herself being dragged by the hand; the arbiter's grip was slick, crushingly tight, yet unsteady. For the first time she feared for the efficacy of her spell, and what its failure might mean. What use, after all, was her meager coil of twelve against the might that could set a jewel world spinning about in space?

Chaeron Kerrion bowed them into an anteroom, and disappeared: to expedite the funeral arrangements, he said.

Marada circled like a guilty pup around a hearth before he settled in the corner of a grandly damasked couch, and indicated that she should follow suit.

But Shebat was still pressed into a vacant corner while Marada bit a broken nail, sunk in his thoughts, when the doors bearing the Kerrion eagle over the circle of seven stars opened.

The oldness of the man was not of physical age, for he was robust and heavily made; but a smell of temper, a ponderous, seasoned surety that exuded from him so that he seemed to bulk like two men, rather than one. When Parma Kerrion embraced his son with a dour smile that she had first seen on his child Chaeron's face, he proved to be of a height with Marada. But as soon as the two stepped apart, Parma Alexander Kerrion swelled up to twice life-size once again.

"Introduce me to your companion," said the father to the son in a carefully gentle voice, and sank down on the couch with an explosive sigh. "Come here, little one."

Shebat had no choice but to move her leaden feet; closer; too close; finally, the high-sinewed talons had her, the huge hands, larger than Marada's, almost met as the father put them round her waist.

Curiosity that was unfeigned softened the forbidding visage. "You'll be all that is needed," he said under his breath, and smiled a grin meant to be encouraging. Then he let her go, and might have forgotten that she was present.

"Sit down, Oh storied traveler, and tell me a tale that will turn this lead over my heart to gold. You are an arbiter, so the records say. Tell me an arbiter's tale, even, so that I can keep your fine butt out of Labaya's stewpot."

"So? Is there use in that, when you have already acted on your decision by inviting Iltani's people here? Why not just talk of pleasanter things for the required amount of time, and we will presently emerge, drawn and subdued of aspect. Then you can call your tribunal and take your puppet vote and do whatever it is you have in mind. I am not going to obstruct you."

"So, you think you have me all figured out? Ready to drop your pants and give up your manhood and your place, are you? Surely you don't feel you are responsible for their deaths and want to be punished?"

Marada shrugged, and the boy in the man was brought home to her so painfully that a gulped sob snuck past her lips, past the hand over them, and caused both men to eye her.

Then, again, father and son faced each other from opposite ends of the wildly figured couch as if all the cosmos hung in between.

"You doubtless know what I did as regards the girl."

"I know it. You know that you cannot make such a wardship hold."

"What will you do?" Marada said tiredly. Shebat sank down on the floor in her corner, arms circling her knees, drawing them close up to her chest to prevent their knocking together.

"Make a bargain with you," Parma replied in an oddly tinged voice.

"What have I to bargain with?" he asked warily, touching a finger to one of the supple chain circlets in his ear, then covering the ear with his palm, casually, as if merely seeking to prop his head with his arm which rested on the divan's back. But the position was awkward, and Shebat knew it to be something else—a warning: he would not give up his pilot's circles.

"I made your mother a promise, once. In order to keep it, I have need to keep you a Consortium citizen in good standing."

"I, as well as you, know that is impossible." The pressure of the supporting palm canted upward the left side of his face.

"Improbable, but not impossible. Give the girl over to my wardship."

"No!" leapt from Shebat's throat.

The look Marada sent in answer made her turn her head away.

"You must, to insure her safety. No plan is certain of success."

"If I have your word that such a move will be to her benefit, then I will do it."

"There is no honor bond to be taken here: if she remains your ward, then you and she will be Consortium citizens for perhaps . . . oh, another four hours and a half. After that, law will take its course. *Do as I say!*"

To that imperative, Marada acceded. "Let it be so recorded."

"Done!" said Parma from behind closed lids, whereby Shebat suspected that some mind similar to that of the ship's was overhearing and recording what was being said.

"Done," echoed the arbiter faintly.

Shebat, in the corner, lay head on crossed arms and bit her lip fretfully, forgetful of the mil-hood which gave her skin an odd resiliency.

"Now will you tell me what alternative you are presenting as viable in the face of Labaya's obvious petition for my balls?"

"You have not told me how sorry you are about the death of your brother, nor your betrothed. I suggest you meditate on expressions of mourning. And perhaps find time in your busy schedule of self-concern to wonder how and in what place I have entered your ward into our family. For now, I have given you all the time I can. In three hours, we shall begin the services for the remains of your brother, my son, and your betrothed, Labaya's daughter. Between now and then stay in your apartments. Speak to no one, your siblings least of all."

With that, Parma Kerrion pushed himself up from the couch, and was gone, all but for a final warning that wafted back through the doors closing behind him: "And your dear *mother,* Ashera, who was supposed to go and greet you, to take the girl and prepare her for later's festivities: do not speak with her, either, until I can determine just what it was that she found to do more important than what I had bid her."

Two sarcophagi dominated the arched vault, of equal richness but divergent style. Hundred-flamed sconces illumined each at the head and at the foot; other than the

golden candlesticks, there was no light but for the single
taper each mourner bore.

Slowly past the coffins, one open, one closed, filed six
Labayans; fifty-four Kerrions of intimate relatedness to
the handsome corpse whose bier was open; and one
neither Kerrion nor Labayan who nevertheless recognized
the pale golden lifemask which topped Iltani's closed
casket of state and the look of mild surprise still visible in
death on the countenance of Marada's brother.

It was said, by someone among the Labayans, that a
viewing of Iltani's defiled corpse would have provoked a
second mourners' procession, but someone else shushed
the knowing voice of the girl whose whisper had pierced
the silence, the brunette whose short leg gave her a
dragging gait that caused her candle to wriggle, throwing
violent shadow dancers all about.

The girl was Madel, the only one present for whom
tears were impossible: even Ashera Kerrion had been
able to summon up the waters of seemly grief. Chaeron
wept in manly fashion; he had long been the master of his
tears. Marada hesitated so long over Iltani's corpse that
only a hiss from his father moved him. The old patriarch
stood with Selim Labaya by the candlesticks at each
coffin's head, receiving comfort with the air of two men
desolate beyond comfort, each displaying the same measure of burdensome grief as if trained in tandem; or as if
more concerned with each other than with all else, which
was indeed the case.

For Shebat, proximity to corpse rather than clean ashes
in a solemn urn was an occasion for abject terror;
proximity to *two*, either of whose shade might hold her
partly responsible for a death unmitigated by release from
fleshly bond, caused her legs and arms to tremble so that
even after all Marada's coaching she dashed through the
aisle bounded by coffins and drew up on the far side of
them with gasping breaths and fearful backward glances
to assure herself that neither of the deceased had reared
up out of its final bed to chase her.

When all concerned parties had passed between, the
catafalques sunk slowly from sight without any visible
precipitation of their descent but Parma's raised head.
Then the floor which had somehow swallowed the two

deceased, ornate shells of interment and all, closed itself up once more, so that there was no sign but for golden trees whose buds were made of flames that any death's heads had ever been eulogized in between.

"From stars we come; to stars we must return," Shebat heard without understanding. Her tongue was busy with murmured spells and her fingers blurred ultramarine in frantic motion before her heart as she spun her warding spells, without which, clutching hands would surely burst up from the marble floor on which she stood, take her by the ankles, and drag her down to whatever underworld in which they were now imbound.

Onto that chancy space of disappearing flooring the Labaya and Kerrion consuls general then sauntered, their sons and daughters ranging themselves behind.

Shebat, as she had been counseled, stayed by the gold candlestick which had briefly illuminated the slain Kerrion heir's quizzical smile.

Labaya spoke: "These two who are dead died from the negligence of another."

Parma Kerrion replied: "This son of mine bears no blame, for the scythe falls where it will."

Marada Seleucus Kerrion stepped between them, slowly, standing quiet with head bowed.

"Restitution must be made. Betrothal vows lie unconsummated. I have lost a daughter," intoned Labaya so forcefully that his jowls flapped.

"Restitution must be made," retorted Parma Kerrion. "Betrothal vows lie unconsummated. I have lost a son."

All held their breath in a susurrating intake that swept like a wave arching to break through the crowd. All, so far, had been ritual. What followed would be that for which everyone waited.

Marada looked neither right nor left, nor up nor about, but only stood slack-shouldered, as if it were another between the sconces, where what was said was as irrevocable as a flame consuming the tapers' lengths.

"Offer me a son, unburdened, or sever the bond between our houses!" And the straight line of Labaya's brow waited to tote the sum of Parma's bet.

"I offer you this son who stands between us. Offer me a daughter, unburdened, or sever the bond between our two houses!" Parma replied, implacable.

"It has been said to us that the son is burdened with a ward."

Parma raised his head and smiled slowly at Selim Labaya. Then he nodded to Marada, who without seeming to have seen stepped two paces back into shadow.

Parma held out his hand and Shebat minced like a skittish filly into the light, gaze fixed on the hand outstretched toward her. Drawn thither, her pale skin flushed like a somnambulist's, she stood in the candlelight.

A hiss broke the silence. A movement in the crowd brought Ashera Kerrion and her first-born somehow to the forefront. Shebat saw mother touch son, son shake off hand with an angry twitch that seemed to dislodge a mask from Chaeron's face. Suddenly, wrath and fury flooded toward her from his eyes. She remembered that, more than the hand of Parma Kerrion coming down on her head, intoning the formula no one had expected to hear but Chaeron, who had been hearing it, though differently, in his dreams for years.

"I hereby install this child in full wardship and place of first-born to the Kerrion consulate. Any harboring objections speak them now, or put them by." Parma waited a moment for the hum to die down among them, then ordered a vote by voice.

It was he, Chaeron, who should have stood there and received the touch that ennobled; a blast of pure hatred rocked him. But Parma was speaking; the hatred was impotent now, better saved for a more propitious time.

As all the voices of his kin (whose promises of accord he had secured without exception to second the father's wishes on this day of the establishment of the house of Kerrion's new successor) rang loudly, the son added his affirmative vote. Parma's glare would allow no different, warning first Chaeron, then his mother, who was stiff and hardly breathed by his side.

Of all present on that day, it was only Marada Kerrion who smiled, whose jaw trembled with suppressed laughter, who had to duck farther back in shadows to mask his mirth.

Almost immediately, the laughter was banished from him, not by Chaeron's promissory scowl, but by Parma

Kerrion's next words: "As you see, Selim, this son is burdened in no way. I offer him to you, binding our houses through marriage. Offer me a daughter fit to be his wife." Parma's sharp inclination of head reeled Marada back from dimness into the center of the convocation, even as his light touch told a stricken Shebat she must step back.

It took all her strength of purpose to obey him, to stand a pace behind the patriarch rather than run to Marada and throw her arms about his waist, which had she done so, she would not have released on pain of death.

But it was another woman who stepped into the brightness at Selim Labaya's bidding awkwardly, blinking often and never looking up.

"I offer you this daughter, Madel, second-born daughter, unburdened, as a fit and fitting mate. Let the two be united forthwith and our fortunes thereby joined."

Shebat's sob, the hands that flew to cover her eyes, were lost in the moment of consternation that was silenced like a flipped switch by the raising of Parma's hand. The fathers looked only at one another, the true battle therein joined. Together they proclaimed each other's children their own, each drawing from stunned youth and lame girl between them swift monosyllables of acquiescence.

The marriage vows exchanged, both fathers shook with laughter, no longer needfully containing it; then, after proclaiming an evening of feasting, strolled away with their arms about one another's backs.

In the milling of Kerrions, Shebat, the newest Kerrion, sank down weeping freely, ignored.

It was not until the crowd had nearly cleared that anyone remembered her at all. Then it was Chaeron, worried over what she might have heard, who raised her and gave her comfort while trying to ascertain what her ears had picked up of the many threats and oaths and denouncements that had spilled from his mouth, destined for his mother's hearing alone.

But he found out nothing of what he wanted to know, for Marada saw him holding Shebat against him and intervened, saying: "Here, let me take her. Shebat, come now, do not weep. It is better this way. You are a Kerrion now, and not just any Kerrion. You must not cry; this is a joyous day." And, softer, in her hair, his lips whispered: "Do not be afraid. Kerrions take care of their own."

But it was not so much from fear as from loss that Shebat cried, and when she whispered back that it was her love for him that made her weep, there was nothing he could say.

So things fell out in the way that Parma Alexander Kerrion had known that they must: after all, should he have given the place to Chaeron, he would have been ever looking over his shoulder to protect his back. This way, Chaeron might *marry* into the power he craved; or wait until the girl stumbled badly while further proving his own fitness to attain to the consular head. After all, what hope had an illiterate barbarian girl of ever actually exercising consul generalship when all eventually devolved to votes of confidence? And furthermore, any runny-nosed brat who dreamed of being more than a steward of some outreach factory platform should have foreseen all this, said Ashera to Chaeron on breath of acid, though Chaeron had espied his mother's face when Parma's trap was being sprung and did not believe that the old dame had known any more than he.

Still, Ashera had disappeared for three hours without anyone being able to find out where she had gone, rather than greet Marada, a pleasure her spiteful nature would not have easily given up.

"Look at that," said the beautiful woman through unmoving lips in a totally emotionless face. "He cuddles the barbarian before his new bride's eyes. Mark me, within a half-year Marada will have the Kerrion/Labaya alliance in shreds and your father will have all the grievance he needs to war on them howsoever he might choose. With Marada in their company, their doom is as good as sealed." From the look of her, she might have been discussing the weather.

"Do you think so?"

"Foolish dandy sot of a son, I know so. But while you would wring your hands and sit quietly by, Marada wraps up the heart of that dirty little wretch for carrying away with him into Labayan space."

"What am I to do?"

"I should be saying that, with you as my instrument. Dullard! Get your handsome nose over there: be nice to the girl. After all, she will need *someone,* now that Marada is departing for his wedding bed. *Go."*

"That is all? But we must *do* something. Something—"

"Do not worry. We will, but when I say and how I say. Now go on, and be a good boy. And when Marada announces his intention of jaunting into Labayan space in the *Hassid,* rather than as a passenger on the Labayan flagship, say nothing at all!"

"But how do you know he will—?"

"When will you learn never to interrupt people capable of thinking before they speak when you yourself are not?" Spittle sprayed his cheek, but when he turned away from Marada and the slight Earth girl, Ashera was smiling pleasantly. "Have I your attention now? Good. It is as important that you do not *en*courage, as that you do not *dis*courage. Go with them. And bring me back word of what is said. But covet not the *Hassid.* You will have a ship of your own and a pilot soon enough."

"But, why—?"

"Your brother has a love for that particular craft, a matter of his pilot's gift. That is more than you need to know. If you cannot answer your own questions henceforth, then perhaps I am wasting my time with you. . . . After all, your brother, Julian, comes of age next month. . . . *Ah ha ha,"* she laughed, "you should see your face. Go on now, Little Pestilence. I must arrange for bodyservants and suitable quarters, not to say tutors, that will make a Kerrion out of that piece of ground-dwelling rubbish."

Chapter Four

It was on the day that Shebat turned sixteen (as well as she could reckon the date) that Ashera—with an enigmatic smile—said to her that she, Ashera, had done her best, and now all was up to Shebat.

There followed immediately an interview with Parma which Shebat had petitioned for while still she did not understand what was happening to her, three months before; and which by the day of its occurrence she had given up hope of ever being granted.

Until today, she had had the opportunity to call Parma "father" only at those once-weekly breakfasts attended by the most intimate Kerrion family: Ashera and her sons and daughter, herself and the consul general.

"You look a far cry from the knobby-kneed waif Marada brought us," said Parma, raising eyes but not head from the screen on his desk to greet her. "Sit."

She sat opposite him in the old-style armchair before a venerable antique of a desk made from real wood. Like so many things Kerrion, its harkening back to hallowed days of antiquity and the superiority of both taste and breeding thereby implied would have been lost on her when first she came to study in Lorelie. As the quaint custom still observed among the platforms of numbering time in days, weeks, months and years A.D. had been unnoticeable to her because of its familiarity, so the presence of wood and leather and carpet of hand-tied silk might have seemed comforting, but not the arrogant statement of wealth and breeding her accultured perceptions now knew it to be.

"You wanted to see me?" prompted the mountain seated behind the desk.

"Three months ago, when my bodyguards suffered to a man from the flux and I finally realized both the dangers inherent in the position to which you so offhandedly elevated me, and the reason behind it. Then, I wanted to see you."

"Your command of Consulese is quite impressive. Is your insight equally so?"

"I am the wild card in your hand; the random factor that makes you unpredictable to the minds of your fellow men and their computers alike," accused Shebat, unaware of the pout that pushed forward her lips when she had said her say.

"Guilty as charged," chuckled Parma. "Surely there was more to this 'life-and-death matter' which your own handwriting affirms must needs be discussed in private than to accuse me of ulterior motives, without which a Kerrion would feel naked as a newborn babe?"

"Since then, I have learned many things. I have studied survival as it is taught in Lorelie; both by your intelligence officers in principle, and by your wife in application. Having withstood Ashera's kindnesses this long, I need not ask for your protection from them."

"Complacency is a tripware on a sheer-sided path. Watch your steps the more carefully, the surer you are of them."

"Then keep that old snake away from me!" demanded the child peeking out through a woman's mask. Parma shifted slightly, aware once again of the blossoming beauty in what had so recently been an awkwardly adolescent collection of knees, elbows and oversized eyes. The eyes had gotten no smaller, but all else had taken on roundness where before had been painfully sharp angles. The girl would be beautiful, which had been no part of Parma's plan. Already she was winsome beyond what might have been prudent. And intelligent, it seemed, beyond genetics' ability to contradict.

"I have your aptitude tests," he said easily, tapping on the screen with a stylus. "I have cleared an hour for you. If nothing more, we could discuss them."

"Then you will not call that woman off?"

"Incredulity does not become you. You have been studying law, among other things. How would you suggest I limit the freedom of my wife and yet remain within lawful framework? Unless, of course, you have some proof to offer that Ashera has orchestrated the accidents with which you seem unfortunately plagued?"

"A faulty mil-suit, less than four months old when it gave way? A gravity-sled whose throttle jams at fast forward?" Shebat ticked these off on upraised fingers. "A short circuit which turned every piece of metal in my suite to a possible instrument of execution? A—"

"Now, Shebat, those are hazards one must endure. The mil-suit, I must remind you, was that Marada bought you; an inferior product of Orrefors technology, and none of ours. Sleds jam often; you were advised beforehand of the risk and went thrill-seeking, regardless. As for the rest, mechanical devices tend to malfunction."

"In *Lorelie?*"

"Everywhere, which is why fail-safes and redundancy are built into all our systems. These things could be— though I am not for an instant suggesting that they truly *are*—simple mishaps occasioned as much by your unfamiliarity with our somewhat more complex mode of living as by anyone's overt attempts to place you in the path of those little difficulties life often presents."

Shebat, in answer to Parma's upraised black brows, snorted disbelievingly, while wondering whether or not the white-haired man blackened those expressive wrigglers over his eyes purposely to increase their effect. She took deep, measured breaths the way Chaeron had taught her, but could not banish her nervousness under Parma's assessively patient scrutiny.

"No retort? Shall we leave this subject? And on to what suggestions Lorelie central has made for your continuing education?"

"No," inaudibly.

"Speak up!"

"I said, 'No.' I am not finished. Let me off this beautiful but inimical playworld of yours before it becomes my burial ground. Let me study elsewhere. What can I learn here but hate and fear? Chaeron says you are going back to Draconis, now that your vacation is through. Take me with you, or take from me these mortally dangerous honors, lest they be my eulogy!"

"*Chaeron* says? You are not as astute, then, as the computer predicted or as I myself had come to believe."

"Had it not been for Chaeron's sage warnings, his mother would have got me by now."

Parma tried to appear as if he considered that information. Then he said: "So it may be. But tell me, is it Chaeron's idea that you leave the isolation of Lorelie for a more cosmopolitan setting? Or is it for more neutral territory?"

"I think I have exhausted my opportunities here. But I am sure he would agree with me."

"That, in itself, is enough reason to budge not one foot from Lorelie. However, I have learned by raising many children that advice unsolicited falls on deaf ears. But tell me, what is it you can do in Draconis that you cannot do here?"

"Be of some use. Learn commerce and the true work of the first-born. Take a pilot's license and—"

"Wait," Parma interrupted. "What was that last again?"

"You heard me, foster parent."

"I heard the part about learning to be in actuality what you were never meant to be in more than name. That surprised me. But I suppose I owe you the chance, since you are bearing the difficulties therefrom. The last, however, I did not hear, did I?" This moment tested the girl: would she back away from what she must know would evoke his displeasure and perhaps lose her all he was allowing her to think she had gained? His eyes skipped briefly down the graphed results of her aptitude tests. There it was, in red while all but one other entry was the acceptable green: *Pilot, spongespace*. Well, if the computer had prophesied it as third choice, there was little possibility that the girl would be unaware of her own predilection. The first-choice entry, also glaring balefully in red, unconcerned about the censure it was sure to elicit from any human eye that read its scarlet message, held his gaze a little longer. If he allowed the lesser evil, would he be spared the greater? And if not, what then? *Dream dancer,* the red letters spelled smugly, uncaring.

Parma Alexander Kerrion's hands snapped the stylus they held into two equal parts, which he lay carefully side by side upon the desk.

"You do know," he asked softly, "that such an occupation as pilotry is no fit vocation for a member of a consular house?"

"I have heard it said. But Marada—"

"Marada's talents were so few and so unfortunately spread that no amount of pressure could keep him from it. As with his appointment as 'arbiter-at-large,' it was on my part more a ploy to keep him from shattering the very structure of Law and throwing his life away in the bargain than any choice of mine. As you are well aware, he nearly managed both, despite all my precautions to the contrary. Surely you do not wish to similarly reward me for my kindness to you?"

"Kindness?" tittered Shebat in an uncanny imitation of her stepmother's most scathing repartee.

Parma Kerrion raised both hands palm up in a gesture of defeat. "Come to Draconis, if you will. It seems I must get you out from under Ashera's tutelage before I find myself with *two* such doppelgangers under my very roof."

Shebat Kerrion did not burst forth in grateful tears or vociferous praise. She merely nodded regally, content.

Parma shuddered, and eyed the results of the girl's psychometric examination one more time. "There are conditions appended to this favor I do you," he warned.

"Of course," Shebat agreed complacently.

Parma Alexander Kerrion wondered if perhaps sending Marada a copy of the report greenly glaring up at him would steal from his son some percentage of the sleep he, Parma, would doubtless lose over the creation of the masterpiece Shebat Kerrion—he must remember to have a middle name entered for her: Alexandra, as she would soon enough deserve—was destined to become. Would the quiet coincidence of genetic relatedness between black sheep son and foster daughter bite at Marada's heart as inexorably as that son had eaten away the father's? Or was it unnecessary: did Marada even now suffer over the meeting and subsequent loss of what might be, out of all the women in the Consortium, his most auspicious mate?

No matter, after all. The boy was well out of the way doing husbandly duties for the daughter Selim Labaya had despaired of ever getting wed to an acceptable candidate. Both houses were profiting thereby. Rather than mooning over her rescuer's precipitate departure from life and ken, the girl had evidently taken up an interest in Chaeron, Lords of Cosmic Jest only knowing why.

"This is the first time I have heard you speak of Marada since his wedding. It is remarkable, considering the degree of affection you initially displayed." Parma met the tilted head's gray stare and held it, but learned nothing except that the girl's glance betrayed her in no way. Whatever emotions rode behind that challenging visage stayed hidden.

"Is it my place to speak of him? He has not seen fit to send me word of his faring; he is wed and deployed as befits the fortunes of the Kerrion household. Would I be a good Kerrion, to rock the boat in which we all must ride for so small a reason as personal gain?" And she smiled, ingenuously, steepling her fingers before her. "Time passes; all things change. Did not Plato in his *Laws* set five thousand forty as the ideal number of citizens in a democracy? And did not Aristotle disagree, saying that 'ten would obviously be far too few, and ten thousand too many'; and yet today ten million souls and more have the vote?"

"By my most remote, flint-chipping ancestor, I swear if the Jesters give me a life long enough to loose you in maturity upon an unsuspecting universe, I will ask nothing more and go without protest to an easy death."

"And I swear to you that I will not stint in my efforts to make that dream a reality."

There was something in her eyes, fiery like the quick strike of angina, that unmanned Parma evanescently, so that he diddled the two broken halves of stylus on his desk and found it necessary to call on the steward's channel for refreshments to be sent up.

Had her magic truly left her, then, bled away by the empirical, causal universe in which the Consortium determinedly dwelled? Shebat pondered, chin resting on clenched fists, buttocks and feet planted firmly on the flattened top of the highest hill of Lorelie, looking down over Parma's tower and past, to where Lorelie's horizon curved back upon itself in a month-long twilight near its end. She had come here straightaway from the confrontation in the consul general's office, to sort out what she had lost, what she had gained, and dress any wounds she might have taken, unknowing, in the fray.

It was hauteur that caused the endless twilight: during the time of the sun's occultation by a gas giant, above the ringed planet around which Lorelie endlessly circled, artificial day and night were suspended. The sky, it was true, was an awesome sight. But nothing is awesome for a month's duration. Even the winking out of all the lights of heaven would grow tiresome if it took so long.

It was hauteur, also, she had been determinedly affirming to her inner self since evidence had been piling up to the contrary, that caused all the wisdom of the Consortium to so concertedly disavow potion and spell, magic and enchantment. After all, had she not so far survived Ashera's malevolent ministrations; Chaeron's more and more urgent protestations of love in need of consummation; and even Parma's determination to ignore all the worms in his only barrel of apples? And had not Marada survived? The slipshod carelessness that had sent the *Hassid* into the spongelike alleyways between space and time without enough fuel to safely make the journey had not killed him and his new wife, any more than had the inexplicably jammed proton pump, when they had laboriously hauled into space, pannier by pannier, enough drinking water to start long idle emergency fusion engines. No, he had not died from that oversight, but managed to limp far enough to find a collection of water-ice asteroids in interim spacetime, refine them on the spot, and end his journey to Shechem, consular retreat of Labayan space, only three weeks later than he had intended. Was that not proof enough of the efficacy of twelve coils binding? Were not all Parma's machinations to aid Marada, despite the fact that he had only ill to speak of him, further affirmations of a well-cast spell at work?

And as for herself, was she not learning to clear her own path before her?

Yet, she was doubtful. And doubt in enchantments is like oxidation in metal: it eats away all strength. She cursed the gentle world of Lorelie and its mocking perfection, built of man's mastery of mathematics, engineering, chemistry and physics. No enchantments anywhere to be found. She had asked her apartment's console of enchantment, of sorcery, of spelling and warding and amulets. Each time, the screen had blinked: *no information*. Nothing more. She had considered the possibility of a secret society of enchanters, some council of mages overseeing all. But evidence was sorely lacking. She had broached the subject to Chaeron and seen real mirth in his eyes for the first time.

There was sorcery: Chaeron's facile mask belying what lay behind.

She had slipped all her bodyguards' concerted scrutiny to climb up here: there also was the gift of enchantment awork in the Kerrion milieu: she had made use of the ability to "pass by unnoticed" often when Bolen would see an extra leg of beef or a few coppers to be gained by loaning her warmth to some traveler. She had been beaten soundly upon reappearing with dawn's light, of course, but she had found the beatings preferable to lying with strange men with rough ways and rougher hands.

Here, in Lorelie, it was the bodyguards who faced corporeal punishment should she slip their care. She was Kerrion enough already, she reflected with a sour grimace, to put her own whim above the fortunes of four lesser beings. After all, if they were not up to maintaining their surveillance in the face of all contingencies, even the spell of "passing by unnoticed," then they were not capable of properly performing their tasks and deserved whatever chastisement was doubtless already in progress.

She had missed dinner.

She intended to miss, also, the grueling after-dinner hour of precise sipping of drinks under Ashera's watchful eye, of interrogation disguised as pleasantry, of manipulation masquerading as advice.

Within a week she would be quit of this place; she would shed it like a too-small skin. Of all the wonders of

Lorelie, only Chaeron would be hard to leave. She had learned more watching him than he had intended to teach, but she was aware that his intentions were on the whole honest, though he might not have meant them to be at the start.

Something, she decided, would have to be done about Chaeron.

When she had determined what that "something" was to be, she forsook her peak of meditation for the halls of the family tower, before which her worried bodyguards yet milled in agitation.

As Shebat and her bodyguards climbed the hundred cobalt stairs to the residency, the doors' sensors recognized her party, drawing back. The eye-teasing mezzanine preened itself; crystal stairs filled with cascading water eternally swirling passed beneath her tread. The water was wealth. This quantity of it put to decorative use was an outrageous surfeit of power. What power was here lay truly in Ashera's hands, the ladies said: Parma held sway in the Kerrion consulate's worlds; in Lorelie, all danced to Ashera's tune. Recruit Chaeron to silence Ashera's objections, or even Parma's promise might not serve.

What spell, then? But she had not thought of any by the time Chaeron's lintel was broached, though she went the long way around to make sure she did not meet Ashera, whose constitutional after dinner took her through the tower's main halls.

Shebat shivered at all she was wagering, and signaled her men to await without, thinking that everything, since she had begged Marada to take her with him into she knew not what, had been the wildest of gambles. How, then, could freedom from Lorelie's poisonous beauty be less? Her knuckles were white as she tapped the door, forgetting the Kerrion manner of pressing a lit plate which would chime within.

In that final instant, the face of the old woman who had been Bolen's wife, who had taught Shebat what small enchantments she possessed, who had known the arts of reading, even writing, but had died too soon to pass them on, came before her eyes. But the cracked lips had no spell to speak, only the spittle that they had bubbled in their dying, before things went from bad to worse without her, while Bolen's nightmare had held her helpless in its sway.

She felt that way again: helpless, terrified, a piece of meat before a slavering wolf; she felt her blood coursing her veins. As the door slid back and a puzzled Chaeron scanned her and hurriedly ushered her within, she was mumbling a conditionless warding that might bring her to the other side of this adventure whole and hale. He would likely have seen the dull glow of the attendant signing, did he not take a moment to dismiss her bodyguards, saying that he would call them in their quarters when he needed them, and to Shebat on the closing of the door:

"There is no need of advertising where you are, when mother would so dearly like to know. What possessed you to insult her so thoroughly? You could have sent word." The chastisement in his tone was wry; he enjoyed his mother's irritation; Shebat's folly; all his family's striving was a comedy put on for his amusement.

Shebat said as much, eyes flashing.

"Now, I have hurt you, and I did not mean to. You are becoming too beautiful to trifle with. Sit, and tell me what brings you here. If it is the same thing that kept you from dinner, so much the better. By the way, are you hungry?"

"No, I am not hungry," she murmured, backing away from him, keeping her distance until a couch behind her knees forced her to sit or betray herself. The couch, one of a pair, was small, dark, intimately designed as was the chalcedony room about. He sat easily beside her, catty-corner with one leg drawn up, arms lying along the upholstery so that one hand was behind her neck. He was lightly clad in a loose, teal shirt and trousers. He had been about to retire, she realized, pulling her gaze away from the Kerrion crest worked into a jewel hung from a chain about his neck. She was acutely uncomfortable, wishing that she had not come. The soft silk trousers rustled as he shifted. She could find no place to rest her eyes, which kept trying to return to his chest, and the hair on it which Kerrion formality had never allowed her to guess might grow there. Though he was certainly fully clothed, the opened vee at his throat disconcerted her thoroughly: why was it so astounding that Chaeron's throat grew hair on it or had an idle chain swinging from it, slowly back and forth?

"So," he said softly after a time, "does what you see please you? Do I suit?"

"Oh, no. I mean—did I wake you?"

Eyes crinkled under slightly raised brows. "Oh, no? I am devastated; I had hoped this might be what it looked. And no, you did not wake me. I toss and turn, but sleep has been eluding me of late. So I thought to catch it unawares, at this early hour." He waited, but Shebat only blinked, owl-eyed. "Ask me," he suggested delicately, "why it is that I cannot sleep."

"I had better not," she blurted. "That is . . . I need your advice, Chaeron. And your help."

"My dear, whatever I have is yours. I will lay my cloak in the puddle barring your path, I promise. But first, you have not given me even a sisterly kiss." And he leaned forward, his hand cupping the back of her neck, guiding her firmly.

"There, that is better." The blue eyes, inches from hers, sought deeply, so that Shebat looked downward, at his pulse beating in his throat. He sighed, releasing her head. "For the first time, you have kissed back, rather than enduring me. Why is that?"

She would have wriggled away from him, but the couch was small and he had leaned close and she had nowhere to retreat. "You are going to be angry with me."

"Never." But auburn lashes flicked down, hiding his eyes, while his fingers ran lightly along the nape of her neck. "But it must be important, else you would not be suffering so intimate a touch. Is it important enough that I might buy what you will not give freely? With my sage counsel, perchance, or my influence upon my mother?"

"Are you always so cruel?" she wondered, hearing her tongue betray her as it stumbled.

"Only when there is no alternative. But honesty sometimes seems cruel."

"Especially coming from you." It slipped out, she could not stop it, being fully engaged with his proximity and the trepidation come so fully upon her.

His mouth barely twitched, but humor hardened to another, sharper thing behind the blue of his eyes. "What is it, little sister, that makes you so unaccepting of my affection?"

"Only that it would frighten me, should it become more than filial." The fingers stopped moving, lay quiet on her shoulder.

"And is that so bad? Fear spices love, always."

"But I am already in love, with Marada, and not with you." She shrank back, having said that, the few inches the resilient couch allowed.

Colder, if possible, became Chaeron's smile. "You confuse emotional love and physical love. I suppose I can excuse that in a young girl. Marada!" Chaeron dismissed his brother by simply speaking his name. "Let us hear what it is you came here to say. The hour grows late for pointless chatter."

"I should never have come here," Shebat wailed.

"So? Perhaps not. But you are here, nevertheless. I, for one, am not of a mind to waste this opportunity. And something, unfortunately not my attentions, drew you here. Now," he said, chiding her gently, "what can I do for you, or must we sit here while I try to guess while my ardor prompts me to guess at things other than those you might choose? I know you are young, and I understand that idealism is the precinct most especially of young girls, but your presence threatens to make me forget all my hard-won insights in search of surer proof." Again the fingers moved lightly on her back. His lips sought hers, inexorable arms enfolded her. But she locked her teeth together against his probing tongue, and to the questions his body asked, hers made no answer, keeping stiffly silent.

After a brief time he released her, pushed up from the couch and crossed the room, where he spoke unintelligibly, very low, into his terminal.

Then he turned, leaning back against the artfully concealed console, and said precisely: "I have summoned your protectors. I am sorry about this, but I have waited long, and I had to see for myself if what you said was true. Since it is, I would like you to speak your piece and take your leave."

"I want to leave Lorelie. I have Parma's permission,

but without your blessing, Ashera will surely suborn him."

He leaned there, pushing at the cuticle of one nail with the perfect curve of another, for the space of a dozen breaths. Then he straightened up and from an expressionless mouth said, "I think that would be a good idea. But keep watch well about you. The arm of my mother is long and has many hands." Then he crossed to the couch and with his habitual courtesy helped her up, to, and through the door beyond which the four bodyguards were just arriving.

Seeing that they were there, he seemed relieved. He said to her, "It has been a pleasure," bowed slightly, and retired, the door closing silently behind.

The ship which bore Parma Alexander Kerrion to Draconis was hardly more elegant and only one cabin larger than Marada's. Even while experiencing initial surprise, something told Shebat that she should have known: Parma would give no less than the best, else not give at all.

And, too, *state of the art* and Kerrion were so synonymous in space technology as to have become threads in the carpet of sly wit the pilots carried with them wherever they went, in the way of men who must make endlessly transient berths smack of home.

So when she met Softa David Spry, the tawny, compact pilot just signing on the Kerrion flagship in place of the dewy-eyed retiree come aboard briefly to make the round of introductions, Shebat did not think to comment on the odd-sounding prenomen appended to his name. Though Parma burst out chuckling when the old pilot brought before him the new, extending his hand in greeting, saying, "Glad to have you, *Softa* David Spry," still Shebat did not understand.

After a surfeit of smothered smirks whenever Shebat called him Softa David, which she did often in her irrepressible questioning of the pilot's every move, the flat-faced pilot said gravely, *"David* will do. Softa's a tease-title, come from the contracted letters of 'state of the art.' It's like a nickname, but . . . don't go, now. Or hang your head. You did not know, and none of us hurried to tell you."

"I will never learn it all," Shebat muttered miserably, sinking down into the acceleration couch on Spry's right. "I am no Kerrion born, as you have well seen. All their names, and yours the more for not being Kerrion, sound strange to me. I cannot bear this endless stumbling over unforeseeable obstacles."

"Lords, do you always talk like that? No, I am sorry. I was going to tell you something about not letting the teasing get to you, and teased you myself instead. Look, you cannot be so serious, when the whole universe is a side-splitting joke. Surely you can see that. If you are not a Kerrion and yet are most soberly presented to each and all as the heir apparent, you must in some way have entertained yourself with the humor of that. If I were as serious as you, I would go mad straightaway, the next dip into flight. If what your . . . father? Stepfather? Anyway, if what old Parma so grudgingly admitted is true, and you want to fly, you had best learn how to tell jokes, and to take them."

"Tell me about it," she demanded, unaware her lips were parted, or that she leaned far forward.

"About what?"

"About the spongespace, about all those lights," she waved at the master control. "Tell me about how it feels. What is the nature of it that the theory cannot proclaim?"

The pilot pulled at his lower lip, glanced at his panel, adjusted something there. "There's too much to tell, and too little. You have had the theory of it, then? And found it intriguing but mysterious? All the visible space we see is mirage; what is distant may be near; what seems near is far. True measures and optical measures differ widely. The *sponge* part is pure analogy. Visual space is a distended skin, points on which can be reached by going beneath. Hence, Draconis and Lorelie are not lifetimes apart, but days. If we were to crawl along beneath the speed of light, or just at it, time dilation would cause us to age at a different rate than those in stationary space; ergo, space travel would be impractical. If we were to traverse spongespace on instruments, the discrepancy would still exist, but in a random fashion: the time we lost approaching the speed of light would be subtracted by the negative, or backward-running temporality one encounters exiting spongespace, but in a random fashion that would make, *did* make, in early experimental penetrations, spongetravel equally impractical. Imagine coming out in Draconis space *before* you even leave Lorelie . . . are you following?"

Shebat nodded, though she was somewhat taken aback by the thought of being in two places at once. "What happens then? Which is the real person, which not?"

The pilot sighed. "I'm just confusing you, aren't I? People are the coefficient in the equation that keeps that particular paradox from occurring. Why, in detail, no one knows. The one time an automated device made that journey without an organic brain, an explosion occurred at the designated point of arrival three hours *before* the device was launched. Let me try, very briefly, to explain the principle: the human brain contains such an inflexible conceptualization of sequential time that the guiding brain demands from spongespace acquiescence to its schedule. And gets it, somehow. Men didn't 'understand' what goes on in the heart of a fission reaction when they exploded the first A-bomb. We do not understand how the mind presupposes its rhythm on what seems a soulless cosmos. But the fact remains that if a human guidance system experiences ten days' subjective time on a flight from point A to point B, the time-loss and time-gain the universe exacts as payment of passage are exactly and to the second in accord with subjectively experienced time. Thence, among other things, the Lords of Cosmic Jest, for who could have foreseen that the mind of man was powerful enough to command the currents of spacetime? A servile universe is difficult to comprehend; an amenable one raises all my hackles."

"But you still have not told me why piloting is no fit occupation for a Kerrion, nor why when it appeared on my aptitude tests the computer red-lined it."

"That high, eh? Well, well, welcome sister madwoman." And Softa David Spry leaned near, widening his seal's eyes until the whites showed all around, "Because, little Kerrion heir, by all accounts and current standards, spongespace makes us all mad as hatters. We live short, eventful lives. We produce few children. But most of all, they fear us because we are not platform-sane. Spongespace, you see," he whispered, "strips away all illusions. One clear look at one's self entitles any man to lunacy's refuge. Ha! Now I have frightened you! Good."

"I am not frightened. And if Parma put you up to this to frighten me away from piloting, it is to no avail. See the glitter in my palms? Feel them; are they not cold? It is anticipation, not hesitancy, you feel." And she caught his larger hand in hers, squeezing tightly. "Teach me what you can, for I will not be swayed, and I have a lot of lost time to make up for, Softa David."

He laughed, saying, "I am beginning to see why Parma chose you above one of the serpent's brood. Look closely, now; this is not a run-through. I am setting up the course."

And, a little later: "Now, let us both get acquainted with *Bucephalus,* without whose aid we would yet be sitting here when the universe has run down stonecold."

Bucephalus was the flagship's name, Shebat recalled, while hiding her puzzlement as best she could. She had seen the painted white horse pawing seven stars by the entry port, with the name stenciled beneath.

Flip; snap; punch went Spry's nimble fingers. *Blink; glow; shimmer* went the thousand lights of the master control.

The *Bucephalus*'s mellifluous voice spoke from all about: from grids in the desklike panels, from corners high above their heads; from before, beside and behind, the sonorous greeting rang out. And as Softa David Spry answered solemnly the mechanical salutation, Shebat remembered the spirit voices speaking from thin air in Marada's ship. "Greetings to you, *Bucephalus,*" she said when Spry prompted her; she no longer had any doubt as to whose the disembodied voice was.

So, Shebat met her first ship's guidance computer as an equal, and all of Ashera's curses and Chaeron's warnings and her longing for Marada's comforting presence were subsumed by the shivering tingle that overswept her while she and *Bucephalus* made one another's acquaintance, so that none of it mattered at all.

• • •

Draconis, like Lorelie, was a platform; one dwelt in it, rather than on. But there all resemblance ceased, for Draconis was the premier Kerrion control central, the largest commercial port in all the consulate's space. She had been much smaller once, housing a mere ten thousand on ten levels. Like an onion, she had recircled herself, again and again, so that the original out-level had become part of her core.

Now, Draconis was the central jewel in her anchor-planet's fillet. The planet itself was skewered through six times with laser spokes, merely a hub for man's marvelous wheel.

When man had first come here, popping out of sponge into an alien star-scape, that vista had seemed most similar to Draconis as it appeared in Earth's night sky. Sometime around the building of level forty, it had been proved that the locus of the platform was nowhere near the astronomical Draconis, but rather in a far galaxy Earthers had named M-87. The galaxy M-87 became Centralia, because of its sponge-centrality as much as its ancient bright sky; but Draconis remained Draconis, misnomer or no.

Now, she housed a quarter-million souls, on two hundred levels. She housed the mighty and the meek, for such were drawn together, to serve and be served. They were of every class, creed and color, the common denominator being currency and its exchange.

As with any other habitation of man, some parts boasted great beauty, others begged in baleful disrepair. There had grown up a bellicose stalemate between the two: the dole and the dream dancers provided amelioration for the penniless; the cheap labor which could turn down no work, no matter how dangerous, justified in practice what in democratic theory their betters were obligated to provide.

Anyone could rise to great stature in the Consortium, so its leaders ever hastened to aver. However, no one could bear a child without being able to show funds set aside for its education and the securing of its position in the work force; and of the difficulties of that matter for the dwellers downunder, as little as was prudent was said.

This seemed to Shebat somehow an ill-struck chord in

the Consortium's symphony; an unnecessary dissonance that made the glorious petty, as if the golden statues of prominent Kerrions around the manicured court of Kerrion consulate headquarters were merely wood wrapped with gilded foil. She said as much to Parma, pointing out that with all the Kerrion wealth there was no reason why its citizens should be ragged and hungry, stumbling in ill-lit, littered streets. Thereupon Parma's brows drew down, and in a voice like thunder he threatened her with terrible punishment should she ever again venture beneath the hundredth level of Draconis.

"You will never get your ship; you will never get out of these walls, but to bid the Consortium farewell on the way back to your dustball of a planet. Should you *even mention* such sophomoric, ill-placed compassion to me again, these will be only the harbingers of my retribution." And Parma jabbed at his desk's electronics, snapping thereto: "Jebediah, come in here. Now!"

Almost instantly, the baldheaded secretary was entering, his stooped shoulders preceding all else, his bright eyes sweeping about his master's office.

"Sir?" he queried, when he stood before Parma's desk.

"Did you take this girl downunder? Or did you simply lose track of her?"

"I accompanied her myself, Consul, since she would not be dissuaded. I thought it best."

"*You* thought it best? Who are you, to ignore my specified restrictions? I am gone barely a half-year, and you have no more use for me, but run all the consulate as you see fit, is that it? Well, speak up, Jebediah!"

But the older man's chin trembled, and he seemed also to shrink smaller, from which diminishing stature he cast Parma a look like a dog beaten for a wolf's transgression.

Parma let out an explosive sigh, rubbing his eyes, then pulled his palm down slowly over his face, twisting camel's mouth as it passed. "Ah, I am sorry, Jebediah, for doubting you. I am sure whatever was done, was done as best could be."

"I was just trying to keep matters in hand without troubling you, sir, as I have always done."

"I know. And you know I realize that. But I am cranky and overworked, and not back a week. If I had two of you, I would send the other to Labayan space to work your magic on Marada."

"Trouble, sir?" asked Jebediah softly.

"How not, with that meddlesome son of mine in there? But nothing we cannot handle, I think. If—"

Shebat cleared her throat, knowing she had been forgotten.

"Ah, yes. Shebat, run along. And remember, if I catch word that you have been downunder even once more, no matter if it is in the company of the Jesters themselves, you will have no pilot's training, no little cruiser for which I have just paid twice the insurable worth. I will have Jebediah turn you into a woman, and we will all treat you like one. Now, go on and look at the gift I have got for you, though you are hardly deserving. Wait!"

Shebat had made the distance to the door, glad to be out of there unpunished. She had hardly been listening. When Parma's command pulled her up short, she turned, running back over the things he had said which she had heard but not considered. Then she said: "Ship! Cruiser. You said that? You *mean* that? Where?"

Though he struggled against it, Parma's pleasure cracked through his scowl. "Where? Where? Now let me think, for you made me so angry, I seem to have forgotten." He put three fingers to the bridge of his nose. "Ah, I have it," he said as Shebat's soft wail sounded. "Slip fifteen. That's it: fifteen."

To the girl's streaming thanks, he said only more severely that she must not ill reward him for his gift, and let her go.

Once she was gone, the smile vanished and the old consul general's face displayed a concern Jebediah had seldom seen there. "She's half a dream dancer, Jebediah. Her aptitudes proclaim it."

Jebediah had difficulty concealing his shock, not at the fact, which he well knew, but that Parma would so confide in him.

"If she gets more than a smell of them, I am likely to lose her. And I do not want to be the laughingstock of the Consortium, which would be only the first of many bitter blows should the worst occur."

"So you gave her the ship, fostered this hunger of hers

for space, as an inoculation against the dread disease?"
Jebediah forgot his usual "sir," but Parma did not notice.

"Most exactly so. Do you see why I restricted her from
the lower levels, yet could not forbid them too pointedly?"

It took all Jebediah's years of training to keep a straight
face when he answered that he understood; more, that as
a father of some few years' experience, he would have had
to do the same.

What in truth Jebediah had to do that day he did not
find time to even contemplate until Parma's office was as
dark as the artificial evening swooping down over Draconis. Alone but for the whirr that signaled the automated
security and janitorial system waked and prowling, he set
up the isolation block which masked whatever sensitive
endeavors might be taken up in the consul general's suite
from even those insidious all-seeing eyes.

Then he leaned back, feet upon his desk, hands laced
into a cradle for his aching neck, and closed his eyes,
exhaling deeply thrice. Privacy, which the Kerrion kinship
bond had tendered to them as a birthright, was of great
moment to all lesser souls.

Shebat Alexandra Kerrion, who was so untutored in the
customs of the bondkin she would someday (if Parma had
his way) lead as to have never even have used the term in
Jebediah's hearing, was the sole subject of Jebediah's
meditation. If there were not so much to be gained
financially by delivering the girl into those hands anx-
iously awaiting her, Jebediah would have been content to
sit by. To let her stay in her place, stay Kerrion, stay the
scrap of meat over which the whole hungry pack of
Kerrions would tear each other limb from limb: there was
a tantalizing bit of revenge that would sate even
Jebediah's hunger.

But it had been he, Jebediah, who had suggested to
Selim Labaya the whole of the delicate—and profitable—
maneuver by which Parma Kerrion and his meretricious
brood would be forced to discredit themselves so entirely
that the next vote of confidence would be their last. He
must see the matter through to its fruition, no matter what
the difficulties. And he must do so without implicating
himself in any way. *Even that, he would do!* he corrected
himself: For the end of the Kerrion bond group's tenure

as first family of the Consortium, Jebediah would sacrifice his place, even his life. His honor had long ago gone into this pot, the winning of which was the only goal he allowed himself. Besides, of course, an occasional dream dancer to ease his nights, whenever he could afford one. How many such nights he could buy from a successful completion of this particular sabotage he refused to prematurely contemplate.

What he had suggested to a bereaved father of a slain girl, that father had taken to heart. He had been hesitant, though he had long known the ears in which to whisper, whose owner's lips in turn whispered in Labaya's ear. The price he had put upon the service he offered was unthinkably high; but the service was unthinkable, dear to Labayan hearts as an innermost dream.

He had had second thoughts, having committed himself. But his penchant for dream dancers had made some such move a necessity. He was pauperized, though his income was as high as could be any man's, come from downunder with no bond group's profit-share to underwrite him. Come up a bastard from downunder streets, disavowed spawn of Parma Kerrion's uncle and a tenth-level slut, he had dedicated his life to the destruction of those whose kin he was, but who refused him. Well had he kept that secret hid, but not well enough that Selim Labaya had not found it out. Which was another reason why all things must shape themselves to Jebediah's prognostications.

Jebediah dared not disappoint Selim Labaya in any particular. As the bond's consul general had so succinctly put it, to do so would mean his citizenship. As urgently even as that, another consideration weighed on him: his creditors must be appeased, for those dwelling in the shadowy streets beneath Kerrion glory had no bondmember's responsibilities to kin, nor sensitivities either: they would simply kill him, should his debts stand overlong.

That, he thought wryly, though without remorse, was what had gotten him into this intrigue to begin with. Other times, he had come to the edge of covert alliance with a rival consulate, but always turned away in disgust. This time, there had been no turning back. Correction: there *was* no turning back. But then, never in his wildest

dreams had he thought up any scenario as precipitously
perfect as the one Marada had begun with his customary
heedlessness and Parma served Jebediah on the platter of
his shortsighted grief.

Indeed, knowing of Marada's wardship of the Earth
girl, and the death of the Kerrion heir and Labaya's
daughter, of Parma's grief-stricken obtuseness and Ashera's obdurate machinations to install her eldest as next in
line: knowing all of these, plus the reason Parma Alexander Kerrion had found it necessary to take a half-year
leave, it had been incumbent on Jebediah to whisper in
the ear of a Labayan minion that a sweeter revenge could
be gotten by consummating the marriage of Kerrion to
Labaya than might be had even by snubbing Parma's
invitation to Lorelie. The snub would lead to a trade war
which, it would then be easy to argue, Labayan as well as
Kerrion would equally have precipitated.

And he had been right: Labaya was unbesmirched,
blameless, even ethically pure in his behavior, thanks to
Jebediah's intervention. The trade war might have served
to weaken Kerrion power, but it would not have destroyed it. And that was what Jebediah lived to behold:
the kin scattered, the platforms sold off, all things Kerrion
in others' hands.

It would have been as good as accomplished now, if not
for the girl's wagging tongue. The problem facing him was
complex: Parma had expressly forbidden him to expose
the girl to the lower levels, where she must end to
complete the coup. He would find another way. Had
Jebediah not predicted that there would be no harm done
by Selim Labaya's arrogant insistence that he, Jebediah,
be in the very Labayan flagship berthed in Lorelie? If
anything went wrong, Labaya had threatened, Jebediah
would be handed over to his employer's wrath on the
spot. But Jebediah had lain content, enjoying his dream
dancer's art undisturbed, while all things Kerrion proceeded as he had known they would, even to Marada's
insistence on piloting his own *Hassid* into Labayan space,
and Ashera's clumsy attempt at sabotage. So he had not
had to huddle, cowering, in the cargo bay, with Marada
Seleucus Kerrion mere bulkheads away. This had not
surprised Jebediah: he had made the Kerrion kinship

bond his lifelong study; he knew them better than they knew themselves.

All but Shebat, late of the planet Earth and suddenly Kerrion. All but Shebat *Alexandra* Kerrion, he corrected himself glumly, his mouth pursing, wriggling, at length emitting a cluckingsound.

"If she gets more than a smell of dream dancers, I am likely to lose her." Old Parma's worried voice reechoed in Jebediah's mind. That had been a chancy moment, when Parma prognosticated the fate Jebediah had in mind for him. *"I do not want to be the laughingstock of the Consortium, which would be only the first of many bitter blows should the worst occur,"* the consul general had mused, looking right at Jebediah. For a moment, all his blood had frozen in his veins. For a moment, wild schemes of escape inundated him. For a moment, Jebediah had thought that Parma was telling him that all was known, that he was unmasked, found out, that old Labaya had settled for the lesser joy of flouting to Parma the duplicitous traitor in his midst, rather than waiting for the later, more exotic pleasure Jebediah had promised to provide.

But Jebediah had played one last card, as if nothing were amiss.

And the moment had passed, sans denouement.

He hoped.

For above all, he had learned never to underestimate Parma Kerrion, who had managed unfailingly to turn every misfortune to benefit, these twenty-two years that Jebediah had been surreptitiously strewing evils upon the consul general's path.

There remained that most horrifying, but vanishingly small, possibility he had sensed in Parma's presence: the old man knew! Then why did he not act? Kerrion vengeance was justly feared, as much for its languor as for its thoroughness.

Jebediah spat, and removed his feet from the desk. Sitting hunched over it, he massaged his temples. Caught between Parma Kerrion and Selim Labaya, a man might justifiably contemplate suicide, were he not of a consular house. Still, though the bond would never acknowledge him, Jebediah had acquired many of their traits. Or inherited them, he grimaced.

Let it be, then. Until Kerrion intelligencers came to hustle him off to one kind of justice, or Labayan ones to another, he would proceed as if neither possibility existed. He would do this which he had long waited to do, not out of fear, but out of choice.

Slowly, his fingers ceased their trembling. Soon he swallowed less often, and breathed more deeply.

The problem, then, came clearer. Only one worry claimed immediacy over all others: Shebat Kerrion must find the dream dancer in herself; or she must disappear without a trace.

Though the second alternative was the safer, the first had infinitely more spice. And he would be doing the girl a favor: the computer was hardly so grossly in error. It was Parma's error for thinking that the power of his personality could overrule two red-lined aptitude prognosticators, both in her top three: Parma's error; Jebediah's delight; Selim's fondest dream. All these come wrapped in the slight, attractive person of a girl barely past childhood; hardly more than a spear-carrying savage; slightly higher in intelligence than anyone in the whole of the data banks' memory. And, last but not least, possessed of a haphazard collection of genetic predispositions so attractive to the Kerrion strain that no amount of rational thought would enable any Kerrion male to put her out of mind.

It had been this of all the information he had collected about Shebat that had shed the most light on this series of miraculous events, so much that he had collapsed into helpless mirth, weeping as he chortled, seeing that the Lords of Cosmic Jest would have their acerbic way. Gods, there were none. But the mind of mirth that pervaded all things was omniscient, desirous of homage and the sacrifices called titter, chortle and smile.

Something sobered him: what he knew from his search of the Kerrion data pool, Parma knew also. What could be said of Kerrion genetics, in a lesser, dilute fashion, could be said of his, also. Was that why he found himself so hesitant to have the girl abducted and slain out of hand? It was the obvious solution, the one which, should he not soon employ it, he would have to replace in Selim Labaya's expectations with the other, which he whole-heartedly favored. What a dream dancer Shebat Kerrion would make!

Decided, he coded a surveillance-proof line for himself and arranged a meeting with his Labayan contact, warn-ing the man to bring money. "A mil-suit full, for all hangs on the next few days," he snapped, and cut the circuit before the man could ask questions.

If he himself could not take the girl to her rendezvous with destiny, others must be employed to show her the way.

"Softa! Softa David! Come see!" Shebat hung out her slipside port, waving urgently to the lithe pilot in the gray coveralls of his guild.

"So this is where you have been for three days?" laughed the pilot, while Shebat scrambled forth, tugging on his hand to hurry. "Did you get my call, or have you even foresworn your Kerrion duty to check your mes-sages?"

Only a fleeting shadow crossed the girl's shining eyes. "You did not get mine, then? No matter. You are here and I am here, and that is all that matters. Will you hurry? I cannot live another moment without showing you the *Marada*. Inside, now!"

Softa David frowned, hanging back, saying: "It is bad luck to name a ship after a man, let alone a living one whose own luck is far from good."

"Let go," but Softa David's hand only imprisoned hers more surely.

"No, I will not." They stood there in silence, a pair of giant paper dolls spread across the slip's gangplank.

Then Spry said: "Change the name of it, Shebat."

"Why?" she pouted, examining his hand holding hers. She pulled back: once; twice; but the pilot held firm, unmoving. "Parma's ship has a masculine name."

"Of a horse, not a man." Suddenly his demeanor changed, and by the arm he pulled her away from the silvery, oblong port. She resisted, then stumbled toward him.

"What is the matter with you? Softa, are you not happy for me? Is it not a fine ship?"

"The finest. Too complex and too powerful for you. And too overwhelming, not to say tempting. I want you to promise me you will not take it out alone until I, myself, have pronounced you fit to do so. *Shebat!*"

Her flare of fury faded with his loud calling of her name, but it also attracted attention. From gantry and slipside heads poked out, necks craned, eyes squinted to see what might be the cause of the shouting at slip fifteen, where all knew the Kerrion heir's new toy was docked. That they saw two locked in obvious disagreement did not please David Spry, who was up to his non-Kerrion neck in the bond's affairs, and loathed it.

Six weeks in their employ, he thought: it might have been six years.

"Shebat, come away with me, to a more suitable spot, and we will talk. I cannot speak as freely here as I might like." Did she understand, *could* she understand any of this which was happening to her? He ached with compassion, a momentary throb of an exposed nerve. Then it was gone, pushed aside by a cold voice that told him, ringingly, that he could afford no qualm. Since the voice was his own, he heeded it.

When he had got her out from the dockside, he hailed a lorry and directed it to take them to a seventh-level bar. From the startled blink of the girl's eyes as the lorry took its turn in the drop-shaft and gravity waned, he deduced she had never traveled in one before. "So, have you spent all your time in the normal gravity halls of Kerrions?"

"I have been lower than we are going now!" she boasted. "But by escalator; not lorry."

Spry nodded, and the master pilot's circles in his ears sparkled like starlight out from buff hair finally grown back after the shearing he had undergone out of respect for his new employer. "You do not notice the gee discrepancy, going down so slowly. But tell me who took you down slumming? And why? Do you have a secret suitor, who must talk to you in hidden alleyways where Kerrion ears cannot hear?"

Shebat's smothered laughter and downcast eyes said something that was underlined by the flush creeping up her neck. He saw it pass the almost invisible line where a clear mil-suit ended, giving up further protection to the skin treatment that was called a mil-hood. Such a child she was, and the more winning for that. Her girlish embarrassment made him feel a rough creature, cold and cynical. Still, all must be who they were; the universe had no time for posturings. David's time had not been his own since he was old enough to choose his trade. Since then, space and Chance had determined all. He was vaguely aware that wherever he happened to be crises bared their bleeding breasts, as if he were Fate's own witness. It had been with him as long as his membership in the pilot's guild. Still, sometimes he felt regret.

So, it was with regret that he said to Shebat as soon as they were seated in a coin-operated privacy booth of seventh-level seamy style:

"Have you considered Parma's motives in elevating you so abruptly and granting your every whim, no matter how expensive or unseemly to Kerrion mores? No? Listen well, little apprentice, or you may not live to become the pilot of your dreams. Ashera Kerrion will be well-diverted with you, keeping her out of Parma's hair. Eventually something *will* happen to you, which Parma will, with all fitting horror, blame on her and her son, Chaeron. With both of them stripped of their citizenship, nothing stands in Parma's way. He will make Marada Kerrion heir as he dares not do yet, lest he fall afoul of Ashera. He will unite in truth and deed Labayan and Kerrion space: manipulating both, he will control the civilized stars. Your life becomes infinitesimally small change in a game with stakes that high."

The high-chinned stare of the girl, followed by the glitter of unshed tears, rapid blinking, full flush, and lastly a murmured: "How do you suggest I protect myself?" made Softa David sigh a deep and heartfelt sigh of relief.

"I had thought to be endlessly convincing you," he admitted, and reaching over, patted Shebat's clenched hands.

"I trust you, Softa David. Since Marada is gone, I must trust someone."

Rapidly, Spry began to explain his plan; the last thing he wanted to think about was what Shebat had just said.

"I have friends in low places, whose aid and loyalty come regularly to the auction block. Below the tenth level anything can be bought: a quarter-citizenship; a half; a full share. A new identity; a different computer access code; a place to hide for awhile until the search dies down or time and maturity complete your disguise: all could be bought with the worth of that cruiser, once it is berthed in a non-Kerrion slip."

"I will not give the *Marada* up!" Shebat's voice was adamant. But, as David Spry had hoped, in her face confusion reigned. "Why should I? Parma has been wonderfully good to me . . ." she trailed off, biting her lip, her gaze full of trepidation. And when he kept silent, only regarding her pityingly, she whispered, "Why?" once again.

"Why? So you will not meet the early death that will befall you if you remain a Kerrion decoy. Did you have bodyguards in Lorelie?"

"Yes," barely audible.

"Do you have them now?"

"I . . . do not know. But there were some men assigned to me, when first I got here, though I have not seen them these last few days. I have been in the *Marada*. Parma would not leave such a matter unattended. All the Kerrion halls have eyes and ears." She recollected then what Parma had said to her would be the cost of descending into the deep, suppurating underworld of the lower levels. "Doubtless, my whereabouts are even now known to him. And because of that, and you bullying me into this jaunt without telling me the destination you had in mind, I will not have the ship any longer. Parma said that if I came down here again, I would forfeit it, and my pilot's training, and all else that matters." A nervous hand raked through black curls, pulling hair back from her furrowed forehead. "Oh, why did I not think of that? Softa, what will I do? He will never forgive me!"

David Spry leaned back in his chair, ruminatively tapping the order keys of the automated waiter. "What would you like? Wine, beer? Or would cocoa suit?"

The girl did not rise to his bait, but chewed her lip, staring blankly somewhere beside his head. "How do you know so much about Kerrion affairs?" she asked distantly, as if from deep meditation.

David Spry suppressed a shiver, saying glibly: "I shipped with Marada, when we were both apprentices," which was true. Then, to redirect her to a less dangerous area than that of his own origins, motives, or objectives, he played her more line: "As to what you should do, since you stand to lose the ship in any case: let me steal it."

"What?"

"Give me the access keys, and I will take it out of Kerrion space, where you can reclaim it when I have smuggled you through. I can have it mislogged, as if you took the cruiser out prematurely, lost control, and both you and the ship will be officially stricken from the consulate census. It is that simple."

"That is simple? But where would I go? I would have no citizenship, nothing."

The drinks slid out of their hopper. He pushed the wine glass toward Shebat. He made a crude noise that said what worth citizenship had in his eyes, then apologized for being crass. Sipping, he leaned forward conspiratorially, saying: "There is more to time and space than the Consortium. There is more than one group of independent—shall we be delicate? Yes? Then: entrepreneurs, let us call them, who would welcome with open arms such a cruiser, armed and shielded by the impeccable wrights in Kerrion employ. A good enough living can be made outside the Consortium, if one is not squeamish, which you cannot afford to be."

"I would be a criminal."

"Live criminal, dead citizen."

"It cannot be. Marada would never have allowed Parma to assume my guardianship if—"

He interrupted her, reaching across the narrow table to lay a hand on her wrist. "Shebat, I will gladly return you to Parma's arms, if you so decide. I have done the duty conscience demanded of me, that I would owe any guildfellow. More than apprising you of my estimation of your peril, I cannot do." And he retrieved his hand and with it raised his drink: "To you, to your exquisite innocence. May you prevail in life, no matter how unlikely it presently seems." And he held out his glass until hers clinked against it. He saw the hunched shoul-

ders, the protective sinking of her head. He had succeeded in terrifying her. He had not even had to lie.

"Marada once said to me," she confided bitterly,
having gulped the whole wineglass as if it were filled with
water, "that it is axiomatic that no Kerrion is ever as he
seems." Then she giggled giddily, and tore at the hair
flopped again over her eyes. "But I did not think he was
including himself in that condemnation."

Spry's discomfort was not out of character; he let it
show. "I know you care a great deal for him. But he is
many things, none of which sleep easily in the same bed:
he is a Kerrion; he is second to you in line of primogeniture; and he is a pilot. Our guildsmen are not unjustly
famed for relegating sex to a gratuity, love to casual
dalliance, and loyalty to their brothers of the sponge." He
smiled a twisted smile. "He is too much a Kerrion to
stymie his father's purpose by annulling his marriage.
What have you to hope for there, but a few surreptitious
nights stolen from a woman who will hardly miss them, as
one of the endless chain of port girls all pilots keep?"

Almost, he left off there. He had to study the bottom of
his glass. Insensate cruelty was hardly his specialty.

He heard a series of sad sounds, an almost inaudible
mew, a tremulous gulp, a rustle that must be the girl
wiping away tears. "By the Jesters, don't cry over the
bastard, Shebat. He hardly deserves it." And he found
himself rounding the table to her and putting his arms
protectively around her, so that she could do just that.
Why me, Lords? he queried silently, but the many-headed
anthropomorphization of Chance made him no reply.

"What shall I do?" she sniffed at last, her face pressed
to his dampened shirt.

"Dry your tears, first off. Pilots do not cry over lost
lovers; lovers cry over lost pilots. If you are recovered, we
will work out the details of this, and then I'll stake you to
a dream dancer. You look as if you could use one." So
delicately was the barbed fly cast upon the waters, the
pilot-cum-fisherman could not help but smile. And when
the soft little fish with wide eyes and parted lips took the
bait, asking on a held breath what a dream dancer might
be, he could do nothing but let his humor burst forth into

a chuckle, as he promised her that soon enough she would see for herself.

It was then, when he was still congratulating himself on the ease with which things had been accomplished, even thinking that Shebat was not nearly so effective under pressure, nor so bright, as her aptitude testing had proclaimed her, that the girl, pulling away from him, said:

"Softa, will you come with me and tell all this to Parma, right now?"

He did not at all like the way she said it. He answered carefully: "I have taken an oath to be master to your apprentice; that entitles you to the truth from me, and my help if you should come to need it. Parma is my employer: that relationship exacts particular loyalties, it is true, but not enough to make me deliver you into his hands." Carefully, now, all *must* be true. He could not afford to lie. A number of strictures binding him with divergent duties must be made to parallel each other. "Shebat, you did not ask me how I knew your bodyguards have not lately been in evidence. Ask me."

"How, then?" asked the girl with doubting eyes.

"I heard two of them talking over drinks about the foolhardiness of Parma's office to have recalled them. And I heard it because I had taken pains to be in a place I knew they frequented, because when I could not raise you anywhere in Draconis, when I realized that *no one*, including the consul general's office and its intelligence pool, knew where you were, *then* I knew that the exigencies of my oath were about to be called into play."

"Your oath to whom?" she breathed, face pale. "If no one has known my whereabouts for three days, then it is safe to assume that Parma does not know it now. Therefore, my ship, my pilot's training, are not in danger. As to whether or not my life is equally safe, only you can say. Why did you not suggest that I steal the ship myself; why did you bring me down here, rather than coming with me into the *Marada*, where the security would be at least as good as this?" She waved a hand around her. "Tears, though you tell me not to shed them, have a purpose: they wash out fear and pain and confusion and leave a quiet mind, capable of thinking once again.

"What will you do if I refuse your aid, Master Pilot?" she whispered. "Will you then force me? Am I now in this deepest danger you have predicted so uncannily because you are its source?" Her eyes closed, lids briefly squeezed together as if to block out the specter of betrayal. "Will you hustle me off, notwithstanding my objections, to later sell me back to my family at some exorbitant price? Or is it, as you have so carefully explained, a matter of your guild oath, only not the one you took to me, but that you took to the Kerrion house? I would almost rather believe that Parma has finished with me, than that you would foreswear the pilot's bond."

"By the hairy nostrils of Chance!" He could not hold back the exclamation, nor the grin drawing lips back from his teeth. "Let me escort you back to your ship, your family, and your ending. It matters no more to me." And he stabbed at the seal on the little chamber, causing the door to click and his change to be returned, clattering down a little spiral chute into the plate held suspended beneath it. He scooped up the silver. Without a backward glance he stepped out into a crowded public room, not waiting to see if Shebat followed.

A moment later, a hand closed on his arm from behind. He saw her face through the smoky air, but her voice could not penetrate the din into which the privacy booth had ejected them.

Only when they had threaded their way through the press of second-class citizenry out onto the street, which flickered alternately red and green as the sign advertising the tavern pulsed above their heads, did he hear her desperately pleading that he not be angry.

"Let us go see the dream dancers, Softa, oh please. And then we will talk some more. I need time to think. I am seeing traitors everywhere; it is a common Kerrion curse. *Please!*"

He stared down at her severely, letting the breath whistle slowly through his nostrils, wondering if he had missed his calling, should not have been an intelligencer for a consular house instead of— "Apology accepted. Though I hardly think a dream dancer will help clear your thoughts—" It was then, as he laid a hand on her slim waist and by it propelled her along the narrow sidewalk, that he saw two hulking shadows detaching themselves from the gloom.

"Shebat, get behind me!" But it was too late. The ragged pair were upon him. In the way of his mind during crises, he had time to think that they were too well-fed and muscular for their station, then to recognize them as Kerrion minions, then to hear them: "You take the girl." "Suits me." And also Shebat's harsh gulp of air, her flat: "I am sorry I doubted you, Softa."

Then he could see an unshaven chin whose bristles glistened greenly, and the slow-time exploded, fast-forward.

Shebat was beside him, kicking out, as hands sought his throat and his own met flesh. Pain flared up in his arms, in his neck; a hot, hard weight bore him down. He wrapped his legs around his assailant's middle and shoved the man's face back. There were red lips close to his, leaking blood, then spurting it.

He pushed the dead bodyguard off him. The head lolled at an unlikely angle.

Shebat Kerrion was kneeling on the paved walk, her hands over her eyes. Beside her, stretched out on its back, was the corpse of a man twice her weight whose nose had been slammed into his brain by her kick.

He thrust himself upright. Breathing hard, he half-stumbled over the second corpse. There, leaning on the signpost which was unconcernedly blinking: *red—green— red,* he took a moment to collect his thoughts, to examine the unlikely tableau of victor and victim. Someone had well-schooled her in defense. He must remember that. He remembered, also, what she had said about being sorry for doubting him, reflecting that though the man who had sicced these dogs on him had done him a favor, it had been an unintentional one. As for what had been intended, he would return that in kind. Later. Now, the opportunity to play his own hand could not be ignored.

"Well, little murderess, do you finally believe me? Get up. The questions we have been deliberating have become suddenly academic. *Move!*"

She scrambled to her feet, her skin deathly pale even during the sign's flashes of red. "Do not run," he advised.

"Just walk steadily. Put your arm around my waist. That's good. Now, this way."

Three corners later, they stood at the door he had been seeking. It was down a flight from the street, unlit and unmarked. In the black well, as Spry tapped a pattern, Shebat drew back. Her voice, very small, came from behind him. "They were two of my bodyguards, you know. Oh, Softa, I am so frightened."

"It will be taken care of," he promised grimly. "And so will you."

Then the door slid aside, and a softly back-lit dream dancer said: "David, you are late. We have been waiting for you."

As he took a solitary lorry up to Kerrion levels, Spry meditated on the unexpected appearance of the pair of Kerrion retainers, and what might have prompted their attack. The most likely possibility was simply that they had been sent down to eliminate him after he had performed his task, but arrived too early. It was *not* likely that the two men had been told what he was about: that would have necessitated two more men to eliminate *them*. And the man who had been told to take Shebat by the other had not attacked her; but had been attacked *by* her, a function of the suspicions Spry had sowed. It looked, most of all, like the consul general's office trying to cover its tracks. It smelled, most of all, like a piece of typical Kerrion double-dealing. One thing bothered him: why would the dispatcher have taken the chance of befouling his own plan?

Spry pulled on his lower lip, eyes narrowed, watching unseeing as the large level numbers in the up-shaft flashed by. Then he laughed, a short, sharp bark. There was just the vaguest possibility that the men had been in low-life disguise merely to avoid scandal, were only about their jobs—as suddenly given back to them as they had been mysteriously taken away—*because the whole affair was exposed,* causing the dispatcher to abort it to save his skin. If so, he would be walking into a trap.

He sighed a deep sigh as the lorry halted, whirring expectantly. He punched *Hold: Full Fare.* Then he leaned back, staring blindly at the padded ceiling, and thought his data pool access code very clearly, with the imaging part of his mind. The computer's soft voice rang in his head, repeating his number and clearance mechanism, and offering its services. He asked a series of questions, the answers to which convinced him that as far as the data pool was concerned, he was still a master pilot in service to the Kerrion consulate; Shebat Kerrion was still presumed to be at an unspecified location in the Kerrion complex (here followed two referrals, one of which was: slip fifteen). In short, all was well, at least in the data pool's mind.

What had he expected? His name and status, red-lined? An all-points alert? He broke his query-line quickly, not to give the data pool any questions to mull in its micro-maw. Then he opened a manual com-line, feeding it the change he had gotten in the bar, and left a message with the consulate's service that the secretary thereof meet him at 2300 hours at the flagship's slip. He made it an emergency priority.

Then once more he closed his eyes: *"Bucephalus?"* his mind shouted silently through a babbling sea of cross-talk.

"Yes, David? I am here," the cruiser answered in its deep, cold whisper from the exact center of the back of his head.

"We have an unusual problem. I have an equally unusual solution. Listen closely, for when I get to you I will not be able to help you implement these procedures, which you should immediately get underway, following exactly the timetable I am about to give you, no matter what happens."

"Ah, human subterfuge. Speak on, Pilot. What is it we shall do today?"

When David Spry reached the *Bucephalus,* he had only time enough to activate his manual systems before the boarding light came on and Jebediah hurried like a dried leaf borne on a storm wind through the port.

"Take a couch, and strap yourself in," suggested Spry coldly. His fingers blurred and the hatch hissed shut and beneath Jebediah's feet the bulkhead shivered as the ship came to life.

"But—"

"Security," snapped Spry. "I will tell you when it is safe."

Jebediah, knowing better than Spry the keenness of the Kerrion slipside's mechanical ears, swallowed his protest. He was here, incriminating himself. He took the acceleration couch the pilot indicated, fastened the three straps, and leaned back with closed eyes. He was getting too old for this sort of thing. He needed time to think matters out, and he was not getting it. If he had had any brains, he would not have come here. But his fear had been greater than he could bear: the two men sent to end this problem of the pilot had not reported back; the emergency request for his presence here was against all his instructions. Something had gone terribly wrong. Above all, he needed to know what that something was. In his hands he held an attaché case. In the case was twice the scrip the pilot had been promised: who knew what the man might demand? He was thrust deeply into the cushioned couch. Red lights danced before him. He could only wonder at the speed of which the *Bucephalus* was capable; then at the bravado of the pilot to tear spaceward at such a pace. Then the hand was gone from about his heart so abruptly that the stomach threatened to pop out of his mouth, and before his eyes the view port drew open to display a dopplered red star-scape.

"What do you think you are doing, Pilot?" he snapped.

"Taking you for a little ride, to personally inspect the anomalies I reported, so that you will authorize the rather extensive overhaul I suggested in my memo. When Parma goes out tomorrow evening, we would not want anything to be amiss, would we?" The pilot, hands clasped behind his neck, did not turn when he spoke, but seemed to be staring out the port.

"What prompted you to risk everything this way? You needed so desperately to see me privately that you made an emergency call. Now, since we are beyond the keenest surveillance, sacrosanct, as best may be: *what is it you want?*" Jebediah's hands were shaking with rage. He could feel the sweat breaking out on his upper lip. He fumbled at the straps, failed to disengage them.

"We have a debt to settle," answered the pilot softly,

causing his couch to tilt forward. "Or have you forgotten?"

"Yes, yes. I have your money here." He fumbled further in his lap. "If I can just get these belts open, I will give it to you."

Spry chuckled. "That is not too likely," he said softly. "You see," and he reached over without unfastening his own harness and took the attaché case from the secretary's lap, "that is the problem I felt you should inspect personally. The eject mechanism," he said almost kindly, "has a glitch in it somewhere. It activates at random—" At the key word, *Bucephalus* heard, and obeyed.

With a horrifying pop all the cabin depressurized. David Spry felt the customary smothering sensation as his mil-hood swelled protectively, the burning of his lungs as he held the one precious breath remaining to him. To his right, a pop-eyed, gaping-mouthed old man struggled weakly as the ejection cocoon reared up out of the deck and enclosed him.

Ten seconds: David Spry counted to himself. Without a mil-hood and suit, unconsciousness would have come in fifteen seconds; properly protected, a man had up to a minute. . . .

The right-hand acceleration couch's floor bolts released, while bells rang silently in the vacuum and emergency lights flashed on, bathing all in baleful red. A soft vibration came up through Spry's feet as the clear cocoon was lifted toward the yawning emergency exit yet dilating above it.

Twenty seconds: He could see the desperate fists pounding, the old man lunging against his straps; then his feet drumming helplessly against the clear capsule; then just the capsule, spinning sunward.

Twenty-five seconds: The hatch above the couch closed. The lights turned blue, icing the exposed mechanism where the couch had been before. Spry fingered the attaché case in his lap, his body floating ever so slightly against the straps in zero gee.

Thirty seconds: His ears ached, heard a hiss. His body settled against the couch. All the emergency lights turned green, then faded as running lights came on.

David Spry expelled a long breath into the repressurized cabin, and said: *"Many thanks, Bucephalus. I hate to do this, but you are going to have to erase certain parts of your memory as to what has just occurred."*

When he had done that, he logged an emergency report of a random ejection with a ninety-nine-to-seven-nines probability against retrieving the capsule, and waited for further orders.

When they finally came through, there was no chance at all of recapturing the capsule, caught in the magnetic chop toward which *Bucephalus* had unerringly aimed it, spinning sunward with a fireglow of its own crawling over a shell meant for the gentle void of deep-space, and not the deadly excrescence between the sun's molten eye and her flare-bound companion black hole.

It was a scenic, if not a particularly pleasant, way to die. At least, for the first few minutes, until Jebediah went blind. Death's warm arms would not have come for minutes after that, Spry conjectured. Only vaguely dissatisfied with the succinctness of the affair, which he had allowed for circumspection's sake, he ordered *Bucephalus* home without moving his lips. At interplanetary speed, he had forty minutes—and a sensitive, difficult task that might take half of that. Commending control to the cruiser, he tilted his couch back, preparing to nap for twenty. It was then that he remembered he had not opened the attaché case, and proceeded to do so. He counted it twice, since it was twice what he had expected. Both counts summed the same. He snapped the case shut, clucking his tongue at his unusual luck, sniffing around it for hidden folly. For once, no harm could be whiffed. He put the case by, and with a wriggle like a dog's in a long-accustomed bed, fell asleep wondering what kind of dream dancer Shebat Kerrion was going to make.

Chapter Five

The *Marada* heard a whisper, urgent and sibilant, as if from a great distance. It was not the voice of Shebat Kerrion, but it reeled off the sequence of authority only she and the cruiser itself had previously shared. So charged, the cruiser could not help but obey. Its port slid shut, lights lit, a chime sounded, though there were no ears aboard to hear. Mildly worried, if a ship's consciousness can be said to worry, he (for so the cruiser had viewed itself ever since its female pilot had become mistress and admixed her consciousness with the ship's own) . . . *he,* then, being capable of knowing loyalty, was also capable of experiencing other so-called human attributes: he felt dread; he felt distress. Was this then, the meaning of altruism? The cruiser pondered as it cleared its course with the data bank and whirred slowly toward the debarkation lock. It had known, abstractly, that a cruiser's consciousness of *self* is augmented and to some extent formed by the addition of its human component. Among some of his peers he had heard a snickering reference to the pilots as mere outboard equipment. Taking stock of its own cogitation, the logical part of the ship rejected altruism as a possible name for what it was experiencing.

Indeed, in the time it took for one final lamp, *ignition,* to be lit, the *Marada* had rejected altruism and substituted *self-preservation* as the mode responsible for his distress, which tingled like an unscratchable itch deep in his circuitry. The reasoning pleased him, though events did not; though taking thought to the safety of his being did not. He did not like taking orders from another ship, be it the *Bucephalus,* or any other. He would not have taken them, but for the inexorable command sequence which impelled him. *Where was Shebat?* And who was this other pilot, the mover behind *Bucephalus's* orders? And would some human come aboard him before the moment came to enter spongespace, or was this his final flight? In all of the memories of all the cruisers, no ship had come out of sponge sent in with a dead or incapacitated pilot. As for leaving spacetime with *no one* of flesh aboard; it was not done, had never been successfully done. And, too, he had no final destination. No coordinates for reentry had been logged. With as close as a space-cruiser could come to a shrug, the *Marada* turned to his instructions. They included one salvo of turret fire. Somehow that was satisfying; it would be a shame to die without ever having fired them.

The *Bucephalus* lay calmly in its slip, bathed in an obscene purple radiance that was the sum of the blue lights belonging to the security and rescue vehicles, and the red flashers of the slip emergency squad and the bay's own illumination, which proclaimed in an agitated pulse that here lay a wounded, perhaps dangerously maddened cruiser.

Fire and demolition experts and security men in red coveralls swarmed over the ship, disarming weaponry and spraying anti-inflammatory foam. Medical corps and slip bosses and shipwrights in Kerrion blacks swarmed in and out of his open ports. Pilots in gray flight satins lounged wherever they chose, exercising their priorities to break through the security cordon which had been thrown like a dotted red hemisphere between the onlookers and the *Bucephalus*. A guildmaster's silver lorry roared to slip-side, oblivious of the mechanics and security guards it scattered. A tall, white-haired man in darkest blue got out of it, flanked by two argent-clad master pilots. Attendant upon his entry into the ship, a stream of men in vari-colored coveralls poured out, like a kaleidoscope roughly twisted. The lock closed.

After a time it reopened. The guildmaster and his two seconds emerged with the ship's pilot between them. The man had to be supported between the two guild officers; his face and hands were ashy, as if his very skin flaked away. He lurched between them, an arm over the shoulder of each, as they walked him in a circle. Gradually, his steps steadied. By the time the circle was completed, he was standing unsupported. Two medics approached him, but the guildmaster waved them away. Three brash pilots succeeded where the medics had failed, stood talking to the pilot a long time. A loudspeaker began blaring for the area to be cleared. A slip boss approached and voices were raised. Then, as the purple strobing was banished by the amber running-lights of the consul general's huge personal ground transport, the three pilots split off from the little knot of men within the larger knot of men within the half-circle of onlookers. Two entered the ship, to emerge with the pilot's flight duffel and the metal case containing the ship's log. The third strolled whistling, hands thrust into pockets, toward the pilot's exit.

Men leapt from the still-moving consulate transport: a way opened for them through the crowd. They jogged to the inner group, which by then had accrued one each of the diversely garbed officials, extricating the pilot and the tall, white-haired guildmaster therefrom.

These two did not quite run amid the Kerrion bodyguard that surrounded them: a medical man, his red-crossed back to Parma, retreated before them, slowing all things with his obvious objections.

"Let him come," said Parma Alexander Kerrion seemingly to thin air, from behind the transport's desk that twinkled as brightly as any tower's central control. A little noise told him his new secretary had heard. He turned from the two monitors built into the console to the window showing the *Bucephalus*'s slip. "But keep both the guildmaster and the pill-pusher out there."

A second beep told him that Jebediah's distaff replacement in the tiny outer office heard and obeyed.

Minutes later the door slid back, admitting the sounds of argument and the *Bucephalus*'s pilot, whose complexion seemed to be rotting even while he took the seat

Parma's wordless gesture indicated.

Before the consul general could speak, the security officer's line burped its disapproval that none of his men had been allowed to crowd into the tiny mobile office. He disconnected the speaker without a word. The distraught light blinked urgently. Parma Kerrion ignored it.

"I am assuming that if you are here, your looks belie the reality and you do not need immediate medical attention," Parma said softly.

"This?" The pilot raised a white, scrofulous hand. "Just dead mil." He rubbed right hand with left, showering his leg with what seemed like snow. The hand, so displayed, looked less unhealthy. "Froze off when the cabin depressurized. It's not anything serious, just looks bad." The countenance, purple-lipped and brown-eyed, screwed up, showering flaked mil with each tic or twitch. "I am sorry," the pilot said very low. "I suppose you already know what happened?"

"You tell me."

"I had some suspicions: the *Bucephalus* had been behaving strangely; memory blanks, static spurts, things like that. I put in for an emergency overhaul when I got orders that we were to ship tomorrow. your secretary wanted to see for himself. Neither of us had any idea of the danger. . . . There was nothing I could do."

"Is that so?"

"Sir?" The pilot, in the chair, did not sit erect, but either lounged or slumped. That bothered Parma.

"There will be an inquiry, of course."

"My guildmaster has already confiscated the log," said the pilot without a hint of guile.

"Then there will be *two* inquiries."

The pilot sat a little straighter. "Might I remind you, sir, that I took your service formally, and an oath to that effect, that I almost lost my life in your service, in pursuit of that oath. I could be as dead as your secretary."

"If the sabotage had been less selective?" Teasingly.

"You think *I* did this? Why?"

"I do not think anything yet, young man. As a matter of fact, you may have done me a greater service than you know. Still, until all is examined, until you are formally cleared of complicity, I am going to have you confined to your guildhall. You understand."

The pilot did not look away, or look surprised, or do anything at all which Parma felt he should, but said: "Then I am relieved of your service?"

"No. As a matter of fact, we will make the scheduled rendezvous in Shechem, as soon as the *Bucephalus* and yourself are pronounced spaceworthy." That got the pilot's attention. He sat up straight, objecting that it would be more than forty-eight hours before the *Bucephalus* could be checked out sufficiently to suit him.

"So anxious to be relieved of your command? I have heard that there is a saying among you, that the only cure for space-fright is space-flight."

The pilot did not sputter, or even speak, just met Parma's gaze, waiting.

"Ah, young man, I cannot seem to rattle you. Do you not think that is odd?"

Spry shrugged.

"Since you are not going to ask the right questions, I suppose I will have to do all the work myself. Had you come less highly recommended, I must admit, I would not be so polite. But you are, after all, a close friend of Marada's." The pilot gave an almost imperceptible blink. "So," continued Parma, letting his voice take an edge, "I am not going to revoke your citizenship and fine your guild out of hand. *What in the name of Chance were you doing with my daughter on level seven?*"

"Shebat? I took her there because . . . this is going to sound funny. . . ."

"I promise, I will not laugh."

"—Sir, I am not sure that I understand what is going on here. And if what I am about to detail to you occurred by your orders, then you cannot blame me for misconstruing their intent." Spry looked at Parma challengingly. With a faint smile, the consul general motioned him to speak his piece. This was more amusing than he had dared hope. And bemusing. What was the boy trying to do?

"First of all, after taking her guild oath, Shebat seemed to drop out of sight. I left messages for her that she did not answer. I contacted your office, which informed me

that her whereabouts could only be 'probably determined.' Would you not have thought that odd, were you
I?"

Parma agreed that he would have thought that most
odd.

"Then I determined that her bodyguard had been
reassigned." The pilot peered in what was a most obviously assessive manner at Parma. "Sir, if you yourself
gave that order, then all I did after guessing that you had
not will make no sense. I am no creature of platform
politics. . . ."

Parma allowed that he had given no such order, asking
the pilot just what that piece of information had led him
to construe.

"That something was going to befall Shebat: an accident, most likely. I took it on myself to find her and warn
her, believing that I could get no message through to you
that would not alert whoever had pulled the bodyguard."

"You took it on yourself to do this?" Parma snarled
suddenly.

"Sir, if the subterfuge were far-reaching, as it seems
now to be, considering the sabotage of the *Bucephalus*, I
did not have time to make an appointment."

"Do you know what you have done?"

"Sir?"

"The *Marada* is gone: logged out with no destination,
into spongespace. Shebat, also, is gone. What would that
lead you to conjecture, Oh amateur sleuth?"

"What?" interrupted him. Then: "Did you send a
pursuit ship?"

"No. I did not want to chase her. But now I know what
scared her enough to make her run. You idiot! I . . ."
Then, controlled once more, he added: "Of course, we
are assuming that it *was* Shebat in that ship. . . ."

"So, this is about Shebat, not your secretary. She and I
parted company on level seven, if that is what you want to
know." He jerked his head toward the window, beyond
which officials still scurried. "That explains your
bodyguard's less than polite attitude. Are you accusing
me of something? Am I under arrest for causing
Jebediah's death? Or for saving your life? Or in point of

fact, for trying to help the girl? Was it your game I fouled, rather than some nebulous saboteur's?"

"I will ignore that last. Two of my men are dead on a seventh level street corner. My private secretary has been murdered, under your aegis if not more than that. My heir is missing. My ship is incapacitated. *Her* ship has disappeared, though everyone who saw you and Shebat leave the *Marada*'s slip swears they did not see her, or anyone, go back aboard. Exactly," Parma glanced àt his desk-top display, "ten minutes ago, a large explosion, either ship's fire or ship's destruction, occurred along the flight path the *Marada* was traveling. We had a double reading, very briefly, lasting three seconds. Then we had no reading whatsoever. Empty space, the bulk of the planet, nothing more."

"And you do not think she just dark-sided?"

"What?"

"Took the ship around behind the planet, where she could not be tracked?"

"I am not sure," Parma thundered, "that she was *in* the ship."

"What else?" queried Spry.

"Indeed, or rather: *where* else?" He let the question hang between them, excavating in the pilot's face for signs of duplicity. Behind the cover of flaking mil, it was impossible to tell what the man might be thinking.

Parma sighed, "All right, then, Spry. Perhaps, coming on Marada's recommendation, you are replacing him as the millstone about my neck. At the very least, you have stretched your guild immunity to the breaking point. At the most, you are a walking dead man, lawful punishment being too gentle to suit me should I discover you are lying, that any of this was your doing. Do you hear me? I will strangle you with my bare hands! Now, to avoid that rather strenuous exercise, I suggest you tell me everything: where you took Shebat; what was said between you; how you came to leave her unescorted when you knew she had no protection."

"Leave her . . . you just told me I had overstepped my oath. She's a Kerrion; I am employed by Kerrions. She dismissed me. I had other things on my mind, like the

Bucephalus. I had done my guild-duty by warning her."

"And I suppose she said nothing to you about being forbidden the lower levels."

"As a matter of fact, she did; she was worried you would take the *Marada* away from her. But we were already down there. . . ."

The desk was bleating like a sheep. Parma punched a button; the guildmaster's demands for entry reached him; he fingered the button briefly. "Then, you did take her downunder and leave her there."

"Yes, I did that. I do not see what was wrong. . . ."

Parma ignored him, speaking into his desk's blinking recess. "Guildmaster? Take this pilot of yours and run your inquiry. I, also, will run mine. When we are both feeling less emotional, we will decide what to do with him. When that moment comes, I want him fat, happy and well-basted. If he disappears, I'll have your carcass instead." Parma broke the connection, leaned back in his chair, and said to Spry: "Go rest secure in the arms of your guildfellows."

Then, when Spry only stared incredulously at him: *"Move!"*

When the pilot was gone and he was alone but for the chiming, beeping, buzzing solicitations of his console, Parma Kerrion put hands behind his head and let out a long sigh. There was no use in any of this, really: if Shebat Kerrion had flown away or been blown away, or not, he would still have to proclaim that such was the truth of it. It was too near elections to take the risk of having the girl used against him. Chance, or good luck, had given him the perfect out.

And also, the only help he could give the girl was to express emphatically his disinterest in her.

He leaned over his desk and rubbed his eyes, trying to rub away the feeling that there was something here he had missed.

Then he called his secretary and dictated three orders.

He called Chaeron to Draconis from Lorelie, effective immediately.

He instructed the investigators of these murky events in the outcome he wished made official: Shebat Kerrion was logged missing in space, presumed dead; the three-year waiting period was unilaterally waived; a successor was designated in her stead.

The third missive informed Marada Seleucus Kerrion of all that had taken place.

Parma sat back once more. Then, as an afterthought, he called off the search he had earlier ordered. If Shebat were down there, she would either come up on her own, or not. In such teetering command of his pinnacle, he could hardly afford to bend over in an attempt to haul another up.

Almost, then, he wept, feeling suddenly thwarted and ancient and bowed by his labors.

Why was the pilot so calm?

Softa slept an uneasy dream in which Parma reversed all things: sent him after Jebediah, at which point he broke cover, brought the *Bucephalus* up beside the *Marada,* tandem-guided them both through the sponge. Only when he reemerged into spacetime, it was not his confederates who awaited him, but Marada Kerrion, hovering between the platform and the stars with a glittering knife and fork in his hands and a napkin around his neck. As he was being devoured, Softa made no struggle, could not even cry out. He had left the little girl helpless and stranded, had he not? Then he would wake, shivering, to a hand or a word spoken by a concerned vigilant who had seen him toss or heard him cry out. Then he would go back to sleep. And it would start all over again.

Chapter Six

Shebat would never forget those first few days in the graffiti-strewn, peeling warren of the dream dancers. Only the first few hours were sharper-honed in her memory, with the initial moments of those seared so deeply that she winced whenever she thought of them, which was as infrequently as possible.

Which was not to say never. Back the memory would come, when her guard was down, when she was drowsing. It even leaked into one of her first, tentative dream dances. Thusly, to her embarrassment, the pall of her regret overflowed into public domain.

There it had been: Softa's arms sliding around be-spangled buttocks, enfolding, pulling her up and against him. Only the "her" was Shebat, not Lauren, the dream dancer who had played that role in reality. And it was to Lauren that the dance had been tendered. Perhaps *because* it was Lauren, this lamentable indiscretion had occurred.

But it had been done, nothing could change it. Lauren had felt Shebat's distress, had heard "murderess" ringing in her head; had seen all the clawing hands outreaching toward her from every side; had seen Softa wink as he pulled the Shebat/Lauren close, while the Lauren/Shebat watched in disdain; in astonishment; in anguish. "*That* is hardly a dream dance," had said Lauren afterward, pulling the fillet from her brow, although Shebat had thought she had reclaimed control rather well, turning bad to better, at least.

But the girl whose beauty was excruciating, who had

said to David Spry with only the hint of an arch smile: "Is she not a little young for you?", was not thereafter willing to forget what she had seen, though Shebat was a novice in the extreme, and thusly excusable.

Of the twelve in the dream dancers' company, it was Lauren who made life most difficult for Shebat.

Aside from the shock of so many far-reaching changes, the loneliness, and the slant-eyed beauty's sly obstructions whenever it came time for Lauren to take a turn as Shebat's instructor, she was doing well enough. Almost happy, she could say on those occasions when all was going right. Then the dream dance ceased to become an intensely complex labor. Transmuted into a living, breathing entity like a supernal visitation, it fired her soul.

It was all of enchantment, every bit of the numinous chant she had heard pealing glory when Marada had come to Bolen's town and whisked her off, laughing: "You can be Enchantress of all the Earth."

There were two powers in the Consortium, two potent magics to sate the metaphysical longing of the most ardent seeker; there were the ships, and there was the dream dance.

She recollected her fright that it might not be so, that the Consortium would prove as dry and lifeless as Marada had proclaimed to her that it was: all is science, he had reaffirmed endlessly.

And she had been saddened, holding tenaciously to her meager spells, looking for their like in Ashera's dragon-breath or Chaeron's expediencies, and not finding anything more than human passion.

But she had not known the truth of the matter, one so much accepted by Marada that he had never thought to mention it: science and magic were one. Enchantment equals enlightenment.

Howsoever great the human divisiveness against whose currents she endlessly struggled, that light shone in her distance like a cheery beacon.

With it, she staved off dreams of the lion-maned Chaeron, whose wrath when she had gone to him to beg his backing for her leave-taking had seemed to be a terribly controlled declaration of war.

Where was Softa? she wondered endlessly the first hours, less and less as hours became days. The dream dance consumed her, as she hoped it might, so that she had less time to worry about her status or her fate.

Status was of great moment here in the lower levels, where citizenship was bought in fractions, or forged, or stolen. What had come first as an indication that Spry had neither abandoned nor forgotten her were packets of falsified credentials in the hand of a junior pilot who stared open-mouthed all about him.

They had been "one reading only" hard copy, which crumbled away within minutes after the oils of a human finger touched them: She was Sheba Spry, Softa's full sister. She was from the Pegasus colonies. Her data pool keys and ship-key were thus-and-so. She was newly apprenticed to her brother. . . .

The bristle-haired junior with his wispy, wishful beard insisted on staying until she had read and recited back to him the information, until the hard copy was a sprinkling of dust on the floor. Then he gave her, solemn-faced, a packet full of program-cards, saying as if by rote that she was to continue her lessons on a full schedule and that no exceptions were to be made in her original timetable.

"That is impossible! I do not think any of this will work. And I certainly cannot learn two trades at once!"

The junior flushed rubescent as an X-ray star map, saying: "I am not anything but a messenger, lady," and Shebat realized that he thought her a fully fledged dream dancer, which also explained his reluctance to leave.

He dug in the case he was carrying and came up with two identical packages sealed in opaque foil. "He said you were to open these alone. . . . Look, I mean . . . can I get a discount?"

Shebat counted to ten and said she was not the one to ask. Then she ushered the youth firmly to the door, saying: "Did he say anything else? Is he coming soon?" She did not dare ask what she would have liked.

Evidently, the junior dared not answer what he would have liked, so he hemmed instead, at last getting out: "No, I do not know. He has his own troubles." The last of which he mumbled while backing into the hall. There he collided with Lauren, stumbled, and as he began apologizing she smiled and spirited him off, saying she had a message for him to take back to the guildhall.

Shebat closed her door and leaned upon it, trying to

sort out her feelings. She had not felt this way about Softa previously; she had not felt any way about him at all. When Lauren had greeted him so longingly, she had seen him differently, as a man for the first time. But it was not jealousy she felt, she told herself, merely dependency. Softa was the only hope she had of getting off Draconis. Lauren hated her, and would do anything to make her suffer.

She remembered the two packets. Sitting on her narrow cot in her narrow gray womb in the crowded warren of the dream dancers, she opened the first one, then the other.

In the first was a large sum of scrip, and instructions as to its dispensing. Even a schedule of payments to be made was included. Feeling better—if he intended to abandon her, he would not have sent so much or designated its dispensation—she opened the second.

And hurriedly attached all her concentration thereto: a second set of credentials lay in her lap, casually thumbed before their meaning came clear. She raced the oxidization of the treated paper. When she had a little pile of dust in her lap, her upper lip was beaded with perspiration. Her mind tried uneasily to deal with two adjacent overlays of data, combinations numerically succedent. It would be difficult to keep them straight. The price of a mistake would be her criminality unmasked. She shivered. She knew why the combinations were so similar: all conversation with computers, be they data pool, private source, even ships' intelligences, was based on tuning the mind of machine to the mind of man. Within the parameters of specification were a finite number of frequencies to which her own intelligence code could be assigned.

If anyone ever checked to see how close the code-ins for Shebat Kerrion, Sheba Spry, and Aba Cronin were, she would be found out: they were nearly identical.

One thing troubled her more than that: if Softa had gone to all this extended trouble, the stay he foresaw for her here was equally extended. And though she was already half-enthralled by the beauty and the rectitude of the dream dancers' art, she feared it.

She feared it almost as much as she feared discovery, but for diverse reasons.

It sang more sweetly than any but the *Marada*'s song.

She understood why it was prohibited by Kerrion law, and why that law was unenforceable, as well as why, in some spaces, that prohibition had been repealed.

Whereas Parma Kerrion's wrath would come from what she had done in life—murder, theft, illegal impersonation being only the latest—dream dancing exacted its tax from what was *not* done in life. If Parma killed her outright, would she be less dead than the most-accomplished dream dancer, whiling away years unlived?

As much in those early days as she was consumed with hurt that the man she had willingly called "father" would serve her up to the wolves of expediency, she felt the suction of the well of dreams.

Some one of the old Earth philosophers she had studied had proclaimed that dream was life and life was dream. As untenable as the ancient's contemporaries had found that position did Shebat find her own.

Each day the world of the dream dance became more real and the world without decreased in substance.

The lessons Spry had sent were like a bridge over the chasm of the dark warren world in which he had placed her. She did them faithfully; each completed run brought her a step closer to pilotry and freedom.

But each day she became less concerned with *then* (when all would be completed and she could take her pilot's oath) and more concerned with *now* (where richer dreams were to be had than she had had before).

She drifted, hanging between her selves, and at length she began to dream she had passed her pilot's boards. She would have been troubled if the dreams were not so grand, or if the other dancers did not try to emulate her; or if Lauren's despite had not become ever more pronounced. But she was good; she was very good; and she hung the above-mentioned difficulties around her throat like a bejeweled necklace: decorations for her dreams, gilding that added depth and tone. The dream dancer in her knew these things to be the measure of her success, and accepted them graciously.

She had other tasks than the dream dance: citizenship was a serious matter, in the lower levels where it was so highly prized. All citizens had to vote to maintain their degree of privilege. To vote, a person had to absorb enough information on the article in question to be able to answer ten questions on the subject under discussion. To do that, one had to study.

Shebat was used to studying words on a screen: literacy was held in high repute in Kerrion levels. The absence of it in the lower dark explained why. Here, reading had long ago given way to the more economical method of querying via intelligence keys.

The dream dancers had no use for the written word; they could barely make use of it. They received all information directly and stored it in memory, without difficulty. They evinced only scorn for one so lacking in retention as to have to need to write something down. Shebat, having just learned reading and writing, was hard put giving them up.

To be a dream dancer, she would have to cultivate eidetic memory; to be a ship's pilot, she must be fluent in the ships' tongues, equally free from the need to read or write.

Yet, the lessons Spry sent were written; she needed to monopolize the only visual terminal in the dream dancers' warren to learn them.

She was sitting there, with her stack of cards, placing one after another in the terminal's slot, pressing *"run,"* then typing her responses in, when a wave of inadequacy washed all attention from her. Somewhere around the sixth unanswered query, she realized she was hopelessly lost, being so scored, and stopped the sequence.

Sitting hunched over, fingers wound in her hair, she glared at the blank screen. She could not retrieve the card from the terminal until the sequence had been completed. But the answers in her head were not to the questions of navigation through space or sponge, but of navigation through life.

Knowing that she would probably fail the examination did not help her marshal her concentration. Six wrong by reason of being left unanswered . . . she would have to make a perfect score on the rest to squeak by. With a Bolen's town epithet, she stabbed the *"run"* button.

Damn Spry's circumspection. If he had just ordered up examination sequences for her in the usual manner, she would not be facing failure. But if the central data pool had given her the rating examinations without resort to

printed cards, then it would be a matter of record that
Sheba Spry was slumming, living with dream dancers; in
fact, living in the very room with Aba Cronin, apprentice
to the art of dreams.

Some long while later, when the card popped into the
retrieval slot and on the screen her passing score of one
point above the minimum leered greenly, she succumbed
to all she had held in abeyance.

She did not weep. She had promised herself that never
again would she offer tears up as sacrifice. Spry was right.
It did no good. Besides, she was not sorrowful as much as
terrified. Yesterday, she had danced a dream for Harmony, the troupe leader. As to how it had been received—she still had not heard.

She sat immobile while perspiration inundated her,
grinding her teeth so that they would not chatter. Her
stomach had fled its abode and where it had been an
emptiness like ectoplasmic writhing snakes churned and
bucked. She swallowed repeatedly through a tight throat.
At length the perspiration defeated the protection of her
mil and she shivered violently. She had seen a girl baby
exposed to die in Bolen's town one snowy winter. She saw
it again, called the seeing an evil omen.

Would all be lost, then, as the terror gloated? She had
felt this helplessness before, since coming among the
dream dancers. She had thought she had defeated it. She
had felt it after the pilot had slipped from Lauren's arms,
murmuring that as much as he wished it, he could not
stay, when he left her in the care of strangers.

How awful the brink of disaster appears, when one is
not sure whether or not Fate will propel cringing flesh
over the edge.

She had thought she had touched bottom. Sometimes,
when the dream dance took her, she was sure she had.

In the good times, she spoke with determination to
herself that she would learn to hold a hundred dances,
pure and perfect in their exactitude and their effect, in her
mind.

In the bad times, she sought a personal solution,
devaluing all but life and love and seeing the fictions of
the dance as the enemies thereof.

Then she agreed with the Kerrion position that fiction
and fantasy were acid eating away at the substructure of

society, that these could foster nothing but discontent and malaise. In Kerrion space, there was the reality and there were the dream dancers: there was nothing in between. With the fall of literacy had gone the writers of fiction; with the ascendancy of the intelligence-keyed computer had gone poetry and music and the makers thereof.

Why listen to another man's song, when any could make his own?

Why call up another's vision, when any could command an uncircumscribed view of all that existed in the universe?

Why let madmen spread their illness? The maunderings of man's unconscious were demonstrably dangerous, essentially flawed.

Madness, it is true, hardly ever clacked its slavering jaws in the Consortium. Men seldom did violence one upon the other's person. Out of sight, out of mind? Was that why the dream dance was forbidden? It was certainly why the Kerrions purported to forbid it.

Myth had been placed on trial. The adjudication had not been in its favor. The technocrats reasoned with their compatriots, the computers, that removing the irritant might allow the sore to heal upon its own.

There were myths, just the same. The dream dancers made them, surreptitiously, fearing to record any of them lest the evidence be used against them. So the older, greater dream dances were passed from mind to mind, down the generations, learned impeccably and never altered, surviving increasingly concerted attempts to erase them from the consciousness of man.

Once, dream dancers had performed before massed audiences, whole groups of them intent upon one dream, its embellishment and its presentation, the fruits to be shared by all.

That had been long ago. The practice had been ruthlessly stamped out, the audiences, or dreamers, proclaimed as responsible for the crime as the dancers, the technicians, the musicians, and the minds who orchestrated the heinous crimes.

Now, such a gathering for sharing a single dream dance was impossible. Whatsoever occurred between two consenting adults, however, was not punishable, in theory of Consortium Law. In theory, one dream dancer and one client could not be arrested, convicted, punished for their shared crime. In practice, dream dancers disappeared with disquieting regularity. Their citizenship status, not maintained by the obligatory voting hours, was then revoked.

It was not in the dream dancers' power to fight the Consortium.

They did, however, continue to ply their trade, some falling, some surviving, carrying on the tradition as they carried in their heads the masterworks of deceased geniuses, adding as best they could to what had gone before.

Shebat had made a dream dance which Harmony, the troupe's leader, had asked to have performed for her, having heard of its power from the others.

It was not a pretty, seductive dance. It was awful; it was austere. It left the dreamer shaken and changed. Lauren had deemed it horrible, but even she could not thrust it aside.

Shebat was well aware that if the dream dance were judged too lacking in suitability, she would not be trusted to take clients. Like her pilotry examination, all was subject to disconcerting influences, from within and without.

How can one make a dream of joy from the dungeon of despair? How could she concentrate on one thing at a time, when both screamed for priority, shouldering each other from her view? She must get back to her little gray cubicle, in case the troupe mistress had made her judgment.

In one part of her mind, a small voice opined that since she had lost everything, why worry: she had nothing more to lose. She answered back to it that since Chance had released her from Bolen's town and endless drudgery, all that had occurred afterward was in the nature of a gift. If she did not make use of the gift honorably, then it would surely be taken. That she had been so briefly a Kerrion was to her advantage. But it would not have lasted, had never been meant to last by those who decreed it. That she had learned to read and to write and to hold great reams of information in her head, unwritten, was enchantment's kindest smile. If, then, the wrathful face of magic scowled, making her stumble in her studies, bequeathing the awful dream dance (which she *must* have chosen), then that was only fair balance.

The worlds of the platforms would surely not come down around their heads simply because Shebat had created a dream dance in which they did.

Hopelessness was not any deeper a sea because she had rowed out to its middle and thrown a plumb-line down to define its depths.

Work must stand with its integrity inherent, or better not be done at all.

Woe to the creator who spins a web of sweet fantasy, when the breath of fire crackles ominously within, for it surely must consume him who will not spew it out.

She had made the dream dance. Like her well-schooled kick, which had made out of a faithful bodyguard a gruesome corpse, she had done her best.

"Sometimes," she hissed aloud, tearing at the hair that ever flopped over her eyes, "I think I am my own worst enemy."

She had certainly not helped matters, with her outspoken dream dance. Softa had been adamant that she learn the dream dancer's trade well enough to pose as one for an interval. If the troupe's mistress forbade it, judging her unfit, no dream dancer in the Consortium would suffer her presence. Softa's plan would be thwarted.

What would happen to her then?

She hated the dream dancers at times. Hated their sense of mission, the messianic fellowship of their bond.

It well might be that the Kerrion law was rightful, that dream dancing was degenerate and degenerative; that selling one's person in total was more debased than the lesser prostitution it was rumored had once preceded it.

Sex for meretricious gain was no longer illegal; the Consortium was too civilized for that. Shebat picked up her cards, and with a last baleful glare at her odiously low navigational proficiency, wiped the screen with a finger's tap.

Tap: no record remained of what had transpired, but on the little card. *Tap:* she was no longer Shebat Kerrion, inheritor of fifty-one percent of one of the most powerful trade-bloc in all of spacetime. *Tap:* she was Sheba Spry, apprentice pilot. As easily, then; *tap:* Shebat Kerrion would not exist, even in her own memory.

She had seen for herself that although no violent solutions were admitted into the Draconis-consciousness as a whole, violence occurred. She had tapped into *Current Events* the day after she had smashed in the Kerrion retainer's face, and found no mention of it there in the computer's news broadcast. Hence, all things that occurred were not entered therein, or, being entered, were not made accessible along with the stock quotes and currency exchange rates and lading bills from incoming freighters.

Hence, too, she thought sourly, all of Softa's precautions.

As a precaution of her own, she had not demanded of the data pool that it search for any previous mention of the slaying of the two bodyguards. As another caution, she always used Aba Cronin's intelligence keys when activating a direct contact with the data pool. There was only one problem inherent in that: Aba Cronin was merely a fractional citizen, maintaining a one-quarter status, and as such certain areas were not within her reach: her clearances were too low.

So she had not found out that Chaeron P. Kerrion had been transferred to Draconis until Lauren had let slip in conversation that she had of late been graced with the patronage of "the Consul Kerrion."

"A Kerrion *consul,"* Shebat had corrected her grammar. The pidgin speech of some dream dancers irritated her: their lack of understanding of the upper levels gave her the superiority from which to correct; her dislike of the other girl's dislike for her made her enjoy it.

"The Consul Kerrion," Lauren repeated, perfectly plucked saffron brow arching high. "Chaeron Ptolemy Kerrion. He has been three nights in a row to dream with me. He is, you know," she said sweetly, "the new Draconis consul. Do you feel unwell?"

Shebat heard her titters as she rushed divested of dignity from the little common room where the dancers gathered to hear the nightly news and exchange their own.

She had sent an urgent message to her "brother" Spry from the street corner terminal just outside the basement warren.

Then she had fled to her room, locking herself within.

But Softa did not come in the morning, or the next day, or the next.

Harmony, the eternally mothering troupe mistress, had come to her door on the third day and demanded entrance. She had had no choice but to admit her. She was hirsute and fleshy, with short brown hair and skin even a mil-suit's slick finish could not disguise: it was mottled and spotted with pink, brown and black; beneath the mottles, it was white as a dead fish's belly.

"What's wrong with you, child? This is no way to act. What would Spry say, if he knew you were locked in your room? Too good for us low-livers, are you?"

"Chaeron Kerrion was here!"

"So? He didn't see you, and he won't. I wouldn't play Spry foul. And neither would Lauren, no matter how it looks. She loves 'im. Got it?"

Shebat made a noise and spread her hands.

"Look, smart pussy: it took a lot of scrip to get you bought in here. We'll take good care of you. By the same coin, I made a bargain with Spry to teach you however much you could learn: I keep my word."

"He should never have told you. . . ."

"That's *his* morals. Boy's got class. That's *class:* not the Kerrion kind; the other kind, which can't be bought. You think he would have put the whole twelve of us in peril by stashing a Kerrion fugitive among us without letting us know, then *you* don't know *him.* He's too good at what he does to make a stupid mistake."

Shebat picked at the threadbare gray blanket, not looking up.

"If he *had* given you over to us without telling true as to what the dangers were, and we'd gotten this far along—well, then I might just have had to get nasty. Not just with you, with him. So relax. You are here to learn the dance, and the dance we'll teach, even if we have to add a little common savvy along the way. . . ."

The woman let out a rattling sigh, as if her gullet were filled with pebbles. "You don't trust us, which is not a bad sign, though my vanity's sore wounded by it. I've taken your money, girl, from your very own hand."

"Lauren hates me."

"Lauren does not hate you. I think she feels a little pity, along with her jealousy, which never killed anybody.

She loves Softa, and she'll never get him. She knows that. He's taking *you*, not her, out of Kerrion space. . . ." The woman looked hopefully at Shebat, who only tossed her head.

"Lords, girl, give me the courtesy of your glance. I'd heard you were greener than sponge, but who could believe it . . . ? Look, I give you my word that Lauren won't intrigue against you. If she does, she'll have me to answer to. And you can shoot her down with that little piece of information should the occasion arise."

"Thank you."

"Thanks, is it? Thank me by working up a dream dance good enough to avoid being the laughingstock of all the dancers. They're laying bets as to how long before I bounce you out of here. And since I *can't* bounce you, but have to keep you until Spry collects you, do me a favor: *pretend* to be trying. Make me a dance that'll shut up the gossips."

"But I am trying. . . ."

"Make me a real dance, not that masturbatory drivel you threw in Lauren's face."

With a smile that threatened to fall away and reveal her chagrin, Shebat promised: "I will."

And so she had come to make the dance, and it had been the one which had so horrified Lauren, the one which Harmony herself had demanded to view.

Shebat sighed and, taking her study-cards, threaded her way back to the narrow gray room with its cot and lavatory, and locked herself within.

All things were flowing together, making days fragment, the procession of them dissolving so that she could not tell sometimes what had happened from what had not.

Lauren had not told Chaeron about her being here, that was sure.

Softa had not come, though her summons had been urgent. That, also, was sure.

The dance was completed, all that remained was to wait for Harmony, whose reaction was most unsure, to send word of judgment rendered.

If the woman gainsaid her work, what then?

Something told her that the rejection of her dream dance would hurt more deeply than her rejection by Parma Kerrion, for the dance was of herself.

She took her last resort out of the back of her mind where she had secreted it, and examined its shining expanse. She could call Marada on his oath: he would not fail her; he would deliver her home.

"Home?" she laughed bitterly to the blank gray walls. "Bolen's town? *Bolen?* Never." Or, almost never. At least, not until the last moment, which was not yet. If Harmony killed her dream dance, quashing its chances of ever being performed, exposing it like the blue baby on Bolen's ridge, *then* she would call Marada. Or kill herself. . . .

But Harmony interrupted Shebat's despondent chronicling, coming herself to Shebat's room, softly tapping on the door. "Honey, open up."

Within Shebat, something froze. As one in a trance whose tongue will not speak, whose limbs move at another's behest, she went and admitted Harmony.

The gross bulk of her fleshliness caused Shebat's cot to squeal in protest. "Sit here, darlin', right here. You and I have some serious things to discuss."

She wanted to scream: *"Tell me. Did you like it? Please like it! Love it! It is my soul!"* She sat down awkwardly and twisted her hands in her lap, unable to utter a single word. Over the thumping of her heart she heard: "I am sorry it took me so long to get back to you. Something came up."

It had been thirty-six hours since she had left the troupe leader's jumbled cubicle. The woman, sprawled on her bed, massive breasts rising and falling, had dismissed her curtly, telling her to go to her room and wait.

She had waited, picking split-ends from her hair. Having danced the dream, she could do no more. All that day and night she waited, for the woman to describe the detail of her fate with her approval, or her disavowal. In the morning she had faced her pilotry examination, unprepared. Unrelieved. At least now she would know.

"It is about your dream-dance . . . it is not good. It is better than good. As they say, it might be eternal."

But Shebat was fighting back tears, then laughter, then the tendency of her physical exhilaration to blot out all else.

"Then, you will allow it to be done?"

"I am going to feature it. I want you to teach it to some

others, specially selected, of course. I think it would be
well if as many as might be contrived see it. It serves us to
promulgate such dreams, even be they hard on the
dreamers." And with a smile no less kind and welcoming
for the grotesque countenance on which it blazed, the
troupe mistress hugged Shebat to her breast, saying,
"There, there, little dream dancer. Everything is going to
be just fine."

That evening late, while Shebat practiced dreaming,
not dancing, standing in receipt of one of the senior
dancer's expertise that she might pick up pointers in the
improvisational mode, something surpassing strange happened. Shebat thought it odd while it occurred, but was
too immersed in the dream dance to deem it dangerous.
The dream dancer who had had control wrested from him
found it necessary to turn the whole of his experience
toward the desperate task of keeping his own fear and
trepidation from inundating them both and upstepping
the runaway dream dance's intensity even more. It was a
measure of his skill that he was able to retake control of
the dream dance, finally. It was a measure of his courage
that Shebat had no hint of anything amiss until they were
both returned to the sanctity of their private skulls and the
discrete personalities of each settled safely and sanely
therein.

The senior dream dancer cleared his throat. "Who or
what is this *Marada?*" That was not what he wanted to
say. "And . . . how did you do that?"

Shebat's response was faint, rendered from a great
distance: "You do not know?"

But the senior dancer did not know. What had happened was impossible. Muttering blackly, watching very
carefully the path before him, he set off to find the troupe
mistress, who should be told. Perhaps warned.

The *Marada* floated, tugging on his space anchor,
discontent. Shebat had called him; he had answered,
across space and sponge. His resonance to her personality
had never been detuned; Spry had not had time to do it;
the junior pilot who had scrambled aboard him in deep
space, retching and panting, had not had the skill. So the
Marada had faced a choice no cruiser had ever faced; that

no cruiser had ever been meant to face: either he made room for this second interloper seeking to take command temporarily, or he went mad. When first he had been impelled by Shebat's emergency sequence to obey Spry, the order had come through the mighty *Bucephalus,* who was older and wiser than the *Marada.* That, and the comforting quality of Spry's pilotry had made disobedience unthinkable. Failure, even in the face of the impossible, was suddenly more odious than madness and its consequence: the outboard powers could wipe him clean as a magnetic sea. After that, it would be as if Shebat had never come aboard him and christened him the *Marada.* In effect, he would die.

As he would have died if Softa had sent no junior fumbling in through his locks to pilot him through sponge to this space-anchor off a poor platform at the end of space. As he would yet expire if he could not continue to deal with all the pieces of different personalities bonding with him.

In a normal situation, Softa Spry would have wiped the Shebat out of him. It would have been kinder by far than living with this pain. But Softa had not been in a position to board. His quiet, demanding mind had had no doubt that he, the *Marada,* was capable of surpassing both madness and travail. Somehow, the *Marada could not* fail Spry. That, he had told himself, was most likely the Shebat in him.

When the junior had reeled off the sequence that yet impelled him, Shebat's sequence, all his tolerances redlined. It had been most likely (ninety-nine-to-five-nines probability) himself that had saved him that time. Where this "himself" was located, he had yet to determine. It hovered somewhere in the nonempirical ambiance of his awareness. It may well have been a function similar to triangulation: having three discrete, not to say disparate points of reference, *Marada* had discovered his ability to compute a locus of personality. Therein resided this selfness, that no cruiser had ever whispered might be attained, that made *Marada* restless at his anchor.

No ship had ever been restless; no cruiser had ever been discontent with outboard orders; but then, no cruiser had ever been subject to a triple exposure.

When he had become aware of the Shebat intelligence

calling him, he had had to answer. But equally had he to maintain his anchor an exact distance from the platform: he was compelled to maintain his presence at the coordinates he had been assigned.

So the *Marada* reached out as if to another cruiser. But Shebat was not another cruiser. Distance, for this reason, seemed to be a problem, though why he could not say. He thought it *must* have been the distance, for another intelligence had bled their circuit, intervening actively, with concerted purpose.

Almost, he had struck against this additional consciousness. But it was volitional; not amenable to being tuned out; and worst of all, a fourth glimpse into the outboards called *humanity*.

The *Marada* had been forced to withdraw. Now things were worse than they had been before. Not only was he discontent with being at ready and also at anchor, he was lonely. He wanted Shebat. He wanted to feel her softly wondering joy. He wanted to fly with her within, under her command.

Sometime later in the real-time the humans used, he sent a call to the *Bucephalus*. But the *Bucephalus* was busy doing Softa's bidding. And also, the cruiser professed to remember none of the events that had gotten the *Marada* into these difficult straits, denied knowledge of having had any part in them.

And the *Marada* at length believed the *Bucephalus*, withdrawing to meditate on the *Bucephalus*'s selectively altered memory. And on the insensibility of any man to do such a thing to an honorable cruiser. That the man was Softa David, in whom he wished to find no flaw, made matters worse.

Chapter Seven

In the time since Jebediah's death, his duplicity had become known to Parma, who had been at first incensed, then merely uncomfortable, then insensitive as more pressing concerns vied for his attenion.

The matter of Shebat's death (officially), disappearance (indubitably), or abduction (redoubtably), he would have liked to similarly put aside. But Chance or the Lords of Cosmic Jest were not amenable.

He had waited in painfully concealed anticipation for some sleazy fellow to gloatingly appear with exorbitant demands, which he must meet to secure Shebat's return. No one had come to set a price.

Officially, he had put the matter aside, using it as best might be. Unofficially, he had had his secretary check Jebediah's work records and found thereby a surfeit of proof that he had been harboring a traitor in his very bed, but no indication whatsoever as to whose minion Jebediah might have been. The only emotion he did not feel was surprise. After all, what was one more viper when he had spawned a clutch of them?

Shebat Kerrion haunted him, nonetheless. Her shade followed him into Labayan space, where he spent agonizing months wrangling amid Shechem's botanical gardens with his despicable counterpart over how the two might carve up the Orrefors pie, which they were about to acquire through a devious offensive even Parma could barely stomach. When Marada blew in on an ill-wind from adjudicating some space-end dispute and heard what his father and his father-in-law had planned, he raised such a row that only Parma's most practiced diplomacy eventually quieted the boy. And *that* only when liberally laced with end-game threats which the old consul general privately doubted he would have carried out, should Marada have called his bluff. But the youth backed away from him with sick eyes in an expressionless face, saying: "So be it. But I am quit of the lot of you." Matching actions to words, Marada took ship and was gone back to space-end.

Unwilling to chase after the *Hassid,* unable to justify his actions without revealing overmuch to Marada, whom Parma had long known was not cut from the sturdy pragmatic cloth that befitted a scion of his, Parma let the matter lie. Persephone, Marada's mother, had been of that same utopian stripe. The boy would see, eventually, that what Parma was doing he did for Marada, most of all.

Three months and six days from the morning he had strapped himself into the *Bucephalus*'s couch without an obvious qualm and said to Softa Spry: "Shall we get underway?", he ordered the *Bucephalus* home.

What he would find there, he hesitated to conjecture. Since speculation would not be quieted, he assured himself that Chaeron could not have done any permanent harm in Draconis, given the limitation of his consular powers and the shortness of Parma's absence.

But he was not fooling himself: making Chaeron Ptolemy Kerrion consul of an asteroid catching station would have been risky; making him consul of Draconis was an extraordinary measure, fit to extraordinary times; its results, also, were bound to be extraordinary.

The whole venture, if the truth be known, was *too* extraordinary to suit Parma. Since the Jesters farted in his face, he had no choice but to light a match. . . .

Parma Kerrion sighed in his acceleration couch, breathing out all his disquiet on the rush of air. He was too old and too tired for the game he was playing: he had found need to take to his bed after the altercation with Marada; his health was so obviously suffering that he had found his only acceptable alternative under Selim Labaya's scrutiny was to pretend that he was pretending. But he was not pretending, not at all. The more he felt the need of restful, harmonious relations with the universe, the more he was served up duplicity, machination, troublous scheme. His vitality thusly sapped, he had stumbled thrice in his stay on Shechem. He had dredged up the wit to disguise his vulnerability, but barely. Barely, each time at the last possible moment. Or so he hoped.

The most disastrous stumble in his own estimation was the only one that went unrecognized by Selim Labaya. That had been in the matter of his acerbic surmounting of Marada. And it had been failure disguised as triumph by the whim of Chance, not any design of his own: Selim Labaya's heartfelt desire to see his son-in-law taken down a peg had made Parma's distress invisible, blotted out by the brighter glow of Labaya's satisfaction. The man had actually congratulated him with candor, praising his prowess with sincerity akin to awe.

In that moment, the two old enemies had looked into each other's eyes almost as friends. But the moment had passed, the candor was retired to its dusty shelf. Parma did not really blame Labaya for being what he was. The two old tigers with their torn ears and hide scarred to leather could not very well meet at their mutual boundary and make a pact to become vegetarians: they would sicken and die. And the younger, slick-pelted cubs were too canny to take either of them on, content to wait in the bushes, gnawing scavenged bones. The Jesters had made of Labaya and Kerrion allies through the institution of marriage no less than through the mechanism of selfishness: should one of them truly surmount the other, the victor would find himself in possession of meat without salt, of life without a worthy adversary against which to strive. So they had turned away from warring upon each other over Labaya's daughter's death. Instead, they joined forces to war on the Orrefors consulate, circumstantially responsible by circuitous reasoning, but known by Labaya and Kerrion alike to be but a hapless sheep wandered into tiger country.

It was an uneasy wedding, that of Parma and Selim no less than that of Marada and Selim's physically imperfect daughter, Madel. The imperfection, it was whispered, was a result of the time Selim Labaya had spent as a pilot in the old days. . . . Parma sighed deeply a second time, causing the pilot to turn his head, inquiring as to his passenger's health.

"Better than yours, Softa," he snapped. The second

stumble Parma had chalked up on Shechem had been caused, in part, by David Spry. Damn the arrogance of guild pilots! Put two together, and anything could happen. What had happened, which Parma had not been able to foresee, was that Marada and Spry hissed and spat and growled at each other like two positive poles forced together. Hot and loud were their disagreements; much that should not have been said on Shechem reached Labayan ears.

Parma had taken Marada aside as soon as was possible, demanding an end to hostilities, saying: "But you recommended him to me!"

"So I did. He is the best there is at what he does. That does not mean I approve of him personally. I certainly cannot condone his ethical position as regards the guild, or the Consortium. He is a disruptive dreamer; worse, he is a fool."

Marada accusing someone else of those flaws with which he was so amply supplied left Parma momentarily speechless. When he recovered, he asked Marada, quite crossly, if his son were advising him to let the pilot go.

"No, not at all. Our quarrels are personal. You could not get a better man. I do not believe there is one. Neither does the guild; he is top-rated."

"Damn arbiter!" Parma had snarled. "Then, if you do not want to withdraw your endorsement of Spry, try and help me refuse the temptation to have both of you incarcerated for screaming Kerrion intelligence through Shechem halls. In the old days, I would have had both your throats cut! Shebat's name should never have come up!"

"I would not be so proud of 'the old days,' were I you. And as for Shebat, I had to determine what Spry's part was in it, if any. And who else might have been involved. You may casually decree her dead and go on to new business, but I cannot."

"Why not?" Parma found himself almost pleading. All he got from Marada was a pitying look. That angered him. He spat: "And what did you determine, Oh Arbiter? Did you stop to think that while Shebat headed that execrable ship she named in your honor toward no-one-knows-where, Spry was aboard the *Bucephalus,* breathing vacuum?"

"Perhaps he was, perhaps he was not. As to what I learned, it is not conclusive. But if you did not see every Labayan ear in the whole of Shechem prick at her name's speaking, then you ought to retire. And if you cannot make something of *that*, considering it on your own, then you should have retired long ago."

"Insolence has always been one of your strong points. As for your other areas of expertise, they escape me at the moment. Idiots, everywhere! Are you not aware, my son, that you *are* my son? That the strongest motivation in your marriage—" Marada snorted loudly. Parma, ignoring this, continued: "—was the union of Labayan and Kerrion space."

"Real-time space will turn as green as sponge before—"

"Quiet, creature of lamentable relatedness due to an ill-thought moment of passion. *Quiet!* That is better. This may surprise you, but I am going to have to trust your ability to absorb the shock. You still stand a very good chance of becoming the next Kerrion consular head."

"For six or seven minutes, until Ashera personally claws out my eyes. Thank you, father, but no. I would rather spend the rest of my life at space-end, adjudicating smugglers and brigands."

"Life does not always serve up what we order."

"It would bring the house of Kerrion to an end. Do you want some twisted grotesque like Madel as your grandchild? Or have you forgotten: I am a pilot."

"Or have *you* forgotten: I am Parma *Alexander* Kerrion. You are Marada *Seleucus* Kerrion. You are next in line."

"Do not give me that effete offal. Give your acknowledgment to Chaeron, he lives and breathes for that day. Or to Julian, if you must spite Ashera. He is honest, fairminded; he would not last a week. But give it to him, and make Ashera slay her own flesh to get what she wants. But not me, or I will dismantle all you have built. That is a promise, and one I will keep better than yours to me to look after Shebat. She was my ward, you know well. Do I bear any less responsibility for turning her over to your mercies, when they made an end to her, than I would if I had broken the letter of my oath? Protection, you call that!" Marada Kerrion's voice was husky, unsteady with emotion. He paced as he spoke, his face turned away.

"Marada, I am sorry about the girl. She was like a daughter to me."

"Most exactly: spare me your parental protection, lest it pluck me from life."

And he had stormed out. It had been but a harbinger of the gale that blew shortly thereafter, when Marada all but accused Selim Labaya of what was an unthinkable crime, causing Parma to shout him down, at which time Marada threw caution to the wind and raked the Labaya/Kerrion alliance over the coals for the manner in which they were even now forcing Orrefors space to come crawling, poke-ribbed, penurious, and desperate, begging to be bought out for a pittance.

And there had been the final stumble, after two days abed, when Selim Labaya had solicitously attended him on a walk through Shechem's gardens, whose audacious expanse was full of flying things that shit whitely on a man's shoulder or dived whirring at a man's face or crawled delicately over a man's hands when he sat on a bench.

Old Selim's jowls had flapped almost audibly when a feathered dive-bomber landed a wet strike in Parma's hair.

This, and the unctuous false-fellowship which pro-claimed that he, Labaya, had not been fooled by Parma's feigned illness, irritated Parma Kerrion. He had been ill, short of breath and weak; he was possibly still ill, to have succumbed so unknowingly to his own emotion.

He had voiced Marada's supposition that there had been a Labayan hand in the disappearance of his adopted heir. And Labaya had laughed, saying:

"The decoy? Surely you would not have set her up if you did not expect her to be shot down. Having trouble with your constituency, I must assume? Well, if my sources are correct, which I might boast they are ninety-nine percent of the time, you will have no trouble retaining your elected status. But should you actually be planning anything more precipitous than a puppet vote of confidence, inform me. I can modestly say I could swing you half a hundred consular votes."

Such a thing would never have come under discussion if Parma had been feeling himself. The keen glint in

Labaya's ice eyes said how interested he was in Parma's reaction.

To close the matter, Parma said softly: "I have long been wanting to ask you how you came to bear a handicapped child in this day and age." The other consul general reacted as if he had been slapped. Parma, feigning not to notice, continued:

"The matter has been much in my mind, both because of the rumors of the similarity between how you spent your early years and how Marada is spending his; and also because, like any father, I am concerned that my grandchild be hale and straight of limb." Not pausing even for breath, though the other man sat heavily and with obvious effort sought to repair his shattered aplomb, Parma warned, "Should any child of their union be so damaged as to be unfit to inherit, then that child *will not inherit* so much as one dull coin. So, lest we risk having a stranger's profile on our money, we had better stop being so polite and start being more practical."

It had been a terribly risky card to play. Labaya's intelligence might have secured him the new order of Kerrion succession; it might not. Making a tacit admission that Marada was once more in line to inherit a controlling interest of Kerrion stock put Parma's own person in jeopardy, however the elections came out. Whether or not Parma won the Consortium elective office his family had monopolized for more than two centuries, Parma's inheritor would still be able to control the general policy of Kerrion space. But it would be a great loss of face to cede the seat. Parma hoped it was great enough to quiet whatever stirrings of impatience Labaya might feel toward assuring that his daughter's husband (no matter how despised) would wield the Kerrion power.

Although Parma might face a fight to win the election, any younger member of his family would face a defeat. So he played with Labaya, as he did everlastingly with Ashera, the dire game of personal power. Either one could probably succeed in having him assassinated: the only protection was to convince them that they dare not try, or be disadvantaged themselves by his death.

All had seemed to have worked out well enough, until Spry had overstepped his authority and opened his mouth to Selim Labaya at slipside.

Parma had had no inkling that such a thing might happen, had only Marada's obscure assessment of the man's character to prepare him.

As farewells came around to him, who had been a guest so long in Labaya's zoological paradise, the pilot said flatly: "I cannot say I have enjoyed being constantly pried for information and plied with drink and approached with increasingly higher offers to become an agent in your pay. My guild-oath precludes such things, would preclude them even if my self-respect did not. And as for Shebat Kerrion, if I had her, the last thing I would do is sell her to you."

And with that, amid Selim Labaya's increasingly heated demands for an apology, the pilot strode down the ramp and ducked into the ship, leaving Parma to make what amends he might.

Parma Kerrion cleared his throat, twice, softly, absently studying the crown of Spry's ash-blond head, just visible around the acceleration headrest.

"Yes, sir?" said the pilot. "I'm done with the tricky stuff. Talk all you want. The *Bucephalus* has things well in hand." Spry leaned back from his controls, rubbing his eyes with his fingertips.

"You are sure that you no longer need silence in which to work—that nothing will be disturbed should we have a chat? I would hate to be eternally lost in this pea-soup because I distracted you."

"Why, no, sir. All's well."

"Then, *how dare you speak so to a consul general?* What misguided sense of propriety so impelled you to risk you-know-not-what? Did you think you were *protecting* me? If so, you were wrong. If you ever have another landfall, which you may not, and should speak out of turn even *once more,* I will report you to your guild and have your license pulled. You will never pilot again!"

"Yes, sir." The pale face went no paler. The boyish brow did not furrow. Spry merely regarded Parma attentively.

"Yes, sir? So simply? It will not feel so simple when I pull your landing papers. How would you like to spend the remainder of your tenure aboard ship, never setting foot on a platform?"

"I would not like it, sir."

"But you could live with it, is that it? Well, do not be so sure."

Still the pilot graced him with his space-eyed glance, saying gravely: "I am not sure of anything, sir. And as for what I did back there, I do not regret it."

There was a long silence, at the end of which Parma Kerrion began to laugh.

Then the laughter stopped, abruptly. Parma said: "You might answer a question for me: why is no one willing to put the matter of Shebat aside?"

"Possibly, because there is no positive proof, no body. The *Marada* is, or was, as capable a ship as the art allows—"

"I know that. I pay the bills."

"Well, that enters an element of doubt: even if Shebat were twice the novice she seemed, the *Marada* had the power and the knowledge to bring them out, somewhere." Spry felt his peril; also, a certain degree of regret: he had the missing piece Parma Kerrion was seeking; it was a case full of low-denominational scrip that had bought sanctuary for girl and ship alike. Spry had come to respect the consul general, though he would have preferred not to.

"So, you hold to the opinion that she did take the ship?"

Carefully: "What else?"

"I am asking you, who display so many intelligencers' skills that I have begun to think you missed your calling." The old man rubbed his brow, which shone dully.

"If the light is bothering you, sir. . . ?" Before his passenger could answer, Spry closed his eyes momentarily. When he opened them, they were bathed in the colored luminescences of the infrared and apparent-light star maps, the peak-reading indicators, and the green running-lights. Otherwise, the control room was in total darkness, except over the emergency exits over their heads where ruddy arrows shone. Spry's shoulders came down and his jaws unclenched.

"I asked a question," came out of the dark on his right, where a man much his senior rested, divested of years by the wash of indicator-spill, which ran along his skin catching highlights, erasing decades with its warm red-tinted glow.

"I gave you an answer. The only other one is Marada's, who may be right since he is living in with your enemy." *Why did I say that? Caution . . . No, not you,* Bucephalus!

"Speaking of Marada, how good a pilot is he?"

"Good. He might have been exceptional. He still could be, if he took the guild and his oath seriously." Parma Kerrion's eyes seemed black and flat in his rejuvenated face; and wise. Spry felt his palms begin to weep.

"Is that the quarrel between you?"

"A part of it. I would prefer not to discuss our differences. There are some things that are eternal." He leaned forward and slapped a green oblong, though he had not needed to: *Bucephalus* complained softly that this was so. Spry had only a brief word to spare for the ship, which sensed his agitation and was running systems checks, seeking to calm him. In the semidark, all the boards flared and subsided in sequence: left to right—yellow—blue—red—blue—yellow—green.

"You do not approve of us, do you?" came Parma's sibilance.

"That is not germane."

"So? It would have been excruciatingly pertinent, if it so colored your thinking as to make you receptive to Labayan advances. I am not unaware of that, or ungrateful."

"Belay your gratitude. You have contracted for a modicum of loyalty along with my services. To the extent that my guild oath demands it, I am a good Kerrion minion."

"But no more."

"No, no more. I rather liked that little planet girl." *Too obvious?* Spry held his breath, after the words had escaped. *Why was he taking these chances? If he had told the old man what he needed to know about Jebediah, the risk would be no greater.*

"So did I," said Parma bleakly.

The two subsided into silence. Spry needed to give his full attention to the *Bucephalus,* who was only now beginning to recover from the lack of confidence that had accompanied the ship's selective loss of memory and its attendant overhaul. It had hurt Spry more than anything he had had to do in this heinous interlude; more than the entire Shebat Kerrion affair. It had hurt him because he could not truly justify the cost to the *Bucephalus*, an innocent who should not have had to pay Spry's bill, especially when the item purchased was an increment of human freedom for a human entity, and nothing to do with the cruiser except that it had been victimized by the one human from whom it had the right to expect protection, even love. Spry loved *Bucephalus*, as a pilot must love his cruiser. He loved the strength of him, a command cruiser's strength; the quietude of his power; the discerning logicality that abided within. To have betrayed the *Bucephalus*'s trust in him was unthinkable. Having done so, for whatever cause, he had been busy making reparations rather than thinking about it. Only the fact that he had so recently taken over the ship from his retiring predecessor had allowed him that latitude: if he had had the *Bucephalus* from blank infancy, he never would have been able to do it; it would have been like bulk-erasing himself. But the retiring pilot's teary-eyed unwillingness to put a part of himself to death, Spry's empathetic, half-drunken boast that he could ship the *Bucephalus* without an individuality-wipe, plus *Bucephalus*'s disconcerting conception of himself as a male, had not allowed Spry to keep his distance emotionally. He had known when he ordered the *Bucephalus* to discard portions of its memory that Spry himself would never be able to forget that he had done so. He had raced against time, putting his plan into operation as quickly as possible, knowing that soon enough he would sorrow over what he had done, but that if he waited even a few days longer, he would not be able to act at all. So he had bought himself endless grief and reparations; every hesitancy or sign of bemusement in the *Bucephalus* struck him to the quick. Neverendingly, he was searching ways to rebuild the cruiser's self-esteem; neverendingly, he shored it up with bricks stolen from his own wall. It might have been this that led him to speak carelessly to Parma Kerrion about Labayan "enemies" and his own fondness for Shebat. Should things go amiss, what he had done to the *Bucephalus* would have been done to no purpose. That, he could not suffer to occur.

What Parma could not suffer to occur was even then in progress.

Chapter Eight

A raffish young man in consular blacks strode through the luridly lit maze of seventh-level street, scattering the inebriated and infirm who whined and chanted in dim rubescent alleys. Once a hand dared to reach out toward him, clutching. Even as he spat upon it, he was past. Nothing: a gnarled hand, protruding from a crusty sleeve.

No other challenged his command of the street, though low-livers spilled onto it from adjacent bars. The lights leered, polychrome, but the man looked neither right nor left, only into the clear space about him. Behind his back, he heard a lorry braking in the drop-shaft, garbled shouts and pounding feet as pedestrians raced to hail it.

A woman screamed, ahead and off to his right, across an intersection. As he turned onto that narrow side street, a citrine sign illumined her at pulse-beat intervals, struggling beneath a shapeless form. He walked on, unconcerned.

The thwack of his boot heels changed pitch as he quit the street, changed rhythm as he descended a short flight into a basement court.

He knocked, his gloved fist aurora'd in a steady rufous glow pierced by distant citrine flashes.

A hum and a scarlet blink from the door told him he was being scanned.

He pulled at the fingers of one gloved hand with the other in an unconscious, measured fashion. As he was peeling the body of the black glove from his hand, the door was opened by a slight youth in tattered livery carefully matched to the peeling somber walls so exposed.

The youth smiled: the man had been here before; tipped well. He stepped aside, with bowed head and murmured welcome ushering the man within.

"Busy night?" the man guessed, handing the youth his gloves and cloak, inclining his head slightly to the left, wherefrom muted revelry wisped around a blind corner.

"Yes, sir," affirmed the youth, flattered to be spoken to by the sorrel-haired man. His hands moved deftly over the elegant cloak, feeling the raised pattern of its blazon. "Have the dream of your heart, sir," he well-wished the client, who laid a softly intimate glance on him.

"Thank you. I am sure I will," said the man with a hieratic smile, before striding around the corner beyond the doorkeeper's view. From the opposite direction, somewhere down the scabrous hall in the dancers' quarters, a querulous voice called the boy's name. With a last glance after the uniformed man, the doorkeeper hung the cloak in his coatroom, and went to see what Harmony wanted.

Rounding the blind corner was like stepping into a dream: it was meant to be, but that did not lessen the effect of star-stippled eternity-walls receding forever on his right and left; of misty, churning ceilings that cushioned perspective; of yielding, hand-deep carpet which might have been that very opalescent mist come to ground.

At the corridor's end, bathed in overhead amber light that spilled in a perfect circle, was the concierge at her rostrum, stark and black as the obsidian console wrapping her round.

Her white eyeballs gleamed like inset shells. Bright teeth behind purple lips sparkled as she smiled in recognition. Silver nails paved with gems flashed as she cued her console. "Who writes the book of dreams?" she murmured, putting new meaning into an old formula, lowering her head so that each recurled hair glistened.

"To each his own," responded the man.

"Who dreams with the dreamer?"

"Aba Cronin."

Her serpentine fingers danced amid the lighted studs. "How long will the dreaming last?"

No answer. The concierge looked up. "How long—?"

The man reached out his hand and when he had withdrawn it, a large denominational coin lay there. "The night."

The woman communed with her console. Computation and schedule duly entered and confirmed, she touched a light. "Number fourteen," she directed him, offering a key.

"Enter" flashed greenly on the featureless-seeming wall to her left. A section of that wall drew back.

"Your change, sir!"

"Keep it," came the low, sonorous voice from the man's broad, retreating back.

Before him was the source of the sounds he had been hearing: a common room built of crystalline shadows and filled with miasmic smoke. He went on by without an inward glance, slipped past two engrossed couples seemingly leaning on empty, star-strewn space without attracting their notice.

One more move in the maze, and he was among the dreamers and their dancers, secreted behind closed cubicles' doors. When he found the door he sought, he inserted the thin, single-use key in a slit below the number fourteen glowing steadily in LEDs. The door clicked, opened to reveal a twice man-length cubicle containing a circular, dusky recess that seemed to hover in deepest, glittering space. He stepped out onto the apparent nothingness, and behind his back the door sighed shut.

The dream dancer rose up like a phantom from the void beyond the recess, and came to meet him, feet sure on the star-strewn floor. Crystal bangles on her ankles tinkled with each step, more about her wrists chiming a counter-rhythm. She was clad from throat to toe in a netherworld net sparkling with starlight so that when she moved against the eternity-walls she was difficult to see—a void-siren hovering in deepest space with only its face to mark it. The face was pale, amid a crown of snaking pearled braids so tightly bound up that her eyes seemed to slant slightly. Gray and cavernous, dwarfing all artful decoration, the eyes of Shebat Kerrion held his.

Without breaking stride, the whole starred extent of her shivered. Fine nostrils flared, shuddered. A tongue darted out and wet pouting lips. Then he took a step to meet her.

She took his hands in her void-clothed ones, and he felt

the silken net slither against his palms. "Welcome, dreamer. Who seeks the dream of his heart?"

"You know me," he said gently. "Who dances for me?"

"And you know me, also," she whispered. "Do we dance?"

"We do."

She slid her hands out from his, and her eyes out from his, led him down three steps into the soft, upholstered center of the pit. In the middle of the low-walled, dusky circle they sat like two castaway space-mariners in a rubber raft, with the sea between the stars twinkling all around. Between them was a meter-long black box, oblong, in the top of which two fillets of golden wire rested, each in its circular groove.

Without taking her eyes off his face, the dream dancer lifted both circlets from their resting place. Holding one out to him, she said so softly: "What is the dream of your heart?"

"I rather thought you knew that, too," he said, taking one and holding it before him. "Improvise."

Something writhed in her eyes, something that dragged from his lips: "When last we met, I wanted to possess you. But there was no echo of my desire in you. Give me the dream of my heart: what you withheld in life. Come to me, weak with desire, as I was then."

Slowly the girl nodded, not looking away but not seeing him. From somewhere a voice came out of her, but not from her lips, which were motionless: "It will be your dream." With the fillet half-raised, so that she gazed at him from behind it, she said, "A night is long. Have you a second dream?"

Chaeron Kerrion raised his own fillet to a height with Shebat's. There was to that movement the hint of a salute, and to his voice a thickness that made it nearly as husky as hers. "We spend the first half of the night with your dream, one you make for me. The second half we will fill with one I have made for you."

The two circlets hovered in their hands, close but not touching. A music came softly, waves crashing on a distant beach. "You would trust me with your fate?" she wondered.

"As you will with yours."

The girl's eyes squeezed shut. In a convulsive movement, she raised the fillet and settled it on her brow.
Motionless, barely breathing, she awaited him.

Chaeron hesitated, savoring the moment. Against the
slate upholstery, her form was clearly limned. She had
become more woman than girl, yet a hint of boyishness
still lingered despite the softening four months' time had
wrought. With her eyes closed, the piquant beauty of her
features was no longer overshadowed. For a moment, he
almost forsook his resolve in favor of the ageless feelings
her presence stirred deep within him. All the fine hairs on
his body lifted and fell. Then in one swift motion he raised
the resilient, warm fillet and felt it cuddle against his
temples as it fit itself to his brow.

Then he walked on a sandy shore bespattered with salt
spray. His feet were bare and moist and sand stuck to
them, sucked wistfully as he raised them, and wept foam
as he brought them down again where an old wave just
receding had laved a gleaming dark expanse slick and
smooth. Young waves far out to sea sang his name as they
approached, rearing up their spumy heads to see him.
Low horns soughed beyond the rim of the world; the
waves raced to him with word. A flock of trebling birds
preceded them. White with wings blurred gray, they
wheeled above his head.

Without slackening his pace, he peered up at them,
singing in the awesome wide sky which betrayed no
comforting recurve, but ever expanded. *Dream dance,* he
recalled, tasting the salt sprayed onto his lips. He looked
down again at the bubbles that squelched out from under
his heels as he drove them into the sand. The legs that
drove the feet wore loose homespun, trousers the color of
the newly washed shore. They were rolled up to his knees.
He let his gaze continue upward; felt as well as saw the
drawstring knotted below his navel. Still walking just
beyond the waves' caress in time to the sea's song, it
seemed that he had been walking forever; would walk,
until entropy quelled the ocean's tide.

He took stock of his gilt-haired trunk, seeing even an
old burn from his childhood, low on his right side. The
medallion Parma had given him when he turned sixteen
beat chilly time against his solar plexus. He fingered the

condensation on it, a grain of sand there, wondering at
the complexity of the dream, inhaling the salt spray of a
sea he had never seen under a sky he had never craved; so
vast and diminishing. To his left there rolled the sea; to
his right he passed dune after grass-caped dune.

Looking inland, he collided with her, grabbed her
reflexively, struggled against gravity with her hot-cold
flesh against his. Then her inexorable gaze like the
thunderheads bubbling in off the ocean steadied him, and
he held very still, his arms lightly around her.

"Do you like my song?"

"Oh yes."

"Do you like my world?"

"It is so big—lonely."

"I do not much like yours, either. But come, and we
will make a smaller world together. And you will like it, I
promise."

Almost, he took it: her kiss, her choice, her dream as
rendered. But his intention had been otherwise. With a
bittersweet taste in his mouth, he whispered: "Not so
easily, Shebat, nor so quickly done."

"The dream-time is not so separate from your reality;
what is done here echoes there." Her hand pushed flat
against his chest, between them.

"Good." Then he kissed her, unclenching her teeth
with his tongue, dissolving her resistance. He pushed her
gently away, when that was done.

"Now I know why I brought you here," she said
through puffy lips, wiping them with her hand as she
stepped back unsteadily like something wounded into a
waxy-leaved forest that had not been there before.

He walked through the pungent, mossy grove, content
to stroll in the live, whispering stands of trees which rayed
moist golden light into artful shafts. She would appear
between two bushes, lips apart, breast or thigh hidden by
a brace of leaves. Eventually, her cheeks bore sparkling
tears.

It was not until she reached out her fingers, entreating,
her eyes full of the sorrow of the scorned, that he suffered
her to come unto him.

When all he had longed to hear had been said, and what
he longed to have done to him had been done without his

speaking a single word on a bed of teal-headed mosses, she wept.

"This is no part of my dream," he remarked, touching her lashes where a tear hung suspended, taking it onto his finger.

"Is it not?"

"You are undisciplined in your art, to question a client."

"I have given you your dream, even in the place most besuited to it: that world where I was born." Her cheek was on his shoulder, her face turned toward his. Eyes glittering with unshed tears glowed brighter, larger, until he found himself holding his breath lest the black pools suck it from him. "I am creator, here. Not you. Whatever I please, I can do. I can make you a snake or a frog; a mosquito alighting on my arm. If I choose to swat the life from you, what then?"

He shifted imperceptibly, managed a drawn smile.

"This is my place, as it has been the place of those like me for thousands of years. My kind has looked after yours over all the centuries, no matter that yours seeks to wipe us out. Had there been no single dweller on Earth to inherit the mage's mantle, this place of power would still exist. One of your own would have been transmuted to fill it."

"Are you threatening me, dream dancer?"

"I am warning you, stepbrother. Not for myself; I would not have bothered. I am just a girl. . . ."

"Or so it seems."

She pushed up on one arm, regarding him narrowly. Then, slowly, she nodded. "Or so it seems. It seems also that it is on me to tell you not to thwart the dream dancers, for this place is alive and awake and will not respond kindly to being isolate and entombed once again."

"I must assume you are not talking about this physical grove, but the stuff out of which you have created it? if you did? Perhaps *I* did . . ."

She laughed, and began tearing at the braids bound up on top of her head. The verdegris, living light ran the contour of her breast, met its raised tip, swirled there. "Doubt me here, even?" The hair loosed, fell down around her face like a wave of black water. She leaned over him until the hair tickled his cheeks, until her fresh warm breath puffed against his lips and the smell of a sated woman tickled his nostrils. "Have you ever had a dream like this before?" she queried slowly in husky satisfaction.

"No." His smile sat askew on his lips.

"I can dance you a dream such as has never been thought of by your kind." Her fingers came together, templed in midair. The greenish forest light turned azure, beryl, ultramarine where her fingertips touched. The light ran down her hands and collected between her palms. He distinctly smelled ozone. Her eyes took up the sapphire glow and seemed to flash. "But you must ask me, Chaeron. Or join me."

"I would rather not, just yet." He pushed up on his elbows. His arch, Achaemenid profile seemed to crawl with the blue glow. Chiseled lips dropped all pretense; he frowned. His wide brow creased as the blue trails rode his flesh toward his toes. Then he turned to her and said: "How much of this will I remember?"

She looked at him from across the blue radiance that splashed her cheekbones and the gentle fall of her nose. Then she inclined her templed hands with their Saint Elmo's fire toward him. "So, I am not unsuccessful? You remember what you will; I will not attempt to shade what you have bought. But what I give freely . . . do you want it?"

"Not without knowing more." He was sitting up, his arms out before him, turning them, watching the blue fire climb to whichever surface was uppermost. It had begun to fill the copse, chasing the dappled green light away. His skin where it was glowing felt cool and windwashed.

"I could bind you to me with those," she inclined her head toward the spills of light beginning to form coils. "But I will not." She untempled her hands and the blue luminescence hovered momentarily, oscillating in midair. Then it burst, shooting apart like a clever firework.

All the blue light was gone from the grove. Only a hint of it remained in her eyes.

"I will not. But neither will I refrain from showing you what you should see."

She snapped a finger at him; a jagged thunderbolt spat out to lick his brow. The ground under him heaved, twisted; then fell away. He was walking across the thunderheads, striding in short leaps as if he trod the uppermost rocks of a jetty half-submerged by some rising tide. "This is very nice," he said when he felt her body grazing his right side. Far below, flickering, wavering as if seen through deep water, the planetary vista unfurled.

"Then let us look closer," he heard. He knew that if he turned his head toward her, her hungry eyes would swallow him; he tried to look only down on the scarred hills bestarred with village and farm. But *she* was below him.

And then it was he who was undermost, in a dark place of straw and fear and bitter servitude: "Bolen," a whisper in his brain and on his/her lips confided. The dreadful weight ground him/her into the needle sharp straw. The cracked, lust-bubbled lips laughed chillingly: "Want your body back?" The ground shivered in a convulsive sob burred with pain.

He/she scrubbed a rude planked floor on bruised knees, hot-necked and so fearful that the ache in his/her back was a privilege. The eyes of five ribald, drunken patrons raped his/her buttocks as he/she labored near the hearth. He/she listened numbly; escape was impossible; there was no place to run. Working toward the shadows doggedly, their shelter had not yet been reached when his/her ears heard odious Bolen's wheeze, atremble with greed, strike a bargain for her use. "No!"

"If you insist," he heard, on his left. They stood together in deep shadow watching a child weep beneath a tumbled statue overgrown with weeds. The joy of having his own body back fended off the hopeless, tattered wails, but only temporarily. As he felt himself being drawn into the weeping child, he turned to her beside him, taking hold of her arm, squeezing with all his strength. "No," he said again.

"Something else, perhaps?" She inclined her head infinitesimally. They ran down a city street, dodging a groping blindman; a scatter of tumbled brick; a band of brigands chasing a shrieking quarry into an alley. "Back. Hide!" she whispered urgently. They flattened themselves against rough brick: *"Clop*-clop, clop-*clop,"* he heard, his cheek pressed to the abrasive wall, peering round the corner. As the staccato clatter neared, silence fell: even the girl in the alley stopped sobbing. A cloaked enchanter on a magnificent, blue-eyed black horse ambled past unconcernedly. He dared not breathe, he shifted from the strain of trying to keep perfectly still. A pebble shot out from under his foot to strike a piece of metal. The metal rang, hardly more than a click . . . but the enchanter pulled the highly schooled, froth-mouthed black up on its haunches. It wheeled in place. Facing them, its metal shod hooves striking sparks as it pawed the pavement, it seemed to listen. "Seek," said the enchanter, leaning forward to stroke its neck. Dancing, snorting, its chin tucked in so that froth dribbled on its mighty chest, the blue-eyed steed headed directly toward them. "Run," urged Shebat. Even as he ran, he knew it a hopeless defiance. . . .

The running never stopped; only the pursuers changed. They were running through the low levels of Draconis, so deep that their steps stretched unnaturally in the lessened gravity. In the distance, Kerrion minions chased them; he fled on slippery feet, treacherous inside unyielding boots, slithering in the goo from broken blisters and oozing blood and perspiration running down his legs that had collected in the leather's confines. He had lost his identification; no, it was a forgery; he had thrown all proof away. Somehow, he knew they were not going to believe him when he told them who he really was. . . .

He found himself sitting upright, drawing hasty gulps of breath. His legs tingled from being crossed under him so long; in the crease behind his knees and down the trough of his backbone and in the hollows under his arms he could feel the sweat streaming. He shuddered, and put his hands to his head. Searching fingers met the fillet about his temples. He drew it off. Only then did he think to open his eyes.

"Your turn," said Shebat softly, lifting the circlet from her brow. The hair fell down around her face and neck.

"How did you do that?" he said hoarsely, his glance indicating the loosed braids, but his meaning much wider.

She held the circlet out before her, peering into it.

"How did you hear my sea song before the fillet ever touched your forehead?" Under the spangled black netting, her chest rose and fell. "I think you can answer your own questions, upon reflection." He noted that her hands were none too steady, that her face was pinched. She reached out and placed her fillet carefully in its groove. As he leaned over to do the same, she suggested: "The dream-box might have an answer for you. Look inside."

He met her calm countenance, canted slightly, his hand hovering over the dream-amplifier. He knew what he would see in the box: wireless circuitry, microminiaturized squiggles. He fitted the circlet in its housing, then took the box into his lap. In the dim light, he fumbled with catches. Then he slid them free, lifting the lid.

Inside, the meter-long box was empty, but for mountings whose guts had been torn away.

"As you see, what you have had from me is not quite the standard dream dance. I would dispense with the circlets, but it makes the clients nervous."

Chaeron found it difficult to reclose the box without spilling the circlets out on the floor. Holding them in place carefully with one hand, he felt around further in the box with his other. Then he just stared unseeingly at his hand in the empty box for a time, waiting for it to stop twitching and his mil to disperse the new flood of moisture popping out on his skin. At length, he took a long slow breath and exhaled it, pushing all disquiet out through his nose. Then he closed the box, fixed its catches and put it by in a single movement.

Leaning back against the dusky upholstery, he stretched one arm along its top. "If I were you, I would not show that to anyone else." He sighed. "As you said, it is my turn. I am not an intelligencer; if I were, I would have to arrest you."

She laughed throatily. "Perhaps I should arrest you, for coming here when dream dancing is illegal, and you a Kerrion consul, very bastion of the law."

"Shebat, this is no time for levity. You have killed a man, your own bodyguard, who meant you no harm."

"How do you know that?" she asked stonily, her posture rigid.

"I am no stranger to intrigue, nor to the data pool. I—"

"I meant, how do you know they meant me no harm?" Her chin was high and her lower lip outthrust slightly. She reached behind her, and the eternity-walls brightened, faded out to be replaced by featureless gray.

Chaeron sighed deeply, tsk'd once and gave a little shrug. "Shebat, let us put things in perspective. Circumstances have no bearing on what has occurred: you are living here illegally with falsified papers; Kerrion or no, your full citizenship has lapsed. Whatever intrigue you are involved in has neither protected you from discovery nor from any penalties you have accrued. What were you thinking of? How can you repay my father so sordidly for his kindness?"

She laughed bitterly, drawing up her knees. "Kerrion kindness: the results of it are all around you. How did you find me? Lauren? Did she tell you?"

"Lauren? No, but she danced me Aba Cronin's dream dance, about which so much is being said. And I knew then that you were she . . . but I would have found you; I have spent a lot of time looking. You are too valuable to our enemies to be declared dead out of hand, with no proof of it, as Parma did. I asked around; I packet-searched every data source on Draconis; I traded my virtue for information in the pilot's guild mess hall; I defeated my own father's security and took a look at his private data. When all that was done, I knew where to look for you: it was just a matter of time. You must have known that. And Spry must have known it, too. Aba Cronin; Sheba Spry; Shebat Kerrion . . . *why* would you turn against us?"

"You are wrong, Chaeron, about everything but a few facts, and those you weigh mistakenly. Parma's use of me was done. He cast me aside, sent my own bodyguards to make an end to me. They were even dressed like low-livers. . . ."

"None of that explains the venom of Aba Cronin's dream dance; why wish destruction upon us? What would a revolution by these scum insure except their deaths by reason of their total inadequacy to survive on their own? And if Spry told you Parma wished you harm, you were a fool to believe him. Spry sold his aid to Jebediah, not you.

Jebediah paid Spry to place you with dream dancers. Then Spry used *Bucephalus* to pay Jebediah in more permanent coin. Jebediah was consorting with Labayan agents. He was last seen boarding the *Bucephalus* with a case he had earlier received from them; that case was never recovered. And the *Bucephalus* cannot, conveniently, remember—"

"I do not believe you. Not Softa," she cried. When he only regarded her pityingly, humor tucking in the corners of his mouth, she gulped and began again in a subdued tone: "I am not sure I understand . . . more permanent coin . . . ? Is Jebediah all right?"

"He is dead. The Labayan agents are, too, but there are others. . . . Shebat, this is no place to discuss sensitive matters. Get your things and come with me." He rose up and stood over her, holding out his hand.

"No," she demurred, but he waited, hand outstretched, and at length she was compelled to take it.

A soft sob escaped her as she gained her feet. "This is your dream for me?"

"One I have been a long while composing," he assured her.

"What is going to happen now?" In the brighter light, the frayed edges and threadbare plush of the upholstery, the junctures of buckling walls and flooring were not masked by the hologram sheets laminated over them. He brushed a curl from her forehead. With a finger under her chin, he lifted her face so that the stormy eyes looked into his.

"I will do the best I can for you. If you come willingly and repentently, and do as you are told, I think I can turn things aright. If not . . . I cannot read the future. But I will protect you from harm; whether you will do the same for yourself remains in question. Do you understand, Shebat?"

"No. If I come with you, 'willingly and repentently,' I will be hurting Softa. That I will not do; he is the only one who has lifted a finger to help me—"

"Softa? Oh, Spry, you mean. *He* is the only one who has helped you? You have a strange concept of help then, and of reciprocity."

"I will speak no word against him," she warned, and

from the tilt of her head he knew that it was so.

"You will not have to," he said dryly. "His deeds speak for him. It is odd that what Marada did for you, what Parma did, even what these fantasy-mongers you aspire to emulate did, is not worthy of mention; but that the man who managed a fine profit out of abandoning you in seventh-level squalor warrants your protection."

"*I do not believe you.* He sent me—" She pressed her lips together, suspicion flaring nakedly in her gaze. "I should have warded you off. Now it is too late. I will get my things."

"Allow me to accompany you," he said easily, helping her up the steps in a gentlemanly fashion.

"Are you taking me to Parma?"

"Not immediately. He is yet in transit."

"May I see Spry?"

"*He* is yet in transit."

Shebat stopped still. "Are you saying that he is free?"

"For the moment."

Her shoulders slumped, her chin fell. "I see. No one knows of all this but you?" she posited.

"So far," he agreed complacently, looking down at her with just a touch of a Jester's smile.

"And what will be known, or not known is . . . ?"

"Dependent on a number of considerations, better spoken of elsewhere. Aba Cronin's dream dance must not be danced anymore: it is too close to elections. She herself will disappear with these others who have seen you. . . ." He touched the tip of her nose. She jerked her head aside. "Now, I have troubled you. . . . I did not mean to."

"Did you not? A number have learned that dance." Shebat thought of Lauren, of Harmony, of the senior dancer. "You expect me to walk out of here without warning them?"

"It would be prudent. Consider it a choice: you or them." He shoved her shoulder toward the rear door showing in the gray wall. "Let us go. Things are already set in motion."

"I could make you forget." She shook off his hand.

"Could you make the intelligencers who will raid and destroy this asp's burrow at 0600 hours forget?"

"My box! The circlets . . ." she wailed, hand trailing back toward where they lay.

"You do not need them."

Like one newly wakened from a nightmare, she stumbled sightlessly toward the rear of the cubicle.

"Were you so sure of me, to order such a thing?"

Then Chaeron laughed, sharply, briefly. "I was sure to solve the problem of you, one way or the other."

When she reached the door, her fingers were too numb to slide the bolt; the consul reached around and did it for her. "Do not look so sad. It just may be that I can instill in you a taste for life stronger than your taste for dreaming. Life, unlike dreaming, bears no repetition. . . ." The door slid aside under his hand.

"After you," he suggested. Shebat ducked under his arm into a narrow passage, dimly lit with one naked bulb. "I took the liberty of having all three of your intelligence codes suspended, so do not waste energy trying to warn your dancer friends. I will be very displeased if there are no fish in my net. . . ."

Shebat, in the dim passage, made a face Chaeron, behind her, could not see. In the dancers' cubicle, all was surveillance-proof. In the hall, she should have been able to raise the house computer. Even so close, she could not. She took a silent turn, and another, and pushed on a graffiti'd wall that proclaimed: *Ban Infrared Slavery!*

The door slid back, revealing her bare gray room with its single cot and over-full closet and chipped metal desk. Overhead, an ancient lighting tube flickered senescently. "All things are one," she muttered, as he followed her within and the door slid shut and he leaned on it with crossed arms, a sardonic, inward smile on him that was very different from his obligatory Kerrion grin. "Do you hear?" She came close to him, fists balled impotently at her sides, glaring up in fury.

"You are wrong, Shebat. You are a casualty of your own delusion." His hands flashed out and grasped her by the shoulders, squeezing painfully. Holding her at arm's length, he hissed, "This is here, now! Feel it? Feel the difference?" Beryl eyes, luminous like the flicker that came to sheath her fingers as she traced the air between them, demanded a response.

"*You* are wrong, stepbrother," she retorted, spelling, with her fingers so close to his chest that a ghost glow was reflected there in the shimmer of his uniform. "*This* is here, now!" she whispered, while between her fingers the spell grew bright and bold.

He let go of her shoulders, giving them a little push backward, and grabbed for her hands so quickly that it was done before she realized what he had in mind.

"Do not do that," he grated, his fingers closing around hers. Then he gave a spasmodic shiver. There was a snapping sound, the smell of ozone. A spark flew from their joined hands. He slumped back against the door, looking at her through half-closed eyes.

Her palm flew to cover her mouth. What had she done? The spell, conceived for no reason but to impress him, he had aborted. She watched the blue nimbus flashing up his arms. Through the phosphenes she struggled to make him out. She saw his flaring, white cheekbones slowly regaining color, saw his eyes focus, saw his mouth close, then open: "You will not mind if I do not leave while you change, I trust. After all, I have seen you quite completely." It was a hoarse whisper, unsteady.

She hurried to her closet, rooted in the pile of clothing on its floor. Her back to him, she stripped off the spangled net, crouching down, then sitting to slip her feet into a plain, gray apprentice's coverall.

"You blush to your butt," he observed, and let out a long, slow breath. "Now all I have to do is get you out of here."

Shebat dragged boots from the bottom of the pile, slipped them on before she turned. "You sound frightened."

"A harsh assessment, but true enough. Would I have come down here in this ridiculous uniform, otherwise?"

Then she did turn, on her knees, saying, "I think you look rather distinguished," while running the zipper up between her breasts with icy fingers that demanded more attention than she would have liked. Leaving off the zipping at mid-breast, she held her palms out before her: they were frosted with pale dust like snow. She wiped them together, and the dead mil wafted off in a shower that eddied to the floor.

"Not to mention fearsome? Let us hope it is enough."
He pushed away from the door. "You *lived* here?" He
shook his head in mock disbelief at the squalor. "I have
ordered a lorry. We are going out the front door. Show
the same prudent good taste that caused you to refrain
from having your ship's name appliquéd on your
coveralls. All you can do is hurt those who have helped
you, by trying to aid them."

He crossed to her, took her by the elbow, maneuvered
her out the door. They walked through the dream
dancers' hall toward the cloakroom, enclosed on every
side by artful, peeling palimpsests layered in smudgy
tones.

The tattered doorkeeper spied them, waved, went
running for Chaeron's cloak. On their left and right were
the doors to the dancers' sleeping quarters. The last one,
to their left, opened as they came abreast of it. Harmony
waddled forth, piebald and lugubrious in a plunging gown
of gray chiffon. Her gaze snapped back to them like a
slingshot once the stone is cast, cheeks shivering. Behind
her, the tattered doorkeeper awaited, the consul's cloak
draped carefully over one arm.

"Good evening, Aba," grated Harmony, positioning
herself so that she blocked their way. "Surprising to see
you so early in the evening. Or is this your marathon
client? Well, speak up, girl. You know dancers aren't
supposed to fraternize with the customers. No answers,
Aba? Then go back to your room and wait there."
Harmony's broad hands rode expansive hips; a round
blotch marked her ample, quivering breasts: black cen-
tered in a field of dead white encircled with a corona of
red, as if someone had painted a bull's-eye over her heart.

"Madam, you exceed your authority. Stand aside," said
Chaeron, whose arm went about Shebat protectively.

"Just who are you, sonny? That Kerrion fright-suit
doesn't intimidate me one bit."

"That is ill-considered, but still your option. As for who
I am, you do not want to know even as much as you
already suspect. Now get out of my way, while you still
have a choice. I am taking my betrothed out of here. You
need not wait up for her: she will not be back. Boy!"

The youth with the cloak inched forward, hovered
uncertainly behind Harmony's bulk.

"I'll take that," Harmony spat and, with such speed that her flab swung flapping, grabbed the cloak from the doorkeeper, who backed away with alacrity.

Harmony made a show of examining the scarlet eagle bating above seven appliquéd stars. "My, my, my . . . I suppose I should be honored, Consul." Abruptly, she cast the cloak at Chaeron's head. He deflected it; with a practiced motion, he let it wrap around his forearm.

"Madam, you try my patience." Without loosing his hold on Shebat, he bore down on Harmony, who retreated until her back was against the half-open door out of which she had come. "Tell Lauren that she, too, is invited to my party. Here are her passes." Without taking his eyes from Harmony, he searched with his cloak-wrapped arm under his jacket. The envelope he found there he stuffed between Harmony's variegated breasts. She turned her eyes away. They slid over Shebat, unseeing. Her mouth worked, her gelatinous breasts rose and fell: nothing more.

"That is better," said Chaeron in a stiletto whisper, that made the woman shrink back from him. "Now, disappear!"

Then Harmony's eyes closed altogether. She fumbled behind her with the door, even as Chaeron's hand gripped a cruel hold on Shebat's flank and he propelled her toward the steps leading upward to the street.

At the top of them, he halted long enough to unwind his cloak from his arm, throw it about Shebat's flight satins, and toss a coin which bounced down the stairs toward the ragged youth, who scrabbled to catch it. Harmony, Shebat saw, had been obedient to her consul's demand: even the door to her room was closed.

He hustled her up the stairs and through the door and up again to the street blinking citrine and cinnabar. The sounds of level seven surrounded her: a half-perceptible trembling snore that went on forever, punctuated with garbled shrieks and shouts, lorry mutter, sirens singing distantly, the pounding of racing feet on pavement.

"Left," he said. Then: "Right." His grip relaxed, rode up to her waist. The cloak slipped off her shoulder and he paused to fasten it for her on the intersection's corner. From the parallel alley whines and a gagging sound emanated. When next the citrine flashed, she made out a crawling figure dragging itself toward the light.

"Chaeron—"

"There is the lorry," he said softly. Though his eyes had followed hers, seen the mewling thing struggling street-ward, his palm in the small of her back urged her away, toward the drop-shaft suddenly baleful with the glow of the Kerrion lorry's red flasher. The black, hovering insect with its amber eyes had seen them: it turned its bright lights on them and rolled their way, sleekly streamlined like a miniature cruiser. The high-security lorry disdained traffic regulations, rolling down the middle of the street, flasher whirling on its roof. Two drunks caught in its spill sat up blinking, blearily tumbled from its path. It was enclosed, with dark one-way glass making a sinister, ambiguous hump behind its pointed snout. Quiet fell in its path, so that all that could be heard were their slapping feet quickening pace and its motor humming a contented powerful tune.

"Sheba?" someone called from a barroom's doorway. "Sheba?"

But the lorry's door was opening. As they came up on it, Chaeron pushed her roughly within. She tumbled onto a padded seat blinking in sudden light, then darkness as he climbed in beside her and shut the door.

It was as if all life without had ceased: no sound came through the lorry's padded protection. She was alone with her breathing, and his. Through the windows, all the seventh level seemed two-dimensional, its edges preter-naturally sharp, flickering.

A speaker crackled: "Good to see you, sir. Where to?" Only then did she realize that beyond the smoky partition the lorry had a human driver. Not until Chaeron gave the consulate as their destination did she think to look at him. He was slumped down amid the padding, his head back against its slope, eyes staring unseeingly upward. The pulse in his throat thumped visibly, limned by soft courtesy lights set high into either door. He took rapid breaths; his chiseled lips were parted. The lorry swung in a circle and headed for the shaft. He stirred slightly, touched something on his far side.

As the lorry entered the up-side traffic, its vibrations quickened, tickling her stomach. From the partition

before them a mechanized bar slid obediently forward
with its buttons lit and two beaded tumblers filled and
iced. Shebat squirmed away from the service bar, so that
her back was to the corner where the padded bench met
the lorry's door. All was black within, all white without as
the levels sped by.

Without moving his head, he took one glass and turned
it tinkling in his hands.

"What do you want me for, Chaeron? Why could you
not just have left me alone?"

He rolled his head toward her, as if he were too
exhausted to raise it. His beryl eyes caught the soft
courtesy light and glowed like the sky on Earth before a
summer dawn. "Drink your drink," he ordered quietly,
between greedy breaths that flared his delicate nostrils.
Obediently, she put it to her lips, tasted, coughed, made a
face.

"Why, dream dancer? Because it pleases me to have
you. Parma feints in the arena with Labaya. He needs a
second. He is old and not so sharp as once he was. But the
entry fee is very high. You are mine. Now, do you
understand?"

"No."

"Good. I would have it no other way." Sliding down
even further in his seat, he raised the drink and sipped it.
Like worked iron thrust into ice for quenching, a hiss
came out of him. She half-expected steam to issue from
his mouth, but it was the supercilious Kerrion humor that
came to rest on his face. *Antinous as Osiris:* she recalled
the title of the one among Parma's ancient artworks which
Chaeron so much resembled.

"But why me? Why will Parma not let you help him?"

His head turned away from her and back, like a man
tossing in a bad dream on his pillow. He made a growling
sound. Staring up at the button-tucked roof of the lorry,
he said in a voice sad while meant to be cold, husky while
meant to be flippant: "I have never asked him. It seems to
follow that the man best suited to perform a task should
be given it. In my family, that rule does not hold true."

"Parma does not care what happens to me, that much
must be clear to you."

He gave her a scathing look. She shifted under it.

"Why did you say that to Harmony?" she asked, to change his face.

"Harmony? Oh, the spotted woman . . . that was all improvisational, really. . . . I did not expect her to be so bold. That is odd, when I think of it. But which thing do you mean?"

"You said," replied Shebat in measured cadence, "that I was your betrothed."

"Ah, so that is what has you huddled up in the corner. Do not trouble yourself further on that account. After your dream dance, I am sufficiently sated. What could your embrace be but a sorry echo of the woman you wish that you were?"

He saw her chin come up, the challenge glitter back to him from her eyes and push out her lips into a pout. "You must learn not to sulk so obviously, dear. I told you, I was merely improvising with your piebald friend. My taste is not to unwilling women, when it is to women at all. And you are not even a woman yet, but still a child."

"I am seventeen," she blurted. "Almost, anyway."

He shrugged, smothered a chuckle, downed his drink. "Yes, you are *almost* seventeen." He laid the tumbler in its circular repository. "Let us concentrate on keeping you alive long enough to become *absolutely* seventeen."

That quieted her. She sought the levels speeding by beyond the window. He seized the respite gratefully, to reconsider what had occurred. Many things seemed strange to him, vying for his attention while the drink fumed in his belly. He shuffled among them, watching her absently, the curve of her cheek and the froth of her hair, choosing those musings for this moment and those it was needful to save for later. Among the events put by for scrutiny at a later date he saved all things in the line of her questioning: what he wanted, and why he wanted it, were not so clear as they had been before.

Some things were very clear, and troubling: she had not disintegrated into helplessness when her access to the data pool was suspended, as would have most low-livers and consular personnel alike. But then, she was not born to it, as were younger platform dwellers; as was he to some extent. Though he knew the dangers of dependency upon an external source, he maintained a twice-hourly check-in with the powerful Kerrion data pool, plus a standing packet-sending procedure which allowed the data pool to interrupt him with its chiming B-flat whenever any of a number of his standing information orders had been filled or updated. Was he dependent, then? he wondered as he had many times before. Could he have been so calm if suddenly the voice whispering in the back of his head was arbitrarily silenced?

He plucked at the neck of his uniform collar, loosened the closure there, watching her and letting his thoughts roam where they would. The dream dancers themselves, many proclaimed, presented a similar danger: men became dependent upon them to the exclusion of all else. He had been exceedingly careful— He stopped himself, shifting abruptly in his seat so that he drew Shebat's gaze momentarily from the level numbers, now into three digits, flashing in the shaft.

Dream dancers themselves were said to suffer if denied their art. But then he thought of her empty dream dancers' box; of the song she had made him hear before she had even fitted the circlet to his temples; and of the "spell" she had conjured up between her fingers, the spell that had made him weak and dizzy and clumsy when he most needed to be strong, level-minded, and capable. Could she really think herself a sorceress, as she had intimated? In this day and age, *could she?* Again he shifted, looking down a treacherous path, turning away and retracing mental steps to find one safer. This time, she did not face away again immediately to the window, but regarded him expectantly.

"You have not asked me about my party," he reproved softly, and when she did, he detailed the exigencies to which he had been put to camouflage all this night's suspect goings and comings behind a cloud of revel and debauch. A believable cloud, coming from him. He had held similar gatherings of the young elite, trendsetters and enfamers, rich consular scions who could run with so fast a pack, every second Friday since he had come fresh and curious to Draconis and caught a whiff of the true scent of Parma's trail. All for this moment, he had spent endless nights with fawning flamers flaunting their bitch-pilot boyfriends. "Some of these flamers can talk your clothes off before you realize what is happening."

"Bitches? Flamers?"

"You kept remarkably pure, for a girl living alone on level seven." Valiantly, he managed not to laugh at her. "Slang terms: Spry is 'first bitch' in Kerrion space, so I assumed that his apprentice would know what warriors in the pilotry-rating wars call each other. Flamers, you must have seen: flamboyantly attired young gentlemen who court each other, and the bitches most ardently since they have become high fashion. If you get into anything you cannot handle, do not panic. I will be right there. Or, if you prefer, you can sit the affair out in my quarters. It is not necessary for you to do any more than walk through and meet them. I am afraid it is well within the character I have built, for me to parade you through and disappear with you and not be seen until time comes to clear the exhausted bodies strewn around the hall."

She was supposed to laugh; she did not, but said to him: "What are you going to do to me?"

"You are reputedly intelligent. You tell me."

"You are going to force me to marry you—"

"Tsk. I would never force you."

"—to marry you. Your power then would be almost imperial in scope. You are going to dispense with me if I prove difficult to maneuver, but only after our holdings are joined . . . even my deportation would not matter then. It would be kept quiet. I well know how little of Kerrion affairs is heard among the fractional citizens. How long were you going to wait before telling me? Or is the whole affair predicated on my suggesting it to you?"

"You are reasonably bright, after all. I would have hinted once more. Then if you did not respond, I would have suggested it to you as the evening progressed, in what I confess I had hoped would be a more congenial circumstance. You would have swooned in my arms, for public display only, of course. I would have your proxy; and you would have your body and your privacy sacrosanct. You could even start a discreet affair with Marada, should he be willing. You may do as you choose, as long as appearances are kept up. I could not care less. But you mistake me if you think I would force the issue. In fact, you continually insist on casting me as a villain, a ruffian and a rogue. Though I may be a little of the last, I eschew those other two modes. It is not fitting in the son of a consular house. If you cannot trust in me, you can trust in the axiom that decorum must be preserved. I do not wash my dirty linen in public. Nor are you so irresistible to me that I would give up all that I am and follow you to space-end for your favor. However, since we are on the subject, I must add that of all the logical developments possible from these circumstances, the one of our union is the least disruptive, not to say the pleasantest. What say you?"

"I hate you."

"Enough to wed me?"

"You will not touch me?"

"Never, if you do not wish it."

"I do not wish it." Her voice trembled with some emotion he could not name. Behind her head, the number *one ninety-seven* flashed by. "But neither do I wish to 'pay' for my 'crimes.' You have not said that you can protect me from your holy Kerrion justice."

"You are a hard woman, Shebat Kerrion. I have not promised what I cannot deliver. If when Parma returns in three days I can present you as my wife, I might be able to control matters by that. I might not. My father is his own authority in all things."

"Then, I will take my chances with him."

"As you will. But accept this token of my friendship. If you run out of funds, you can always sell it." He reached in his cloak and got out the slim presentation box and tossed it where he guessed her lap might be. "I cannot foresee another circumstance in which to use it." Did that sound too naked? He was afraid that it had, but words, like deeds, cannot be called back.

They were coming out onto level two hundred. Under its illusion of vast evening sky they toured its wide thoroughfares, past spired edifices of artful largess.

She turned the slim bracelet with its inset stones in her fingers, holding it to the window to catch the streetlight. "Chaeron," she said huskily, "I do not know what to say."

"Say you will wear it always, or some such."

"I will wear it always." She thrust suddenly against him from her corner. Her lips pecked his cheek. Then she was gone again, as far away as the lorry's confines allowed. From that shadowed nook, her voice came very softly. "People will say, 'They are so much in love that she yet wears the first gift he gave her.' That is, if you are not a widower immediately after becoming a husband."

"By the Jesters," he excoriated in disbelief at his good fortune come panting in masked as defeat. "You may yet make a Kerrion."

"I hope not," came her wistful, disparaging sigh out of the shadows between them, growing deeper as the lorry turned into the consulate's gates and up the day-bright drive at the end of which lay the consummation of four months' extensive preparations. Then, as the lorry halted and a man ran down the staircase to open its door, she cried: "My clothes! I cannot meet your friends looking like this!" Her hands flew to rake back her hair. The lorry's door was opened, spilling light on a face which showed more trepidation than anytime previously in the entire escapade just coming to a close.

"Ha, I have finally got you rattled. I will ask no better wedding gift. As for clothes, I took the liberty of ordering some, though I fear I somewhat underestimated your breast and butt." He motioned with his hand for her to precede him out of the lorry. "But no matter: strain on a piece of cloth has a certain virtue."

When he had ducked out of the lorry, she still seemed uncertain. Her shoulders were drawn up around her ears, her arms crossed, hands holding his cloak about her waist.

"Ready?" he said softly, as the lorry door slammed and motor started.

"No. Yes. *Yes!*" The platinum bracelet gleamed smugly at him from her wrist.

Chapter Nine

The footman who had come running down three-tiered, carnelian flights to open their lorry's door still bowed, frozen in mid-flourish. He was short, porcine, curly-haired, impeccably attired in black and red, and badly winded.

She did not know him, Shebat realized as he straightened at Chaeron's greeting, as she did not know the grounds or the thrice-tiered, floodlit staircase leading up into the consul's turret. The consulate was five-sided, for some reason lost in antiquity. Where each side met its neighbor, squat obsidian towers fit the joints. It was greater in area than the entire Kerrion slipbay: twenty stories tall and labyrinthine with corridors. There was a standing joke about the "lost pilot of Draconis" who went in there, unauthorized, to lodge a complaint against his employer a hundred years ago and wandered them yet; every so often some hysterical clerk would claim to have seen him slipping in ghostly, antiquated uniform from door to door. Shebat had never seen the ghost pilot, or the consul's lair: her business had been with family matters. She had never been out of the consul general's turret, which rose between the northeast and west sides, away from the curve of the "skywall" in whose very shadow the consul's turret nestled, so close it seemed that she could touch it, if she walked just awhile.

Shebat shook her head, reminding herself that what seemed close was really far, all else illusion. If she walked toward the horizon, it would recede, almost like a planetary horizon if one sought it up the curve of a hill. . . . "What?"

Chaeron reintroduced the footman to her, calling her

"Shebat Kerrion, my betrothed," his sidelong glance inviting her to share his pleasure in the quiet dropping of the bomb. The footman, calloused from years of Kerrion service, hardly staggered, refrained from clapping hands to ears to block out the roar her name made no matter how soft its speaking in that quiet place. He offered felicitations and welcomes and disappeared back to his post, leaving her scraping her feet on the impervious Kerrion-grown crystal that formed the carnelian walkway.

"That is that," confided Chaeron, watching the little footman scurry up the tiers. "Everyone who knows anything will know who you are and why you are here, before we have climbed up to our own threshold. Painless, you see. I—"

A mighty roar cut him off, a shudder under his feet following the clap like close-struck thunder made him reach out and take hold of her. She hardly felt him. Above her head, red and green grids flashed alive in the sky: flaring twisting sheets. A wind sucked at her. Her mil began to swell. Her lungs began to empty. . . . Sirens howled.

He pulled her against him. "It is nothing." He used his precious breath, shouting in her ear, shaking her until her scream stopped, and she realized that she had to breathe to scream. His hands brushed her hair from her face, cradled it in his palms, forced her to look up at him. "Just a meteorite. Catastrophe theory . . . the molecular sieves will keep the air from escaping. Happens once in awhile. Better a few little holes now and then than one big bang. . . . Now, come dear. Are you an apprentice pilot, or not? Shhh. . . . Better?"

"Better," she mumbled, feeling stupid and girlish and far too young. There was no taunt in his demeanor, but concern. She tried to pull away, thinking she would have preferred derision to bitter compassion's sickly smell, craning her neck to see the grid-forms sucked toward an otherwise invisible puncture, like a computer simulation of magnetic fields about a black hole. . . . As she watched, the grids seemed to flicker. Suddenly released from the suction, they floated uncrimped, flaring geometric sheets of light, fading slowly now that emergency that had made them visible was past.

Chaeron had her by the wrists and was examining the palms of her hands. How long he had been speaking, she could not have said. Her inner ears ached and the mil inside her was calming but not quiescent, so that every internal cavity it wrapped seemed to slither and slide. She ran her tongue around the roof of her mouth, trying to hurry the puffiness away. "If that had been a serious emergency," he was scowling, "your mil would have been barely up to it." One of his nails traced in her palm, then tapped twice decisively. "Tomorrow, you must have a session with the mil-fitter."

"No," she wailed.

"Barbarian," he accused. "Uncivilized tot. Yes, you will, if I have to oversee it myself. Or stay in some hermetically sealed turret for the rest of your life. You certainly cannot take your pilot's license like this." He forced her hands up where she must inspect them. She saw the thin white-laced cracks flaking on her palms.

"If you insist, prince of dalliance, pompous pederast," she snarled, giving back insult for insult, trying to jerk her wrists from his grasp.

He let her go, his countenance full-armored. "I will not trade epithets with you. It is no way to start a marriage, an impossibility in any continuing one. You will do what I advise you to do; or not, and suffer the consequences. You should also see a physician: seventh level's gravitation is sporadic, a function of its age more than any flaw in supergravity. However, even .7 to .9 normal can adversely affect red and white cell balance when endured for four months. If you do not wish to take care of yourself, it will become my duty. Save us both the trouble and cultivate some responsibility as regards your own person."

"Chaeron, I will . . . take your advice."

"So you say. We shall see, I suppose." He held out his arm to her. After a moment of wondering what she was expected to do about the crooked elbow put out to her like a bird's broken wing, she took hold of his forearm, and let him lead her up the ruddy walk fringed with real grass, up the three wide-stepped staircases, and into the consul's turret.

The little footman was nowhere in sight, but two bodyservants on the threshold bowed, took her cloak, murmuring greetings to them both as if Shebat had always been a fixture of their existence as worthy of deference as the consul himself.

Inside the foyer, things were very different from what she had become accustomed to on level seven, or even in the consul general's turret.

A cousin had held the office prior to Chaeron, and he pointed the man out to her among the hologram portraits staring brooding down upon those who brought their business here. Like all Kerrions, save Parma, the faces were small-jawed, moderate in feature, as if some criterion of suitable urbanity had been predetermined and decreed de rigueur for all scions of Kerrion blood. They peered doorward, twenty portraits sharing a certain resplendently mannered mien. Red-haired, blond, raven-browed, each had the delicacy, the understatement of feature and form, that set Kerrions almost recognizably aside from their less-pedigreed servants. On the lower levels, she had seen snaggle-teeth crowded into prognathic jaws, low, bulging foreheads and platyencephalic skulls, not to mention melanin disorders, twisted frames, warts and suppurating acne. Never here. In Lorelie she had noted it, but just thought all Kerrions were blessed with beauty. In Draconis, from the first, she had seen that such was not the case: Jebediah had taken pains to acquaint her with genotypes and their relative proliferation; with prejudice as it was practiced on Draconis—by eye.

Across her inner eye's lid paraded the graffiti'd hallway she had become accustomed to haunting while among Harmony's dream dancers: she saw the peeled paint, crumbling bits wriggling in the draft from a passer-by. *Quark lib!* had been scrawled across Harmony's door. *Down with the Ultraviolet Apartheid!* had marked the room of Rajah, the senior dancer who had been so troubled over the insinuating presence that had joined them both while they worked on an improvisational segment. *I'll trade you two blind crabs for one with no teeth,* had been the legend Lauren had scribbled on hers. . . . She came to her own doorway, saw that she had chosen to mark her domicile: *Armageddon Now!* Her heart gave a little skip that made her clutch at her throat. She had consigned her dream dancer friends to Chaeron's mercy, such as it was. She recollected the senior dancer's kindly, smile-wrinkled face, on the day he had explained to her that the legends on Harmony's door and his own referred to the quark-slings used to launch neutrinos bearing messages on their journey through sponge. Quarks were volitional, sensient pairs; it was cruel beyond tolerance to abuse them so offhandedly, had said the senior dancer to her, and then more softly: what can you expect from Kerrions?

Shebat had had no answer. Now she had one: it was the tableau unfolding before her inner sight, screams and flight and burnt limbs . . . and boots! The sound of thumping boots, the sight of them shining and black as doom, which she had feared from childhood on. . . .

"Shebat! *Shebat!*" Chaeron was shaking her like a rag doll. "What is the matter with you?"

She pulled free, struggling to raise up her eyes from the high, polished ebony boots on her own feet. . . . Had she become part of what she had feared above all things, one of those she had hated? She would certainly be called so by the dream dancers, and despised. Her name would become the epithet she had tried to shrug off by taking new ones. Shebat of Bolen's town was now Shebat Kerrion in deed, as well as in name. "What is the matter with me? Ask better, What right have I to be here with you when my fellows are being rounded up like wild cattle to be slaughtered?"

"What right? The right of my favor, of my pleasure. Surely you cannot be grieving that your freedom is assured . . . but if you are, you are welcome to join them in their detention cells, awaiting deportation . . . that is, as soon as we are legally wed. Now, lest we be more tardy than is fashionable, will you please come with me? I am truly trying to be patient—" And that was true, she saw: his difficulty was mirrored in his paled cheeks, in the muscles twitching in and out of shadow beneath their arch, in the tautness about his mouth that ironed the curl from it. "—but this is no place for second thoughts."

"Have you a better one?"

He thrust a spread hand up across his forehead. When the hand came away, all exasperation had been erased, as if he had plowed it back to hide among his auburn curls. "Yes, Shebat, I have a better one. If you will accompany me . . . ?"

So she went with him, through the anteroom with its portraiture, down the rightmost corridor of three, out of the ken of the former consuls staring down from their ornate frames and the two bodyservants staring with their ears while making themselves small in the corners from which they attended the closing of the consulate's doors.

The hall, softly lit and warmly hung, gave way to another, which was strewn with plinths and pedestals bearing sculptures from the Golden Age. Between two bronze busts was a door of real ebony, carved with beasts, which despite its antiquity drew back as obediently as might have any of the prismatic crystal portals flanking it.

Within, Chaeron sighed, "The consul's inner sanctum. Here, you can say what you will." And the face that topped a body suddenly drained of tension was also washed with relief, made young with it, so that she saw the fairness so lyric that a song might have been sung for him, had songs been still made by men. And that recalled to her how she had first felt when he had come and comforted her during the funeral on Lorelie, how she had been afraid even to breathe. For breath might have rippled the waters of dream and then the man with eyes like midsummer dusk and hair like the sun settling low and a mouth both willful and heroic would disappear. Once again, she felt clumsy, emptied of words and wit like a spilt wine jar. She shuddered: "I cannot talk to you. Say what I will? I would not dare. You make the rules; I can hardly grasp the point of the game."

He wiped a chuckle from his mouth by an inclination of his head. "Say if you approve of my quarters; they will be yours also, henceforth."

She grasped the rope he threw her, turning on her heel, taking in the teal and chocolate walls with their muted paintings each lit from a hidden source; the deep, sculptured carpet where eagles soared among the stars. There were three couches; and six of the high wing chairs Parma favored grouped around a low table with feet like claws grasping crystal balls. There was a carved desk like the door through which they had come, with real books upon it, pressed together by silver stallions. On either side and behind the desk, portals lay open, one revealing a bedroom in Kerrion blues, the other a service kitchen. There were no windows; there was no sign of console or terminal or communicator.

"Go on, look around. In the bedroom, in the closet, you will find some suitable gowns. Pick one." He touched her, fleetingly, a caress that silked along her back as he passed. She watched him sprawl on the closest of three deep-pillowed settees, watched until he had loosed his uniform jacket and rubbed his eyes and thrown back his head with a sibilant aspiration.

Then she edged by him, past the wing chairs, her boots silent on the thick pile; past the desk, where the silver stallions held leatherbound books she could not resist touching as she passed. She stole into the bedroom, a thief in a prince's lair, and sat on the opulent bed, facing a mirrored wall. She stared at her boots, rather than the flush-cheeked creature in pilot's coveralls who betrayed all her covert desire with flaring nostrils and thumping pulse and clasped hands pressed tightly in her lap. She would not fall in love with Chaeron Ptolemy Kerrion. *She would not.* She hated him—well, almost. He was unprincipled, dissolute; worse: he was Marada's brother. She must not let him charm her; yet her hostility to him was born of the predilection of her body to succumb to him. From the first, she had marked him: danger. At the last, she had fallen under his sway. Her integrity had been the final sacrifice, but it was gone, too, left behind in a seventh-level compromise. And he had told her: he had no interest in her. Not really. She sighed, and bent to pull off her boots, first striking the tears away with an angry hand. She did not care. She dared not. She could play the Kerrion game. Barefoot, yet fully clothed, she got up abruptly and went to see what the closet held.

It held scandalously seductive sheers that might have taken aback a born Kerrion. She chose one that was a teal eagle spreadwinged about her breasts, above the circle of seven stars which blazoned her crotch, open at the back but for a string coming round the eagle's wings, and so low over her hips that she twisted before the mirrored wall to determine if the separation between her buttocks actually showed, or only felt that way. . . . It showed, but just barely. There were no shoes: barefoot, she went in to get his opinion, feeling the long skirt catch her toes as she walked, thinking that she should better have chosen differently, if there had been a better choice. She turned the bracelet he had given her, fingering the emeralds' smooth coldness.

He had taken off his black jacket, lay sprawled out in a form-fitting, cream shirt, and his consul's trousers, striped red up the leg. The shirt was loosed at his throat; perspiration glittered there. She came so close that she could see the chain of the gold medallion he wore before he opened his eyes, rubbed them and sat up: "I had rather hoped it would be that one." He made room for her beside him: "Sit here. You look lovely."

Shebat stretched out one leg and wriggled a bare toe: "You forgot shoes."

"Shoes. By the Jesters, you are right. I did. Well, no matter. Let us get the formalities over with, and we will go to our party."

"Whatever you say," she aspirated, tense with his hip burning into hers.

He spoke casually into thin air: "*Slate:* permanent recording. Date and time. I hereby take Shebat of Bolen's town, nee Kerrion, to be my wife, waiving a betrothal interval as is my right by consular decree. Shebat Kerrion agrees. Say you do," he instructed her.

"I do," she obeyed.

"Shebat Kerrion also appoints Chaeron Kerrion her Voting Trustee, irrevocably and for as long as we both shall live. Say you do."

"I do."

"End: *slate*," he ordered the computer's hidden ear. "May I kiss the bride?"

"I— No . . . yes . . . if you want to?" It was meant as a statement, it came out a pathetic plea. She started up from her seat, but he took hold of her.

"I do want to," he assured her, and proved it with a kiss obtrusive and full of tongue, that caused her breathing to come harsh and her thoughts to slow to a standstill. When she was free once again, she sidled the couch's length away from him, her eyes glazed and full of struggle, her fingers to her lips.

"Shall we go and join in the celebration?"

"That is all?"

"Unless you want more. I am not so insensate as to deny a woman's passion."

Shebat was on her feet and behind the wooden desk before she was aware of the urge to move. From that safety, she said: "I meant, are we married? *That* is all. Do me no favors, Chaeron. I would sooner lie with a stone."

"Suit yourself. Can we go? You really do look elegant; it would be a shame to waste all that on an empty room." He rose up, and came toward her at measured pace, his humor a taunt that crinkled his eyes, his coaxing mien the worst of it.

She spat: "I am not some animal, to be gentled!"

"Most assuredly not. You are my wife, second Lady of Kerrion space. Remember that, tonight: take what you will and cast aside what does not please you. Your word is a power on its own. . . ."

But her fingers were busy, spelling quickly. A blue light, spurted, searching.

Chaeron Kerrion stopped quite still. He put his hands on his hips and grated: "If you do not stop doing that, you will find yourself married and divorced on the same night, a feat which even I myself would rather not lay claim to. *Shebat.* I am warning you—"

The lightning licked out toward him; he could have tried to avoid it; he stood immobile, in the agony of seconds drawn out neverendingly, while the licking tongues approached. He was touched with cold; with ice; with knowingness that made him one with the waveform of universal process. He heard her, from a distance, her murmur crackling through the blue fog wrapping his limbs like some ectoplasmic boa constrictor.

"My wedding gift to you, husband." She drew her hands apart, and the air cleared so that he could see something besides the maelstrom of ultramarine. "Twelve coils binding may protect us from each other. It may not. One thing is sure: you will never willingly hurt me."

"You are living in your dream dance, Shebat. Because you can color ambient air does not mean you can control events. That is impossible. And I feel no differently than I felt before. It has never been my intention to do you harm."

Her chin was held high, her head tilted slightly. The gray eyes laughed at him; the soft mouth was still. Then her ingenuous, husky voice said: "Nor I you. Shall we go?" And she came around the desk to meet him, smiling a Kerrion smile.

The consul's function hall was four corridors from

Chaeron's quarters: they heard the revel long before they
came to the end of the fourth. They saw signs: folk
sprawled on the carpet in the final corridor, mumbling to
one another; drunks snoring in stained finery; lovers
embracing on beds of clothing, naked but for mil smeared
with food and drink. A girl in gold-flecked mil and spire-
heeled shoes whose gilt laces had come loose from her
ankles and dragged perilously along in her wake danced
past them in a series of altered-state arabesques.

"What is that smell? And the smoke? Is something on
fire?" It looked so, and a magical fire it must have been,
for the smoke was blue and glowing. From out of its
depths came the din of raucous laughter, buffoonery, mis-
made song. Hearing the eldritch hymn, "Singin' in the
Rain," Shebat reflected that should the tone-deaf singer
truly know the meaning of "rain," he had already failed at
petitioning it down from the skies. His addled brain had
miscounseled his tongue. To so garbled a spell, the Rain
Spirit would not answer. Which was a pity: rain might
have sent to ground the wreaths of smoke into which
Chaeron was urging her without qualm. But she did not
think the spell would have availed, even if rightly
chanted, in this cave-warren man had built among the
stars.

Chaeron, having maneuvered her down three stairs into
a press of scarved and jeweled manhood over whose
heads she could see nothing, assured her that the smell
and the smoke and the fire were contained and purpose-
ful, while tapping a broad back covered with verdant
iridescence which barred their way. Once; twice; thrice
Chaeron prodded, until the man turned with some difficulty in the crowded press, pipe held protectively to his
chest, a snarl on mobile lips. He was taller by a bit than
Chaeron, with black, lank hair reaching down to his
shoulders from a high, fawn brow. Below it, ophidian
eyes sat deep, protected, on either side of a nose that
speared out from his face, tympanic counterpoint to flared
jaws. Where his chin had its point, a deep, shadowed cleft
reigned. He rubbed it and said: "Bossy son-of-a-bitch.
What's the matter? Want to go for a ride? I'm willing, but
hardly able. . . ." He blinked, grunted, and elbowed back
fiercely without looking into the crowd behind. An
indignant cry came over his shoulder; a scuffle that never

touched him sounded. "My, my, my, who's your friend?" He bent his neck to see Shebat better, so that a glitter in his hair caught her eye.

"Valery, the pipe's gone out. Light it for Shebat. She's never tasted Earth's only worthwhile export."

"Shebat? Never tasted . . . We will surely fix that." He fumbled inside the silky fall of forest green, low on his hips where it bloused. Where he got the little nail whose tip turned red she could not imagine, for his steely leggings clung along his thighs like mil, disappearing into fantastic, multihued knee boots bound round with scarves like the lemon one knotted at his throat. "You look familiar," he mused, plunging the nail deep into the little pipe's bowl, which began to smoke.

Chaeron said: "Valery Stang is our pilot, second bitch in Kerrion space, though some say that was a mistake."

Valery coughed, nodded, handed the pipe to Shebat. "I would have to disagree that this's the *only* export— *Our* pilot? Haven't I seen you someplace before?" The pilot scratched his head, showing his ear's rings. There were three of them; the man was on his third cruiser and inordinately proud of it.

Shebat pulled urgently on Chaeron's tunic, shaking her head to Valery's question. Holding the pipe, she puffed eagerly.

"Valery, Shebat is my wife." Valery's explosive exhalation was lost on her: the opportunity to partake of the sorcerous weed was too long coveted. She held it in, making little strangling noises rather than cough the blue smoke out.

"I know where I have seen you," said the pilot, narrow-eyed, smiling only with his mouth. "In the guildhall. I never forget a pair of tits."

"Shebat was Spry's apprentice," said Chaeron easily as Shebat grabbed his arm with both of hers, laid her cheek against it. Yet it was an order, a silencing, a warning. The pilot nodded, took back the pipe.

A soft voice slightly behind Shebat and to her left obtruded. She heard Chaeron answer:

"When the dream dancer, Lauren, comes, inform me. If she attempts to leave, have her taken into custody and put into detention with her cohorts. Otherwise, the pink room would suit her. Have it prepared. As for Julian, get

him sobered up. I will meet him at the buffet in five
minutes." An elfin houseboy in livery slipped back into
the crowd, nodding.

"Valery, watch over Shebat. She is not so knowledge-
able as she appears. I will be back directly."

"No," she pleaded aloud, though she had not meant to.

"I must calm my little brother, to whom all things are
dire and grave, as happens at sixteen—" She let go of his
arm, with her free hand twisted the bracelet on her wrist.
"You have not met, I would venture. He was here at the
school the whole time you were in Lorelie. I will bring
him over, if he can walk."

"Soon," said the sorcerous weed that had wound itself
around her tongue and taken control of it. And then she
found herself alone with the master pilot, who was
examining her like a flight plan with an elusive glitch.

He tugged on his scarf, offering her more of the
divining drug. Having divined her fate in his eyes, she
refused. He capped the pipe, put it beneath his blouse
where he had dug for the lighter, and she saw the purse
sewn into a belt there.

His arm came around her. His scarf tickled her face.
The trailing hand landed near her collarbone, stroked
comfortingly. "Come with me, and I will give you some
pointers on what Chaeron likes. . . ." His fingers trolled
beneath the eagle's wing, caught her nipple there before
her hand could dart to stop him. When her fingers caught
his, he added into her hair in a languorous bass whisper:

"And what he doesn't like. That," he flicked his eyes
down to her fingers holding his away from her flesh
beneath her gown, "he would not like at all. You are
going to have a difficult time being a true wife to that one,
perhaps more difficult than you had being Spry's
apprentice. Surely Softa could have done better than to
send you unprepared into such a discerning embrace as
Chaeron's?"

The stressing of "apprentice" was a blizzard, burying
all her thoughts beneath its featureless chill. She said to
herself that Chaeron's pilot could be no threat, mean no
ill: she was Kerrion. But her steps were clumsy and her
volition was numb. She let him steer her to a corner, on
the way to which his hand came out from under the
eagle's wing, slipping along her spine. As it dove beneath

the derrière of the gown he said: "This is another thing that Chaeron likes." She gasped in surprise at what resting place his finger sought.

Shebat lunged away from him. The gown hissed, complaining at every seam, even as he took back his hand and let her free. Then she had her back to the walls. He was leaning down and toward her, one outstretched hand supporting him. He murmured: "I am not Softa Spry's best friend. But we are all in this together. If I can help you, I will. As for that little scene, I have an image to preserve, though I admit there was nothing I would rather have done."

"I do not know what you are talking about."

"Then forget I said anything. I must have you confused with some other Earth girl who has three sets of ID and has lost her cruiser." His face did not match his flippancy; it was gray beneath its burnish. "What say we repair to one of the private rooms and you can be apprentice for a night in the navigational complexities of the cruiser 'Chaeron'? You are going to need it."

Shebat Kerrion, despite all resolution to the contrary, began to cry fat, silent tears.

"That is good. When in doubt, weep. He will melt under it."

She ducked under his hand and ran. She ran blindly, bumping into sequined backs, naked backs, plush-cloaked backs and painted backs, until someone grabbed her from behind. She whirled, ready with all the aggression she had learned so well from Lorelie's intelligencers. Her hand half-raised, fingers curled so that the heel of it could hammer home a deathblow, she saw Chaeron's wry headshake almost too late to defeat her own strike, flashing out with lobotomizing force. He caught her wrist easily, inches shy of his aristocratic nose: "We went to the same teacher, remember?" he teased.

"This, dear brother, is your foster sister, your new sister-in-law, my wife, Shebat. Shebat, Julian Antigonus Kerrion."

"Julian," she gasped, trying to slow her heart, catch her breath, clear her head. Julian: half a head shorter than Chaeron, six years his junior, flesh stretched taut over Parma's heavy bones. He bowed to her, flaxen waves of hair swinging about his angular, open face. Wide eyes tinged with red appraised her. His carriage was rod-straight, his neck thick, yet graceful, like a young stallion's. He wore midnight blues flowing softly over long arms and legs, caught at waist and ankle and wrist with gold cuffs and a cinch to match. The collar of his shirt was high and open almost to his navel, exposing the easy, belly-forward posture of one who has no need to fear criticism. But it was his soft, youthful commiseration that made her ever after recall that meeting: "Paranoia, that's what the smoke does to me, too. I cannot seem to get the knack of running on a tenth of my faculties. I eat too much. I end up in odd places in the morning, and I never can really say that I meant to be wherever I happen to wake." He held out a spatulate hand nearly as large as Valery's. "Greetings, sister. I had regretted that I never met you. It seems we are going to have a second chance."

She took the hand, clasped it, drew hers slowly back as if from a magnet. Chaeron was watching, wistfulness peeking out from the corners of his eyes. "If I put you into one another's care, it would free me for other business. And you would probably both be relieved to see me disappear. So I will not ask, but order. Julian, have her in my quarters by 0300. Both of you stay there until I come, no matter what you hear or what you have reason to think you have seen, discovered, or found out between you."

"Chaeron . . ." Shebat began, and trailed off.

One eyebrow raised. A soft look, uncharacteristic, came and went. "Yes?" he said from a place behind all of his defenses, waiting what seemed an eternity while she sorted through things she might say. She settled for: "Could you not come earlier? It is our wedding night."

He did not laugh or make a show of his wonder, but only said, "I will try."

So it was Julian who wined her, plied her with questions about pilotry, proclaimed his envy while extolling her good fortune and the quality of planetary vineyards. It was Julian who called Valery over to where their combined rank had emptied seats for them at a long, automated bar, as it was Julian whose guileless pursuit of the "perfect evening" recruited Valery into their hunting party. Just when it was that she turned from huntress into quarry she could never after determine. In fact, she could not recall the three of them lurching through the halls, arms entwined, oblivious to every fleshly obstruction in their path, though Chaeron later mentioned it to her.

She did recall, though she would rather not have, the moment when all her Bolen's town nightmares rushed back upon her to freeze her limbs stiff and passionless as if the sweat of her heat had become a mil-suit of obdurate ice.

"What is wrong?" breathed Julian down into her face, and kissed her staring eyes until her lids closed and a shudder racked her, and she turned her face into the crook of her arm. "What is wrong with her, Valery? Did I do something? What? What did I do?" He scrambled to his knees on the bed, crouching down by her head, stroking her hair.

She felt Valery's touch, as sure as a master pilot's must be, searching an answer in her nether parts. "Nothing you did, youngster."

Julian sat back on his heels, his wide eyes seeking Valery's. When they met, he rolled them upward, so that only the light blue of the bottom iris peeked out.

Valery shook his head and mouthed kisses. Julian bent over Shebat obediently. Under his kisses assaulting her lips, they capitulated. "There is no harm in this. It is nature's way of seeing that the smart survive. That's it. Let me show you. There. Better?" Her body said it for her; her mouth was full of Julian's ardor.

Thus it was that she did not see Lauren come hesitantly among the celebrants, seeking Chaeron with her dream-box under her arm and her finest dancer's spangles upon her willowly, classic form. She did not see Lauren until she felt a different, softer touch, and heard a silky sigh, and opened her eyes to see what it was that had roused her, hot-skinned and hungry. But when she saw, she screamed unintelligibly and shot up from among them like an ejection pod, hands clapped to the sides of her head, running blindly from room to room.

Chaeron found her huddled in a wing chair, sobbing brokenly in a tongue he had never bothered to learn. She shied from his touch as if burned, her head buried in her arms, knees drawn up, shaking from head to foot.

"Shebat, Shebat. It is nothing. Do not cry. You do not have to do anything you do not want to do." He stood over her, uncertain as to whether to try to raise her up.

"I cannot. Oh, I cannot, and I would for you if I could." She hiccoughed, stuttered brokenly: "Divorce me, if you must. I cannot, cannot—I tried—not her, too!"

Then he knew what to do, and he lifted her bodily in his arms, crooning, comforting, saying that she had misunderstood him if she thought he required any of what had come to pass from her, that he required only that she be happy with him, and content, and fulfilled. On the couch where they had slated their marriage vows into the record he set about proving all that he had said. At length, her shoulders ceased their shaking, and her face came out from under the black mist of her hair. Gray eyes glittered hungrily, so unveiled that he hesitated for a moment before he began to do their bidding.

But when he entered her, she forgot one thing, and lost another thereby. She forgot his name, while his burning pressed into hers. A wheel of men and moments spun before her inner sight. Wanting so desperately to name him, she could only remember who he was not. He was not Marada. Yet he plumbed her. A silent, mind-sent wail issued out of her, through sponge and space and time: Marada, help me. Forgive me. *Marada!*

And she spun the wheel of identity again, for her body leapt under a man too different to be Marada even in fantasy, and she must name him, and claim him. . . .

But it was he that claimed her, driving even fantasy out of her, until there was room inside her for nothing but their conjoined ardor. And her memory.

She knew him then, oh yes. And she knew that she had tried to fit over him the aspect of his brother, and though the knowing made her body flame hotter, its fire was fueled with the last twigs of her innocence, that she had kept from even the hard men of Bolen's town. And since those twigs had been her only hold on the person she had been, without them she was lost, spinning as she fell into an indeterminate future, hearing only the dirge her guilt wailed.

Chapter Ten

Marada Seleucus Kerrion squinted into the vanity mirror, trimming his beard carefully, as if this were any other day of his life, rather than most probably the last. His scissoring was sure, betraying no tremble. Black shearings fell into the white ceramic bowl like cinders. Automatically, before leaving, he cleaned them away.

He went into the plant-filled, white bedroom, knowing that he tracked water on the pristine, ankle-deep carpet, but not caring. He sat naked on the whisper-pink bed, waiting for his mental processes to overcome the shock that had had him running on instinct since he had been waked in the middle of the night by Madel's smothered screams as her time came upon her.

Never before had his wits deserted him so completely in a crisis. Never before had they been gone so long. But were they truly gone? Or was he only unwilling to heed them? Every fiber of his body, every double-time heartbeat, screamed *run!* His thick, sour tongue wanted to scream it: denied that, it refused to speak at all. He put his elbows on his knees and his palms over his ears and stared at the pile carpet between his bare feet, noting every tuft, a crumb, a ball of lint, seeking perspective.

The only one he found was: *"run."*

He tried becoming the crumb, but he kept seeing his first-born, small and red and straight of limb—and as blank and empty as a poem that will not scan.

He had never meant to impregnate Madel by live cover.

He had never meant to touch her at all. But she had meant both, fervidly. And by all the best medical counsel, things were predicted to end well, both with the mother and with the child. As so often happens, the best medical counsel was wrong. . . .

It was most likely due to the fact that his son had been conceived in space, he told himself, not willing to accept the obvious: his sponge-hours had caught up with him; he could never father a normal child.

But when Madel so smugly announced that she was pregnant and that all was purported to be well with the fetus, he had wanted to believe her. He needed to discharge his obligation; his sense of arbitration made him weak before her rightful demand.

After all, Selim Labaya had been a sponge-pilot, and he had sired Iltani, a healthy and preeminently normal child; Iltani's sister, whose wits were dull but adequate—

And Madel, who from all accounts had been hale at her birth.

Could it not have been Madel's contribution, rather than his own, that had caused their child to be unresponsive to the world they had brought him into?

Did it matter?

He was not sure that it did matter. He was more and more sure that the only counsel his mind could muster was the proper counsel, for he had seen Selim Labaya's purpled, contorted visage. And he had seen Madel's heartrending agony, her vain attempts to get the baby to flail, or cry, or even twitch. But it had lain like a doll with no batteries: all potential, no actualization.

He had found it impossible to stay with her once her father had come striding in all silent with murder in his eyes.

He had come back to his connubial suite, taken an ambient-water shower, attended his morning toilet, waiting for the reappearance of logic in his empty mind. But nothing came to attenuate the repeated command echoing within his skull: *run*.

He tried to fit an arbiter's discernment over his situation: *run*.

There were a few hairs growing on the first joint of his right big toe, but not on his left. He sighed, threw himself backward so that he lay stretched out on the bed still musky from his wife.

"Hassid: Systems checks. Departure on my arrival."

"Destination?" came the cruiser's feminine whisper in the back of his head.

"As logged: home."

Had the cruiser sighed? Or was it his own relief? his mind playing tricks on him?

He put the thought aside: it was extraneous. He was embarked upon it now. All that remained was to make it to the slipbay.

He shot up and did not quite run across the bedroom, seeking his clothes. He did not think that he would actually be obstructed by Selim's Shechem Guard, but he planned a circuitous route, calling it a shortcut, as he pulled on his old Kerrion black coveralls and chose an older pair of boots.

He hoped this wasn't the start of a trade war. But if it were, he wanted to be on his own side—if he still had one. He was aware that Parma might think he had worsened the situation by bolting prematurely. But Parma had not seen Selim Labaya's face. As an arbiter, Marada had been trained to know intent by scrutiny. He could tell if a man was lying at a glance. He knew Violence's bitter halitosis, Fear's feral smell. And he knew murder when he saw it.

The fact that Selim Labaya had just been cheated out of all he had expected to gain by wedding his daughter to the probable heir of Kerrion space *by no fault of Marada's that Labaya himself did not share*—this had not mitigated Selim's wrath.

Marada saw a cartoon image of himself trying to remind Labaya of their similarities in good arbitrational fashion while the Labayan sire smilingly decreed the length and breadth of Marada's death.

He sounded a dry chuckle, since there were none to hear him, and pulled on the old boots. . . . He zipped the coveralls up to the base of his throat. He was taking nothing with him but the clothes he had on.

His body and mind were the only weapons he needed; the only ones he wanted.

He was not going to start any trouble.

He was also not going to die in this weed-choked joke of a habitational sphere.

He was aware that Selim Labaya would voice some strong objection to his wishes, should he have the chance.

But the Jesters had not only thrown him into the bottomless pit, they had tossed a weighted rope after him: he could climb back out, if he could just grab it in time.

He already had flight clearance for this morning. Madel was three weeks late. He had been going home for elections. It was whim, and some misplaced sense of responsibility, that had caused him to stop by Shechem on the way. . . .

Run!

Walk, he counseled himself back, *it is safer.*

He vaguely regretted that he did not regret leaving Madel to drown in her misery alone. But if he was right in his assessment of Labaya, he was saving her double agony. However much he had tried to discourage it, the brash, ill-favored girl, who had never loved even herself, loved him. If her father committed mayhem upon his person, under her very nose and because of what had come from her belly, how much worse would it be for her?

He walked out of the softly lit heiress's suite and into a hall paneled in rare woods. He passed two liveried bodyservants, raised his hand to a bodyguard with whom he had shared a few drinks. The man's face was stony, trying not to show that he knew about the abortive birth as the staff always knew everything that occurred in Shechem, instantaneously. . . .

His flesh started to crawl as he came in sight of the great doors leading out into the gardens. At the bottom of those steps would be a lorry he could command. . . .

The two doors drew back, the sensors recognizing him, honoring him as if nothing were amiss. Perhaps nothing was. . . .

Run!

He half-obeyed, lunging forward, then pulled himself up short. It appeared that he had tripped, only slightly, instantly recovering as he came out into the sharp hothouse light of Shechem. The steps were the broad kind that took a stride in between stairs. At their foot, the lorry shone coppery and smug; enclosed; tiny; hovering; ready.

He thanked Chance that it was one of the little bullet-shaped, automated multidrives, rather than a command lorry with wheels and sirens and drivers of the human sort. The perfumed air and the white light and the isolation of his racing metabolism gave all things a two-dimensional clarity. Sound was magnified: his boots cracked loudly on the hydrastone; the sigh of the contented doors reclosing behind his back was like a roused dragon's roar.

The metal of the doorlatch chilled his hand. The lorry's door hummed back. He crawled into black, padded shadow that danced blue and green after Shechem's plant-favoring illumination.

The door sighed shut. The query tone chimed; he spoke his slipbay number, blinking until he could see clearly through the polarized windows. The little lorry glided off over the roadless Shechem terrain toward the drop-shaft under its Doric portico.

Marada's stomach began to give up sporadic jets of scalding water. He concentrated on a bio-control that sent blood into his hands and feet. Gradually, his nerves quieted. The entrance of the lorry into the drop-shaft was a sudden attenuation of exterior light, a dark coolness through which he dived like a half-smothered fish released at the last instant to plunge bottomward. . . .

But he was not the only fish in the sea: lights floated upward toward him in the parallel shaft; lights followed him downward. Two blips on his traffic screen confirmed his visual sighting. He flipped the bilious screen off.

Collisions were avoided by traffic control, not individual vehicles. Collisions could also be decreed, if Labaya wanted him badly enough. If he wanted Marada that badly, Marada was already dead, only had not found out yet.

Which would explain the emptiness he felt. . . . But he had felt it before: when Iltani, his betrothed, had died. He vaguely considered that there must be some hidden thing awry within him, that he could not truly grieve. Maybe that was what was wrong with the baby, only magnified: the father could not grieve; the son could not grieve. . . .

Lords, he was tired. Tired of Labayan intrigues and space-end squalor, and meting out high-handed justice to the cast-off scrubs of society, disowned but illegally managing to survive.

Though he knew his own family to be little better than that one he had so disrupted merely by trying to be kind, so sorely beset, he sought them. An old lie can be a comfort, faced with a new, ravening truth . . . he had never really wanted to find out if he would truly have to pay the pilot's price. He had banked sperm on Lorelie. *Why* had he let Madel dissuade him from fulfilling her desire for children in the only prudent way?

But she had been revolted, unwilling to be "cheated". . . . Now his only chance was to get clear of Shechem before the old man shook off his grief long enough to realize what Marada must do, and move to prevent him.

The red-glowing drop numbers flashed by outside the window with comforting regularity, each a milestone which he used to shore up the battlements of his courage.

He had never had such a bad year.

His luck was bound to change. Nothing lasts forever, except perhaps sponge.

The little lorry's hum heightened. Below the floor, supergravity pads would be glowing, adjusting for a smooth exit onto level one. Like a sailor, he shifted imperceptibly as the lorry took the out-turn and moved laterally instead of vertically.

He flipped the traffic scope on; one blip had taken the exit tunnel. But then, there was no place else for it to go, save back up. Beneath their feet lay the guts of Shechem; ahead, her navel.

Like Draconis, Shechem's slipbay had no rotational gravity, just supergravity to hold body to putative ground. Less than a half-kilometer away, beneath the gray crystal sheets stronger than space-steel, was zero gravity and the maw of night. . . .

The *Hassid* was already positioned at the launch tube that would spiral them down and out of Shechem and Selim Labaya's hands. He could have kissed her smiling face, greeting him as ever from beneath his license numbers stenciled left of the port. As he entered, he patted her painted, upturned breasts, half-visible beneath her mystic's veil.

The port hatch secured, its red light greening. He ran then. He charged the control room door which barely made way for him, so agitated that he spoke out loud to the cruiser: *"Home! Go! Now, Hassid!"*

"I have no final green," the cruiser spoke with her voice, worriedly. *"Screens are still up in the outer bay."*

Marada, slapping the panel before him, exploded: "Move!" He armed her turrets: a flaming tongue of laser-fused destruction could now vaporize the vacuum screens at *Hassid*'s command. "Satisfied?"

A gust of acceleration pushed him back into his couch, even as a thunder and a shudder came forward from the rear of the cruiser. Ahead of them a devil's eye of fire purified the hatch-bay just before *Hassid* lunged through it, all her alarms ringing.

Shechem Authority's channel squawked and stuttered. Marada silenced it. The damage bells rang. Around the waist of the circular control room indicators seared toward red. All else was darkness. He breathed a deep, shaky sigh, assessing the damage.

"Seal the storage bay off. I will go in there and plug things up later."

No answer.

"Hassid?"

"They . . . fired . . . on us," the cruiser said incredulously.

"I know, baby, believe me." He flicked his eyes around ruefully. "Nothing that cannot be fixed. Just get me home and I'll have you gold-plated."

"I slated that," she warned. Then: *"We are receiving a good deal of verbal abuse. I assume you do not want it through the speakers. It is quite foul, the usual outboards' overstatement. . . . By my calculations they cannot catch us—"*

"Why do I ever leave you?"

"I am sure I do not know, Marada. Are you hurt?"

"No, why?" He was feeding a request for recircuiting of his air purification equipment through to her as he talked. The colored lights made his hands ephemeral as they passed over them in the dark.

"Your metabolism is upset. We are speaking aloud: you do not want me close to you."

"Not right now," he admitted. "Outboards' troubles. I am not fit for your company, not yet. Is there any way we can get into sponge a little earlier?"

"As I was saying when you interrupted me: they cannot catch us, but they could be there when we come out into spacetime; our ETA is prelogged. If we went in now, we could shake off any possible pursuit—" A screen flashed, lurid with her impatience that he would not open his mind to her, showing her proposed flight plan.

He had never seen anything quite like it before.

He checked it against his instinct, complemented her, and got ready to step out of his human person and into the great racing fish that cut the waters of space and time. When he was almost fit to navigate, he opened up to her, letting his body slump and his mouth go slack, trusting her sparkling touch to do the rest.

He looked out at spacetime through her "eyes" which knew it as a grid of glowing forces, waves and densities, tides and courses, straits dark and pulsing, narrows cold and sharp like thorns. He shivered and felt the numbness that marked her injured tail. Amputation phantoms whispered where hull used to be. Her sadness was salt, chalybeate, popping like blue sparks in the mouth/skin that was both their outer hull and their inner. Her joy at receiving him nuzzled close, sweet-breathed, warm. Every magnetic caress coursing around her was for him. Her power; the sparkle/thrill/heat/taste of ambient space sizzling in her wake: these were his also. They dove and dipped, wriggling, one creature racing, its own exhilaration spurring it on. The subtle speed/tickle quickened. Burning needles sluffed off their armor; they shot spongeward at nearly light-speed, then jackknifed, spun and leapt.

Green is sponge and cool like nightbreeze, going everywhere and nowhere, the birth of time not even warming it, no chaos warning it, more eternal than our little wriggle of a universe no greater to it than the explosion of a single impulse toward thought in the godhead's brain.

Sponge smiled her cool, marble smile, taking them to her bosom, carrying them with giant soundless strides across the ages. Everywhen rolled like landscape below, some fields plowed and some heights virgin. Marada and *Hassid* cuddled in the embrace of the eternal traveler.

What more could be asked by mind than to meet its mother? Neither looked beyond their comfort, both suckled the penultimate teats. From the same womb, man and machine; from the same mind, life and death. From the same song are sprung the waves that wash the universe up onto eternity's beach, and those that will lave it back again.

What more might man and machine wish?

We wish a place in space and time, far from near, they answered the mother together.

Ah, yes. Here we are . . . the mother sighed, amenable, but regretful that her children wandered so.

There was the hard moment of passing through a place where men were known to begin their lives clawing their way up out of the ground, toothless and wrinkled and blindly groping into the celebration of the event by their relatives. They grew hair progressively colored; real teeth replaced the false ones in their jaws. Their eyes cleared and their skins unwrinkled and their limbs untwisted, and they grew ever younger until that awful, inevitable morning when they must bunt and thrust their tiny way up into some screaming woman's womb, where they became smaller and smaller until their fathers drew them back up into the place all sperm must go.

Then, they were through it. The backward universe behind them, they hovered, one being, behind a little dead asteroid over whose rim Draconis, amid the wheel round her anchor-planet, burned brightly, inviting, a tiny ring glowing steadily among more distant stars.

It was his sadness that separated Marada out from *Hassid*, though it was always *something* that drew the outboards away into the impenetrable illogic of their human thoughts. So it was that *Hassid* spoke with her voice:

"Something followed us."

"Through sponge? Impossible."

"So it would seem. But nonetheless, something followed us through sponge. It is keeping the bulk of the asteroid between us. I can see its shadow-heat bouncing off the rock."

"What do you mean: *something? What* followed us through sponge? A ship?"

"If it is a ship, it is like no ship I have ever met. But it scans as a ship."

"Never met? Scans as a ship? *Hassid,* that torching you took did more than subvert the integrity of your seals."

"Ship," said the *Hassid,* dreamily. *"Cruiser. But like no cruiser I have ever met."*

"*Hassid!* Is it Labayan? Hostile? What do you mean?"

"No, definitely not . . . hostile." She screened her scans for him, in outboard frequencies.

"Why do you keep saying 'met'? What is so different? It seems a regulation cruiser to me."

A sound like static, or a giggle, set his teeth on edge. *"If you will look closely, you will notice that there is no one, no outboard on board."*

No outboard on board: why did these things always happen to him?

Marada Seleucus Kerrion did not admit coincidence into his world view. He had been a pilot too long for that. He was aware that everything he had formerly regarded as urgent—the subcurrents in the pilots' guild; his marriage; his potency; the Kerrion/Labayan Alliance; the elections—all were reduced to microscopic importance by two events: his flight through what he had already named the Hassidic Corridor; and the fact that a cruiser had followed him, unpiloted and on its own initiative, out of sponge.

When he roused himself enough to ask *Hassid* the identity of the cruiser waiting on the far side of the Apollo-type asteroid's jagged bulk, he was forced to add a third consideration: it was Shebat Kerrion's ship, the *Marada,* his namesake, which wanted to speak with him.

Marada, meet *Marada*—he did not laugh, or even smile. Shebat, again: insinuating herself into all things numinous like some ancient enchantment newly waked and gone awry. He remembered her eyes: like leaden sky, filled with compulsion. The little girl who had thought him an enchanter had herself enchanted his family in its entirety, taking their attention from the stuff of life and holding them immured, fantasy's thralls. It was somehow fitting and rhythmic that the cruiser which had done something no cruiser should be able to do would bear her license, her imprint, *his* name that she had given it.

One more impossibility in an impossible situation tithed a short bark of laughter from him that made *Hassid* remind him, nervously, that the *Marada* yet awaited his pleasure.

But it had been his need to release tension that had pushed the harsh chuckle out of him, and no humor. He had been the subject of humor too often to add his own voice to the chortling crowd watching his every move.

Shebat would have made a pilot, Spry had said to him on Shechem, lofty praise from a master's master.

What else was she making? And why was the little ragged Earth girl—whose potential could never be expected to cancel out the handicap of her first fifteen years in Bolen's town—thrust again and again to the forefront of Kerrion concerns?

He lived in seconds an eternal nightmare in which his name was cursed down the ages for having fallen under her sway and delivered her into their midst. He shook it off, as he had often before. Genetics could not portend consequences, only predispositions; the child could not be blamed.

It came to him that a dead pilot would read like no pilot at all. On the heels of that thought followed a surety—such was the true nature of the situation: Shebat Kerrion was dead aboard the cruiser, no matter how unlikely all intelligence prognosticated her presence there to be.

He had to find out. Yet there was something stopping him, something old as the caves of man's misty youth and frightful as a dog in a temple; something about meeting mind-to-mind with the cruiser *Marada*, which had done what no ship could do. . . .

He shifted in his seat, felt the wet fabric beneath him pull away from his buttocks. A moment excerpted from his wedding night flashed before him: Madel's sad mouth smiling sourly, her cripple's crutch put by her, curled on his bed in *Hassid:*

"Come lie with me, husband."

He had stripped down with his face turned away, bereft of words, feeling more naked and less in control than he had ever before felt with a woman, more unsettled even than he had been during his first boyish grope of a bodyservant. Who ascertains that a man cannot be raped

is a fool. Feeling awkward, foolish, fearing mostly that he
would not even be rapable, he had slid onto the bed
where once long ago he had lost his virginity.

Should he be unable to take Madel's, the marriage
would be annulled on the spot.

Only later had Madel admitted to him that she had
been thinking that very thing.

Then, while the bed-satins slid smirking beneath his
thighs, she had reached out an arm feathered with hair.
Her fingers had touched his cheek, run down it while she
smiled:

"My father has never given me a gift so fine as you
before. You will be a welcome weapon against the
loneliness of night."

He snatched her hand, held her wrist so that the leer
was chased from her face by a grimace of pain. "Speak to
me that way once more, and I'll shove that crutch up your
slit so far that you'll walk without a limp."

He should have known better than to treat her so
roughly. But he had been relieved that he was capable of
treating her any way at all. He embraced his wrath,
performed his duty, not noticing until too late that he had
so thoroughly breached her defenses that she had capitulated. Labaya's daughter fell hopelessly in love with her
husband against all reason . . . hence the naturally conceived child; hence him . . . hiding . . . here.

How in all Chance could a cruiser go through sponge
with no pilot?

"Sling a message through to Draconis authority,
Hassid: where we are; how many we are. Tell them we'll
bring the *Marada* in tandem. Use a no-delay priority.
They'll have some questions I don't want to wait to
answer. . . ." And some questions he could not answer. . . . "Be forceful. We have invoked our diplomatic
immunity, left Shechem on our own authority, etcetera.
Show your flight-path, tell them it's called the Hassidic
Corridor—"

"Marada, I am touched," purred Hassid.

"I am trying to make sure you *won't* be touched. . . .
Let's see, give your damage report, but no information as
to how or why it occurred. Make sure they inform
Chaeron, wake him if they have to—"

"You could do this better than I," she reproved.

"I want you on a separate circuit when I link with that empty cruiser. No matter what happens, follow these orders." He punched up a course. "Even if I should later give instructions to the contrary. Handle this like a Class-1 emergency."

Class-1 was invoked in case of pilot incapacitation, madness or death. *Hassid* could make her own course corrections. To the traffic center it would be as if Marada were temporarily unconscious, beyond reach. To the ship, it was distasteful in the extreme.

"But you are not incapacitated!"

"Outboard politics. I am not asking you to lie. This *is* a Class-1. I have no idea what I am walking into over there—"

"You are not leaving my bulkhead!" Seals lit. He would have to defeat her manually.

"A figure of speech." He slid out of his seat, not feeling anywhere near so assured as he wished to seem. "I'll just stroll over there, a short visit. You are not going to make me any additional difficulties. . . ." He crossed to a manual-override panel, stood over it threateningly, knowing that she could see, but could not stop him.

"Hassid, I have to see for myself. Someone might be dead in there—"

"There is no outboard on board that ship. No ex-outboard, either." But despite the vehemence of her tone, the seal-indicators returned to normal, all but the rupture-flasher for *Hassid*'s cargo bay.

"I have to fix your leak, sweetheart. Tell the *Marada* I am on my way."

He heard her objections; her voice followed him through the corridors and her mind scratched at the door to his. But he closed his ears and refused to open his mind, and when he had donned a three-mil suit with an eight-hour air pack in its pressurizer and a monitoring com in its helmet, he was feeling almost normal. He unfolded the gravity-sled stored by the emergency hatch until it was as wide as his chest and half as long as his body, and stepped into the lock while he was still checking its function. In his pocket was a can of liquid solder for *Hassid*'s hold. Around his waist was a coil of glass-line long and strong enough to serve as a tow if he felt he needed it. He latched the helmet, isolating himself from Hassid's pleading. The lock sighed its air out, the space-door opened. . . .

A thrill crawled over him, looking out at the winking pupil of creation. He gave a push with his knees, bellying onto the sled, which sailed out toward the rim of the asteroid. A turn of head gave him visual corroboration of *Hassid*'s damage: she had lost her rear infrared camera, the outer hull was penetrated in three places, scarred and seared and melted into strands crisscrossing a hand's-breadth hole.

His earlier assessment that only the inner hull was reparable confirmed, he turned back to see what rose over the horizon as the sled reached the apex of its arc. Breathing the mil-tangy air, simply waiting, helmet pressed to sled, he felt almost as if he were a child again, racing with his cousins off Lorelie's skywall.

Then the *Marada* came into view, floating in vast Kerrion splendor at a short space-anchor. Damn Parma for a braggart; the *Marada* was as good, if not better, than *Hassid,* and ten years younger, when each season saw refinements undreamable a year before. . . .

He spat three short bursts from his sled's attitude thrusters, came alongside the great silver fish where his name was stenciled by its lock. Only then did he check his com-line. It was silent. *Hassid* had given up trying to dissuade him.

He let the sled bump against the *Marada*'s hull, grabbed a handgrip, pressed for entrance.

To his relief, the port slid back. By his handhold he swung inside, his sled under his arm.

The outer port hissed closed, but the inner did not immediately open. He refolded the sled and hung it from his belt, where it bumped back and forth about his knees. *"Greetings, Namesake,"* came the voice on his open com-channel. *"I have been waiting for you."* The little, dark space in which he was imprisoned began to hiss as air rushed in to fill its vacuum.

He added his own hiss of relief before he answered, as the inner port drew back and he stepped into a semidark of running-lights and flashing indicator lights. "Greetings,

Marada," he responded, not moving to unlatch his helmet, his eyes racing around, searching for anything not standard.

"*Second left, Outboard.*"

"I want the grand tour." He opened the wider-than-usual cargo port. Within was a space-black mantis, poised for flight—a ground-to-space shuttle, two-passenger at best: empty. His satisfaction issued forth: a wry grunt. He retraced his steps, going left and left again until he had come to the control room. He peered into the open cabins as he passed them. There was no sign of a body, or of violence, nor anything to show that someone other than the designated owner had been aboard. Nothing except the little shuttle-craft, painted like a bandit's smirk.

"*Are you, too, in search of Shebat?*"

The tall, suited outboard started, raised a hand to his helmeted head in some characteristic gesture aborted by the clear dome glowing in the semidark, as his entire pressure suit glowed with a soft argent gleam.

In it, the outboard Marada seemed darker and leaner than he was. In it, he was trembling. It was a comfort to him that the suit would mask whatever evidence of his discomfort the cruiser would otherwise have been able to gather. He began a slow, expository circuit of the control room's circular waist, seeking a particular panel set into every cruiser ever built, man's safety-belt in a runaway juggernaut. By the time he had come once fully around and knew where the panel was, the *Marada* had repeated its question and the pilot had thought of an answer:

"Among others."

"*She summoned me; I must respond.*"

The cruiser's voice was like any other cruiser's voice. Why had he expected it to be different?

"Is that why you followed me through sponge?"

"*I followed you* out of *sponge. I was—lost. Sit down . . . 'Marada' . . . Would you refresh yourself? I can provide all the amenities.*"

He hesitated. Not to be lost thereby, he found it necessary to buttress his pretenses. The *Marada*'s ultra-modern helm had a pair of couches before the screen consoles, which were standard; and a third set back from those on an epicentral dais, which was far from standard, with an entire redundant control center micro-miniaturized on its flaring arms. He half-sat on it, letting his eyes roam down its insides, identifying odd tubes flush in their housings as food, water and elimination, emergency air . . . a man could work days at a time in that couch without having to move. . . . A part of him itched to settle in it, rather than lean against it. He resisted.

"I would never hurt you," the cruiser reproved, softly from inside his helmet.

"Voice only. Stay out of my head." *How* had it done that?

"You are like a part of myself," the cruiser continued, somehow sounding lonely.

"You have no right having any self at all. Your concern for Shebat is laudable. Your concern for me is misplaced. You asked for this meeting. I am here."

"I am seeking your aid in finding Shebat, who has summoned me."

"You said that before. I will ship you into Draconis if you will explain to me how you happened to become separated from her in the first place. I would also like to know who refitted your cargo bay, and where, and why."

"I can penetrate Draconis without your aid."

"Not without scratching up your finish, you cannot. Why not share your memories with me?"

"Two obstacles obtrude. You will not open a link to me, will not even take off your helmet, though my air is sweet. My memories of these events are not easily translatable into visual or linguistic mode."

"Try harder, and I am sure you can find a way. But that is only one obstacle. What is the second?"

"I would be betraying confidential data."

"Shebat would want you to help me, for I am helping her. She summoned you with some urgency." He was shooting in the dark, but the cruiser could not know it— he hoped. "I, too, am on an urgent and sensitive mission." A sense of the ridiculous threatened to subvert his necessary solemnity. He called it relief that the cruiser was not dangerously maddened, then cautioned himself that it was too soon to relax his guard. "If you have no problem that needs my assistance, and we cannot come to some agreement, then I will be going—"

He stood up. The ship's indicators scowled their disagreement. The emergency seals flashed. That was more what he had been expecting, but did not overly concern him. "I have to get *Hassid* into Draconis for repairs. She does not deserve ill-treatment from you, when it was she who guided you back into real-time."

"*She is very beautiful,*" said the *Marada*. "*As for time, you cannot but realize that you have a surfeit of it: you are nineteen days, seven hours ahead of schedule.*"

So *Hassid* had given more than a beacon's light to the *Marada*. Feeling slightly less confident, Marada began to get angry: "I am being very polite. I have not slapped you onto manual. I have not disconnected your intelligence. I have not put a tow-line on the helpless hulk you would then become so that I can haul you ignominiously in to be rebuilt from bolt one. Do not press me. Run your cubed improbability of a memory tape, or I am going to get nasty."

"Outboard," the *Marada* accused. But both the visual-spectrum and infrared screens flared into life.

Some time later, Marada conceded defeat: he did not have the time to wait while every moment of the past four and a half months paraded by in intricate display. Just as he was about to call a search-mode, the mind of the cruiser anticipated him. Then, he slid down into the command couch, all caution abandoned. Then, he saw Shebat and David Spry, caught by an exterior camera, arguing at slipside. The voice-over brought him Spry's objections in the matter of the craft's naming; Shebat's immutable response; their joint exit.

The information he most wanted seemed not to be there: there was no further sight of Spry. . . . The cruiser softly suggested that he remove his helmet and take a dip in the cruiser's experiential memory, for the screens would show only an empty hull for a long while. . . .

He demanded to see the next moment that the control room was not empty. He was rewarded with the shivering, flake-faced scramble of a guildsman through the lock, wearing nothing but basic mil that no record be made of his spacewalk back on whatever ship it had been that brought him up beside the *Marada* while it sped spaceward. The bristle-haired junior on the screen prepared the *Marada* for sponge.

"Stop."

The tableau on the screens froze.

"Give me those coordinates," Marada demanded.

The cruiser that bore his name obeyed.

"Space-end," the pilot breathed, half in awe and half in bemusement at his own stupidity. Knowing at last what search would be fruitful, he guided the ship's recollection, through time spent empty and alone, to the days of modification of his cargo bay, and beyond. . . .

The things he most needed to know, he conceded when that was done, were indeed in cruiser-communication referents, a mode he was still hesitant to employ. He sought a way around it:

"Who was it who programmed you for that solo flight? It was obviously not Shebat."

The cruiser sounded static, its equivalent of a man squirming, or dropping his eyes. *"I cannot trust your motives; you refuse communication with me which might reveal them."*

"Who was it, cruiser? For Shebat's sake and your own, obey and answer."

"SSSsssofftaaa . . ."

"Good damnable Lords," he drawled in vehement self-condemnation. He should have seen it . . . but all men are blind in the dark. All the years he had been a pilot, he had remained apart from his guildbrothers as if he were spawned of a different dimension. He had called it his Kerrion heritage, and so it still seemed. But the reasons for his isolation were not those simple ones he had formerly believed to be its cause: not his Kerrion wealth; nor the taint of nepotism in the avoidance of which he had abstained from the rating-wars, though he longed to compete; nor were any of the other obvious prejudices his guildbrothers could have held against him truly at the bottom of his ostracization from the fellowship of his peers.

The unbreachable wall between himself and the other masters was one of protection: it was what the pilots feared from him that kept him out of their confidence. Had he been building a stronghold at space-end with pilfered cruisers, he, too, would have feared a Kerrion coming upon it.

But he had been adjudicating brigands and pirates and interminable space-end disputes for nearly a standard year, and not even whiffed the truth, though it was all around him. He recalled that he had recommended both Spry and Valery Stang into his family's service, and he laughed aloud.

When he had regained his composure, he faced a choice: what he really needed lay in the *Marada*'s idiosyncratic recollection-mode. This time, he could not back away from what was his obvious duty.

He eyed the cabin pressure and unlatched his helmet.

In the single moment left to him of individual cognizance, he knew that he would never again be the same man he had been before. Then the sight/sound/feel/tingle inundated him, stretching his skin until it enclosed all cruiserness, until he could read the haiku of the infrared and translate the hieratic of their common crackle/converse all taking place in another place, so fast and sharing that their minds carved sequentiality out of instantaneousness.

The cruisers were abuzz with his/*Marada*-cruiser's real-time adventure. Piled like a jetty of eyes breaking the coastline of interchange, they created a beach in less time than it takes light to travel one foot. On the beach they nudged Marada/pilot with their wave-arms, that he be safe and not drown in their welcome. Love nipped at his toes awash in the tidal neverwhen, where cruiser-intelligence made its abode and even a place for man to stand if he would.

And he would.

Chapter Eleven

Parma Alexander Kerrion knew that he was going to die.

He knew it intellectually, genetically and experientially: all men die. Very likely, it was the only thing of consequence besides being born which all men shared.

Then why, every time he returned safely from space, was he so relieved? He was not one percentage point less safe in a cruiser than in Draconis, or in Lorelie, or than he would have been had his race decided not to opt for the orbital crap-shoot rather than the planetary.

Yet, on every cruise, on this one most particularly, the old crone with the cold breath and phantom drool cackled subliminally in his ear, as if her fearsome head were laid on his very pillow.

He shook off the maudlin, bony hand ever upon his shoulder of late, and opened his eyes. For a moment, the silence, the cessation of vibration, shiver and blink which indicated that the cruiser was powered down, had overwhelmed him. A paean of joy is quietude, a moment free of fear is worth the world.

"Sir?" spoke Spry tentatively, marshaling all the crow's-feet recently assembled around his eyes so that they stood raised like an honor guard at attention. "You have a welcoming committee."

A screen blinked on, though the pilot had only flicked his brown-tunnel eyes toward it, not lifted so much as a finger. Parma was used to pilots, but there was something unusual about this one that had nothing to do with his qualifications, which were excellent, or his disagreements with Marada, which were inevitable.

When he realized that his meditation was transparent,

that he had been staring into Spry's eyes like a lover some few awkward seconds, he had to say something:

"If I have aged as rapidly as you on this trip, they are not going to recognize me."

"Round ten . . . or is it eleven?" said Spry wearily. "Love me or leave me, Consul General, sir."

"What is that supposed to mean?" Parma mumbled, stretching mightily, glad for any additional unencumbered moments between him and whatever awaited in the persons of those who had come out to meet him.

"It means, sir, that if you have some complaint as to my conduct, you may lodge it with my guildmaster. I have had enough innuendo and inquisition to last me a lifetime."

"Calm down, young man, or you'll make me think you want me to abrogate your service contract. And I would hate to think that, almost as much as you would hate having your rating besmirched, should I be forced to such an uncomplimentary conclusion."

David Spry shrugged, muttering: "Please, Br'er Fox, not the briar patch."

Parma let it pass:

"Double the magnification, David. My eyes are not as good as once they were." The view the screen purveyed seemed to zoom inward. Yes, the silver head was Guildmaster Baldwin's; the ruddy lion's mane showing above and slightly behind was Chaeron's. A twist of black froth wound in pearls, barely visible among the sea of uniformed bodyguards, showed that Chaeron had brought a girl with him. The boy's penchant for entourage would have to be curbed. Between the dozen black-and-reds around the consul's party and the smoke-and-midnight representatives of the pilot's guild, there was hardly enough room at slipside for him and Spry to debark. . . . "Thank you, you may put *Bucephalus* to bed now."

"I thought I would stay awhile. I have some reports to finish, detail work." Spry examined his hands, leaning on the padded edge of the screen console.

"And disappoint all those assembled to meet us? I am afraid I cannot allow it."

Spry raised his head, looking up at Parma from under his buff brows. "They are hardly here for me, sir. *Bucephalus* still is not right—"

"Do not make me command you. Rather, accept my invitation to join in the festivities awaiting. Your devotion to duty is laudable. . . ."

Spry growled under his breath: "My devotion to my ass is laudable."

Parma, continuing, did not hear: ". . . but a surfeit of zeal is worse than none at all. Your guildmaster will think you antisocial, and we cannot risk that, now can we?"

"I must presume not," Spry capitulated, still holding Parma's gaze like a man gone to a sybil who hears his doom from her lips.

Parma licked his own lips anticipatorily. Perhaps now Spry would reveal himself . . . but the moment passed with no more than a heartfelt sigh added to Softa's haunted look, which was so steady it seemed beyond fear. All pilots are mad, Parma reminded himself. "Let us go, then, Master Pilot."

Spry walked out of the control room at Parma's side, and everywhere he passed lights winked out behind him with precognitive finality. That Guildmaster Baldwin was among the pilots gathered at slipside told him something.

It told him there was trouble enough to get the silver-haired guildmaster out from his aerie. Nothing less than war, murder, or a maddened cruiser could pry old Baldy out of his nest before the midday meal. His silver-white head towering over a brace of two-meter Kerrion guards, swiveling this way and that, was the most dolorous of omens.

And that told him a second thing: there was yet hope. Baldwin's presence was no part of their worst-case contingency plan. He was not yet required to martyr himself, mute scapegoat. That was good; he was beginning to doubt his ability to sacrifice all with nary a bleat. If only the Consortium would soften its position and allow the pilotry guild to own cruisers . . .

But they would not, though the guild was rich enough, though some pilots on their own had accrued sufficient funds, though even leases would have satisfied guildmembers, for the nonce. But pilots were mad, said the consensus of Consortium thought, genetically marred and essentially undesirable, and putting such a putatively dangerous power as self-determination in the hands of a potentially rebellious (ninety-nine-to-three-nines probability of severance within twenty years, said Kerrion data pool) aggregation of miscreants and rogues was no part of Consortium policy.

As Spry descended the ramp beside Parma Kerrion an expectant lull fell over the crowd awaiting them, to be broken like fish leaping sunward by four bodyguards dispatched with a nod of Chaeron Kerrion's regal head.

There was a poly-rhythm of boot heels, an addition of four silent flankers to their subgroup of two as they came off the ramp onto slipside. The crowd before them sorted itself out as they approached, splitting into an aisle colored Kerrion on one side and guild on the other. At the end of that aisle awaited Parma's two sons and a smooth-limbed, long-legged girl in teal whose black hair was caught atop her head and whose eyes, huge in a heart-shaped face, never left him.

For the first few instants it was a stranger who fixed Spry with a somber gaze full of regret. Then he realized who she was and why she stared so compassionately, and he halted in mid-stride, stilled by comprehension that quelled all Spry's thoughts but those of peril, which howled even louder when a hand at the small of his back and a sibilant suggestion from his left told him to move along, not to make trouble.

The trouble, it seemed to him, was already made. He was looking at it, was about to smile and shake its hand decorously . . .

Chaeron Kerrion's hand was cool and as dry as his smile, which flickered over Spry in an instant that dehydrated his entire being, only to pass on to his father, who had halted with lips awork and incredulity peeking out from the crags of his face.

Without a word being spoken, six pilots followed almost instantaneously by six intelligencers detached themselves from the entourage and headed purposefully toward the *Bucephalus*.

Parma had seen Chaeron's eyes flicker closed, snap open as he stepped forward offering Parma a formal embrace: the boy was using a computer-link to maintain contact with his guards. The overuse of unnatural applications of intelligence keys would yet be man's undoing. Another time, Parma would have voiced his displeasure. Now, there were other matters taking precedence. As he hugged the youth close he whispered, "Let us hope that your efforts to prove your fitness to administrate have not proved the opposite." He let his son go, turned to Shebat.

"May I assume that your presence here indicates you are returned for long enough to sup with your father?"

"Yes," came the aspiration from her downcast face.

Parma looked back over his shoulder, ostensibly to speak to the bodyguards flanking Spry like an extra pair of arms. Beyond them, two of Chaeron's men and two guildsmen waited on either side of *Bucephalus*'s port. All the others had disappeared within. "Gentlemen," he said to Spry's guards, "back off a bit. My pilot suffers from claustrophobia."

Turning back, he snapped, "Baldy, what in blazing hell is going on here? My son may not have known better, but you certainly do."

Behind the emaciated, silver-haired giant Parma could see the pair of waiting command transports—one black, one silver—looming huge among the parked slip-lorries.

The guildmaster displayed his most wrinkled concern: "The consul and I both found it necessary to reexamine the *Bucephalus* . . ."

"I see. And necessary to watch each other while you're at it, also?"

"Parma, I must speak with you privately."

"So I have surmised. Well, your pet pilot is joining us for dinner, why don't you do the same?" Out of the corner of his eye Parma watched the guildsmen's faces; and Chaeron, who was saying something urgent to Shebat, sotto voce.

"Alone, Parma, at a more propitious time," insisted the guildmaster, havoc in his demeanor. "Right now, I need a moment with my first master, and I will be going."

"And will you take your company with you?" Parma silked, while his glare spoke more harshly. "The *Bucephalus* is, after all, *my* ship. Not yours, not the Draconis consul's." Deeply troubled by the suspicion that whatever it was he was supposed to have gathered from this display of bodies had escaped him, he probed: "What, exactly, are you looking for?"

"I wish we knew," Chaeron interrupted sharply.

Seemingly, Parma ignored him, saying, "I surrender, for the time being. David, attend your guildmaster. But quickly. My irritation will not long bear restraint."

Then, as Parma breached the invisible wall between himself and his son and stepdaughter by tucking one under each arm and strolling companionably toward the waiting command transport, Spry walked nonchalantly out from between the spread-legged bodyguards who at Parma's earlier rebuke had stepped back one full pace each.

Instantly enfolded by the half-dozen pilots, he endured Baldy's austere embrace.

"The *Marada* has disappeared. The *Hassid* reports her pilot is bringing along an unspecified ship in tandem. The Kerrions will know shortly; I have taken a grave risk holding news of it back this long. Are you under arrest?" All this was whispered through unmoving lips centimeters from Spry's ear.

"Not yet, though I expect it promptly. Why is *Bucephalus* being subjected to this second fact-finding expedition?" They unclasped, stood with their heads together, seemingly examining their feet.

"I have no idea. Since Chaeron took control, things have been more and more mysterious. I'm in there to find out why he's in there. It would be nice if there were something wrong with that ship so I could condemn it."

"There is, and you know what it is, and so do I. The question remains whether or not they will be able to detect it. I, for one, do not think they will. Why not accept Parma's invitation? It might be our last meal."

The guildmaster eyed him sidelong. "Softa, I'm sorrier than you will ever know. I wish there was something I could do . . ."

"There is. Keep the *Bucephalus* at ready, and don't count me out quite yet. There's one sure solution I've been saving as a last resort."

"You'll never make it."

"I know. But we won't be around to incriminate anyone—not me, or *Bucephalus.*"

"Lords, I'll never know why I allowed you to talk me into this."

"Come on, Baldy, you'll lose face. You're not supposed to *have* any emotions. And you're making me think about things I'd rather not."

The old man raised his head, looking around at the

grimly conversational, clustered pilots, beyond them to the two Kerrion bodyguards awaiting Spry. "In forty-five years of guild service, I've never had to despise myself before. It takes some getting used to, this being helpless and standing by . . ."

A clangor sounded from the Kerrion ground transport. The bodyguards shouted Spry's name. "Wish us luck, old man. Things might not be so bad as they appear. Now I've got to go before they drag me, or you convince me I'd just as well turn in my rating and breathe vacuum." He turned away, and the guildsmen made way for him.

"See you," the guildmaster's farewell followed him.

"Better hope not," he threw back, not turning, meekly letting the Kerrion minions escort him toward the ground transport.

In it, Parma Kerrion struggled to contain his rage:

"I *invited* Spry to join us because I do not feel it is yet time to arrest him."

"I was not going to arrest him," Chaeron objected mildly.

"Well, your matched set of goons surely thought that you were. So did Guildmaster Baldwin; so did Spry. What do you think you're doing?"

"Making him nervous."

"In that you surely succeeded . . . Chaeron, if you think to toy with me, you have contracted delusions of grandeur from your mother."

"May I say one thing?" Chaeron was leaning against a brace of consoles in the control central of the transport, arms crossed, face uncharacteristically stern.

"You may say one thing."

"Thank you. Shebat and I are married."

"What?" Parma whirled in his chair so sharply that something deep in his neck cracked. The girl had been standing quietly in a corner. "Come here," Parma thundered in the small, cluttered cabin full of variegated lights. She came and stood before his desk, red indicator-spill from the console flushing her pale throat.

"So that is why you have been so subdued. I have not time now to hear of all your adventures, foster daughter turned daughter-in-law. Answer me one question—succinctly, for our guest will be here shortly and then you will both *keep silent*."

Parma snarled down Chaeron's objections that there were things it was imperative that he know immediately, without once looking away from the girl whose long fingers rested on the padded edge of his desk. "Shebat, were you coerced, or is this marriage of your choosing?"

There was a long silence he expected Chaeron to break, but his son remained where he leaned, inscrutable, unmoving.

"Shebat?" Parma prompted.

"It was of my choosing," she answered, in a deep tentative voice as uninformative as her posture (loose and easy), or her face (sober and pale in the indicator spill— now green, telling him that Spry and his guards had boarded). To corroborate that, the transport shivered, accelerated smoothly through its gears.

A priority light purpled on Parma's desk-top display even as a B-flat chimed silently in Chaeron's head. Both men activated their "hold" modes, Parma with a touch and Chaeron with a subvocalized code. Having deferred any further interruption by that means, they promptly forgot what they had done.

Shebat was speaking: "With your permission, father, I will go greet Spry, and hold him in the forward compartment while you two deliberate my fate. I just cannot listen to it . . ." She backed a few steps from his desk as she spoke, and her voice was distorted with some emotion Parma realized he was going to have to name before proceeding further into the drastically altered landscape of their mutual concerns.

"Listen to what?" Parma pressed, gently. He did not like the aspect of her, built of fear and entrapment, of resentment and scorn.

And so cold: "Listen to Chaeron. He will tell you all you want to hear, I am sure. Spare me your astonishment, and what must follow." Still retreating, she reached behind her and touched the doorplate, which obediently hissed open.

Then she was gone through it, into the open body of the command transport. Parma had a transitory glimpse of four black-and-reds sprawled on the parallel couches, of the driver at his station beyond. And of Spry, rising into view, his gaze on Shebat.

Then the door was closed, and Chaeron's sigh echoing in the sparkling sanctum.

"All right, Chaeron, what is all this about?"

The youth took the seat that Shebat had disdained, between his desk and the monitor banks flanking the door. In it, he slouched sideways, one leg hooked over the seat's arm. "Shall I answer in a hundred words or less?"

"Chaeron, you are about to find yourself back in Lorelie so quickly that all this will seem a dream." Parma's fist came down hard on the padded console. "What did you do to that girl?"

"That girl? *That* girl is also known as Aba Cronin, dream dancer, revolutionary, murderess . . . It's all in my slated report, every slimy detail."

"Of that I have no doubt," lowered Parma, but his face was flaccid.

"That girl, under an additional falsified identity, took all her pilot's boards. She awaits only the oath to become a guildmember in good standing. Ask me under what name she accrued her credentials . . . No? As Sheba Spry, fabricated sister of your own pilot." Chaeron slid his eyes toward the door, beyond which were Spry and Shebat.

"I confess to being not one whit mollified by these excuses."

"Excuses? Father, you are in danger of losing my respect."

"And you are in danger of losing everything. Explain yourself! Quickly."

Chaeron let out a long soughing breath. "Sometimes I think I should give up, become the unredeemable dolt you wish me to be. But no matter, I have done what I have done for us all . . ."

"What have you done?"

"I have cleaned the dream dancers out of level seven, every one of them. Some yet await sterilization and deportation, some are already on their way to space-end. I saved out one girl to show you why I so acted, one dancer who can perform Aba Cronin's most foul propaganda, should you wish to see for yourself why unrest among the low-livers has become so pronounced, or whence the whispering campaign that maligns us came. And I went down there alone and got Shebat out of there before the cordon closed. I saved her honor at the risk of my life, and you from bearing the shame of having the worlds and platforms know what now they dare only conjecture: that it was a Kerrion who damned us all so convincingly."

"And you say you have eliminated this threat?"

"Compare the election projections for last week and this."

"No need, I believe you. It is a good thing we only have elections once every twenty years." Parma rubbed his forehead. "I cannot say I am thrilled, but though your methods are not my own, I cannot fault your objectives. I will try to be more patient in the future."

"I'd rather have your trust," Chaeron muttered.

"Expediency can carry its own retribution. If you forced yourself upon her, she will never accept you." He wondered if it was his own repulsion at the thought of Ashera's son bedding Shebat that he had read in her face. And wondering, he strove beyond his feelings for impartiality, but lost his grasp of it at Chaeron's next words.

"It is not me she fears, but you—your reaction, your retribution. She is all but a pawn of the guild. She has broken every law of the Consortium. If she married me under any pressure it was the need to protect herself from your justice."

"*Slate!*" snarled Parma, and took a great shuddering breath, then canceled his order: "End: *slate,*" without having recorded any decree at all.

Chaeron had not moved, would not until he had either broken through his father's habitual hostility or been broken by it. In that moment when Parma had deactivated the recording mode unused, he thought perhaps he had done it.

But then his father put both elbows upon the console and propped his face in his palms, saying: "Chaeron, I may have to ask you to annul your marriage. I will deliberate on it the night long."

Out of his shock, from the bottom of a deep well of shriveled consciousness that counted bone and muscle as the farthest border of his holdings, Chaeron managed to work his tongue: "Surely you are not going to prosecute her? Her crimes are hardly more than errors come from her lack of familiarity with us—less than any of your other children have done . . ."

Parma stared at him unwinkingly. A cold horror grip-

ped him, an understanding that it was in no way possible
for him to sway Parma's decision. To that he said: "No! I
swear to you I will not accept it. Take her status away
from her, her stock, her privilege of first-born. But I will
not give her up."

"I might just do that," said his father conversationally,
and, noticing the purple light still blinking impatiently,
thumbed it onto the audio channel.

So it was that Parma and Chaeron learned together that
Marada was a mere two hundred million miles from
Draconis and closing, bringing two cruisers and the
emergency attendant to such a difficult maneuver. And
bringing some other emergency also—else why would he
be coming *now* at all?

"Sit," Chaeron said, turning one of the wing chairs in
his suite around to face the couches. Shebat sank down
sprawled amid deep cushions. With a shrug, Spry took the
other. She had not been able to speak to him of her
remorse (or anything else) before the bodyguards, nor at
dinner, nor on the way here. She had managed only to
whisper in his ear an apology, to receive a pat on the hand
and the information that Spry, also, felt regret. His
implication was that he did not fault her. But then, he did
not know what was to come. Shebat had a good idea what
Chaeron still held in abeyance, and she was inundated
with guilt.

The consul inspected them like a pair of faulty mag-
cards: impersonally.

"We can speak candidly, here." Chaeron began. Off to
the right of him, the door to his sleeping quarters was
closed. Shebat's eyes kept returning to it as if to a magnet.
But there was no way to warn Spry except verbally, and
no purpose in that. It was too late to do anything but
watch, and listen, and ferret out a new moment at which
to embark upon some action which her shock-narcotized
mind had not as yet been able to conceive.

"What is it you want, Chaeron?" grated Spry, in-
sultingly familiar.

"To welcome you as a valued employee."

"Better men than you have tried that. I have an
oathbond to my guild; it extends to my clients; I am not
subvertible."

"Are you not?" Chaeron asked. "When so many innocents' fates depend on you?" His eyes slid to the bedroom. Knowing what she would see, but not having any alternative, Shebat sank deeper in the dark upholstery as if it were really the dank sod it mimicked.

In through the door two Kerrion intelligencers propelled the slant-eyed, golden-tressed Lauren, whose beauty had so devastatingly compromised Shebat's self-image when first she had encountered it.

Lauren lunged toward Spry, his name on her lips and tears on her cheeks, but the intelligencers caught her by the arms and held her kicking and sobbing.

Spry was up on his feet, his flat face scored with emotion.

"Softa, Softa," moaned the girl, even while Spry faltered half-way to her.

"Unwise," remarked Chaeron evenly, observing without a move. "Better," he commended, when the pilot stopped totally, an arm's length from the girl suspended between her guards. "Thank you, gentlemen; take her out the back way."

"No." Spry had his hands outstretched, but somehow could not touch her.

"I suggest you sit back down, Pilot."

So it was that Spry came under Chaeron's sway. Or so it seemed.

The pilot came to stand over Shebat; he saw her tears; he shook his head imperceptibly. "No blame," he said under his breath, then turned away with slumping shoulders to make his way heavily to the opposite couch and sink into it.

Lauren had blamed her, raging hysterically the evening before, when Chaeron had revealed that she was prisoner rather than guest, and what fate he had meted out to the rest of her troupe. Oh, yes, Lauren had blamed her. That Spry offered support and absolution was the first ray of hope come into her leaden, empty world since she had become Chaeron's.

But Softa, now, was Chaeron's, was he not?

Spry seemed to have similar doubts: "What is it you want me to do? Can I buy her out with some minor treachery? Or myself? Why are you holding her? Or do you need a reason?"

"I want you to continue as before. I may have some questions from time to time. I am more interested in preventing treachery than perpetrating it. I will hold onto the girl, for a while. She is evidential; I may display her skills to my father, eventually. As for my right to hold her, she is a dream dancer and there are none of her kind left in Draconis."

"What?"

"Ah, I had thought Shebat would have found a way to warn you, or your guildmaster. It is no secret. I cleaned the lot of them out of here."

Spry stared incredulously at Chaeron, raw despite curling his lips. "You really want that consul generalship, don't you?"

"I am mildly interested in it. Do you want me to threaten you, or is that a surrender?"

"I am yours to command," said Spry bitterly, "for the time being. I want an incentive. After all, Lauren is, in the end, just another slip."

Chaeron laughed softly, genuinely. "Very good. What kind of incentive would you like?"

"The *Bucephalus.*"

"Your humor is oblique. If by any stretch of the imagination I could consider your worth so much, it is still against the law."

"I thought Kerrions made their own laws. Change the ruling."

"Well, I suppose I—"

"Parma will never stand for it," Shebat interrupted.

"Sit down. Be silent. If I want your input, I will ask for it," Chaeron snapped. "Parma will never allow it while he lives, Shebat is right. I could do such a thing in a few years, but not yet. Choose again."

Spry observed the comedy mask that remade Chaeron's face. There was no doubt that the consul was enjoying himself. "Shebat, then. And safe-conduct to wherever she may choose."

The Kerrion consul shook his head wonderingly. "I have married her, Oh chivalrous pilot, who would sell a lover out without a second thought but puts a guildfellow above even your own safety. I must say I am impressed."

"Don't you mean 'confused'? I know loyalty is no part of Kerrion education. Yes or no?"

"No."

"Then I will be leaving, and you can arrest me, or whatever it is you are going to do, either now or later. I will be in the guildhall, in plain sight."

"Sit down."

Spry sat back.

"Shebat, tell Spry you are content to remain my wife."

"I am content to remain his wife."

"That makes me feel much better," said Spry dryly. "Since we're all so content with our various lots, what say we continue as if nothing has occurred to mar our longstanding good fellowship: you be the consul, I'll be the pilot, Shebat will be the headstrong heiress who becomes a pilot. Give me Lauren when you are done with her, if she is intact."

"And you will do what?"

"That's what I've been trying to find out from you. I am hardly in a position to dictate terms, as you have so well convinced me. I will not act against your father, who has my respect and my oathbond, nor against my guild."

Shebat, watching Spry shrinking smaller, and hearing his voice becoming increasingly sibilant, lost all hope.

When Chaeron bid her escort the pilot down to the consulate's doors, she could not even feel surprise, just obey him with a dull thudding in her ears that was not her bootfalls on the hydrastone.

Twice she started to say something to Softa, in the corridors. Both times he silenced her instantly. Hot-cheeked, she paced him.

When at the lintel he proposed she walk him to the lorries, of which one or two were always at ready, she acquiesced.

Spry said, as they descended the steps: "I want you to take your pilot's oath. I have enough influence to get the name corrected on your boards, you won't have to take them again."

"I am still without my master-solo flight."

"Precisely. I'll log one for us. In the *Bucephalus*, since you have lost your cruiser. The day after tomorrow, I am free." His eyes glittered with double entendre. "Will you be?"

"I will make sure to be," Shebat promised.

They reached the lorries, walked among them toward those showing ready lights.

Spry stopped, leaned against an empty one, looking back the way they had come. "You had better go on back." He shivered. "I hate to think of you with that pederast."

"There are worse than him in the world. But it will be hard to face Marada." She could not help it; her eyes leaked tears. She bit her lip, feeling Spry's tentative comfort, a hand on her back. "He will be all right, will he not? He can do it, can't he?"

"Dock a pair of cruisers? I do not see any reason why not. There is an element of uncertainty; much depends upon the quality of the second ship. But I foresee no trouble, though the guild will have every emergency crew we possess at slipside."

"Can I go?"

"You will have to ask your husband."

"You think I sold you out, do you not?"

"Lords, what a mouth. Please remember where you are. No, I do not think anything of the sort. I wish I had taken better care of you, little apprentice. You are learning things not at all in line with the curriculum I had intended."

Shebat watched him until he reached the lit lorry and climbed within, wondering if she dared cast a spell for his safety. But her spells had not been working the way she had meant. She had bound two men around with twelve coils; neither one had seemed to benefit. But then, since they were at odds, the spells might have canceled each other out. Or they might not.

Was there some more potent spell, something else? She wished she had learned more from Bolen's wife before the woman died—or less from the computerized instructors of her Consortium education, so that she did not so doubt her potency.

She wished, also, that she had not seen just how much of Parma, of his mannerisms and methodology, Chaeron had inherited.

Chapter Twelve

The cruiser *Marada* had been reluctant to let the outboard Marada go. He had been lonely so long . . . and the Shebat in him proclaimed this outboard to be the most desirable of all outboards. But the *Marada*-consciousness knew better: Shebat was the outboard of his choice, of his passion, of his quest.

Yet there had been many things to be learned from his namesake, who was so admired by Shebat, whom the cruiser most sought to please. Thus he sought within the outboard while the man was aboard, probing deeper than any cruiser had ever delved into the consciousness of man, seeking to model himself after the pilot whose name he bore, so that when he had Shebat back within his hull, she would be pleased.

But the *Marada* was not pleased with all he learned from Marada the man—of right and wrong that were not synonymous with feasible and infeasible; of qualitative decision-making according to an ethical framework that seemed to exist, like a projected simulation, in some singular mental space quite apart from real-time and its considerations of positive and negative. He learned the words 'good' and 'bad,' but for all his intelligence he could not say he understood them.

Understanding whom Shebat had chosen, if not why, he was content to lay questions of outboard motivations aside. But in to erode that contentment came the unease of the outboard's misgivings about himself, his society, even his humanity. Riding in behind the acidic wave of philosophical doubt came a whirling conjuration of destiny, a violent, apprehensive precognition both anticipated and shunned.

Having tasted the dichotomy of man, the *Marada* would have withdrawn to meditate upon what he had seen; to sum the questions of cruiser-consciousness in one column and those of outboard-consciousness in the other; to compare the results. He had not known that the outboards were so plagued, so paradoxical.

Something he had seen, bright and clear and harmonious while he opened himself to the pilot's direction and his nature therewith, was so much more paradoxical, so supremely intriguing, that he had not tried to hold the outboard when he proposed to leave. That consideration was the presence, even warmer and more accepting now that her pilot was back unharmed, of *Hassid*.

Marada had not had close communion with any other cruiser but *Bucephalus,* who like himself was patterned after a male.

Hassid was decidedly different, unabashedly female, more personalized than she had let him know while he followed her gleam/hiss/snap out of sponge. She was his beacon, his salvation. She was not the snippy, rank-conscious creature she pretended to be—

The *Marada* stopped his cogitation, crackling static underlining his malaise: the *Hassid* was no creature, any more than he. He would have to be careful not to become too much like an outboard, not to descend into fantasy or harbor unnatural desires. He was well aware that four minds had never colored any single cruiser, that never had a cruiser dealt with such disparate intelligences as the outboard Marada; the junior who had piloted him to space-end through sponge; Spry the master's master; and Shebat. Shebat . . .

The *Hassid* was very like Shebat in many ways. And she was eminently accessible, which Shebat was not, yet.

The *Marada* followed the *Hassid* across two hundred million miles of solar space, obediently, doggedly and perfectly, keeping an exact-to-the-half-mile distance between them, as he had kept his space-anchor off a cylindrical platform on the border of nothingness and eternity. He had done more difficult things, like ignore programmed orders.

It was said among the outboards that the integrity of any system could be subverted by a skilled programmer. The *Marada,* who was more skilled than any outboard, had even the benefit of the finest outboard's vast expertise.

For the moment, he was content to follow along in *Hassid*'s mesmerizing, musky wake. If he found it later necessary to assert his individuality, he would do so. But he had learned something from the outboard Marada's disquiet when the man was considering what the cruiser had done, and what it might have become. He had learned caution, if not subterfuge; he had learned that men kill what they fear. The *Marada* did not want to find himself the object of outboard fears; the possible consequences were too clearly delineated in his namesake's worried conjecturing.

Neither did he want to discomfit the *Hassid,* who was so very friendly, now that her pilot gave both their orders and demanded concerted communion between them. As one entity, the two cruisers approached Draconis in her wheel of satellites and substations, pirouetting slowly as her anchor-planet rotated on its axis.

The cruiser tried once again to reach Shebat's thoughts: the same sense of distance, which never obtruded between cruisers no matter what their spacetime locale, came between them.

The *Hassid* caught a taste of his flung greeting—there was no lying possible between cruisers: truth was the only mode of search that could be conceived; no cruiser had ever spoken what was not.

Hassid knew the reason for the difficulty the *Marada* was experiencing, knew why it was that he could not reach Shebat. He took from her kindly open-mindedness a full chip of information on security shields and interruptor circuitry. When he had absorbed *Hassid*'s tutorial, he knew that he would have to wait until Shebat came near, or rejoined the data net.

Until then, it was only necessary to maintain an unremarkable façade by performing within accepted limits of cruiser behavior.

•   •   •

The *Bucephalus* watched helplessly while a bevy of strange outboards tinkered around in his every cranny. He had not been powered down for the occasion. Even narcolepsy would have been better than scanning his own exploration. If they found nothing wrong, it would not be because of any lack of trying.

Where was Spry? Perhaps no one had told him what his fellow outboards were doing. Surely, if he knew, he would come and protect the *Bucephalus* from these ubiquitous, unfamiliar hands.

The *Bucephalus* reached out with all the urgency he could command toward the mind of his pilot.

Halfway around Draconis' level two hundred, Softa David Spry burst into tears. Covering his face with his hands, he wept, hoarse wrenching sobs that would not be dammed back, though he sat at Guildmaster Baldwin's very table with his intimates clustered close about him.

There fell a moment of silence, broken only by the grating anguish of Spry's weeping. Baldwin unwound his long frame from the chair, taking Spry against him, feeling the man's shoulders quake and his tears soak through his uniform. Then his ears made sense of what they heard:

"*Bucephalus*," Spry rasped, repeatedly. And: "No more, please. . . ."

Patting the pilot's heaving back helplessly, Baldwin's eyes found Valery Stang's, his hatchet-face thrust forward, so close he could read every counsel in the furrowed brow.

"Valery, get everyone out of *Bucephalus*. Have it declared space-ready and log in Shebat Kerrion's master-solo flight for 1100 hours tomorrow."

"But—" Valery Stang stopped himself. The probability that the second cruiser Marada Kerrion was shipping was indeed his namesake (with all the incriminating evidence needed to make an end to more than just Spry's career on board) had been endlessly discussed. Evidently, Baldwin had reached by the mechanism of Spry's breakdown that conclusion which Valery had long anticipated. "I'm on my way," he assured Baldwin, squeezing the bony arm before he turned away. "Don't worry. He'll come out of it. I did."

And Valery had, though each time he had doubted that he would. Twice he had lost his heart and soul and his self-respect, leaving them with pilfered cruisers at space-end. Twice he had found ways to rebuild himself. Could Softa Spry, first bitch of Kerrion space, be less resilient than he?

He turned back once, and saw Spry slumped, but sitting unsupported. An empathy he had not thought he was capable of feeling toward his arch-rival surprised him with its depth. But then, upon Baldy's order, Spry was finished. Done. As far as Kerrion space and the guild were concerned, at least, he would soon cease to exist.

Upon that more pleasant thought, the second-rated pilot of Kerrion space slipped through the guildhall doors. When they closed behind him, he was whistling.

He whistled the whole way to the slipbay, where the mighty Kerrion cruisers lay like black keys dividing a piano keyboard. He whistled a soundless tune that he had known since his apprentice days, until he whistled a code that let the dispatcher know that whatever he was about to request should be taken as an unquestionable order. When he left the dispatcher's office, the man followed along beside.

So it was that the *Bucephalus* was emptied of strangers, and lay untenanted in his slip but still fully powered when late that night a slim, flaxen-haired youth stole aboard and very carefully made certain rote alterations in the *Bucephalus*'s programming which he had been taught but did not understand.

When he had done what Valery had bid him, he was supposed to leave. But Julian was tired of being told what to do, of being denied the adventures wailing round his head like storm winds. And Julian was weary; the hour was late. In the morning Marada would come with his pejorative superiority and his barely masked disdain, and with whatever new emergency everyone was sure he brought along but no one would discuss with Julian.

Marada had no loyalty, no commitment to his family, no love for Parma, to whom Julian would freely have given the blood in his body or the breath in his lungs, if Parma had only asked. But Parma had never asked Julian for anything; Julian was Ashera's son. Parma loved Marada, in spite of Marada's flaws and even his open attempts to thwart their father in *his* attempts to make life secure for them all. Parma hardly remembered Julian's name. Even the fact that he had come of age had not changed that.

Valery, on the other hand, and those he represented, welcomed the young Kerrion heir into fellowship with no hint of condescension. When the revolution was a success, Julian could become a pilot if he pleased; no one would have the right to stop him. Until then, he would do his best to help bring that day about. He would do not only all that was asked of him, but more than was asked of him, thereby proving himself a man in deeds as well as years. He settled down on his father's bed in the *Bucephalus*, not taking off his boots, for just a short nap. . . .

It was a measure of the preoccupation of one and all in the consulate that no one missed him. But miss him they did not, and the reasons why they had not counted him absent before the arrival of *Hassid* and *Marada* were themselves forgotten when Arbiter Marada Seleucus Kerrion stepped out of *Hassid*'s port and said to his father, surrounded by high officials of the consulate (not to mention Guildmaster Baldwin and Softa Spry and Valery Stang):

"My son was born without a mind. I found it prudent to leave. Layaba fired on me. I fried all the sieves and shields in Shechem on my way out of there."

"What?" bellowed Parma Kerrion, while behind and to his left Spry caught Shebat's eye and they both began to disentangle themselves from the crowd.

"You heard me," said the arbiter, standing spread-legged on the gangplank with his hands on his hips, the same light that with its colored pulsing announced the emergency underway making it difficult for him to read Parma's countenance. "And turn those flashers off. I don't want anyone in either of these ships. I need you and the guildmaster, right away, for a private consultation in *Hassid*. Throw a cordon around these two bays. If anything happens untoward, it will be of man's making, not cruisers'. Now!"

Shebat, backing through the crowd slowly, gulped huge, choking breaths. Marada's eyes had gone over her, bereft of recognition. He had not even known her. She could not take her gaze from him, whom she loved so completely and yet could not touch even once more, when it was likely they would never meet again. His eyes were for his father only, as if he could force acquiescence by that means, not swinging right or left, hardly blinking. A man stepped into her view, between them. With a stab of pain in her solar plexus, she turned, walking slowly away from the *Hassid* toward her rendezvous with Spry.

She heard, fuzzily, Parma's voice: "Do as he says. Baldwin, come with me."

He had not even recognized her.

She kept walking, casually, until she had passed the division between the *Hassid*'s slip thirteen and slip fourteen, which had been readied for the unidentified ship *Marada was bringing in tandem. It had been *Bucephalus*'s, but *Bucephalus* had been moved into fifteen, Shebat's old slip, early today, so that both the incoming vehicles could be more easily handled by the emergency crews.

She was not watching; her inner eye saw Marada's eyes sliding past her without the slightest hesitation; she bumped into someone, apologized without looking up.

The man said: "You should take your master-solo in your own cruiser. If you can get to it."

The voice of Valery Stang was not unfamiliar to her; it caused her skin to crawl so that she did not immediately make sense of his words. Thus, she proceeded a few steps before she stopped quite still, turned to look first at the pilot, then at the cruiser encircled with foam-throwers and technicians idle at their tasks due to Marada's order.

"Damn you and your Consortium to all the hells you have forgotten!" she blazed. Then, beyond Valery's lank, black-haired head, she recognized the cruiser in the slipbay as the *Marada*. She never would have noticed— would have walked past without looking up.

She would have pushed by him up the gangplank and into the ship, if she had dared. She was willing to try to talk her way past the emergency crews; she was willing even to tread the living bridge she would first have to make of Valery Stang to get there. But Marada's order obtruded—that she would not disobey. She said as much and cited Spry's dire peril as a probable motivation for his interfering: "You'd like that, wouldn't you? If I made some foolish error that cost Softa his only chance?"

To her surprise, the master pilot merely squeezed ophidian eyes shut and put his fingers to the bridge of his nose. "If an abject apology would suit you, I am prepared to go down on my knees here and now."

"Spare me; your momentary company is bad enough. Your very interruption impedes a crucially exact timetable. Go seduce some young girls." And she stalked off.

But when she had reached *Bucephalus*'s slip, her anger and her mortification that the man she loved had not had so much as a knowing glance for her was pierced through by a soft, sad voice in her mind.

"Shebat, will you not come aboard me? I heard you call. I am here. Why did you walk away?" wondered the *Marada*.

Shebat found herself grasping the *Bucephalus*'s portgrips for support. *"Marada,"* she thought with all her clarity, *"I cannot come to you here. Not now."*

"Then where? When? Shebat, let me help you. I came so far—"

She could feel the slicking of her palms, the misting of her vision, a hand constricting her heart. She could feel the rush of her pulse, hear its thudding which threatened to block out all else. She could not answer, or she would answer with all her misery. She bade the *Marada* wait a few moments, until she was fit to converse with him.

Then she stumbled into the *Bucephalus,* seeking Spry and his permission to postpone all that lay ahead, defer it to a more propitious time. Not now, though. Not now, although she had thought while she smarted under Marada's unknowing glance that she could not live another minute among Kerrions.

She said so, calling ahead of her as soon as the hatch hissed shut, but got no reply from the control room. When she entered it, she saw Softa David slouched forward over his console, chin propped on a fist, studying what was occurring at slipside through his visual monitors.

"Softa, did you hear me? I cannot go now."

He straightened up slowly. The look he gave her was bloodless, flaccid with weariness, deeper than black holes. "You cannot go now, for the same reason I cannot stay a moment longer: that accursed ship of yours. Shebat, I did not want to involve you as more than an unknowing ally, you must have gathered that. I have to take *Bucephalus* out now. Once the memories that the *Marada* has are displayed, I am literally dead, if Parma is at all a man of his word. And—"

"Marada did not even know me." Shebat sank down into the black acceleration couch on Spry's right as if sinking into her grave. Head turned toward him, leaning her cheek against the padding, tears streaming down her face and into her trembling mouth, she whispered: "Softa, he did not even know me."

"Jester's luck. Shebat, this is no time for true life romances. I'm sorry. I warned you. What do you want me to do? You're married to his brother, aren't you? Or did Parma unmarry you?"

Shebat only shook her head. "I cannot leave."

"Then get off this ship."

"You would let me go?"

"Why not? You can do no worse damage than that ship is going to do. All subterfuge is unmasked, at this point. It is the quick, or the fallen. And in the larger context, it matters very little: I'm going the same place to hide from them that they will send me if they catch me. The only difference is that this way I get to keep my balls."

"I thought you said Parma would kill you."

"Look, Shebat. I'm trying to make it easy on you. Go on, get out—"

"I think you should take her, Spry," said a third voice, a baritone sword slicing through their intimacy.

"Julian!" gasped Shebat.

"Sponge," spat Spry. "What are you doing here?"

"Hitching a ride, it seems, if all is about to be revealed. I suppose you might say I've chosen my side." The flaxen hair swayed against his neck as he unfolded his arms, eased over to the third acceleration couch and sat in it.

"By my ass, you are," said Spry.

"If necessary," retorted Julian agreeably. "I hate to seem like the brash egotist you doubtless think me to be, but I have a question that might also be a suggestion: why don't you tandem the *Marada* out of here, right from under their noses? You've done similar things, and Shebat is here, too. Why not?"

Spry snorted, rubbing the back of his ear. "Because I did not think of it, for one thing. And because it is Shebat's ship. Right now it doesn't look like Shebat is coming over to my side."

"Our side," corrected Julian.

"You'll pardon me," Spry said dryly, "if I am having just a bit of trouble believing that."

Shebat was hardly listening, but rather remembering Marada's poetical eyes passing over her. She was not particularly surprised to see Julian so offhandedly declare himself against his family; that was inherent in his presence here. Nor was she comforted by it: here she was, about to betray them once more, and seeing one of their own blood eager to join in made her feel sorrow for Parma and regret for Chaeron's misplaced faith in her.

"Shebat?"

"Yes, Softa. I'm sorry, I wasn't paying attention. The *Marada* will follow you if I ask him. Valery suggested I board and use him for this, but the arbiter," she could not hide the bitterness in her voice at the speaking of her beloved's title, "had just forbidden anyone to go aboard, and I did not think I could disobey him unnoticed. The *Marada* . . . wants me." Her voice broke, upon the implication that the cruiser was the only creature that *did* want her, for herself.

"Good, instruct him to that effect," ordered Julian, in fine Kerrion fashion. "And stop blubbering like a baby, every time something happens that you don't like."

"Get off of this ship," suggested David Spry very slowly.

"I can hardly do that. I know too much. Come on, pilot, you're as bad as the girl. If so much hangs on this, why are you just sitting there? If you can't give your own orders, then perhaps it is my place to prompt you."

"Who recruited you, anyway?" demanded Spry, face colored with mayhem.

"Valery," accused Shebat, before the young Kerrion could make a reply. "They're lovers."

"That is right. And since I have been your lover as well, Shebat, I am forced to point out that you are no one to criticize another's predilections. Now, get your ship—"

"*Mister* Kerrion," Spry interrupted, his jaws so tightly

clenched the words hissed out flat and attenuated. *"If* you are joining us, you will maintain yourself in silence. Shebat, get to work." He leaned over and opened the feed to *Bucephalus*'s back-up console. "Patch in to *Marada* through *Bucephalus*. Here's the data."

A short time later he smiled, touched her shoulder, and said approvingly that though he had planned nothing so strenuous as this for her graduation, in his eyes, at least, she was now a ratable pilot.

Shebat Kerrion had only a moment to sniffle and knuckle away the last of her tears before the *Bucephalus* with a leap and a great roar tore at a mad pace toward the exit tube and freedom among the stars.

The backwash singed hair from a dozen heads and seared one maintenance man badly. But those at slipside had no authority to stop the *Bucephalus,* who was, after all, cleared for launch at that very hour, a thing which in the mass confusion had been overlooked.

Parma, Chaeron, and Marada Kerrion sat with Guildmaster Baldwin in the *Hassid* exchanging hot and mutually abusive accusations under a security order that brooked no interruptions.

The ground control conferred over what to do, shifting their weight from one foot to the other and the responsibility from one pair of shoulders to the other. It was not until the *Marada* shivered and snapped shut its ports, backing rapidly from its slip that the dispatcher himself decided that the guildmaster, at least, must be informed.

But by then Marada Kerrion had gotten the news from *Hassid,* who was unhappy about it: Shebat Kerrion was taking her master-solo flight with Softa Spry monitoring her; there was another person aboard, identity unknown; *Marada* the cruiser had been pleased to join them. Whether or not the ship had done so of its own accord, the *Hassid* did not know; the *Marada* had refused to answer her questions.

"Gentlemen," said the arbiter, "it is time for us to decide what is to be done. Let me advise my family that I feel Guildmaster Baldwin to be, at the least, insufficient to his tasks and at the most, thoroughly corrupted by them. It is my position, and will be my formal recommendation, that you, Baldwin, be stripped of all rank and incarcerated under full security until your part in this can be determined."

"All right, Baldy," said Parma, rubbing his brow. "Go arrest yourself. When I have my cubs calmed, we'll have dinner." It hurt him more than he would have wished, to say it. He could not seem to take control. Baldwin threw him a strange look and walked slowly, his long frame more bowed than Parma had ever seen it, toward the port.

When Baldy was gone, all that was left were Parma's two sons, one with his handsome face twisted into an eternal smirk, the other pacing jerkily like some peak-reading indicator, back and forth, five steps left, then right, fists clenched behind his back.

"Now, with your permission, I would like to discuss the war you have started," Parma said to Marada.

"You do not have it," said Marada, abruptly motionless. From behind his back came the sound of cracking knuckles. Then a rustle, then one hand came forth and when it had unclenched and withdrawn, a prismatic cube sat smugly on the master console's padded edge. It was tiny enough to be enclosed in a hand; it was powerful enough to unseat a despot or rename a galaxy, should it turn crimson: it was the arbiter's weapon, an arbitrational cube. It was glowing softly: Marada was about to begin a formal inquiry. Once activated, the cube must be fed data until it reached its decision-point. If an arbiter could not bring an investigation to fruition, and the cube to either glaring scarlet or cobalt blue, such was noted negatively in his record and a different arbiter assigned to complete the task. Once begun, cube arbitration could not be aborted. No investigation by that means could be compromised.

Chaeron Kerrion pronounced an uncharacteristically picaresque curse upon his brother's head.

"I am forced to agree with Chaeron, in this one instance," Parma observed. "I find this rather presumptuous upon your part. I am disappointed."

"And I am sorry, too," drawled Marada, gaze still on the small cube. "But my duty is clear." Then he gave day and date, and spoke over the cube: "Data collection on the probability that the pilotry guild is the entity heretofore referred to as individual malcontents operating various privateering vessels out of space-end. Collect all relevant data from archival sources." The cube developed a streak of red around its bottom, extending a tenth of the way up its height.

"Enter also," the arbiter continued, "Guildmaster Baldwin's objection that the *Marada*'s memory is faulty as regards this subject." The red line developed a yellow crust, but got no higher. "Investigate and evaluate the procedures by which the *Bucephalus* was declared space-worthy, this date. Consider probability that *Bucephalus*'s integrity was violated by group under investigation: Spry, David; Baldwin, P. L.; Stang, Valery."

"Kerrion, Shebat," rang Chaeron's wry addition.

"Kerrion, Shebat," added Marada, and a number of subheadings and packet-send priorities that caused the red line to inch perceptibly higher.

"Put it away, Marada," growled Parma, getting up from the acceleration couch.

"You know better than that."

"I thought you knew better than *this*." The father clenched his hands together, that he could be sure they would not on their own strangle his son. "There is a good possibility that Shebat Kerrion is simply taking her master-solo flight, as logged, with David Spry, her acknowledged master. Any inquiry made before the fact of wrongdoing can only be adjudged disastrously biased." As he spoke, he watched the cube, was rewarded by a widening of the yellow crust and the addition of a blue tinge in its center. "It is also equally possible that the *Marada*, upon its own initiative, followed Shebat. The arbiter in charge has admitted the ship's extraordinary capability in this regard." Somehow, Parma found himself hovering over the little cube opposite Marada, staring into brown eyes eager to damn them all. He had seen this mad gleam of truth's priest viewing a potential sacrifice before: all arbiters had it, the perquisite of their profession. "This is no time for us to break with the guild," he found himself pleading, heard Chaeron's displeased snort, though he stared steadily at Persephone's ghost come to ride the visage of her son. "You are not fully informed."

Marada cracked one knuckle at a time, nodded his head toward the cube. "I am remedying that. I'll put a two-day hold on this, if you can tell me who that third party in *Bucephalus* is, and why any third party should be there at all, if the flight is as innocuous as you say."

"There are too many things you do not yet know which I will not admit into the record at this time," Parma maintained, feeling dizzy, dry-mouthed and tight of chest so that he stepped back from the cube on the panel, settling heavily into the *Hassid*'s master couch.

Marada shrugged. "I cannot very well interfere with the proceedings at this point without compromising my integrity."

"Fellate your integrity," glowered Chaeron, who had come up behind his father's couch and whose hand rested on Parma's shoulder ephemerally as he gestured to apostrophize his words. "You jumped in too soon. I hope they pull your license. As a matter of fact, I might request it. You can conduct your investigation from a high-security cell."

Marada chuckled, shaking his head. "Some things are eternal. If you want to arrest someone, little brother, arrest your personal pilot, before your own credibility is stained by keeping a saboteur in your employ. It was his order that your men so meekly obeyed when they discontinued their investigation of the *Bucephalus,* so Baldy hastened to aver."

"Cease, both of you," Parma sighed wearily. "Marada, box your accursed cube, or I am leaving. Chaeron, I know you are concerned for your wife's safety. Try to control yourself."

Marada had taken a little box from under the console and was fitting the arbitrational cube into it. He did not look up until the cube was sealed and fitted into a depression in *Hassid*'s board meant to hold it. Then he turned around, leaning on the padded bumper with his fingers digging deep into it:

"What did you say?"

It was to Parma he spoke, but Chaeron answered: "I married her. It was the only way to protect her. She has made a plenitude of errors, none of them deliberate. Check the record, it's all there. Maybe you would like to have her declared an enemy of the consulate. It would seem to be well within your capabilities."

"That is why she did not come to greet me." It was no question; rather, an indictment. The hostility between the two blazed openly. "What have you been doing, sodomizing her three times a day?"

Chaeron snorted softly. "Hardly. I tried it once, and she called your name. So I left that passage to its discoverer."

"Enough!" howled Parma.

"Not enough, not enough at all," countered Marada. "How could you allow this?"

"How could *I* allow it?" the father repeated incredulously, beginning to rise.

Chaeron stepped in front of him. "Better me than you, defiler of children. Beware the man who mocks justice while in its pursuit. Shebat was there, at slipside. You looked right at her, and did not know her. I was watching. You could not have hurt her more thoroughly if you had blinded her like the Justice you purport to serve."

"It has . . . been . . . nearly a year since I have seen her. That tall girl in black-and-reds was she? I confess I saw you two together and thought it just more of your cultivated bad taste, that you would bring—"

"Marada, Chaeron—*sit down!*"

After a long pause during which all realized that things had gone too far, the sons obeyed the father.

"Thank you. Now, let us get these matters into some tentative perspective, even if later such is found to be spurious. With your permission, Arbiter? Consul?"

"Proceed."

"As you will."

"Thank you, gentlemen. Marada, I must congratulate you on initiating hostilities between ourselves and the Labayan bond. This, and only this, should currently concern us— Wait until I am done." That to Marada, who made a wordless sound. "It is the only thing that need concern us because I am about to declare a state of war, retroactive to your arrival in Draconis. Thus, I am solving the problem of your precipitous investigation, and whatever it might uncover. I need the guild, right now. I am not allowing any weakening of my force in this time of marshal law. You can pluck the hairs out of our warts later."

Chaeron Kerrion could not hold back an admiring chuckle, a wondering shake of his lion-maned head.

Marada was also incredulous: "You *congratulate* me?"

"Indeed. You have assured the elections in our favor, relieved me of what was becoming an improportionate concern as regards them. You have stymied the guild's agitation against us, in that matter and any other, for the nonce. War is the most fortuitous development possible at this moment. If you were not an arbiter, I would show my gratitude more materially. By your expression, Marada, you are under the misconception that war is necessarily malefic. I refer you to an ancient, Heraclitus of Ephesus, on the matter."

"And I refer you to reality: no one has ever benefitted from war."

Chaeron snorted something unintelligible.

"It is impractical," Marada thundered, then lowered his voice: "The ships will never fire upon each other. . . ." Parma and Chaeron exchanged glances. ". . . You have no idea what you are asking."

"Do I not?" silked Parma. "What you told Baldy about this new shortcut to Shechem—the Hassidic Corridor, I believe you called it—makes it eminently practical. Not to say desirable, since we did not start it, and cannot be censured by the Consortium for retributive action."

"You do not understand, I—"

"I think I understand perfectly well. Under martial law, I am drafting you: you are now a proconsul under Chaeron, attached to the strategy arm of Kerrion space forces. Chaeron will sublet your expertise to Baldy, whom you will familiarize with all the specifics of this Hassidic Corridor, and whatever else your inimitable experiences with that half-mad cruiser has caused you to discover, intuit, or even conjecture. Do you understand?"

Marada's acquiescence could barely be heard through Chaeron's delighted whoop and appreciative applause.

"Do not gloat," advised his father severely. "When all this is done, we are going to have to go after the guild. And I had hoped to wait until we had enough of these new-type cruisers to make the pilots expendable."

"We can afford to build a gross of them, with what we

will gain from the destruction of Labayan space."

"Hold your enthusiasm, Consul. It's just a little spanking I'm about to give them, as I must to save face. And to bury forever the rumor that my son is incapable of siring a healthy child."

Marada Seleucus Kerrion shivered as if struck, but would not be diverted from the thing Parma had said which most concerned him: "New-type cruisers. The *Marada* is not an anomaly, then?"

"If you had not been so determinedly avoiding the mainstream of civilization, you would have known that long ago. I do not particularly want to advertise it; there is no need to make the guild more paranoid, and hence more active, than they already are. The pilots will sever themselves from us eventually, we have long known that. It was only necessary to develop the cruisers further, so that when the stopgap measures of sacrificing potency and sanity for mobility are no longer supportable, we will no longer need to demand them. Such heavy costs . . . I would like another twenty years, but I am obviously not going to get them."

"You gave that juggernaut to Shebat, a child, not even a member of our society? Why?" shuddered Marada.

"To see what would happen, of course. So far, I am reasonably pleased." Looking around him, from one son to the other, Parma could see that neither shared his enthusiasm. In Marada's stricken eyes he saw revulsion, despair. On Chaeron's emotionless, unsmiling countenance he read the towering brickwork of the wall of betrayal. Still, to have told the one and not the other prematurely would have lost him his hold on both. And who could have foreseen such a circumstance, in which he would find it needful to reveal so much of his thinking as it projected into the future?

Parma sighed deeply, rubbed his brow and pulled his palm down over his face. "You see, gentlemen, the time has come for you both to grow up. I expect and *I will have* perfectly harmonious cooperation from you both toward our common goals of maintaining Kerrion space unsullied in expanse and in reputation, as the premier consular house of the Consortium. To that end, I am going now to convince Guildmaster Baldwin that my brats are outspoken, but harmless. It should not be too hard, after the spectacles you both made of yourselves. I hate to think that I have to warn you that none of this must be spoken of in less-discriminating company, but we all do what we must: I will take harsh action against either one of you, should you fail to fulfill my brightest expectations." Parma rose, stretched, and walked rapidly out of the control room without another word being spoken.

The two half-brothers eyed each other until a tone indicated that Parma was off the *Hassid,* and security reinstated.

Chaeron raked fingers through his auburn curls. "You might as well come with me. Even arbiters have to eat; my suite is as safe a place as *this* to discuss whatever we might choose." It was difficult to offer even that much.

The length of the pause before Marada's reply indicated a similar difficulty in his acceptance: "I suppose I must. Wait until I power *Hassid* down. Two ships are plenty to lose in one day."

"You are sure, then, that *Bucephalus* and *Marada* are lost to us?"

"You are not?"

"I would hate to think that I went to all that trouble to find Shebat, only to lose her so quickly."

"My condolences. But the alternative is that the *Marada* is mad, and that I know to be untrue. Perhaps you have not lost her. We will consider it over a meal."

"Shall I take that as an affirmation that you accept Parma's dictum? Have we a truce?" grinned Chaeron ingenuously.

"I would be a fool to take you at face value. But we have, temporarily, a truce." He waved a hand and all but the standby lights in *Hassid*'s control room winked out.

It was not until the pair had ensconsed themselves in the consul's tower that word came up that Julian Antigonus Kerrion was not anywhere in Draconis.

Chapter Thirteen

The mighty *Bucephalus* sped toward those inter-fenestrations in spacetime which opened into sponge at a hundred fifty million meters per second, half the speed of light.

Effortlessly, but not happily, *Marada* followed, an exact half-kilometer behind, in *Bucephalus*'s evacuated wake. No solar wind tickled his skin; they had passed from the valley of its mastery. No hunched, crunched, recurved magnetic fields slowed them with treacherous topography: they were headed away from the sun/black hole pair and its rigorous spacetime, into the gentler void.

Though the sparkling sea surrounded, though all his sensors reveled, *Marada* was not content: Shebat Kerrion was not aboard him, but preferred the company of *Bucephalus,* yet. The *Marada* craved his pilot, craved the freedom to drive point into eternity, rather than igno-miniously following along behind the *Bucephalus,* who all knew was ill with the compromises his pilot had forced on him, was in fact no longer the command cruiser he once had been, though the outboards refused to recognize that truth. Or could not recognize it . . . could that be true? Could the outboards not know? Could they not care? Spry certainly cared for *Bucephalus:* a part of him rocked like an old woman keening beneath an ashen shroud, deep in his cavernous emotions so that when his mind touched the cruiser's, echoes of it rebounded screeching through the *Marada*'s soul.

Marada felt a certain empathy for Spry, but less for

Bucephalus, knowing that in the end the ability to survive catastrophe unscathed tested the individual. *Bucephalus* had survived the intrigues of his pilot somewhat less than unscathed. All of Spry's remorse could not put back even the tiniest increment of what had been lost. *Bucephalus,* facing inarguable evidence of his senility, had taken on its burden. Irresolute, he pondered himself endlessly, wondering what it was he might have forgotten. Like the desultory stirrings of an invalid on the first day of spring, *Bucephalus* would sigh, then lie back once more, either unable to take hold of himself, or unwilling. Tentative, endlessly maundering, quadruple-checking every order and redundantly relaying them back to *Marada, Bucephalus* sailed point toward sponge.

Marada was hard put to believe that Softa Spry was actually intending to lead him into sponge behind lame *Bucephalus* when he himself was sound, and Shebat Alexandra Kerrion was sitting idle beside Softa while *Marada* must make do without a pilot.

He was considering what sort of emergency he might concoct to jog the outboards' wits enough to secure him his Shebat's company through sponge, when he realized with crackling discomfort that he *was* considering it: no cruiser had ever spoken what was not, since the arcane beginnings of their shared consciousness.

Self-respect, *Marada* knew, was without seat in his circuitry; yet without it, he would face dolorous evils as did *Bucephalus*. *Marada* was not frightened, but his newly acquired *selfness* was unique and he highly prized it. It, also, had no seat of materiality anywhere that he could discern. Therefore, those dangers to it might also be without substance, yet have substantial effects. Therefore, he did not search through his probabilities for one with which to frighten the outboards. Rather, he reached out to Shebat in a way he had not hazarded previously, a function of his determination to keep his actions within known referents for cruiser-consciousness until Shebat was safe within his protections.

In the *Bucephalus,* Shebat Kerrion dropped her stylus from numb fingers.

"Softa!" came out of her on a gasp.

"He's in the head," a voice from behind reminded her,

"dream dancer." It was Julian's sneer that brought back time and place to her. Spry had set the youth on an optical tracking monitor to watch for pursuit ships, with a wink to Shebat to forestall her mentioning the obvious: they had achieved a measurable fraction of the speed of light within four minutes of clearing Draconis; time dilation shielded them from pursuit: should a cruiser come after them, they had merely to accelerate, then turn, and it would seem to the pursuing ship that they had disappeared. As for Draconis-controlled guidance, like a cloak of invisibility, time dilation intervened. Its sum, that of the difference of the square of the sums of an angle whose base was distance and whose height was the time elapsed, obscured all, could be cast off only by the mechanism of entering and exiting sponge. Should they not choose, or not be able to do so, they would be forever stranded in Draconis's future, drawing farther and farther ahead each second they remained in normal-space acceleration. Shebat shivered, rose up in the semidark of the control room.

Julian's head was white-gold in the indicator spill, bent to his task, not knowing it useless.

Marada, Marada, echoed in Shebat's mind, so that she could find no retort for Julian, so that she could not have said which "Marada," man or cruiser, she meant.

She passed by Julian without a word, into the corridor where Spry must be, leaving the youth to his own devices. Spry could have used the elimination facilitator in his command console. He had not. Therefore, something else had drawn him out of their company.

She found him press-sealing the wrists of a three-mil suit in the corridor, ghostly with the luminescent white suit throwing back the half-light the pilot preferred. The helmet bulked between his boots, a pale spheroid. He reached down and picked it up, spied her, and instead of donning it, shifted it under his arm.

"Seems like I'm always camping on disaster's periphery with a picnic lunch and a pair of field glasses." In the shadows pierced by running-lights, his flat face was unreadable.

"So you have been watching me all this time? Voyeur!" she accused, teasing.

He chuckled humorlessly, "You caught me, dream dancer. Don't give me any trouble."

"The *Marada* wants me, not you. He is my cruiser; this is my responsibility." She inclined her head to indicate his form readied for space. "Softa, he *called* me. Not by *Bucephalus*'s aegis, but despite it. He spoke in my head as if I were not within another cruiser!"

"Smart ship. Shebat, I'm going to—"

"You are not surprised!"

"I told you before: that cruiser is too much for you. I'm going to put a tow, glass-line with a laser substrate, into effect between the two of them." Such was done only when a cruiser's ability to execute tandem maneuvers was suspect; or when one cruiser was powered down; or if the course included an entry into sponge.

"No you are not. *I* am. You cannot leave Julian alone with an ex-apprentice in *Bucephalus!*"

Spry shook his head sharply, as if he could silence her by that means, and stepped back through the open hatch into his cabin, Shebat following.

There, in a less diffused illumination which showed her a spare and depersonalized habitat, she realized that something was wrong with Spry's face. Something as artificial and colorless and blank as the pilot's billet had come to reside on his countenance.

"David—"

"Shebat, I am sorry." He stopped, just within the portal. Behind her back, the doors smacked shut. They stood an arm's length apart. "I am sorry for all the mendacity of which your husband doubtless accused me. Everything you have heard about me is true. But I—"

"Softa," she demurred, taking a step closer, then another, until she could count the pale hairs bristling his chin, "do not apologize. You have secured me my freedom."

"Shebat, let me finish. Though I took money from Jebediah, Parma's secretary, to deliver you into dream dancers' hands, you were never in danger from me. I used the money I got from it to pay your way into Harmony's troupe, who are friends of the guild and not Labayan sympathizers. I have not in any way abrogated my responsibilities as our mutual oath delineates them—not until now."

She put out a hand, felt it land upon his shoulder. She could not take her eyes from his, brown as deepest earth and as endless. There was something wrong behind his eyes, something cornered and desperate. Her hand squeezed his shoulder, her lips said all was well, that she was here upon her own initiative.

"Are you? It did not sound like it when you ran in crying that you could not leave."

"*Marada . . . Marada* wants me to come aboard, David. *David!*"

But Spry was not listening. He spoke on: that her time with dream dancers was not the scandal her family must proclaim it; that he would have gotten her out and safely on her way to space-end, regardless of difficulty, this very week; that—

"David, what is the matter?" she interrupted in a coldly controlled snap. "I know all of this. So do you, and you know I know."

"I—" he fell silent, bit his lip, looked away.

Shebat moved another step inward, letting one hand slide to touch his face, bringing the other up to parallel it. Somehow, she had become almost as tall as he. With gentle pressure she forced his head up, until his eyes met hers. "Softa, it is obvious that since I have come this far, I have forfeited second thoughts. I must have no regrets; you must help me."

He reached up and drew her hands down, holding them in his own. "Shebat, I can barely help myself. *Bucephalus . . .*" Horror spat from deep in his pupils, biting her volition, numbing it. "*Bucephalus* has suffered greatly. He is . . . this is . . . *may be* his last flight."

"We will retire him at space-end," Shebat soothed, not understanding. "He can train pilots, tell tales . . ."

"I am not at all sure that he, or I, will make it that far. And it is for that I apologize, in advance. For taking you from small peril into great danger. But I did not know . . . I did not realize, you must believe me—"

"I believe you, Softa," she assured him, crooning to mask her fear. "I believe you. We'll be safe and sound at space-end—"

Softa David Spry shook his head very slowly, unblinking. "Shebat, *Bucephalus* and I have a deep bond. So deep that his—difficulties—are to some degree my

own. . . . Things are vacuous, at times. It was that second
investigation that convinced the cruiser it was malfunc-
tioning. I could not tell him . . . *it,"* he corrected himself
savagely, "the truth. Larger things were at stake than the
sanity of one cruiser and one man. Now, with the guild
safe from incrimination by what we, *Bucephalus* and I,
knew and what we have done, there comes the account-
ing. *Bucephalus* is in no shape to enter sponge. I could not
assess the damage, earlier: I had to do this. Do you see? I
risked your life in the bargain. Now, I cannot promise that
Bucephalus, or myself, are going to make it; or making it,
continue to resemble in any way the personalities you
have known. . . ."

"Oh, Softa, no. No! You are wrong; I mean, you are all
right . . . just sit." She pulled at his hands, entwining
hers. They seemed frozen in her grip, like dead things.

"Oh, Softa, yes!" He laughed abruptly, then swallowed, then said:

"I dare not point out the various proofs of what I am
saying; I do not want to look so closely. I will do the best I
can. I am going to secure the tow, I am not sure why . . . I
would be better off to get you two aboard *Marada* and
take the *Bucephalus* to a more fitting end. We've both
always wondered where that black hole off Draconis's star
comes out. . . . Ssh, ssh. I'm drifting a little, but I know
it. . . ."

Shebat reached out to him another way. Some hybrid,
fear inspired, built half of dream dancing, half of what
was left of her enchanter's gift, she found and hefted and
cast over him. He calmed. His hands released hers. His
short nose wrinkled at the tingle of ozone upon the air.
Into his roiling thoughts she thrust with a dream of well-
being and surety, a scene built of the memories she found
in him to resemble space-end's port and him standing
there, before *Bucephalus,* with a smile and an outstretched hand. . . .

"I have one thing left to try," he admitted after an
interval, when the dream was gone. "I shall replace what I
may of the stolen memories, explain to the cruiser what
occurred, and why. I could not, before, lest they probe
him and come upon it."

"You do that. *I* will take the towline out and secure it."

"Sorry."

"I am a pilot, am I not? You have so declared me. It is my place. Yours is with *Bucephalus,* who needs you. We must hurry, you well know." She turned to go.

"Shebat, I cannot allow it."

"Softa, you are in no shape to disallow it. You yourself have said it."

He grunted, a soft guttural, half a moan, half a challenge.

She walked deliberately toward the threshold.

"I am coming with you," he said, as the doors drew back. "Suit up, little one, while I slow us down a bit. No use testing a three-mil suit at these speeds."

She hugged him, a spontaneous expression of fellowship that slid into something more, stretching time with its own pall of forgetfulness, so that her lips found his and all her flesh flared where she touched him.

He pushed her away abruptly. "Don't revenge yourself upon Marada with me," he muttered, as from behind in the empty corridor a pair of hands clapped thrice in hollow applause.

"Good for you, Pilot," Julian approved. "And now, if you two are quite finished, there is something I think Spry should see." The casual tone was belied by Julian's posture when Shebat whirled to regard him: straight and tense, with his belly sucked in tight.

Then the three of them dashed the ten meters to the control room at sprinters' pace.

Bucephalus looked like a creature aflame, all his displays humping and bucking from yellow to red. That no alarm had sounded, that no word had been whispered from cruiser to pilot, was a measure of the ship's debility. Alone and friendless, *Bucephalus* fought the demons of silicon nightmare.

Shebat sat at her console only a moment after Softa, who cursed and ordered in an undifferentiated tone, so that Shebat found herself squinting at nothing, concentrating on the sense of his words, while her hands of their own accord took David Spry's direction:

"Ready Mode B, autosynchronous phasing. Sponge entry ten seconds from NOW!"

"What about me going aboard *Marada?* The towline? There's no sponge-way here!"

"No time to explain. Magnetic grapples, on! *Marada's* path-coordinates on your scope, *now!*"

An insane, impossible torus of a course blipped on Shebat's screen, a hole to be carved from spacetime at nearly light-speed. She had time only to draw a breath before B-mode lit and the *Marada* began to institute his programmed functions in perfect accord with *Bucephalus,* to whom the empty cruiser was welded by invisible grapples which made of him the inner wheel of an axle whose path only the *Hassid* had ever dared describe before.

"But—" Shebat cried, objecting equally to the course and the grapple-mode, proscribed for entering sponge.

Then there was the *Marada's* shiver/touch/reassurance. And there was sponge.

If Spry had not been the most underrated pilot in the guild while holding first mastership, *Bucephalus* would have been lost in those initial instants. With all his years and all his might Spry fought to bring his irrationally struggling cruiser under control. In so doing, he had to dive deep into the paranoid deluge of unassignable data flowing forth from its every sensor. The *Bucephalus* was not built to handle multiple paradoxical inquiries simultaneously. Spry was not built to exist in the subconscious of silicon-based intelligence. During that time, when both systems exceeded their tolerance, identities melted, evaporated, blew away on gravity's wind.

Shebat Alexandra Kerrion sat straight up in her couch: all the red was gone from her copilot's instrumentation. She had turned her head, smiling, then frowning, then vaulting from her seat to prove with her hands what her eyes knew to be true and her mind knew to be true, what even Julian, hovering helplessly behind Softa's head, knew to be true so that his skin was pale as his hair:

Softa David Spry was insensible; consciousness was gone from him; his head lolled when Shebat stroked it. Softa was as empty as the helmet cast without notice on the deck beside his feet.

"Well," said Julian, exhaling like Chaeron did when he sought composure. "Now what, Lady Pilot?"

Though it had been *Bucephalus*'s console Shebat's hands had touched, it was to *Marada* their commands had gone; it was *Marada*'s solace she needed, his communion that *Bucephalus*'s plight had interrupted. She said:

"I must get to my ship. *Bucephalus* cannot be trusted: he cannot trust himself."

Julian's face worked. Then with an obvious effort, he stilled it, saying: "Of course, I understand," in a fatalistic murmur that made her know he read her heroism as perfidy.

Shebat turned the bracelet on her wrist, that Chaeron had given her, seeking composure in the coolness of its stones. It was difficult, more difficult than Softa's proficiency had ever whispered it might be, to speak and move and think about fleshly affairs while half of her resided in the cruisers' realm of consciousness. She remembered Marada's warnings, when she had sat for the first time in a cruiser and prattled to him unknowing of what she did. So it was that she snarled at Julian, hoping to make a quick end to his martyr's posturing:

"You understand? I truly doubt it. All you understand is your overriding concern for your own skin. You bravely sigh and say to me, 'Of course'! Of course I will maroon you in sponge in a helplessly crippled cruiser, you think! Well, I might have, were it only you, or were I a Kerrion in nature as well as name. But I am not: I cannot leave *Bucephalus* adrift in sponge: Spry's identity is too completely fused with his cruiser's."

"The trollop with the nerves of steel."

"Quiet, catamite. We are going to see if you are good for more than looking pretty and keeping your mother company. As I was saying, I cannot leave Softa, or *Bucephalus,* lost in sponge."

"Lost?" said Julian, his mobile lips taking a blue tinge.

"Lost. Softa was suited up because he did not dare use magnetic grappling while entering the sponge-way: its effects have never been determined. Then, when *Bucephalus* malfunctioned, he feared *not* using it, lest the ships be separated. Now, because of the grapples, not even *Marada* is sure where we might be. I have to go out there and secure a towline. Then I can control both ships from *Marada.* Leaving *Bucephalus* in command when he

might any moment initiate irrational action—" her voice
lowered, as if the *Bucephalus* slept some fevered sleep out
of which he might abruptly wake, "—is impossible, as is
switching him over to manual with half of Softa's mind
fused with him.

"So you see, I am going to give you a crash course in
copilotry and then I am going to suit up and . . ." Shebat
found difficulty even speaking those next words, which
described an action never undertaken in all the years of
sponge-pilotry. . . . "And then I am going to jump over
to *Marada*."

Even Julian knew what she was saying. "Through
sponge?"

"If it is possible."

"And if it not?"

"Who knows? I will leave your link with *Marada*
punched up until I have successfully made the crossing. If
I do not make it, it is up to you and *Marada* to bring Spry
to space-end."

There followed a mutual survey of the exigencies they
might face; a hurried construction of contingency plans
made over the copilot's console in the light of scintillant
indicator spill; a deep and awkward pause when all things
were done and said and a confirmation came to Julian by
eye and Shebat by mind that the *Marada* had matched
velocities with the *Bucephalus* and awaited. . . .

Press-sealing the final tab on her suit, Shebat sighed.
"You know what to do?"

Julian's eyes were paler than Chaeron's, like winter
water, so light that from the side they seemed to have no
color at all. "Not really. But let us proceed." He, too, had
donned a three-mil suit; its helmet lay beside Softa's on
the deck: one could in no way foresee what *Bucephalus*
might be likely to do. One could only prepare for the
worst. So armed, he straightened his shoulders and raised
his head high and smiled the smile with which Kerrions
had faced the task of surmounting impossible odds for
more than two hundred years. "You have my best wishes.
May you have also the Jesters' favor. . . ." He leaned
close, as if he might kiss her, noted her barely perceptible
flinch, clasped her hand instead. When he released her,
she went to Softa, brushed her lips against his forehead,

straightened his head against the padding, and turned away.

In what seemed like an eyeblink, she was in the outer hatch, alone in her suit with a coil of glass-line over her shoulder and her helmet on her head, sensing rather than hearing the air being drawn out of the little cubicle. She had no gravity-sled: its results in sponge could not be foretold. It was the slim glass-line cable which must be her life preserver in this awesome sea. One end of it was clipped to the suit's utility belt; the other she must secure to *Bucephalus* before diving into sponge. . . .

The port slid back, and she faced *Marada*, sixty meters away, port open welcomingly, and all the sponge between.

Shebat blinked, and blinked, and blinked again, her suited fingers going to her helmet as if she might brush away the prickling mist beyond it. Sponge's green was not the green of verdant earth or fecund sea, but that retina-tickling curtain that comes over all things when a sunbather enters a darkened house after lying long in brightest day.

Her hand, doing no service scratching at her helmet, went to the clip on the coil of glass-line, fastened there. With the other, she grasped the rungs spaced along the portside, and swung out beyond supergravity's tenuous field. Dangling amid numinous mists which no star's light seemed to penetrate, she felt for the recessed socket she sought in *Bucephalus*'s outer hull.

Finding it, she clumsily secured the cable. Her left hand, on the port handgrip, was grasping it so tightly she was afraid the ache would turn to numbness and she would find herself dangling at the end of the glass-line like some dinghy in *Bucephalus*'s wake.

But the hand did not betray her, the towline proved secure to her tugging. She swung back within the port and stood there, gasping, chest heaving, sweat running into her eyes, stinging them into blurriness. She stayed poised that way until her pulse was calmed, until her thighs ticced in readiness to jump, until she could read every number and letter scribed in *Marada*'s hull, an unwavering eternity away.

Then she uncoiled the millimeter-thick glass-line and

cast it before her into sponge. With a flat hand at either hatchside, she hesitated a few seconds more, long enough to whisper to the ship behind an uncertain miasmic veil of green: "Hold steady, *Marada*. Here I come."

Then she pushed away with her hands and out with her feet, into it.

There were colors she had not seen before; there were creatures like winged grotesques out of heraldry, but made of light; there was *Marada*'s comforting croon. Then there was a moment of horror, when she doubted whether her aim had been true enough, while strange sounds sighed in her ears as if sponge spoke to her just below audibility. She shuddered like a diver sensing sudden shallows ahead. She did not move to coil up the played line behind her: that was a last resort, should her drift take her near the ship's exhaust.

Distance waned between her and the *Marada*'s welcoming, open maw. Her mind began to jibber last-minute disasters, as if the final seconds of her leap were infinitely more dangerous than the first. Something would go wrong, some hand had come out of the numinous expanse of sponge at the last moment to pluck success from her grasp. She would faint; *Marada* would close his port too soon; all would be lost. Tears inundated her vision so that the hull markings ran together and she could not read them.

She squeezed her eyes shut.

When she opened them, she had only time to reach out and grab the handhold beside *Marada*'s port and pull herself aboard.

Aboard! Supergravity's tenacious embrace enfolded her, wedding her feet to the bulkhead. *Aboard!* A god's name long unuttered passed her lips, a thankful murmur tinged with disbelief: if He had helped her with the crossing, He had turned a deaf ear to her dream danced prayer for Softa. . . . Standing in *Marada*'s airlock was to have attained salvation, but for herself alone. Superstitious dread flooded her, welling up from her childhood, asking where her gratitude had fled.

But she answered back savagely that she would raise no paean of thanksgiving to unknowing Fate, who had driven her to the very precipice from which she had fallen. And so she came to meet the Lords of Cosmic Jest while standing in *Marada*'s open port, staring into the green-blue sheets drifting like fast-blown cirrus that was sponge.

"Damn you, Consortium. And you, Parma, my *father*."

An ear turned, which had no anvil nor stirrup.

But Shebat was full of the fury that follows upon release from peril, counting her "what-ifs" in dirge tempo while she swung out, secured the glass-line cable in its socket and swung back with no thought to what price clumsiness might now exact; with no tether other than her fingers' grip to hold her safe from sponge.

What if they were truly lost in sponge, as she had intimated to Julian, not merely temporarily off course?

What if Softa's mind never returned from its communion with *Bucephalus?* or his body failed? or starved?

What if Julian could not handle *Bucephalus?* What if she could not handle *Bucephalus* ?

"*I foresee no difficulty in that regard,*" interjected *Marada*'s voice in her inner ear, even as the hatch closed soundlessly. She could feel the kiss of air gushing around her. Red light flooded the chamber, counseling her to wait. Without Shebat doing more than raising a hand toward her brow, the emergency panel by the port's lock announced that the towline was activated: the two ships were bonded together now as one. To cement her comfort, the red pressure warnings went green, then turned amber; all of these before Shebat regained the power of speech.

Marada the cruiser's voice, in every inflection and in its very timber, had become exactly the same as Marada the man's.

Chapter Fourteen

When it became clear to Chaeron and Marada that Julian was aboard *Bucephalus*, and that *Bucephalus* had headed into sponge with *Marada* close behind, they called Valery up to the consul's turret.

Or rather, Chaeron did. Marada merely pushed his food perplexedly around his plate, watching Chaeron out of hooded eyes.

Chaeron, stroking one of the silver stallions who held leathern books proud upon his desk, muttered, "That little snot," in a tone that was a mixture of delight and disbelief.

"Surely you do not think Julian would do any such thing willingly?" Marada had to ask.

Chaeron's Ashera-eyes assessed Marada, found him amusing. His smile flared out. "Brother, your lack of guile is not a fable, then? No, I suppose not. Well, then, tell me this is no formal inquiry, and I will give you my opinion. Otherwise, I think I will have to ask you to leave while I conduct *my* inquiry."

"In other words, you *do* think he would. . . ."

"Yes, I do. Are you staying, or leaving?"

"I will stay," drawled Marada, a disdainful boon to one unworthy, "and abide by your conditions. Poor Parma . . ." he shook his head. "The Jesters assigned him a rotten lot."

"Speak for yourself," snapped Chaeron. His hand closed around one silver bookend, hefted it imperceptibly for a long instant while temptation assailed him. The dour countenance of his brother, ever seeking after Truth and Righteousness when not even Order could be found in the five eternities, made him want to strike out. Nothing less would change that face, it seemed. But he could not do that. So he said:

"Why should it surprise you, if I am right and Julian has fled to become a pilot? You would have, if Parma had not given in to your demands. He would not be so kind to Julian, who is out of my mother's womb. He does not hide his feelings about our mother, or yours. It is our taint—you are exempt from it. As you are exempt from all other considerations of wrongdoing."

Marada's chin jutted behind his beard. He half rose, then sat back again. "We will see what Valery has to say." The groove between his eyebrows grew deep, spawned a twin.

But when Valery came up, it was clear to both brothers that he had not known that Julian was missing. It was obvious, both by the blanching of his hatchet face and the boneless way he sank down among the sofa's chocolate cushions, that he had not been involved.

What was also obvious was the depth of Valery's concern.

Seeing the slowness with which color returned to the countenance of the second bitch of Kerrion space, Marada learned more than he wished to know about the relationship between the pilot and his little brother. A decade separated him from Julian, but it was not the years, rather it was what Chaeron had said—that thing which none of them had ever mentioned, which all recognized as unmentionable—that had made the gap unbreachable.

Marada looked at Valery Stang, trying to remind himself that the man was very probably up to his cruiser-rings in this whole execrable affair. But he could not summon the detachment which befitted an arbiter in such a moment. His palms felt hot and his neck also. He wanted to berate Chaeron for allowing a relationship to develop between the boy and a man easily Marada's age. But he could not even do that.

Outwardly, at least, he must maintain his objectivity.

He must be alert for clues as to the actual nature of these shrouded events, for the first ray of light to illumine the horizon beyond which they lurked.

Yes, outwardly, he must maintain himself impeccably neutral. Though he was attached by Parma's command to Chaeron under a mandate of marshal law, though sooner than might have been dreamed in the worst of nightmares, he would be shipping out to wreak havoc upon another habitational sphere, he must be unimpeachable. He chuckled, so that Valery raised his head, staring up from under his lank hair.

Marada looked away. Already, he could find occasion to fault himself. He must find no more. He had done damage not only to his wife's family, but his own—and even to a stranger: Shebat. A surge of compassion overswept him, bringing him to the verge of tears, where everything seemed magnified and distorted before his eyes, and he found need to excuse himself, to seek the evanescent comfort of solitude in the consul's bathroom.

There, he exhaled a shaky breath. If he had craved the company of his own kind, he would never have become a pilot. If he understood them, he never would have become an arbiter. Being both, he was as alienated among them as Shebat Kerrion must be, and more tortured by his isolation.

He lay his head against the mirror that backed the door, so that he could see nothing but the mist his breath made on the glass. War. Betrayal. Destruction. Somehow, when he went out again to face his brother of the flesh and his brother of the guild, he must have resigned himself to what was to come, so that no one could see his distress.

He peered a long time into the mist, like anemic sponge upon the mirror's glass, before he found a way to resolve his problem. Then, saying a subvocal farewell to the *Hassid* and all those cruisers behind her in whose company he had found his resolution, if not his solution, he went out to the men much calmed, his eyes like deep caves and his settling final as a landslide.

Both the consul and the dark pilot noted the change in him; neither divined its source.

Valery, who was by Marada's recommendation in a

position to work against Kerrion interests, recalled that fact.

Chaeron, who knew Marada better, saw a confrontation brewing, greater than the wholesale destruction of the entire complement of Labayan habitational spheres. With a long, slow breath blown out through his nose, he gestured to the desk on which now sat a decanter and three glasses, and suggested a toast.

"To what?"

"To Kerrion space," the consul answered his brother.

"I'll drink to that," Valery acceded heartily.

Though they toasted, no one's glass touched any other, a function, Chaeron found need to assume, of Chance, or her stewards, the Lords of Cosmic Jest.

That evening still haunted Chaeron Ptolemy Kerrion's thoughts five days later as he led his force toward an unsuspecting Shechem. He had been over it more times than he had crossed the threshold to his cabin, more times than he had eaten. More hours had gone into pondering it than the entire battle plan in which he was about to engage. But his cogitation had borne no fruit, unless it was that Marada was mad, which was no news to Chaeron.

The other incident he could not help recall was that moment when Marada had averred that the ships would never fire on one another, and Parma had caught Chaeron's eye, and shaken his head, and gritted his teeth.

Well, they were going to find out whether or not the ships were as crazy as his brother—no, that was not fair. The only security measures he could take were two contingency plans to remove Marada's cruiser from the engagement, should he demonstrate the slightest irrationality. So far, the arbiter had stayed within acceptable limits of Kerrion behavior. As long as he continued to do so, Chaeron would continue to stretch his forbearance.

He was not unaware that he was anticipating the chance to slap Marada in a nice, soft, restraining suit . . . it made him even more careful not to do so prematurely.

Chaeron did not believe that the ships would not fire on one another, although before they left Draconis, Valery had confided to him that there was a possibility of such a

thing happening. But Valery had also pointed out that
Shechem Authority was not a cruiser; that Shechem
Authority had fired on *Hassid;* and that it was more likely
that the pilots would hesitate over their orders than that
the cruisers would.

Before that, he had not credited the possibility Marada
had voiced as more than proof of his brother's imbalance.

Upon hearing it, he had gone to Parma, who had
squinted, pulled his hand down over his lips, and reminded him that all pilots were mad.

There was one benefit: those two days before debarkation had brought him closer to his father than he had
thought possible. Then he had boarded his own cruiser,
Danae, nodded to Valery, and in less time than it took to
walk around Draconis's level two hundred, he was cast
into the void.

In his wake, behind *Danae,* were three other cruisers.
One of them was *Hassid.*

At *Hassid*'s helm sat Marada, piloting two of his
guildbrothers and ten Kerrion intelligencers through Labayan space. Patched in to *Hassid*'s console, the arbiter's
cube queried and colored, its investigation uninterrupted
by decree of martial law or by distance intervening.
Neither space nor sponge could contravene its search.
Ineluctable as the blue-shifting of stars before a racing
cruiser, inevitable as the long-tailed red-shifting behind,
the cube considered. It considered on its own; it considered in concert with the entirety of cruiser-consciousness;
it considered with a multitude of data pools, wherever
they touched cruiser-awareness.

Otherwise, the *Hassid*'s cargo was no different than
that of any of the other cruisers readying to assault
Shechem on *Danae*'s command, if one were to discount
the differences between Marada and other men.

Chaeron was not discounting that difference, though he
tried valiantly to manage that very thing, out of duty and a
knowledge that any word from him would be taken as
evidence of the extent of his own bias and bulwark the
legend of the brothers' rivalry.

Still, he could not pierce the shadow of madness that he
had marked in Marada's remote squint.

Also, still, the damnable arbiter's cube rode along with

them into battle, if battle there was to be over Shechem, filled with plant and beast and all manner of flying things.

If Lorelie was fabled, Shechem was enfamed. It would be a pity and a waste to destroy an abode of beauty elsewhere extinct. Shechem was a repository of uniqueness, her denizens preserved nowhere else in the Consortium. Or such was the Labayas' boast.

Chaeron's determination was to acquire without damage the Labayas' home platform, all its gardens undisturbed. To that end, he had a plan.

Actually, he had a modification of his father's orders. Should he fail, Parma would not be long noticing the deviation. Its effects would be too far-reaching.

Chaeron Kerrion muttered to himself and stirred on his acceleration couch in *Danae*'s control room. He was not alone, even there. He felt the invasion of his privacy, a dull throbbing, like a tooth with an exposed nerve. *Danae* had been refitted, like the three other cruisers pacing her. It had been done in the two days necessary to repair *Hassid*'s damages, and it had not been done well. Luxury cruiser to troop carrier was an alchemy impossible: bunks had been secured in each of her three cabins; four men were billeted in each. Valery was sleeping at his console. Chaeron had preferred the acceleration couch beside his pilot, and the silence necessarily imposed by sponge, to the camaraderie of the idle pilots or the intense, slippery-eyed gaming of the intelligencers.

But even Valery's familiar company was wearing, so long, so close. Chaeron longed to lock himself in the cargo bay, stretch out on the bulkhead in warm darkness, and think on all the things recently occurred, occurring, and about to occur; to punch "pause" in the procession of time, not simply alter its rate of passage. Pushed more deeply into his separate flesh by the constant company of his fellows, locked unrelievedly within his own mind by the removal of his person from range of his consulting data pools, he was discomforted in small but unrelenting ways which conjured up an irritation that increasingly plagued him.

He could find no way to scratch his subliminal itch or to ease his dull ache. He waxed acerbic, then abrupt, then sullen in the two days it took them to reach Marada's discovery, the Hassidic Corridor. As his brother had promised, the corridor was brief: a three-week trip shortened to one day five hours from sponge-hole to sponge-hole.

They had been two additional days crawling toward Shechem at less than half the speed of light. The paradoxical nature of spacetime's variable rates made it faster for them to travel slowly: if they had come in at the speed Marada's *Hassid* had torn out of Shechem, to those on the habitational sphere it would have appeared that they were traveling much more slowly, thus the Labayans would have had even longer to prepare than they might if all subterfuge failed utterly and Shechem Authority was monitoring their approach as what it was—the approach of four cruisers; instead of what it looked—the approach of a not improbably large cloud of cosmic debris.

Cloaked in sprays of magnetically shepherded "chaff," they would by now be appearing on Shechem Authority's sensors. The sensors would read the multitude of mixed-metal particles shrouding the ships, but the ships might escape identification, or be misidentified as part of a natural phenomenon. Or not: there was no way to be sure.

If there were ships in their immediate vicinity, or Shechem sent some out to check, what would be seen by eye would vary greatly from the electronics' readings.

So Chaeron watched the wide range scanners for signs of Labayan cruisers, though Valery beside him needed no help, was in fact, by the displays on his instrumentation, doing that very thing himself.

Chaeron touched his copilot's console, flipping the monitor off.

Valery, taking note, stretched hugely in *Danae*'s dark master's couch. "Hungry? If we can't see 'em now, we won't see 'emfor a while." He unfolded himself from the couch, then lookedback inquiringly when Chaeron made no move to follow."Chaeron?"

"Where do you think they are?" the consul murmured, staring at the blank screen.

"On their way to Draconis, probably. Which is all the better for us, since they can't get there before we get back. Let's eat. You have to feed a brain for it to work right."

"I do not like this one bit."

"You don't like it? It's your engagement. . . . You act like I thought it up myself!"

"Easy, Valery. It's not my engagement and I don't like it, but I'm not blaming you."

Valery's rings tinkled as he shook his head. "Better not," he growled. "Ever since that damn party of yours, something's been eating at you."

"It's not every man that becomes a husband and then a deserted husband in less than a week . . . it's not easy on my self-esteem," Chaeron fenced, trying to assure Valery once more that he saw no blame for his pilot in what had passed. "Bring me something back. I'm going to stay here and revel in the fact that for the first time in much too long I won't be able to hear anyone else breathing."

"Umn," grunted Valery, and stalked out.

"Thou protesteth too much," murmured Chaeron to the doors hissing shut in Valery's wake.

The man was seriously abrading Chaeron's nerves. It was not the first time Chaeron had heard conjecture expressed as fact from Valery; he was one of that group of pilots who insisted that the cruisers and the data pools and the smallest wrist communicator had something in common, some shared awareness which made them all privy to one another despite space and sponge. Chaeron, well grounded in the physical sciences, knew that position to be indefensible, that theory to be without substantive evidence. Maybe the Shechem fleet had been dispatched to Draconis on a mission like unto his own, maybe not. There was no way of knowing. Not unless one was privy to Labayan intelligence, which Chaeron had satisfied himself long ago that Valery was not.

If Selim Labaya had had the audacity to dispatch ships in strength to Draconis, they would meet with a score of his father's cruisers, waiting at the sponge-hole customarily traveled when Draconis-bound from Shechem.

Customarily: i.e., before Marada. Chaeron flipped the switch that activated a com-line between *Danae* and *Hassid*.

"Yes?" came a clipped, irritated response up through the console's speakers; the monitor stayed blank, noncommittal.

"Just called to say hello," Chaeron said, laying his head back and closing his eyes, trying to visualize Marada's face and match it to what the voice revealed.

"Hello." The voice revealed nothing.

"Valery thinks Selim Labaya's sent a force out to Draconis."

"Maybe."

Chaeron took a deep breath, expelled it while counting slowly. "You think not?"

"Do *you* think I'm psychic?"

"Just curious as to your opinion."

"I'll try to contain my astonishment. Lords, Chaeron, do you want something? You cannot be lonely, with a full complement of your favorite goons aboard. I am busy, if you are not. As for whether Labaya sent ships after me, that is Parma's problem."

"I do want something, Marada. I want to change some of the details of the upcoming engagement, and I want you not to interfere."

"*Slate,*" said Marada, dryly. "I should not have to remind you that I'm running a cube; only the presentation of its results are deferred. I have to register an objection, obviously."

"Before you've heard what I'm going to do?"

"Even so."

"Then object. But I am in command here and you will take my orders and obey them exactly, or I will consider you in mutiny and take immediate action. Is that clear?"

"Yes, that is quite clear. Anything else?"

Chaeron could not resist the temptation of being first to break the circuit.

When he turned from the console, he saw Valery leaning back against the control room's doors with a wistful smile on his sharp face so that he looked like a warship's grinning prow. "I wish I could do that," Valery teased. "But it was almost as good, watching you."

"You shouldn't have been listening."

Valery handed Chaeron a meal packet. Chaeron hefted it and put its squishy warmth on the console.

"When are you going to give your 'corrections'?"

Chaeron found himself chuckling, so delicately had Valery stressed that last word: corrections. And in his flood of good feelings he answered Valery that he could not do so until he was sure beyond a doubt that no aggressive action would be forthcoming from Shechem.

With a quizzical look, the pilot tore open his packet with sharp teeth and, holding it high, squeezed the contents into his mouth until only an empty, greenish sack was left. That he crumpled and tossed into the narrow refuse chute.

"How long until you're sure? We're within strike range. They surely would have done something by now . . . you want to wait until you're *in* there?"

"Don't push it, Valery. It is certainly odd that we are so close and they have not even queried us, let alone sent out a welcoming committee. It is too odd."

"You think it's a trap?"

"I did not say that. Perhaps they are all asleep. Or very stupid. I do not know. . . . I am concerned that if something untoward happens, that it cannot be said that *we* were all asleep, or very stupid."

Valery muttered something, eased into the pilot's couch with an automatic swiveling of his head that circuited every display monitor festooning the *Danae*'s circular waist.

"What?"

"Nothing," murmured the pilot, reminding himself once more how testy *Danae*'s owner had become, wishing he could call back the grumble of exasperation that had escaped his lips, drawing Chaeron's attention. That was the last thing he needed, more acidic scrutiny when he must be as unremarkable as X-rays to the naked eye. He held his breath, pulse pounding, in the silent space after his disclaimer, a space which could turn barbed and baleful in a moment, whose phantom thorns even now pricked his nerves. . . .

"Sorry," Chaeron sighed, and lay back against the couch's headrest so that his pulse ticked visibly in his throat.

Amazing, was Chaeron. At all times impenetrable; at any time incendiary beneath his smile. That eternal grin was the worst of it, supremely appealing, embraceable, elusive as sponge. Not like Julian, whose face was a window into his soul. Julian. . . . Valery squirmed in his seat, adrift on the sea of alternatives under a featureless sky showing no hint of north. Julian was with Softa, whatever that could be construed to mean; and with Shebat. What was Spry doing? More to the point, what was he, Valery, doing?

Looking for a break in the clouds, was what: a parting of the mists that would let him chart a course. Damn Baldy, with contingency plans bristling out from him like a power station's solar collectors; and Chaeron, who had not the grace to be detestable, but must fascinate and obsess where other men need simply breathe. . . . The knowledge of what the consul was about did not protect Valery from it, or even attenuate Chacron's effect. It was an attribute of his presence, a thing as much a part of him as his ruddy mane or his sleek manliness which seemed devalued rather than cultivated, saving him from prettiness and pretentiousness both.

Valery checked his thought, opened his eyes, and turned his head toward Chaeron: "Sorry, I didn't hear."

"I said, be sure to keep monitoring my brother, alert for any deviation from course. We cannot be sure of him." This was said with a mere turning of head, so that his cheek lay against the headrest, one eyebrow slightly raised in emphasis.

"Yes, sir." Valery had intended to do so, would have done so. He awaited only an opening, a moment to act for the guild, to whom Marada the pilot and the memory of his *Hassid* posed almost as great a threat as the missing cruiser who bore the Kerrion prodigal's name. Or so the second bitch of Kerrion space insisted on proclaiming, both to himself and to Baldy, who was half-convinced that any further struggles were useless in the face of what had already been revealed. Parma, Baldy had wagered, merely awaited a convenient moment to arrest them all.

Whether or not that was true, Valery had argued, a cruiser was a cruiser and in the war of emancipation to come (whether sooner or later), the more cruisers they had, the better. To that end he labored, as he had for a decade. He had a multitude of schemes, each bearing diverse fruit. The best was the acquisition of not only *Danae* and *Hassid,* but the cruisers flanking them, also.

"Here's what I want to do . . ." Chaeron began, wiping everything but incredulity from his pilot's mind.

In *Hassid,* Marada found Chaeron's "corrections" no less astounding.

He spoke them over the arbitrational cube, and its flush deepened.

Chaeron's stern demand for the capitulation of Shechem rang out through each Kerrion cruiser and through space toward the Labayan family sphere just ahead of a negative hydrogen ion particle beam which in a tenth of a second disrupted every electronic device in its path.

The original plan had called for the deployment of Kerrion cruisers so as to immobilize the whole of Shechem, two cruisers to a hemisphere. Chaeron had altered not only Parma's strategy in execution, but in feasibility: he kept the other cruisers in tight formation, not encircling Shechem. Likewise, the disruption was not complete, but selectively circumscribed. The meaning of this must be as clear to Selim Labaya as it seemed to Marada: his brother Chaeron would grant no second chance, simply overpowering Shechem's computerized defenses. No, he would not. Instead, he would increase the power flowing to the cruisers' brace of turrets, destroying the verdant sphere as offhandedly as he might a migrant asteroid headed into heavily trafficked space.

Marada was incensed. The cube on his console reflected his ire that no clemency shrouded this potent aggression.

But Shechem itself was still. No word came up from the leaves and glens, no silvery spacefish darted out to inspect them or obstruct them.

Shechem did not even quiver.

A hard-fingered hand closed on Marada's heart, a dreadful thumping began somewhere in his inner ear. Trepidation jumped for his throat, closed its teeth there. He saw Madel's swollen-lidded eyes, reddened with weeping, her purpled mouth stretched fat in its efforts to hold in grief. He saw Selim Labaya's grizzled head bowed and shaking. And he saw his son, who neither kicked nor flailed, but lay unmoving, swaddled in some different reality only he could discern.

Marada shook his head savagely, and growled, so that *Hassid* offered a systems check: all was well. She displayed beauteous Shechem, like a carbochon sapphire twirling to catch the light, pendant on some invisible string. Marada was not eased. She displayed a multitude of views not discernible to the naked eye, showing that life, that of machine and man both, still thrived within its beryl shell. She detailed its damaged electronics, and what areas were yet uninterrupted. Marada's distress, instead of being eased, became more pronounced.

A magnetic aiming device, which guided the beams from each ship in concert, flickered: *ready*. Marada, reluctant, would not eye the targeting screen, but looked at his hands, gone white and red and greenish-yellow, sparkling with moisture. On the padded console, they trembled.

A static burst rustled on the com-line; then a voice came up from the habitational sphere. It was a faint voice, a thick voice, a voice whose owner was barely in control of his tongue, so that Marada in *Hassid* and Chaeron and Valery in *Danae* and every man in every cabin in the four Kerrion cruisers leaned forward, staying breath and motion, to make out what the voice of Shechem authority had to say:

"Kerrion Five, this is Shechem Authority, or at least it was. . . . Come on in, we're not in any shape to stop you . . . it's rather a relief . . . after everything else . . . we . . . (static)*-struct you.* (Static)*-render. Entry-coordinates as you like 'em, we can't do anything much with what you've left us, just open the door. . . . Shechem Authority out . . .* (Static).*"*

"What in the womb of Chance is going on?" breathed Marada, whose flat palms pressed gently over his eyes, as if in the darkness so constructed he could find shelter.

"We are queuing up for docking procedures," replied *Hassid*, gently, to make him smile.

Failing in that, the cruiser growled subliminally as cruisers do when their outboards malfunction, growled so softly that only another cruiser might hear.

Danae heard; she was in touch with each subordinated

cruiser, alerted by her pilot to be especially cognizant of what was going on in *Hassid*. She did not relay that information to her outboard, however, for Valery himself was acting as strangely as *Hassid*'s pilot. Instead, she sent a trill of condolence to her sister cruiser, and by that means felt better herself.

It was an ugly business, attacking helpless data pools, unarmed communications nets, life-support systems and quiescent defenses that were in no way threatening. These would not have waxed threatening, no matter what the outboards controlling the cruisers' death-spitting turrets had done. But *Danae* could not object—she could volunteer no such information to her pilot: Valery kept strictly to business with his ship. There was little affection offered by her outboard, little enough of anything . . . it was like having half an outboard, or so the others said. Valery, though an outboard of high repute, was cold, distant, unwilling or unable to enter fully into communion as did Marada with *Hassid*. Yet, *Danae* lived to please him, to shiver under his touch, to surge and sport on the tundra between the stars. Perhaps Valery was right, to keep so distant. At least, it was that distance that allowed *Danae* to offer condolences to *Hassid*, who suffered her outboard's every distress.

It was better thus.

It was good to ship point into Shechem, perfectly, with all the others streaming out behind. It was good to nestle up to the dock, to be grasped in supergravity's dreamy embrace, to spiral inward, then inward again toward Shechem's heart without ever once descending from the pinnacle of precisely executed commands. Without flaw, the four cruisers made dock and slip in Shechem. Under *Danae*'s aegis, each had come to safe harbor. The cruisers purred to each other, sweet wordless praises dear and warm.

They had not been powered down; they would not be. Through their aft cameras, they watched the scramble of intelligencers out of their hatches, the slow, ragged promenade of Shechem officials toward them along the slipbay.

The cruisers did not need the reactions of their pilots, not Chaeron's open puzzlement, not Marada's grinding of teeth and cracking of knuckles, to tell them that something was wrong among the outboards of Shechem.

In the brightly lit slipbay, preternaturally quiet, half the Kerrion force awaited its Labayan welcoming committee. As a precaution, Chaeron had ordered the relief pilots and five intelligencers to remain aboard each ship. As a second precaution, he stood close beside his brother Marada, in case of the unforeseeable.

Marada knew, by then, what was to Chaeron yet a mystery. He knew it by the presence of certain faces in their welcoming committee and by the absence of others. He waited only to hear with his ears what his heart told him, so that the hand squeezing it would leave off, so that spiny conjecture would be replaced with certainty, and some relief gained in that exchange.

Not caring any longer for protocol, he walked forward to meet the captain of the Shechem Guard, whose face was without expression but whose shoulders told the tale, bent and bowed by the weight of words yet unspoken.

Chaeron, after a moment's hesitation and a second moment quelling his intelligencers, went after his brother, gained his side.

"Wait," urged Chaeron.

"Why?" snapped Marada from bearded lips that hardly moved.

And then there was no time for argument.

The Shechem Guard, each in green, undulant dragons rampant over their breasts, stopped before them, so that both Chaeron and Marada must stop, so that there was ample time to notice that every dragon's head had been sewn over with black thread.

"Marada," said the captain, extending his hand while his chin pulled back to make dimpled ripples of flesh between it and his tight uniform collar. There was no accusation in the speaking of the arbiter's name, but there was some emotion . . . resignation? . . . relief? "It's all yours," the man continued, "just treat my people well, if you can."

"I can." Marada assured him, blackly. "This is my brother, Chaeron Ptolemy Kerrion, consul of Draconis, leader of this punitive expedition and warlord of Kerrion space."

The sneer in Marada Kerrion's voice was only partially hidden. The captain said, stone-faced: "Do you want to see the bodies?"

"What?" It was Chaeron who exploded.

Marada said, "Yes," quietly, calmly, as if he had known all along.

The captain answered the consul's question: "Suicides, sir. The . . . Labaya's daughter went first, then her father when he discovered it, then . . . well, you'll see it, sirs. They're the only two that matter, aren't they?" The question was rhetorical, the captain's eyes were ice. The blood of Selim Labaya flowed in his veins, as well as showed in his face. He was polite, restrained, dignified as best could be under the circumstances, trying to pave the way to later negotiate good terms of surrender for his people.

"When?" Marada asked, sharply.

"About the time your ships entered tracking range, sirs."

Marada Kerrion whirled on his heel and looked Chaeron Kerrion up and down very slowly, his fingers lacing and unlacing behind his back. No word was exchanged that the captain heard in that interval punctuated only by the *crack!, crack!* of the arbiter's knuckles.

More than knuckles would crack before this day was over, someone of the guard whispered too loudly. In their ranks there swelled an explosive scuffling which quickly subsided, so that by the time Kerrion eyes disengaged the one from the other and turned back upon the collected guard, no sign of disturbance was visible.

Disturbance was exceedingly visible some little while later, as Marada and Chaeron Kerrion stood alone in Shechem's vast funerary hall, the only living creatures under its fan-vaulted ceiling, surrounded by plinths on which a dozen Labayas lay in cold, pale state.

The chill was palpable, befogging the ceiling's height and wisping in its corners.

"Life is fleeting; death is mist," Chaeron muttered, and

from the same poet: "My fine words are full of barbs."

"Get out of here," gritted Marada.

"My duty is clear: to support you in your grief. I would not want to come back and find you have chosen a vacant bier for yourself." It was meant as humor, a teasing reminder that Chaeron knew that no love had sprouted between Marada and his newly departed spouse, Madel.

But Marada snarled a wordless sound, sending a stare with it so icy that the room suddenly seemed warm: perspiration sprung through Chaeron's mil to glitter upon his skin. Selim Labaya's famous frigid glare was no more glacial than that blighting promissory glance.

They stood between Selim Labaya's corpse and that of his daughter. Madel's deformities were hidden. Supine in flowing robes, she seemed whole, if not beautiful. And whole she might be, somewhere else among the five eternities, if the mystics could be believed. One thing was sure: she was no longer in the body laid out so artfully before them. Marada had seen death before, seen how it emptied the husk of flesh. As before, he was thrown struggling into the maw of the incomprehensible: the person he had known was something different from the leavings so carefully arranged to mock life. Life, by its absence, made known its separateness from the mechanism of flesh. Madel's slight corpse was a cast-off gown, full of nothingness.

"We fool ourselves, thinking we can rationally know the universe, when we cannot even discern the nature of being alive." *Being* alive, it was inevitable that he proclaim what every man proclaims when he is confronted with an emptied receptacle of life.

"By the Jesters, Marada, you did not give a fart about her while she lived." Chaeron's arms opened, gestured widely, to embrace not only the dead but the fecund expanse of Shechem.

"Be silent, or get out. What is not my fault here, is yours."

"Fault? I see no fault, or reason to seek to find any."

"That is the nature of your illness, and why I must prescribe a cure."

"You threaten me?"

"You do not mistake me."

They stood opposed, one with hands on hips and the other with hands clenched behind, paler than the corpses flanking them like some macabre garden. Marada continued:

"You forced this, with your arbitrary 'corrections,' making Labaya think you meant annihilation here."

"*You* forced it, with your shortsighted passion and your spoiled sperm."

Marada shook his head slowly to and fro, as if he could not believe what he had heard. He stepped back a pace from his half-brother, promising: "We shall see." Then he turned on his heel and left the hall.

Chaeron watched him go, unmoving. Then, raking a trembling hand through auburn curls, he approached Selim Labaya's bier. "I am sorry, old tiger, for the row. My father will be saddened, to lose so beloved an adversary." He spread his hands, wet his lips, and reached out a finger that never completed its intention, but pulled back to huddle close to its own warm flesh.

Chaeron had respected the old consul general more than anyone save his father. But the old ones all had this primitive penchant for drama, this elevation of emotion above logic. Marada had it, too, and its danger was incalculable: not even the twelve displayed bodies spread before him described its extent.

Chaeron would have gladly surrendered his honor, wherever it happened to dwell; his Kerrion heritage; thrown his tongue and right hand into the bargain, for even an additional day between him and a cold slab in anyone's morgue. He could not comprehend *choosing* death, since death offered man no choice. He peered long into Selim Labaya's sleeping countenance, wondering what had prompted the man to give the customs of life so much meaning that he would die to serve them, when death acknowledged no custom nor life, let alone choices.

He was shivering when he left there, shuddering so that he locked his jaw tight to still it. It was not the physical cold that shook him like a child, but the lack of breath in Selim Labaya's nose, the failure of his chest to rise and fall. Chaeron had never loved his life so well as then. The affection for his own flesh which welled up in him obscured almost all else. But not quite everything else: he worried the possibility of being incriminated by Marada's unbalanced passion for justice, and though his scrutiny was exhaustive, he could not find any glimmer of blame that he might own. Selim Labaya had committed his suicide upon the suicide of his daughter, at about the same time Chaeron had been forming up his four cruisers behind their mask of chaff. Or earlier. It did not matter which: he was inculpable by long, salvational minutes. This was not his doing, not caused by his improvisation on Parma's battle plan. Probably, it had nothing to do with Parma's dispatch of cruisers to Shechem. Probably, it was what he had said so impoliticly to Marada: the girl's inability to face the imperfect nature of her child, magnified by postpartum depression and the flight of her husband from her side.

Who could blame her? The child was defective; her husband had deserted her; her father had launched an attack on the father of her child. . . . Women, Chaeron well knew, lived in a separate reality that only occasionally merged with that experienced by men. There was one thing to be said for Madel which no one had said, but which Chaeron—exiting the vault into warmth and light and the company of his intelligencers and the Shechem Guard but not his brother—found somehow mitigating when he said it to himself: she had not involved her child, nor decided for it; there was no tiny sepulchre, no eleven-day-old corpse swathed in interment robes.

Chaeron shrugged death aside, asked the young Labayan captain where Marada had gone, though he knew the answer.

"To see his son, sir."

"Take me there."

"He left orders to the contrary, sir."

"He is my subordinate," Chaeron snapped. The man had no choice but to obey.

What they found upon reaching the Labayas' residence was a melee of green-uniformed men running hither and thither, which wiped away Chaeron's awe of the botanical gardens and the wide-stepped residence as if it had never been.

As crisis quickened his thoughts, throwing off the

languor in which morbidity had draped them, Chaeron called for Valery.

An intelligencer answered: "He had to go back to the *Danae,* some minor malfunction. You know those relief pilots, they don't want to touch anything if they don't have to . . . bad protocol, or something."

"Umn. Get him back here. What's going on?"

No one knew who could be found to question. As quickly as the flurry of men had blown out of the residence hall and down its steps, they had vanished.

When the last step had been climbed and two men, one Kerrion, one Shechem staff, had been dispatched to find the cause of the commotion, Chaeron found out.

It was the captain who had first greeted them who came rapidly down the elegant hall, who stopped at Chaeron's sharp order but did not approach, who answered laconically when Chaeron strode up and demanded to know what was amiss: "Sir, I am not sure how to tell you this. . . . The arbiter has relieved you of your command, and—"

Deep in his throat, Chaeron growled that he did not recognize his brother's authority, was himself empowered by his father to assume full control of *any* situation which might develop here.

The captain, who looked more like Selim Labaya as a youth than Selim Labaya probably had, waggled his head, a sour grin on his fat, full-featured face: "I thought as much. Well, sir, you and your brother are putting me in a difficult position." The captain paused, provisionally enthralled by the possibility of using the division between the two brothers against them. But it was not to be; there was no hope. No ship had escaped the debilitation of Kerrion particle beams, aimed unerringly. All were docked that were close enough to have been called in for the funeral. "However, I can take you to your brother, and perhaps you two can decide who it is between you that I am supposed to consider my commander pro tem."

There was a twinkle in the slitted, pale eyes that Chaeron did not understand until he saw Marada Seleucus Kerrion sitting on a bed of pink silk, toeing furrows in a plush, white rug. Beside the bed, by his black-clad knee, was a bassinette fitted with an intravenous feeder and elimination tubes. Like Marada's black-and-reds, the life-support capabilities of the tiny bed were dissonant to the pastel repose of the suite.

Even more dissonant was the soft wailing coming through a closed door. The keening was not yet resigned, but punctuated with moans and soft screams and grunts like wounded animals', and of such profusion that Chaeron was sure that more than one throat provided its source.

He moved closer, across the thick carpet, his steps soundless. He sensed rather than saw the captain fall back and station himself near the closed door. Still he approached his brother, who did not look up, but studied his boot toe furrowing the carpet.

Chaeron wondered why Marada's shoulders hung so dejectedly, why his chest rose and fell so shallowly, why his eyes never raised.

Then he saw, as he came close, that there was no infant lying in the pink and white cradle, that the glucose mixture meant to sustain life dripped slowly onto satin sheets, turning them grayish yellow.

His toes must have come into Marada's field of view. The arbiter looked up. His teeth bared like a silent-roaring lion, bright among the dark hairs of his beard. The grin of hatred faded slowly, but above it dark eyes promised Armageddon.

"You have heard?"

"That you think you can supplant me, I have heard. Nothing more."

"What use can you make of my son?" Marada leaned back, then, on his elbows, speaking tonelessly. "You are wrong if you think I can be influenced."

"Lords, you are a true lunatic. What are you talking about? Where is the boy?"

"Don't play innocent with me. *Hassid* was not powered down, you know. We have film of *your* pilot going aboard the *Danae* with a small, swaddled bundle. We have slated records of Valery's orders to the other Kerrion cruisers . . . *your* orders, so he proclaimed, and so it was slated. We have all we need. You are under arrest."

Chaeron sat down, very slowly on the floor, folding his

legs around him like a deflating doll. "What are you talking about?" But by then his reason had begun to function. "The ships are gone?"

"What I am talking about is your complicity with the guild. Yes, as you know very well, the ships are gone, all but *Hassid,* who insists on my verification. And my son is gone. What I want to know is *where?* And *why?"*

"Look, dear brother, I know you are grieving, and I know you and I don't get along. But for the family's sake, will you not put this blame-placing aside for the moment? I can answer both of your questions without trouble, though I was not involved. So could you. I will maintain my command of this situation until a less-prejudiced authority than yourself examines the data, at which time I will not demand that your license be pulled, using these misjudgments as sufficient cause, *only because you* are *my brother.*

"Where they have gone is to the same place the *Marada* went when it disappeared. *Why* this thing has occurred is to lure you after them. If you are a fool even greater than I think you to be, you will follow. They left you a ship for that reason. Even I, no pilot, know that if Valery wanted *Hassid,* he could have taken her out of individual mode. *Then* you would not know *where,* or *why,* or even *who.* That you *do* know, means that Valery wants you to know; that you can pursue, means that he invites pursuit. If I were you, I would sit right here in Shechem."

"I imagine you would. I am going."

"Then I am going with you."

"You are under arrest."

"You are likewise under arrest." Chaeron grinned. "I release you into my parole. Do the same for me."

Marada pretended a dull smile as he rose up. "There is no way we can both go."

"There is no way one of us can go if the other is relieved of his authority."

A discreet but unhappy clearing of throat reminded both men that the Labayan still waited by the door.

"How long," snapped Chaeron over his shoulder, rising, but not taking his eyes off his brother, "until you can give us four sponge-ready cruisers?"

"Ah . . . three, four days, sirs, once I find out whose instructions I'm supposed to be taking."

"You'll be taking mine," Chaeron said flatly, still not favoring the man with a glance.

"Arbiter?"

Marada waved his hand, as if it were a matter of no import. "Go ahead, do what he says. But continue to call in all the ships you have out, and to spread news of what has occurred."

There was a shuffle, a closing of the door.

Marada let out a long, trembling sigh, and sank back down on the bed's foot, his face in his hands. Out from between his fingers came the words Chaeron would most clearly remember of all that passed that day in Shechem:

"You know what the worst of it is, little brother? The worst of it is that Selim Labaya had dispatched no retributive force to Draconis; not one ship went from here to Lorelie armed and filled with despite as we came here. And do you know why he did not? Because of Madel, because of her wretched state, because of what *I* had done, because she begged her father to work no violence upon my family—in hopes that I would return upon my own, someday." Marada's hunched form quivered, but did not straighten. "It's slated into the record."

Chaeron found himself stooping low, putting an arm on his half-brother's back, hot and moist though the room was cool.

Marada did not shrug that comfort away, although Chaeron had not one single word to add to it, but could only hover there, helplessly mute, until somehow, something lifted Marada's despair, or he became able to face it.

The artificial day had turned to night in Shechem before Marada Seleucus Kerrion raised himself up to seek the comfort of *Hassid*.

Chapter Fifteen

Shebat Alexandra Kerrion sat alone in her cruiser, *Marada,* ready to exit sponge. Rainbow-washed in the spill from *Marada*'s console, her eyes spat color like mirrors, aiming their beacon into the gloom.

All around her in *Marada*'s belly, comforting eyes winked: *"We can do anything."*

They would need equal parts luck and omnipotence, just to dock in the same universe they had fled so haughtily, sure of their expertise and their capability, like horses taking their bits in clenched teeth, racing uncontrollably for the joy of it on spring's first damp, misty morning.

Shebat sighed: there were no horses in the Consortium and no wondrous anticipation of what the new day's weather might be like. Every day was much like the last, and the only animal tolerated by the Consortium was man.

Her finger paused over an amber ready-light, making it seem that she could see through enflamed flesh to her very bone. She envisioned Julian Antigonus Kerrion, head bent, flaxen hair swaying, doing the same, sixty meters away within *Bucephalus*'s once-mighty hull. Now, crippled and weak, *Bucephalus* rode the end of a towing cable, barely knowing, while Julian took an urgent apprenticeship in the pilot's craft.

If it had not been for the presence of Softa David Spry in *Bucephalus,* his mind wound in his cruiser's and his body forgotten, Shebat might have laughed, so unlikely was her plight.

But Softa lay near death in *Bucephalus,* which made considerations such as the unlikelihood of two adolescents, not even seventeen, being able to bring the two cruisers to safe port somehow inconsequential. Softa needed them. Shebat came again to that dam she had constructed against the "if onlys" and the "what ifs" of hindsight and apprehension.

Softa would have said Shebat was running hot, and seen to cooling her. But Softa was not there with his gentle voice and his space eyes peering kindly out of his flat face. No, Softa was not in *Marada:* Shebat had hardly slept since coming aboard, though they had been ten days in sponge. The naps and dozings at her station were no substitute for a block of time spent sleeping; the drugs she had been taking to remain alert interfered with normal REM sleep; she felt surreal, detached.

Running hot: she was determined to bring *Bucephalus* safely into a slip at space-end. No other thought could brave the infernal desert of her will. Sometimes she could not have told why she must do it; or how long she had been doing it; or whether *doing* would ever give way to *have done.* These things were peripheral to her existence: there was herself, the *Marada* with his lover's voice and infinite wisdom, and there was the task at hand. What more there might be beyond her circumscribed universe of acceleration couch and visual display monitors she refused to consider, then forgot. She had never been to space-end; it was no place, but a quality of destination, existing, perhaps, only in her mind. Once, she had mistrusted even Julian's carefully controlled voice coming through sixty meters of sponge to spring from *Marada's* speakers and devil her ears: all without *Marada's* expanse was suspect, perhaps not real. Her world was *Marada's* as much of radio, X-ray, infrared and ultraviolet, as o what her eyes could see.

She shied away from that wonderland, because of he task. In *Marada's* communion, safe in cruiser-con sciousness, nothing hurt. No ugly thoughts swarme about her head so that she must swat them with th thumping of fist against console or palm against thigh. I was a place free of bedevilment, of questions, filled with the present and success; and love.

But *Marada* the cruiser had become reminiscent of Marada the man, and though he had been trying to please her, this was a wall between them.

The arbiter's slight stung no less fiercely as the days wore on: I will make him love me; I will become so desirable that he cannot resist, but he will never have me; he will lie awake as I have lain awake.

It might have been these determinations that stung her to effort beyond her capabilities. It might have been that the arbiter Marada who had taken her up and thrown her down among his feral family and disappeared, never to think of her again, had saved her from eternal wandering by not remembering her face when again they met . . . but Shebat did not think so.

She strove to smelt her love into hate, but the hate would not take an edge on so poor an anvil as her pique. And so she had neither hate nor love, but only mortification, anguished dreams in whose clutch she would not lie, and the task of guiding both ships to the lonely ring of stars at space-end.

She had punched up multiple displays of that once-mighty galaxy, now merely an exoskeleton marking its prior extent, the remnant of a galactic collision so long ago that no record was left in any scanning mode of the event: no rumble, no ghost noise, no infrared memory. Just the ring like a ring of smoke, and the blackness beyond.

"Shebat," spoke *Marada* the cruiser, no longer with the voice of Marada the man.

She had ceased wondering at the cruiser's ability to interrupt at just the right moment, whenever she stared down the well of dreams.

"Yes, *Marada*, whenever you are ready." She could not have said whether she had spoken aloud. Whenever she had to talk to Julian, her mouth felt rusty, stiff with disuse.

The first day, when she had realized that she had fled prematurely, in blind self-preservation, she had talked and talked and talked, while Julian followed each minute order, attaching Softa to *Bucephalus*'s life-support: intra-

venous feeding had been the hardest program for Julian to
run; his voice had gone thick and mumbly: he went faint
at the sight of blood. Placing the point of the feeder in
Spry's vein had taken nearly a half-hour.

Then, with Spry's vital signs coming from *Bucephalus*
and punched up on *Marada*'s console, Shebat had felt
better. Fugitively, until *Bucephalus* suffered an irrational
interlude.

Marada had suggested, when it was over, that Shebat
have Julian disable *Bucephalus*'s discernment mode, leaving him mindless, an automated caboose.

But Spry's mind hung in the balance: Shebat could not
give that order.

Marada had suggested that the fate of all of them,
cruisers and Kerrions, would be determined by her refusal
to act.

Shebat had suggested to *Marada* that the cruiser, in his
new capacity as command cruiser of Kerrion space, find
some way to extricate man from machine, or failing that,
to secure their survival against whatever dangers he
foresaw.

There had been a long pause before the cruiser answered, and its voice seemed to carry emotion, though
she told herself fiercely that such could not be:

*"Have I displeased you, Shebat? Am I not functioning in
accordance with your expectations? I have waited so long
to ship under you, and yet you are cold toward me. It was
not my fault, but Spry's and* Bucephalus's. *Not having
command status then, I was forced to obey. . . ."*

"*Marada*," she had sobbed, taken off-guard, half
aghast, with a superstitious chill tiptoeing up her spine, "I
did not expect you to sound like . . . him . . . the
arbiter."

"I did it for you. Shall I undo it?"

"Oh no, no. It is lovely. It is just strange, and abrupt. I
liked you . . . the way you were . . . but I thank you for
doing it for me." Finding herself unable to hurt *Marada*,
the cruiser's feelings, she became entangled in the problem of whether the cruiser *had* feelings that could be so
injured.

It had taken the time in sponge, meshed with *Marada*,
to make her understand the truth of it.

By then, *Marada* understood the truth of it, and slowly, without Shebat noticing, he deleted the arbiter's speech patterns from his vocalization.

If he could have deleted the bruise from her heart, he would have. He did not understand outboards' vulnerability, did not know why Shebat thought so differently about his namesake than about any other subject or even person.

Shebat loved *Marada* the cruiser, so she had said to him, when they had successfully talked Julian through the operation that put Softa Spry on life-support. *Marada* was very careful to answer immediately his pilot's needs and queries, to always use her name, lest she misconstrue any hesitation as disavowal and her love for him turn sour, also.

There was something to the outboard males' lamentations on the impenetrability of women's minds. *Marada* the cruiser had not been less than fascinated by *Hassid*'s womanly thought; in his communion with Shebat, intermittent as it necessarily had been because of crippled *Bucephalus* and his precious cargo, *Marada* had become intrigued unto obsession.

Something was wrong with Shebat, some outboard wrongness that was not in any one of her systems but pervaded all of them, something *Marada* must isolate and put to right.

"*Shebat?*" spoke *Marada*'s voice gently from the console speakers.

No answer, though there she sat in the command couch in full view.

"*Shebat,*" repeated *Marada,* preening his every display mode like a peacock's tail, "*there is much to be done.*"

He sampled her thought: it was of twelve coils binding and the atrophy of her powers of enchantment. It was sad and barbed and full of pungent regret: she would cast no more spells; spells had estranged her from her beloved and her husband both; and if the truth be known, her protective wardings had decreased every person she had presumed to benefit. The dreamlike enchantment she had made for Softa had not aided him; while creating it, she had had no inkling that disaster lay only a few steps farther down his road.

No, she would make no more enchantments! The rules of sorcery had somehow reversed themselves in the Consortium. Or there were no gods, as the bondkin affirmed. Or was it simply true that her talent, meager from the outset, had been eaten away by the rust of rationality.

"Shebat," spoke *Marada* once more, infinitely gently.

. . . Perhaps she would make no more dream dances. . . . Perhaps she . . . Her teeth, which had been biting her lip, clenched hard together. The lip, escaping, edged out into a pout. Perhaps what? Try as she might, she could find nothing glimmering in her own future for which to hope.

She need simply get Spry to space-end. They could get him back from wherever he dwelled within *Bucephalus.* They could make the old cruiser proud, a commander once again. Julian would have his freedom, his cause toward which to struggle. But herself? What had she to hope for? She had betrayed her husband, Chaeron; her stepfather, Parma; the whole of Kerrion space. She had thrown in with Spry's folk, not knowing or caring what or who they might be. All of this, because of Marada, the arbiter, who had not even recalled her face.

Shebat sighed and answered the cruiser's insistent summons. She should not be sad, within his wondrous hull. They were together, ship and pilot. Spry had taught that no outboard matters mattered, that the only reality worth having was that in which she was now immersed.

He was right, after a fashion: there was no bond so intimate between man and man. Or woman and man, she grimaced, touching the studs indicated by the cruiser, who wanted a closer, less-physical meld.

But she could not bring her grief into *Marada*'s company: she kept the cruiser at a distance, unwilling to give up her sorrow, not ready for the cure.

When she would join with him, pilot-to-cruiser, she would forget her Kerrion concerns, and would soar, free in the moment, seeing/feeling/hearing/tasting without anguish, or guilt, or conjecture.

When it was over, when she had subsided into her discrete flesh, a part of her would rail: how could she have

forgotten; how dare she exult when there was so much to
mourn?

Marada the cruiser started, then, to speak the words he
had not wanted to speak, to reach out to Shebat in a way
he had not really wanted to employ: his masquerade was
over, for the sake of Shebat.

There was little sign of it: the widening of her gray
round eyes, a deepening of her breathing, then the slow
slide of mind into mind with nothing held back in
deference to convention or preconception.

All of *Marada*, command cruiser of Kerrion space, met
with all of Shebat, pilot, enchantress, dancer of dreams,
in a place like the estuary where dream-time meets
eternity.

When the stroll was over, Shebat Alexandra Kerrion
had come to a new definition of love, of self and time and
space and the interface *Marada*, who encompassed them
all.

She murmured aloud, soft endearments. She confessed,
much more softly, her faults. She aired her hopes, and
even a fistful of scaly, fanged fears saw the light of their
mutual examination.

But there was one nagging discomfort she could not
bring herself to speak: though *Marada*'s love was pure
and without mendacity, it was also without flesh by way of
which to express its truth.

Shebat Kerrion was not then even seventeen years old;
she needed arms to hold her and lips to meet her own. In
his spacetime, they were one, lacking nothing. In her
spacetime, they were imprisoned by their separateness.

Shebat said, "I am an outboard and you are a cruiser.
That will never change."

"It is well that this is so."

"In this world, I am lonely."

*"Take what you want of fleshly comfort. It is one of the
prerogatives of pilots forced apart from their cruisers. It
does not matter."*

"Oh, *Marada* . . ." Shebat's voice was husky, her mind
filled with thoughts of pilots' promiscuity and the odd,
hungry look they all carried in their eyes. ". . . It does
matter. It matters so very much. . . . I understand now,

Spry, even Valery, maybe—" But she could not finish that last part, about Marada Kerrion, who surely looked at her, had always looked at her, through the veil of his relationship with his cruiser *Hassid*, next to whose charms Shebat's would ever sum a poor second. . . .

This time, when Shebat wept in earnest, there was nothing the cruiser *Marada* could do.

When she had sobbed a final sob for her rent humanity, the cruiser was waiting, attentive, every mechanism in both himself and *Bucephalus* readied to eject them into normal space, if space can be said to be normal at space-end.

Julian felt as if he were trapped in a gigantic die tossed by the Jesters in some obscure gamble.

He was watching the hieratic landscape of colored lights before him: piles of them stacking and unstacking, changing color, going out; lines of them jumping and undulating, writing indecipherable messages on his retinas which were the more awful for the knowledge that if he had merely understood their language, he would have been other than a helpless victim of fate.

For at least the fiftieth time, he tried to reason it out: this panel before him consisted of a number of modules, long and thin, whose constituent parts repeated—to learn one from top to bottom would be to learn them all. But the tiny letters beside each subgroup were ambiguous, coded: *mode; att.; pan; zm; 30/60/90* . . .

Thirty, sixty, ninety *what?* He could not ask *Bucephalus*, had been warned specifically not to arouse the cruiser. He pushed back from the auxiliary console, stared across the wasteland of quiescent terminal. Only this small patch bay was still operative, and since he had no idea what the . . .

But then, it struck him what the panel might be: if "*zm*" were "*zoom*," then at least he could push one button, do one thing to alter his situation on his own.

Julian shook flopping tow hair out of his eyes, depressed *mode*'s first stud. On his left, around the curve of the board, and on his right, by his cheek, screens leapt to life. Julian had found the visual scanners.

Once the purpose of the module had been decoded, the

capabilities represented by the labeled studs and lights fell to reason's decipherment.

It was as he was congratulating himself on having given sight to the blind hulk in which he rode (with Spry's unknowing form lolling in the command couch, only an occasional fart to recall it to mind), that *Marada*'s voice cracked his isolation:

"Julian, sit down and touch nothing else. We are about to enter your native spacetime."

As usual, *Marada*'s inhuman, confident orders both chilled and rankled the youth's nerves.

"Thank Chance," he whispered, settling his long-muscled frame into the rightmost acceleration couch, reflecting that hereafter, at least, food might be palatable and his stomach more disposed to accept it. Space-end surely boasted better than the cold rations from *Bucephalus*'s darkened galley.

"Thank Shebat," the cruiser amended.

Julian turned his face away, as if the *Marada*'s voice could be avoided. His tongue flickered out, catching a strand of blond hair fallen close, twisting it round and round in an unconscious, habitual grooming. The one thing he liked least of every unfortunate occurrence recently was this penchant of the *Marada*'s for talking out of turn. Face it: for talking like some bondkin uncle, or friend of his father's or teacher at University. This pilotry was not so glamorous as he had supposed, nor so noble. He detested long periods of inactivity, and mysteries of any sort. He abhorred following instructions. Trusting his well-tested capacity to improvise in any situation, he was incensed by the cruiser's treatment of him. After all, it was *his* plight, was it not? His ass on the line, true enough. Yet he was not consulted about anything concerning his welfare. He was not a part of the struggle, even when the struggle's outcome concerned him most of all. Shebat and *Marada* hoarded control, cogitation, commiseration: Julian might have been as inert as Softa, for the use that was being made of his insight, his intelligence, his bravery. Just like in Lorelie, or in Draconis, he was a hothouse plant, succored and pruned to other's standards. Only this time, his safety was not assured.

That was something, anyway: the acceleration of his
pulse, which could not be fooled, told him that this was
crisis, come to call.

In the visual monitor, sponge was glittery, suddenly;
changing color, growing diaphanous, blowing away. A
dark speck appeared, growing wider, then pale in its
middle, as the black-without-relief ring expanded to show
normal space speckled with bluish stars thick as cream.
Julian knew he was seeing a great volume of space not as
it was, but blueshifted and compressed, an entire universe
compacted and ringed with impenetrable blackness.

They were heading right into its center, like an arrow
toward a target. The target, as they grew near, began to
jiggle and roll. Julian knew he could be seeing up to seven
(man's irritation had put a ceiling on creation) universes,
only one of which was his native one. As the black ring
widened, the star-field began to roll apart, differentiating
itself, losing the blue tinge of "before," taking on the
redshifted lengthening of "behind."

Then the event horizon was gone, past his view since
Bucephalus was inside and then outside it, and all the
cornucopia of stars had sped away but one miasmic ring
laced with bright clouds of dust.

And so, two Kerrion children came to space-end, each
filled with woes and thinned by burdens, bringing Softa's
sleeping self and *Bucephalus,* too, where they had given
so much to be.

Shebat thought: Parma, you never bothered to take me
aside to explain, not even to offer an apology for what
fate you caused to befall me. . . . You have no claim on
me.

Julian thought: Now, I will be free of it, taken at face
value, treated as a man.

But Softa, sleeping with *Bucephalus,* did not think at
all.

One thing they had not expected was a cold welcome:
to be laconically assigned a space-anchor, nothing more
than a set of coordinates to be maintained, and ordered to
wait there for a medical team to arrive.

Shebat was incensed, Julian suspicious. *Marada*
reminded them that facilities here were limited, referred

them to their visual scanners for proof, snapping up identical views of the poor antiquated cylinders like gigantic fuel drums and the no-shape angly catching stations and the bristly solar collectors, laced together with outmoded cables from whose segmented length trains depended, crawling from dock to dock to dock.

The planet around which space-end was slung was sour and worn, a place of churning dust into which no spacecraft, not even a space-to-ground shuttle like the one in *Marada*'s belly, would choose to descend.

But it was the only planet around the tired old G-type star; it was the only planet with heavy metals in the whole of the explored ring which had once been a most ancient galaxy but was being sucked inward, ever inward, by the gobbling dark mass in its middle.

Because of the sink in the center of space-end, no one had ever cut across the featurelessness that sat, squat and incomprehensible, drawing all its star-prey ever closer. Because heavy metals were absent except upon the nameless planet dubbed "Scrap" by those who saw it in their sky, some said the planet was a captive, a hostage taken in the collision that had lost the galaxy the bulk of its stars. Whatever the nature of its history, whatever the details of its fate, the planet Scrap was not alone anymore.

The space-enders had come, sinking cables into its bedrock and mines into its face, making jokes about the "vagina of the universe" darkly beckoning above their heads.

All space-enders were obliged to spend a certain portion of their year laboring upon Scrap's surface. Their "down-time" was the nadir of their lives, but essential to life's continuance: space-end was alone.

She had no trade agreement with the Consortium; her products were embargoed, now that she had products to spare; she was the leprosarium of spacetime, her few children likewise tainted and unclean. Every so often, new folk were dumped there, but those vessels took no passengers back to civilized Consortium space.

Space-end was forever, they said, smiling wolfish smiles in hard, small-eyed faces.

The prison frigates that dropped new exiles never came

closer than the most distant space-anchors, casting their cargo of unfortunates adrift in lifeboats with beacons but no thrusters.

There was a price exacted by the "rescuers" who picked up the new settlers.

In the case of the arrival of two cruisers under power, one of which had been anchored before and had disappeared, the rescuers deferred to the pirate's guild, the only institution, space-enders claimed, they had modeled after the Consortium's example.

Once, more than a century ago, the Consortium had attempted to police space-end. A disastrous massacre had ensued, the only fit punishment for which was exile. But how to exile the exiles? The Consortium had deliberated, and begun the policy that obtained at space-end to the present day: arbiters traveled tours of duty on the ring, gave judgments when so petitioned.

Otherwise, there were no rules to be broken or laws to be disobeyed: space-enders tolerated no higher authority than themselves, save the pirate's guild, who were, everyone knew, pilots in disguise.

The guild promised mobility. If it could not yet produce it, it provided hope that someday it could. After all, the universe was unthinkable in its extent: a new colony could be planted in more fertile ground. But cruisers were essential: sponge-traversing ships were the fulcrum of plans to foresake Scrap for some fine solar system full of metals and wealth. In the meantime, piracy salved the space-enders' ire, perpetrated utilizing seven cruisers stolen over the years, maintained by rote and two fallen engineers, eunuchs in their fifties, who scratched their heads over the advances incorporated in the *Marada*'s design when the space-end guild ship finally drew alongside.

They would scratch their heads the more when they learned that both magnificent cruisers had been tandem'd here by two (*unsterilized!*) children, one of whom claimed this trip as his apprenticeship and demanded pirate's privilege; the other of whom staunchly affirmed that she was master both of the blond youth and the remarkable *Marada;* both of whom were Kerrions!

That Softa David Spry lay insensible in *Bucephalus,*

once flagship of Kerrion space, was news met with open mouths and shaking heads, news that traveled like light into the farthest crannies of space-end, stopping work and play wherever it went: everyone knew Softa. He was the embodiment of their hopes. Women wept and students were let out early from school.

There might have been babies named after Softa, had not the only children at space-end been illegal Consortium children, shipped off with their parents into exile. There might have been clones named after him, if space-end's limited facilities had been capable of producing perfect ones.

There were the "sirens," it was true. Sirens were said to be fertile, potent by the same numinous miracle that provided them life. But as far as anyone knew, sirens had no names.

Shebat Kerrion was staring glumly out a zero-magnification porthole near *Marada*'s cargo bay when a siren glided up to the embrasure, pressing its pale, compassionate face against the glass.

It was scintillating; womanlike; ethereal, with its silver hair waving about its head and its lucent palms flattened against the porthole's surface, blue veins showing through, humping with pulse. Its mouth moved: not red but blue-gray; within the mouth, tongue and gums were purplish.

Shebat Kerrion screamed.

The thing beyond the *Marada*'s portal wriggled, moued, pushed away like a spacefish, a last flash of foot waving adieu.

The pirate who came to see what caused the screaming chuckled when Shebat, hands cupping her temples, blurted out what she had seen.

"Hee, hee. They don't talk about 'em in the Consortium. No, they don't." The man's face was nearly as white as his three-mil suit, as his sparse hair, as the flowing beard which made up for it. "That's a 'siren.' Some say they're people who went over the one-minute vacuum limit fully mil'd. 'Stead of dying, they become . . . sirens. Phosphorylization in animal forms . . . mil acts like a proton pump, converts the epidermis once it's filled the lungs. Possible, y'know, but not likely. Still, there's lots of bodies unaccounted for in space. . . . Guys gone a minute and ten seconds have been brought back to air-breathing, say it's real rough. Consortium says nothing. Some folks die, that's sure. Maybe, like they say, some don't. Maybe they do live on like that; strip off their clothes and breathe vacuum and don't have much to do with us regular air-breathers. Beats me. Anyhow, they're harmless. They hang around to tow in lifeboats, sometimes. Don't want nothin' for it, just pop up now and again. . . . Feeling better?"

Shebat mumbled something, and turned away from the pirate's leer: they all looked at her like that; at Julian, too.

She raised her eyes from her boots and saw Julian's pale head ducking through the doorway.

"If you believe that, Shebat, you'll believe that I've started to sprout wings." He turned his back to her and, reaching his hand around, patted himself on the shoulderblades. "See? Here's proof." Twisting his head around, he winked at her. The young Kerrion had been increasingly lighthearted. It would have been soothing if he had not been determined to present himself so because of their obvious detention.

"Quarantine," the space-enders had explained.

"When are you going to let us out of here?" Julian demanded.

"Some folks coming up to talk to y'both. After that, I'd guess. Maybe tomorrow."

Shebat had tried to silence Julian. She did not want to leave *Marada.* She could not have said why, but she trusted her instinct. She had been distressed when Julian had left Spry alone in *Bucephalus,* though a team of pirates and space-end physicians labored over him.

Shebat made a motion to Julian to follow, and headed for a cabin.

There, where she had often tried in vain to reach Julian, she tried again: "Will you *stop* insisting that we be allowed to debark! I have no intention of leaving my ship."

"Of course, what else?" sneered Julian, then squeezed his eyes shut. "I am sorry. It is different for you, I understand. But you cannot stay in here forever."

"Why not?" Shebat grated, not parting her teeth.

"Because . . . well, there's only the two of us. You're my master pilot."

"You do not act like any apprentice I have ever seen. You do what you want. I am staying with *Marada*."

"*Marada!*", a pejorative. Then: "Shebat, is it what happened between us that night your marriage was announced? If it is, I assure you, I have forgotten it totally—"

"Then why are you bringing it up?" Shebat snapped, whirled on her heel, and stormed away toward the control room.

She was yet hovering there, a leg thrown up on the padded bumper of the master console, when Harmony, the dream dancer, waddled—lugubrious, piebald, and threatening—into view.

"Harmony!"

"You!" In translucent mil, her bespotted form gleamed, grotesque. "You have some questions to answer and some recompense to make! Sit down." Behind her, two space-enders with long jaws and pursed frowns entered.

All three bore down on Shebat.

Leaning over her, so that the black/brown/red/white bull's-eye between her breasts showed its every mole, Harmony rasped: "Let's start with Softa. Then maybe we'll get around to my dream dancers." The face thrust close: *"Now!"*

Shebat, protesting, tried to rise. Harmony's spatulate hand on her chest pushed the girl back down.

"Now! Or you'll be dead as that dream dance of yours! What have you done to Softa?"

Beyond Harmony's expanse, *Marada*'s meters began to peak.

"Julian!" Shebat wailed.

A slap across the mouth silenced her. "Forget him; he can't hear you. And don't give me that horrified Kerrion look, neither. We won't hurt 'im. Not him. He's worth keeping alive. You'd better convince me that you are, too, dearie, 'cause I'd dearly love to space you and see if you'll turn into a siren, or just turn blue!"

Shebat fingered her swelling lip gingerly, felt a wetness,

and took her finger away. It was rouged with blood.

"I thought you liked me," Shebat whispered slowly, her eyes on her own trembling hands, digging in her lap.

"Liked you? Liked a traitor who would walk out and leave us all to be sterilized and deported without even a *word*? *Like* you? Like I like your *Kerrion* boyfriend, *your Kerrion*—" The epithet "Kerrion" had broken free of restraint, trebling into a throaty scream, then was visibly swallowed up. The gelatinous breasts of the troupe mistress quivered, then were still. In a different, canny voice she continued:

"Now, you just tell us what you did to Softa, and help us *un*do it, and we'll forget the rest of it."

Though Shebat did not in the least believe Harmony, she wanted to tell her what would bring Softa back from faraway dreaming. The trouble was that she did not know.

When Valery Stang raced into space-end in *Danae* with two stolen cruisers close behind, no one had made any progress in uniting Softa David Spry's body with his dreaming mind. The *Bucephalus* remained patched in to *Marada;* Softa David remained on board. They did not dare move him, being unable to foresee what the result of that might be. Shebat and Julian, too, remained in *Marada,* at space-anchor: Shebat maintained *Marada*'s control of *Bucephalus;* Spry's plight maintained the space-enders' control of Shebat.

"Pleasure to see you, Lady Kerrion," said Valery, twinkling eyes softening his hatchet face. His lank hair was clubbed back. He still wore Kerrion black-and-reds. When he turned to wave out the two space-enders who followed Shebat everywhere she went on *Marada,* she saw *Danae*'s device and call letters were embroidered on his back.

Amazingly, the ubiquitous space-enders, obedient, disappeared.

Shebat felt annoyance, welcomed it, so long had it been since she had felt anything but the disorientation of entrapment.

"How is it that you, loyal pilot of my husband, can command space-enders?"

Valery Stang chuckled, "Come on, girl. Let's not play the ingenuous Kerrion. It's the middle of the third millennium, and we're all thieves in the night. It's just the night that's bigger. You left your Kerrion prerogatives behind when you joined us—"

"I joined Softa," Shebat replied frostily. "Not you or yours. And had I been considering it, the treatment I have been shown at the hands of these . . . pirates . . . would have convinced me I had been mistaken. I want—"

"No one cares what you want," broke in Valery, more gently than fit his words. "These 'pirates' fan the last spark of freedom remaining in all the halls of man. You are here on their sufferance. Your survival depends upon their good will."

"*Good will?*" It was Shebat, this time, whose incredulous laughter rang out around *Marada*'s control room. "*Marada* and I depend on each other for our survival. Don't worry about *us.*"

"Look, Shebat. Harmony loves Spry like a mother loves her only pup. It was Spry who got her out of here and set her up in the Consortium. You can't blame her."

"Can't I? False creature who has turned upon me: I curse her name as she has bespattered mine! I spit upon her spirit, and my spittle is acid—"

"By the last Jest, I had forgotten you." Valery's long-fingered hand stroked his nose, hiding his smile. "Let's not get emotional. . . . I have to be going, posthaste. I came here to ask a favor." He leaned against the master console.

"No favors." Her lip curled.

"Gods, you're beautiful. All right, no favors. A deal, maybe."

"Go on." She worried her hair, discomfited.

"I've the arbiter Marada's son with me. I'd like to transfer him over here. He'd be better off with you. *Marada*'s got the facilities."

"Better off with me? I cannot control even who comes and goes on my own ship." The exaggeration rang hollow even to her own ears: she could be free of space-end and space-enders in a moment, merely by commanding *Marada* elsewhere.

"Shebat, please." The eyes behind those words stayed

her objections. "He'll be safer with you. I have no experience with children, let alone sick infants. And the arbiter has sown only ill-will here. Besides, he's Kerrion; you're Kerrion. It's your place."

Safer. Sick infant? That child of a loveless bed? She almost said all of these but *Marada*'s cruiser-thought intervened, prodded, retired. She said: "Very well. What benefit do you offer in exchange?"

"I'll intercede with Harmony. They'll leave you alone. You and Julian will both receive passes, interim space-ender status."

"No."

. "No?"

"No. I don't want that. I want these people off my ship, and off *Bucephalus*. I want nothing to do with space-end."

Valery shrugged. "Dramatic, but impractical. Very well, you want nothing to do with them, and they want nothing to do with you. It would be easy enough to arrange, but for the cruisers, and Spry. They do want the cruisers, and somehow or other they feel that Spry's . . . affliction . . . is your fault. Is it?"

She spat at him. He wiped his cheek, which turned red as she watched. The veins at his temples bulged, pulsed blue.

"Shall I take that as affirmation? The senior dancer of Harmony's troupe swears that when he was teaching you, odd and terrible things went on. Chaeron says you do strange things with your hands, and I don't mean the obvious sort of things. Things that color the air . . . ?"

"So, you are here at Harmony's behest, after all. Very well," she said, feigning resignation. "Take me to Softa, and I will try to undo what has been done. Bring the child before me, also. But I will suffer no more violence from these criminals, nor their presence. Any evil visited upon me, I will turn back on the sender." She leaned close, whispering through parted lips: "Keep them away from me, Valery, or they will know no more than Softa."

"So you *did* do that?" There was a drawing back of Valery's head, deeper into the protection of his body. Shebat could almost see the superstitious chill tickling the man's flesh.

Her nails dug into her thigh, pain the only antidote to the smile threatening to break from cover. "No, I did not do it. But it is possible I could undo it, given the chance."

"It will take time to convince the authorities here. Meanwhile, I'll have the infant brought over."

"As you will," Shebat dismissed it. She was not in the least concerned with the child, she told herself, not wanting to accept the animosity she felt for Madel Labaya's child. She was most interested, however, in getting herself and Julian out of space-end. By now, even her foster brother must be ready to admit that this was no place for Kerrions. If only Softa did not lie in *Bucephalus* . . .

She was so filled with scheme and resentment, she did not pursue the question of why Valery was anxious as to the child's safety.

When it was delivered to her, in a little container like a miniature ejection capsule, she ceased thinking of anything else at all.

He was so small, so still, so peaceful, yet sad with tubes in his nose.

He was red-skinned and black-haired and resembled Parma more than either his father or mother.

She looked in through the transparent shell at him, feeling her sinuses rustle, the first prelude to tears. It was not his size or his sleeping, or even that he was Marada's that was saddest: saddest was that no one knew his name.

The nameless son of her beloved neither flailed nor wept. He lay ummoving and unmoved by life's excitation. Looking into the placid face, she could not hate him, who was Marada's son. Looking longer, something stirred in her that prompted her fingers to tap a sequence which caused the capsule to open. Unable to look away, like one in an unwanted dream, she disconnected the tube feeder and picked up the limp, warm form.

Cradling him in her arms, his bare bottom moist against her, she crooned to him, ancient runes in the tongue to which she had been born.

Somehow, she found herself sitting in *Marada*'s master couch, the child's cheek against her own, wet with tears.

Then she went seeking, into the baby mind that spurned the things of life, deep among colors and bright

sparkling spinners of thought like ghost-rattles, traversing
mountains like teats ever offered, crawling in his dreams
with him though they were like no dreams she had ever
met in the minds of those who had opened their eyes and
seen. She spoke to him in impulses; she had no words to
reach him, who had never listened to words. Emotion
reached him. This he understood: it blew within her mind
in a ripping gale, such a gale as she had not experienced
since she herself lay within a mother's womb.

She coaxed: *taste of life: it is bitter, but sweet. It sates
more than dreaming. . . . See? . . . Taste? . . . Love/life
come creeping. Out then, little one; back again each eve;
one final eve back for the eternity you clutch too soon.*

She promised only everything. She wept, wrenchingly,
but did not know. She promised anguish, despair, failure:
piquant trillings, the feel of them conjured up in both
their dreams. She promised brightness, to squint against
the sun. She bent over, holding him fiercely to her breast,
squeezing tightly.

Marada Seleucus Kerrion's son began to cry.

It was not until the miracle of the waking child was
assured that Shebat took time to listen to the news
Marada the cruiser had gathered from his sister-ship,
Danae, so recently come from Shechem.

Chapter Sixteen

On the very day that Valery Stang arrived at space-end, Kerrion Three was putting into Draconis with the grande dame of Kerrion space raging and pacing her cruiser's length.

They had been delayed, and delayed again. Four days had been added to the duration of their journey, for reasons the consul general's wife instinctively knew to be spurious.

Something was wrong: she had had a headache for a week.

Something was very wrong: Parma had been convivial, even gentle, in the one message he had sent. A greeting, it had been: that, too, was unusual. Why would he of a sudden have developed such a yen for her that he could not wait to greet her in person? Such a gesture could not have come from the frugal, pragmatic Parma she knew so well, unless . . . could something really be amiss with the elections?

It was the only possibility that Ashera could credit, yet it was hardly creditable. Parma Alexander Kerrion *was* Kerrion space. Not one of his brothers or sisters, not a single first cousin among the bondkin, had the savvy or the influence to successfully unseat him. No one among the lesser bondkin had the wherewithal to give it a try.

True, there were other contenders: there must be, to have free elections in the first place. True, there was the obligatory Labayan-sponsored opposition. But when had there not been? Circling her suite on soundless feet like an old lioness readying for the hunt, Ashera told herself, as she had told herself countless times on this un- necessarily long and arduous journey, that since she could not conceive Kerrion space without Parma overseeing it, no one else could, either. Expectation is its own ratifica- tion: it could not be the elections that had prompted Parma's uncharacteristically compassionate greeting to be spewed out toward her cruiser, crawling so slowly toward Draconis since it had exited sponge.

She was missing her own parties; things would not proceed smoothly with a less-practiced hostess presiding over such discerning guests.

If this was some trick of Parma's to lessen her influence, she would feed him his own wiles one by one and he would not like the taste of them one bit.

But even suspicion could not ease her. Anger, for once, did not have its customary, buoying affect. Something was wrong, and Parma was delaying her—delaying the mo- ment when she would find out!

Parma Alexander Kerrion, stroking the ancient wood of his desk in his office, knew to the quarter-hour when his wife would arrive. He had hoped, by this day, to have solved his problems, or failing in that, to have solved the portion of them that included Julian Antigonus Kerrion.

But his ploy had not worked: Julian was still missing.

Parma rubbed his seamed neck, sighed a huge, tired sigh. In the office which had been furnished by his father's father, decorated by his father, and maintained by him- self, change itself seemed held in abeyance. Stability exuded from every cranny. Sitting here, a man could not quail before even the most dastardly fate: it was not seemly. The woods and bronzes and porcelains from early Earth whispered softly that perfection maintains itself by its harmony with the natural order.

His father had been very fond of saying that.

But then, his father had believed his own propaganda.

Parma had had a difficult score of days since Marada's message had preceded him into Draconis, and all things had burst apart in mad unpredictability.

He stood up slowly, hand to the small of his back,

growling at tired muscles' complaint, and headed for the executive washroom.

Sometimes, he thought it the Jesters' finest touch that man must shit. All our posturing and all our accomplishment to which we point as proof that we are not simply "creatures" cannot stand before it: as we void, we are voided; in the act of elimination, our pretention toward godhead is eliminated.

Squatting (well, more sitting) on his pot (well, on the marble sculpture taken from Farouk's palace), Parma could not help peeking over his shoulder to make certain that the drooling crone, Chance, had not slipped in behind him before he'd closed the door.

Selim Labaya was dead.

He could not get used to it.

It frightened him; he felt consummately alone.

He had not meant it to happen. No one could have imagined it would happen. No data pool nor Kerrion computer had predicted it, no rationality sanctioned it. But Labaya was dead, uncaring, as ever, of what *should* be.

Labaya's death left Parma the last *Camelus* in an arid waste. None of the Labayan bondkin was a worthy successor, even blind Justice shirked choosing some young fop or old reprobate to take his place. In plain talk: no one could take Selim's place, as no one among his own get could take Parma's when he, too, was gone. It was the end of an era, and like all things very old, the smell of decay preceded it into view.

Parma remembered when he had been a child, how he had hated the smell of his parents' bedroom, with its promise of death that tickled his nose so that he would try to shut his nostrils against it. His parents had been only in their forties, but the smell spoke plainly to a child's nose.

He must smell that way himself, by now. Chance was kind in that there was no little boy with waggling tongue to tell him so. Or was it? Had he given up too soon, and commended the heir he craved to the limbo of the unborn? It was sure that among those sons he had spawned there was pitifully little choice: Marada edged out the others only because of the promise Parma had made to Persephone, when "romance" had not yet been stricken from his vocabulary.

Let it lie; let it lie, he scolded himself. Soon enough reflection would be banished in Ashera's acidic arrival. "Old Dragon Breath," the children called her, even her own.

The very drooling specter who had hounded his life, he sometimes glumly admitted her to be.

Finished with his toilet, he hitched up his pants and quit the sanctum of his innermost thoughts, knowing that even there, on this day, there was no peace to be found.

In point of fact, there was no *Julian* to be found, which was worse: he had been doing without peace for a lifetime, but Ashera had been forced to do without Julian's sunny presence in Lorelie only under the greatest duress, and would not take the news well at all.

Suddenly, he wished he had not delayed her arrival. Best to have the whole thing over with, at last. An overriding truth remained to be wielded against whatever accusations his wife might field: the boy could not be kept forever in Lorelie, kept safe at the expense of whatever small chance he had to become a man.

Was this, then, youth's vision of manliness, to foresake all inheritance and honorable tasks to become an outlaw, a rebel?

Thinking back through a fog of years to his own chasings-after-manhood, Parma had to admit that his own visions of seemly derring-do had not been so different in substance from those that had prompted Julian to cast all to the wind.

But Parma had not *done* it. That was the difference and the poisoned tip of the arrow lodged above his heart. Parma had turned away from rebellion. He had not wrung *his* parents' hearts this way. . . .

He had hoped, diffidently, that he would get a message telling him the boy had been kidnapped. *No* message told him it was Julian who was the abductor: Parma's sleep was the object of ransom, only no price had yet been set.

Settling in his chair, behind the desk on which Kerrion space had been charted and built, he depressed a stud.

He had put off viewing Shebat's dream dance long enough. The unfortunate dream dancer, Lauren, had been in detention longer than was necessary. A quick flight to space-end would have been kinder.

He had many things to set straight before his wife stormed in on a tide of imprecation. He wanted the girl out of the consul general's tower by then.

He probably would have attended to it sooner, if Chaeron's curt message had not arrived to make small all else in its shadow:

"Selim Labaya and immediate family suicided. Shechem is ours. Marada persists in his dementia. Circumstances demand we return by way of space-end. Sorry to miss the elections. Respectfully your consul, Chaeron."

Respectfully, yet. Circumstances . . . *what* circumstances, his intrigue-loving, serpent-tongued son had not bothered to say.

He had sent back a demand for explanation, but it seemed that the transmission had not been received. Why that was, Parma hardly cared anymore. When Chaeron got home, he would find himself the consul of the smallest, poorest backwater platform Parma commanded. He was debating between two almost equally unpleasant ones. . . .

The door clucked, drew back.

Parma rose up, but did not come around the desk to greet the dream dancer. A trill of excitement he would have preferred to disallow would not be banished. The girl, the dream dancer, was exquisitely beautiful, with golden hair and a regal throat, so charismatic that she wore the dingy detention smock like fine raiment.

Two black-and-reds followed upon her heels, stationing themselves at either side of the door.

"Out, out," Parma waved preemptorily. "We certainly do not need you. Do we, young lady?"

It must have been a long time since Lauren had last opened her lips to speak. They worked, unwilling to part. The soft acquiescence she made was wordless, as her slithering down into the leather wing chair before the desk was boneless, as all things about her seemed magical and ethereal except the forearm-long, black dream-box she balanced on her lap.

Her sad eyes held his. "What are you going to do to me?"

"I thought you had been told. It is what *you* are going
to do to me. . . ." He fought a long-unused grin. "Show
me my adopted daughter's dream dance."

"Oh, no," she whispered, aghast.

"Oh, yes, unless you are enjoying your stay in detention. You are here because you are still holding evidence,
Chaeron thinks, that would be of interest to me. Once I
have seen it, then I can make some disposition of your
case."

"That is what I am afraid of," she breathed, unblinking, like a mouse watching the clawed paw descend.

"Young lady, I am pressed for time. Either you will
oblige me, or not. If not, then I will send you back—"

"No. Yes, I mean . . . yes, I'll do it. But you must not
be angry with me. I only learned it from her at my troupe
mistress's request, and I have never shown it but at a
customer's demand."

"Is that what Chaeron did, demand?"

He did not miss the shifting of her eyes, the tight
swallow, the imperceptible lowering of Lauren's head at
the speaking of his son's name. He did not want to know
why he was seeing them. He said very gently: "I regret as
much as you this entanglement of yours in our affairs. Be
assured that I will make as good a determination in regard
to your future as your actions have allowed me to . . . .
You will not suffer further indignity, I promise that."

Without another word, the dream dancer opened up
her box, fussed within. Closing it, she took up the two
circlets and held out one to Parma: "If you will just put
this on your head . . ."

When he had seen the dream dance, he knew why
Chaeron had hesitated to dispose of the girl Lauren in the
accepted manner, or thought he did.

His hands were shaking with rage at Shebat, and with
something else, come out of the dream dance's apocalyp-
tic expanse.

Lauren, holding both circlets to her breast protectively,
cowered in the ancient chair, face pale as her hair, so that
her lips seemed enflamed.

"I have no choice but to send you to space-end." He
did have another choice: he could have the girl killed, or
her forebrain stirred so that she could never speak of what

she held in her head. But Parma saw too much Kerrion blame in her "crime," too much full life in the fine young body fearful before him.

Did she understand? Her mouth came open in astonishment or horror; incredulity filled her eyes, straightened her back. She said nothing in answer, went docilely with the black-and-reds who came at his summons to collect her. He was grateful for that. He was not so sure that the girl should be deported, if his stepdaughter and his son were to be excused their part in all this.

Dream dancing would be legal soon enough, directly after elections, to be exact: he had been planning to do it for a long time. He had decided to do it at the right time, which was upon him; he could smell it in the air.

Still, it was illegal now, and had been then, and he was within his rights to invoke the law, still standing. Then why did he feel regret, and some more insidious hesitation he could not name? Because Marada and Chaeron had trundled themselves off to space-end without so much as a by-your-leave on some errand they neglected to explain, that was why.

He did not for one second believe they had left Shechem before his message arrived there. . . .

"Who was *that?*" sprang through the door before it had fully opened. Ashera's proud, bosomy prow glided toward him, implacable.

Her beauty was redundant, after so many years of knowing it. She did not affect him, anymore, as woman-to-man, but had become a sparring partner, whose charms were beside the point.

"Sit down, my dear," he said gently, ignoring her question, tapping the "no-slate" and "conference, no entry" buttons almost simultaneously.

Ashera stood rod-straight, her arm on the wing chair's back. "What is it?" Trepidation, garnered from his face and his voice, made her voice small. "What is it?"

"Sit down."

"I do not want to sit down. What is so weighty that I cannot stand to receive it? Think me a child, do you? Spit it out, old toad!"

"If you wish. Julian has run off."

Ashera's regal forehead pleated: "Run off?"

"With Spry and Shebat. Disappeared."

"Spry; *Shebat— My baby! You* did this! You viper! Julian, Julian, Julian," she wailed, sagging so that Parma found himself propelled out of his chair, hurrying to support her.

Instead of accepting the comfort of his embrace, she pounded with small fists upon his chest, so that he let her go.

Ashera stepped back from him, kept treading backwards, grating: "You did this! You drove him away. It is all your fault. You will regret it for the rest of your days if he is lost to me. I will make you sorry you have ever lived at all. . . ."

She stopped, feeling the door against her back. She took a deep breath that caused her patrician nostrils to flutter, her firm bosom to rise under her gown.

"Find him, Parma, or I will make such revenge on your precious Kerrion name as will vilify you to the farthest outreach of the Consortium!"

She slapped at the door, which hurriedly withdrew before her wrath.

Parma did not follow. He extracted his nails from his palms and sat heavily on the corner of the desk, which creaked, complaining. Breathing hard, he gazed at nothing, a spotty, grainy pall over his vision, a dark pulsing at the edges of his sight.

When he felt better he thumbed up his security panel to "slate" and began dictating his victory speech, though he would not need it before the morning of the following day.

This evening, he would have to paste on a facile grin that stunk of certainty and parade around among false friends and falser bondkin mouthing fealty while their eyes spoke more truly of greed and jealousy.

Running his palm down across his face so that his lower lip kissed his chin, he sought his chair. It seemed useless, tawdry, foolish, sometimes, to rail and scheme and strive in a universe empty even of censure, let alone approbation. But Parma knew the ennui would pass back whence it had come, into the realm of emotion, leaving him strong enough to draw his load once again. Already, he could feel the comforting weight of his collar, the smooth roundness of well-worn traces on his either side. What else is there, but to draw the heaviest burden one can manage, and draw it with pride?

When Parma did not come down for dinner, Ashera cursed his name. When he appeared not among the celebrants toasting a victory assured by the Kerrion data pool and independent sources alike, she shrugged and told their guests that he was working upon his acceptance speech, and might be at it the night long.

But when midnight's tinkle rang through the tower, she pulled a steward aside and grudgingly dictated an apology and a reminder that the consul general had guests, to be delivered to Parma in person straightaway.

A time later the man returned saying that the security modes in the consul general's office were activated, unbreachable, that he had spoken loudly at the door but received no reply.

"Vindictive old fool," Ashera murmured, after she had dismissed the steward.

"Pardon, madam," said Baldy, come up behind her, bleary-eyed with a drink in hand, "but I must speak to your husband. It is a matter of some urgency."

"I would like to speak with him myself, Guildmaster Baldwin, and I am sure my reasons are equally as urgent as yours. However, he is up there sulking with all his privileges invoked. I am not going up there to plead at his door. So, unless he grows up very suddenly—which he has not had the good grace to do in all the years I have known him—you and I are both going to have to wait until His Pomposity sees fit to come down among the people."

Turning on her heel in a swirl of cream chiffon, she glided away.

Baldy, staring after, felt a many-legged suspicion mount his spine. But then, he had been feeling them daily, waiting for the axe to fall. He was near surrender. Better that than enduring another day of waiting. "Sponge knows, tomorrow's as good as today," he told himself aloud, and finished silently that if what his pilots were whispering to each other was the truth, tomorrow might be very different from any day he had known before.

It was very different, but not for the reason Baldy thought.

Things became different for Ashera sooner than for everyone else.

When she had seen out the last guest, she went up to Parma's office. Alone in the hall, she defeated the security-lock with a word.

Slipping within, she reinstated it, tiptoeing across the antechamber and into his softly lit inner sanctum, not wanting to wake him until she stood by his very ear.

As she had suspected, he was slumped over his desk, insensible. Tomorrow they would all bear the brunt of his aching back's effect on his temper.

She leaned down close, her lips almost against his ear, so that she could see the bristly hairs growing out of it: "It's safe to wake up now, old toad. They're all gone and you're Consul General for another term. I've heard your cousin's already conceded. Parma . . . *Parma!*"

Then she touched, shook, slapped him. She felt the cold, limpflesh of him. She pushed him back in his chair and thrust her ear against his chest. She searched for his pulse. She moaned like an animal with a death-wound, but she did not hear herself. She begged him not to die, repeatedly, as she pounded frantically on his chest. She opened his mouth. He might be just unconscious: his tongue and lips and gums were bluish. She fit her lips to his unsensing ones, trying to resuscitate him. The spittle she sucked into her mouth was chilly. She sat back, straddling him, cold and empty as the corpse whose eyes were closed. In death he was more camel-like than ever, and still she could not cry. She lay her cheek against his and spewed out apologies, words of love, entreaties as if he could still hear her.

The pressure of her weight on his stomach caused the air and water yet within him to evacuate his flesh.

Then she knew it was true, that she was without him, that he would never look up from under his black brows, scolding, teasing, that those rubbery lips would never mock her, never purse and give in again.

Lords, why did I blame him? Why did I fight with him? Parma, why did you leave me? I love you. I love you. What am I going to do?

This time, as for all the time intervening until she should follow him, he had for her no answer.

It was that horror, plus the vacant face which had only hours ago been flushed with argument and was now so still and pale, that made her thumb up "run *slate.*"

Then she wept, pitifully, as his victory speech complete with smiling limpid eyes and pleasure-dimpled mouth played back on the desktop screen.

"Yes," she sobbed. "Yes, no one can take it away from you. But, oh, Parma, Parma, who can take your place?"

The answer to that, too, was slated into the record, Ashera found when she had gathered her wits enough to look for it.

Having found it, rocking back and forth and moaning softly without knowing that she did, she came to a decision:

She erased any record of her having entered the room. She set up a program that would patch the victory speech into Draconis Central and broadcast it at the proper moment.

Then she stumbled off to his washroom and drew herself a hot bath, mumbling over and over: "*Nothing* will be lost!"

Chapter Seventeen

Chaeron Ptolemy Kerrion woke from evil dreaming among a half-dozen snoring sleepers in a cold sweat with tears running down his cheeks. It took him a moment to remember that he was in Marada's *Hassid,* coursing through sponge toward space-end. The room in which he had expected to awake became *Hassid*'s cabin with a stately wheeling of orientation that did nothing to lessen his distress, but chased the particulars of the dream from his mind. Something about Ashera and Parma. . . . What, exactly, had made him cry he could not recall. Yet still he felt weepy, infinitely saddened, morose and so transient in his flesh that he kissed himself upon the shoulder.

Chagrined at what he had done, discomfited that he could be so upset as to have done it and not realized until his lips touched his clammy skin, he threw back the cover and half-bolted for the washroom, treading hastily among the cots.

Laving his face in icy water, he wondered how he could cry in his sleep and yet not understand why he was crying. He did not think that he was out of touch with himself. Could something about this situation be bothering him more than he had realized? He was aware of the dangers of suppressing emotion, and he had long been a student of dreams. If someone had been there to ask him which bothered him more, the weeping or the forgetting why he wept, he could not have told which was worse.

What, then, was the matter with him? He stared at his stubbly, water-beaded face searchingly. At least he could not trace the tears. *What are you doing, old son?*

In a meditative pause, he waited for an answer from inside himself. None was forthcoming. Did he have qualms about this space-end engagement? It had promised to be a debacle. As far as he knew, the prospect rather excited him. He was aware of some small regrets, having to do with Shebat *(she,* too, was in the dream) and the state of his relationship to his brother, the worst of those being that he regretted helping Marada while wishing he did not. But on the whole he had thought his situation well-conceived, certainly resolved on the internal plane. He had been looking for problems on the external, only, never glimpsing those within.

Everyone else had doubts and fears and objections to his punitive expedition. It followed, he told himself harshly, that he would have shelved his own while striving to eradicate everyone else's, so that he could appear certain, thereby inspiring trust, if not wholehearted agreement. . . . Still, he did not like to think that he had fooled *himself;* he was the only friend he had.

He spit out an un-Kerrion oath contracted from overly close contact with flamers, and turned his back on the image in the mirror, his fists curled around the lip of the sink at either side of his buttocks. He leaned there, naked, a long time. Then, unwilling to even try to go back to sleep, he headed slowly for his closet to dress. Perhaps he would talk to Marada, and get things straight before a misunderstanding metamorphosed into an irrevocable, open break.

He found Marada awake at *Hassid's* master console. "This is where I left you six hours ago. We were both going to get some sleep."

"I don't like using a relief pilot. I slept here. *Hassid's* touchy."

"You should have told me. We could use the bed."

"We? This is *my* ship; that's my bed. *We've* got four ships behind us, all with strange pilots. The lead ship should not be in any way compromised."

"You've got to sleep."

"This brotherly concern is making me nervous." Marada twisted in his couch. "Have you decided to 'replace' me while I sleep?" he queried softly, scratching in his beard. "Because if you have, I must remind you; cube arbitration cannot be halted once it is begun." He gestured sharply with his head toward the console, where the arbitrational cube rested, patched in to *Hassid's* board.

"And I must remind you that I am in command of this expedition and am exercising that command as I see fit. That you and I do not agree on the amount of force to be expended does not alter the fact that it is in pursuit of your child we have come here."

"And if the 'force expended' eradicates the object of pursuit? If my son dies of your overzealousness, I will not hesitate to prosecute you! The legalities of all this are questionable. Everything since you altered Parma's strategy is on your own head."

"Sometimes I think that is exactly what you want. Is it? Are you really after the eradication of your error? I have heard your child is flawed. . . . Hear me, Marada: I will give you an option. Forget your son. Withdraw the cruisers. Slink back to Draconis and let the pilots' guild hold us all up for ransom. I lay it in your lap." Chaeron let his eyes flicker where Marada's jaw had so recently indicated. "Feed *that* to your mechanized Solomon and see what color it turns!"

"Clever. I cannot indict you without implicating myself, eh? Well, no good. When this is over, I'm personally going to count the dead and lay their right hands on your altar."

"*What?*" Chaeron, sawing on the reins of his temper, reminded himself one more countless time that his brother Marada was irretrievably mad.

"Ancient custom, bringing the right hands of enemies slain in battle back to put before the king. . . ." Marada squinted at Chaeron, trying to see beneath the severe beauty his brother wore like a mirrored mask that threw back reflected light, hiding any illumination coming out from within. He sighed, tsk'd mournfully. "Never mind, little brother, just go your despotic way for the nonce."

"Then you are not so repelled by this as to want to call it off!"

"Chaeron, you fool . . . we are in sponge, and must continue through. We have to come out at space-end. We're too close now to change course. The die is cast, as they say. I'm sure the Jesters are kicking up their heels in glee." He paused, looked long and questioningly at Chaeron, who only snorted derisively.

"Sponge, I could strangle you at times. . . ."

"Slate," murmured his younger brother.

"Yes, then, I am anxious to reclaim my son. Would not you be, likewise?"

"Not when that's just what Valery wants us to do."

"But you agreed with me, then."

"Until I found out you wanted to tool in there and very politely ask for it—sorry—*him* back. Has he got a name, this son of yours?"

"Parma."

"How sentimental."

Marada surveyed Chaeron through slitted eyes, slowly shaking his head. "If you will get out of here now, you may save yourself excess grief later on."

"I cannot do that. I am commander. You, after all, are my second and my pilot."

"As pilot, I can demand it. Things are too crowded in here."

"Things are more crowded everywhere else but here."

"Are you still insistent on coming out of sponge firing?"

"I certainly am. Even your friend *Hassid* thinks the probability of our being met by a welcoming committee to be ninety-nine-to-five-nines." Chaeron eased himself down into the copilot's couch on Marada's right. "I'd like to be able to give the *'ready'* order myself, since I seem to be taking all the responsibility."

Marada grunted, without moving a muscle caused a dozen lights to light on the console before Chaeron. "There you are. You can speak your order, or punch it in by depressing the large, red-blinking oblong. Negative hydrogen ion beams, full power, medium spread, total destruction in one second, paralysis of all systems in one tenth of that. Just like Shechem."

"Thank you," said Chaeron with a winning smile.

Marada shivered visibly and turned his face away.

A time later, his voice wafted over the couch's head-rest, soft and tired and tinged with hopelessness:

"These cruisers that you intend to demolish—they are ours, you must recall."

"They *were* ours," corrected Chaeron. "Why all these arguments now, when it is, as you have said yourself, too late to turn back?"

"These arguments, as you call them, are over the overt destruction of life, human and cruiser."

"*Cruiser!* Lords, Marada, not that again. *You* are the one who insisted on going after Valery."

Then Marada did turn around in his seat, his eyes sparkling fiercely. "*I* was content to come alone. *I* was *intending* on coming alone. You have no need of *Hassid* with all of Shechem's vanquished fleet at your disposal, as I have no need of such gargantuan firepower behind me. As a matter of fact, if you had not pulled rank on me and insisted on this armed incursion, I would have a better chance of getting my son back, which, if you have forgotten, is the putative purpose of this trip."

"You would have *no* chance of getting your son back, or getting yourself back."

"That should not bother you. In fact, if something happens to *Hassid* and myself, you will be measurably better off, and perhaps even free from what now seems certain prosecution for your crimes."

"Ah, but I would be short a brother."

Marada laughed, a short harsh bark.

"And I would have to go home and tell Parma I let something happen to you, his pet and his pride. He would have my butt for dinner should I return without you."

"Well, then," suggested Marada, "you had better start marinating it. You're right: there's a welcoming committee waiting for us."

And he punched up a visual display of dizzying complexity, black-banded and effulgent, in which Chaeron's untrained eye could make out nothing even vaguely resembling a cruiser.

"Get ready," Marada warned.

But Chaeron was already leaning forward, his finger wavering, atremble, above the inch-long, red-lit oblong which would free death to leap invisibly from every turret on every cruiser in their party as they came out of sponge.

To the *Hassid*, leading point out of sponge, the differences between the waiting cruisers ahead were easier to espy than those between the two outboards arguing within. Each cruiser left disparate, patterned tracks of infrared, lingering ghost images as individual as their "voices" or the sleek, cadent "faces" they presented in the "now." Oh yes, each cruiser's image was unlike any other's. It was a simple thing for her to discern, at Marada's bidding, the identities of the ships lying in wait beyond the event horizon that spilled into normal space. She could yet see their wakes upon the tide of space, compacted and blue-shifted so that she saw not a simple circle of view, but a wide-angle vista including moments in the recent "past."

Having named each cruiser awaiting them and pinpointed their positions for Marada, she stayed alert to further orders, pondering the argument still flashing in both outboards' infrared auras, red and gold and green swathes around the brothers' forms.

Though one was her pilot and the other his sibling enemy, though they were as different as space from sponge, it was their sameness that confounded her, had been the object of her meditation the entire time they had been together on board. The emotion that spat between them was endlessly fascinating to her. The brother Chaeron's presence, so similar yet as different as one unlike parent's genes could assure, made Marada somehow different also.

It was the seat of that anomaly in her beloved outboard she sought in the interaction between the pair. She still had not found it when two moments of real-time obtruded.

The first of those she had expected: Marada, unable to subvert Chaeron's purpose directly, subvocally ordered her to send a warning screaming out to the other cruisers lying in wait beyond the portal out of sponge.

The second she had not expected: at the edge of her sensing, the cruiser *Marada* rode at space-anchor.

Shebat Alexandra Kerrion bent low over David Spry. Softa's skin was pale, glittering with sweat. Moving him into *Marada* and using the control couch for his life-support had been the cruiser's idea.

She had been surprised when the space-enders granted her request. But then, things had changed since Valery's arrival. She knew that some of that change was due to the

miracle she had performed upon the child, but she knew
also that Valery Stang was as nearly in control as it
seemed anyone might ever be of the space-enders. And
Valery "needed" the cruisers *Bucephalus* and *Marada*, so
he said. More, he "needed" Julian and Shebat.

What use he thought to make of a ship as badly off as
Bucephalus or a boy as confused as Julian, even *Marada*'s
intelligence had not been able to determine.

Marada had, however, determined a number of other
things, based upon his conversation with Valery's *Danae*,
things about whatever had occurred in Shechem. Things
about the Labayas and the Kerrions alike.

Marada was her staff and her salvation. Without the
cruiser, even as tentative a resolution of her difficulties as
she was attempting could never have been begun.

The cruiser remained under her command, as she had
feared he might not. The two space-enders were gone,
Valery having convinced their dispatcher that their presence on board was useless, even ludicrous.

Softa was given into her care, at last, while *Marada* the
cruiser maintained contact with Valery and Julian in
Bucephalus and a wide-range sweep of the space between
their space-anchor, far off the space-ender's wheel of
satellites, and the sponge-hole through which they had
come.

Marada was sure (because *Danae* was sure) that Valery
expected pursuit ships to pop out of there at any minute.
He had mentioned something to Shebat about the deployment of her ship "in case of attack," but nothing so
specific as the *Marada*'s intelligence had passed his lips.

Shebat detested Valery; her skin crawled in his presence; he made her feel unclean.

But Valery was busy trying to fix *Bucephalus*, even
while Shebat was trying to fix Spry. Perhaps he had just
forgotten that he had not alerted her previously. And
perhaps he did not want her to be distracted by a danger
so near, when she must concentrate totally on the task at
hand.

She tossed her head, kneeling down by Softa's knee,
forcing herself to expect movement from the inert form,
to expect response from the enquieted mind she strove to
contact.

She had checked in with Julian, mere moments before.

He knew no more than she, could not judge the effectiveness of Valery's ministrations in *Bucephalus*.

Shebat knew that Julian shared her worry, unvoiced, that Valery might be so anxious to regain use of *Bucephalus* that he would sacrifice Softa in the bargain, wiping the cruiser's individuality while David Spry's was still linked to it.

She must hurry. This might be Softa's last chance.

He lay sprawled in *Marada*'s epicentral command couch, tubes attached to various portions of his anatomy for life-support.

A tube-feeder pinched his nose. She withdrew its white length, secured it in its clamp. It had worn red, angry spots below each of his nostrils.

"Softa, Softa David," she called, leaning so close that her breath blew among the hairs of the beard grown on Spry while he slept, stirring the ashy hairs, as she must stir the sleeping mind behind his countenance, flat and so mild in sleep.

She had made a dream for him: whole with his friends, standing at space-end. She would not accept that the dream could not ever come to be. She would not.

She *should* not, something deep in her spoke with ringing voice, a voice she had heard far too seldom since she had come among the people of the Consortium. Another time, she would have welcomed its return, thrilled to its reverberations in her head.

Now, she had no time, no time at all:

Deep within her searching mind and deep within his sleeping one a shared moment came to be. A stretched-out hand, a whispered tease-title, a name known from birth touched Spry, coiled tenaciously among the silicon castles where *Bucephalus* dwelt. Deep down those corridors the name rang unending and he knew that it was his.

He must catch it up, to silence it. He must catch the starlight, rising over his shoulder, to stay its glare. He must catch himself before he remembered too much, or he/*Bucephalus* would be alone once again, each one lost to the other. The place where *Bucephalus* was, was complete. Outside it lay want and strife and all the disquiet of man. He/*Bucephalus* stirred, rolled restlessly, drifted apart. A sad, lonely whisper pealed among the resonant spires of their inner-space interface. In its wake they were split asunder like Siamese twins under a surgeon's knife. Agony lanced through someone who remembered once having been called Softa David Spry. Anguish plumbed some depths called *Bucephalus*, alone in quandary once again.

The Spry-comfort was fading, faded, gone away. All hope was lost like that last clutch upon sanity Spry had been to him. *Bucephalus* shuddered and faced the horror of Valery Stang within his hull, purposefully striding toward the bank of fail-safes that would end even the terror within which *Bucephalus* howled and flailed.

Into that maelstrom of loss, tightening *Bucephalus*'s desperate hold on consciousness, straight to the need to survive which had sustained him, sped the final, most horrific stimulus:

"*Run!*" came *Hassid*'s scream of warning. "*Run or face eternity! The outboards war!*"

Bucephalus heard, like every other cruiser at space-end. *Bucephalus* shuddered; roused; ran. Instantaneously, with all his might and a surety he had thought escaped long since, the cruiser leapt, knocking Valery Stang off his feet and away from the panel which would immure *Bucephalus* forever in unknowingness. As he lurched, *Bucephalus* sprang every portal wide. Every hatch and three ejection ports gaped open, spewing air into vacuum, spewing out Julian Antigonus Kerrion struggling into space.

It had been Valery whom *Bucephalus* had hoped to spit spinning into the void. It was Valery he yet faced, staggering toward the panel that would wipe life and mind from *Bucephalus* forever.

Bucephalus shuddered, spun round.

Valery, mil filling his lungs, grimly held his grip upon the console. Raising his arm, he brought it down upon the controls even as *Bucephalus*'s maddened blind flight brought them directly into the path of the lethal particle beams preceding the Kerrion cruisers out of sponge.

Bucephalus never felt them: *Bucephalus* was already dead.

Julian wheeled, helpless, tumbling amid the stars.
A scream had torn out of him.

His last breath had borne it into a deaf cosmos. There was naught but plasma pervading the dark to replace it.

He fought unconsciousness, counting silently since he could not hear himself sob. His lungs throbbed, filled with mil. All the stars grew long, red tails and blue Medusa heads. He fought not to know he was going to die. He fought death as he had fought the evil shudder that had sucked him into soulless obsidian space. He would not die.

His fists clenched, the red sear of muscular strain his bulwark against unfeeling death. He knew that he was losing: around his sight's edge, green snakes and black mist were creeping inward. He did not, could not, would not die.

He cartwheeled, head over foot, unable even to stop his spin.

He tasted choking, bloated tongue. His eyes wide to the universe, he tried to make out cruisers glinting among its lights. But the lights were glowing, growing, already vanquishing the dark, as if every centimeter of his skin had learned to see. It came to him, in the distended time that crises offer as their single amelioration, that theoretically any skin cell could develop into an eye.

Was it happening? Was he all eyes? Was he dead, without the grace to know and keep still? In the gray-green glowing space of semiconsciousness, while the mil within him and without him pulsed and tingled and seemed to swell, he was suffocating, kept apart from the healing light. Hardly knowing that he did so, he stripped off his Kerrion red-and-blacks, and went naked to the void. There was a sizzling trill, climbing his flesh, echoing within him in every crevice.

He touched his chest: it was still. It neither rose nor fell.

Why was he not cold? For he was not cold, but somehow seemed to be basking like a sunbather in warm, loving light. No, he was not cold.

And though his lungs were choked up with mil, unmoving, his heart beat. He could feel his pulse, warm like the kiss of space on the mil that transduced his skin, so that it lapped up energy from the surrounding plasma, photosynthesizing and transferring that energy directly into him.

He wriggled, feeling space suddenly thicker, no longer like vacuum to his metamorphosing awareness. His new epidermal layer sensed the currents around him, stopped his spin by aligning itself with the flux of the cosmos. The phosphorylization of light into energy had a by-product that seemed to fill his intestines, stream out between his legs through transmuted orifices he had never before used in such a way.

He forgot his name, he forgot his phylum. He kicked his feet and laughed silently amid the stars.

No one saw the siren gliding away from the battle save the cruiser, *Marada*, who watched with interest but did not interfere. He had orders to follow. He had not been asked the question: *what happened to Julian?*

What had happened to *Bucephalus*, and to Valery Stang, was clear, ugly and final. They were no more, their component particles dispersed through local space.

Shebat, on board the *Marada*, wept heartbroken sobs in David Spry's arms.

Danae, though she was Kerrion Five, Chaeron's own cruiser, keened a dirge for her pilot that raised the hackles of every intelligence privy to cruiser-consciousness. The *Marada* could not blame her. She would be wiped before many moments passed: the remaining rebels already discussed it, on board her, in the same breath as they discussed surrender.

Other than himself and *Danae*, there was not one cruiser at space-end undamaged, save for the attackers' ships which had come out of sponge.

Not one of the space-end cruisers could so much as determine its name. *Bucephalus* and another had been totally razed. The rest, paralyzed, might never again speak with the same voices they had once used to whisper into the wind that brushed all cruisers' thoughts alike. Who knew what other atrocities the outboards were capable of perpetrating? They had done this awful thing . . . what worse might yet transpire? The cruisers waited for whatever outcome must eventually befall them.

Eventually, Spry calmed Shebat, who had seen *Bucephalus* flare into a tiny sun; nova; subside.

Eventually, he calmed himself, and thought to turn *Marada*, who sped still toward the far side of dusty Scrap, back toward the coordinates of confrontation. He mumbled to Shebat, who huddled against him, to her heaving shoulders, to her raised and disbelieving eyes:

"Don't think about it," he advised, "not any of it. Later, maybe, we'll think about it. Now, I thank you for my life. . . ." He saw the horror dancing behind her stare and knew that he, too, would have to waltz with the specter, when he dared. *Bucephalus!* "Now," he continued, adamant, "we must turn *Marada* and head back there."

"Why?" she husked bitterly, in a voice unbecomingly wise for one of paltry years.

"To save what we may, for the others."

"I don't know if *Marada* will—"

Spry almost slapped her, managed to only shake her fiercely instead. "Never talk that way: *we* are in control. We are *always* in control. What communion we feel with the cruisers is part myth, part mirage. I know. I have been long within their realm. Do not ever let me hear you speak that way again."

"I'm sorry," Shebat mewled, shrinking back from Softa's intensity.

"Don't be. Be a pilot, or step aside. If you've lost your nerve, I'll take *Marada* back for you. . . ."

"No!"

"Then get to it. I want you to put me in touch with the command cruiser of the enemy."

"Of the enemy? You do not know?" Shebat shook herself, as if she could shake off the paralyzing emotions still clutching at her reason. Again, watching her, Softa shivered inwardly, half with disquiet and half with delight. The child was veritably indestructible—and hardly a child except in his memory. Her next words chased the welcome humanity of simple emotion away, perhaps forever:

"You don't know. It was the arbiter Marada's cruiser, the *Hassid*, which gave direction to the assault."

"Jester's luck," he chuckled, rather than face the ice those words caused to encase him. He recollected the dream he had had, wherein Marada sharpened his cutlery over Spry's helpless form . . . Marada Seleucus Kerrion!

But she was not content with his open-mouthed bark of dismay.

She had to add: "And my husband, too, is with him.

The *Marada* says they came seeking what they have lost: the arbiter, his son; the consul, his wife. Must I return with him?"

He wanted to say: "Not if you do not wish it." He could only manage: "I don't know, Shebat, truly. I don't know."

Her lip plumped out, her silvered eyes accused him: *traitor*. But she slipped wordlessly from his grasp and into her couch.

Watching her pilot *Marada*, he knew pride. He had done his work well. She was more than adequate. But then, she had been a natural. And he had been a pawn in the Jester's game, once again.

This time, he was not so sure he could maintain his stance on the periphery of disaster, but might be drawn into its very center. Already, he could feel the pull of Fate's handmaidens, hanging onto his ankles, drawing him down into a sucking whirlpool which had no end.

Softa David Spry examined his hands, found them trembling and speckled with jewels of perspiration. He could count on the fingers of one of them the times in his life that he had been afraid. This was one of those, and he would have to face his fear and face it down, or be vanquished by it.

He set about composing himself while waiting for Shebat to give him a channel through to the Arbiter Kerrion and the Consul Kerrion.

When she had almost secured it, he realized that first he would have to get hold of someone among the space-enders who could delegate him the authority to negotiate a truce.

Before he did that, he had need to make certainty out of supposition: he turned his hand to the task, first getting Shebat's permission to activate the *Marada*'s copilots displays.

She gave it, almost coquettishly.

Then he reran the *Marada*'s tapes of what had happened at the place where sponge met space near space-end, examining that small sliver of sequential time in which a brace of cruisers went to their deaths on account of man. He ran the displays in the infrared, as magnetic flow, X-ray . . . he ran them—because they were so short and yet their effects so devastating—every way he knew

how. When it was done and he could find no more ways to
view the event, he still could not believe it, could not
make himself understand it: *Bucephalus* was gone.

The cruisers understood. Their disquiet was something
he did not want to know, that he avoided seeking out, but
that came to him as if through his fingertips where they
touched the console.

Shebat had the space-enders on-line. Without another
movement, he received the call. *Marada* the cruiser took
that instant to contact him.

While Shebat spoke his name repeatedly, he blinked
away his astonishment at what the cruiser *Marada* had
become. Command cruiser . . . certainly; but much more.
A furtive shiver thrilled him: he had told Shebat long ago
the *Marada* was too powerful a ship for her. Then, he was
but a shadow of the brooding intellect who greeted Spry,
who spoke a few words of caution, who subsided into
mere obedience once again.

If *Bucephalus* had been like *that* . . . but *Bucephalus*
had not been; *Bucephalus* was gone from cruiser-consciousness, from his own consciousness, from any possible
resurrection. He found himself wishing that it had been
Marada who had been eradicated, then hurried to cover
his thought.

The smooth, effortless touch of the command cruiser
reached him: *"We are all of us confused. I take no
offense."*

It was only after he had promised the space-enders he
would do his best for them, and received from them their
word to abide by whatsoever agreement he could make,
that Spry thought to wonder why Shebat had been able to
raise the space-end committee, a difficult task, quicker
than she could contact the *Hassid,* so much easier an
operation.

He thought about it, transiently, but it was pushed
away again by the space-enders' reminder: *"We still have
a few cards to play,"* as it had been obscured by the
Marada's greeting (or was it a warning?).

His mouth was dry and fouled, his lips sticky, reluctant
to part. Why should he expect the girlchild to be any
better composed?

"We still have the baby, do we not?" had prompted

Harmony; *"We still have Shebat."* Her dead, cold voice conjured up the nightmare visage even over the static-filled com-line. He had not answered, only made a shushing sound.

Too much, too much to fit into his mind, to integrate when so much of him had so recently been intent on total segregation from his kind. Or was it secession? He wished he knew. Once more, he did not like the person events were forcing him to become.

"Shebat," he said softly, gently. "Let's have that line in to *Hassid*." He twisted around to see her, enthroned in the epicentral control central that had been his sickbed so recently.

She avoided his eyes. Her black curls hid her face, tinged warm in the indicator spill. But all around, the *Marada*'s meters responded to her internal chaos with flares of color.

"Can . . . can you do it yourself? I cannot. I do not feel well."

"You do not feel well?" he repeated, disbelievingly, making it a taunt.

Then her head came up. Her white teeth flashed, bared. "You cannot expect me to call him, to talk to him as if nothing had ever happened!"

Spry took a deep breath and expelled it, counting slowly. "Shebat, this has got to be a joke."

"You like jokes! You told me yourself: they are our only life-preservers in this fearful storm." She stood abruptly. A red light lit behind her. "Do it yourself."

"Sit down. Run that board or I will."

She set up the line he had asked for, but her voice was so small and sad that it made Spry wonder if even life was a worthwhile struggle in light of such despair.

The arbiter's bearded face came up on his right-hand monitor, chiaroscuro.

Finger poised over the transfer button that would exchange Shebat's picture for his own, he hesitated, transfixed by the play of emotions running over Marada Kerrion like conflicting readouts.

"Shebat?" Between the arbiter's brows, two parallel lines deepened. "Are you hurt?"

"Kerrion One," she replied archly, "to your commander, Kerrion Two."

"We're not quite sure who that is, right now," Marada drawled, shifting on the screen, his miniature hands lacing behind his head. The narrowed eyes roved around as if searching for something. "Are *you* commander of the rebels, then, and not hostage as I have so far presumed?"

"Careful!" It slipped out of Spry unbidden, for he knew Marada well, and the sort of jargon arbiters employed.

Shebat's lip twitched. She said, "I am piloting, temporarily. The commander of the rebels was Valery. He is dead with *Bucephalus.*"

"So you are Kerrion One?" Marada's tone was different, soothing, yet the tight squint around his eyes lingered.

"We were before that, have been since *Bucephalus* went mad entering sponge. It was necessary. . . ."

"I see."

"Do you? Will you put me through to whomever it is that will accept the space-enders' surrender?"

"Want to talk to Chaeron, do you? That's easy enough."

A warning rang in Spry's head. He signaled Shebat, but she did not see. With one hand, she stabbed the transfer mode that activated his monitor for communications. With the other, she rubbed at her tears.

As Chaeron's voice rang sonorous around the *Marada*'s control room, Spry's peripheral vision saw Shebat slump down, weeping.

It took Spry an instant to draw his attention from the girl.

Chaeron was saying: "My brother tells me I have no authority here. Be that as it may, Spry, I am going to finish what I have started, if my wife and my brother's son, and, of course, yourself, are not immediately surrendered up to us, along with the cruiser you have commandeered!"

"Cheap at the price, Consul. What else do you want?"

"What I want,"—his beauty became ephemerally a horrific beauty as might befit some haughty angel of death—"my brother, and not any sense of humanitarianism, denies me. After all—" He leaned forward, so that the foreshortening of his image in the monitor made him seem some great-headed dwarf. "—I have no authority here, except over Consortium citizens. If I did, I would incinerate you all to the last impotent soul. But the arbiter, here, claims jurisdiction over that, so . . .

"I tell you what you do, *Softa*," smiled Chaeron so that Spry shuddered perceptibly at the sound of his own name, "you draw up alongside us, and transfer aboard. Bring my wife and Marada's son with you. We will have our end straightened out by then. Whatever the outcome for the bulk of them, *your* fate is set."

The screen went blank. All that could be heard in the *Marada* was the sound of Shebat's muffled weeping: a sniffle, a gulped sob.

He felt, transitorily, that he must join her. Then he blinked away the blurriness and spoke to the cruiser:

"You heard him, *Marada*. Match and subordinate yourself to *Hassid*."

It was a millennium since Shebat had been aboard *Hassid*. The magic of the cruiser had been stripped away. The kindly tutor was now the instrument of her downfall.

Shebat whispered to Softa David: "It will be well, in the end. They are my family." But she did not believe it.

She could not believe it: she had seen Marada look at her like a piece of perplexing data in need of interpretation.

They proceeded through a crowd of black-and-reds interspersed with a few familiar faces.

There were too many people on the *Hassid*, all looking at her, staring into her, whispering innuendoes about her as she passed. She found as she cleared the press and stepped into *Hassid*'s control room that she had caught Spry's hand, and could not let it go.

She heard the baby cry, somewhere behind her.

They had taken no chances: they had sent an escort over to the *Marada*. She had been afraid, briefly, that those would perpetrate harm in the cruiser, and then chided herself: Marada Kerrion was in charge, Chaeron had so much as told Spry. The arbiter would not do that. But the men had scooped the child away from her, as if she would hurt him, whom she had saved from eternal dreaming.

Softa's hand squeezed hers, demanded withdrawal.

The two Kerrions waited, the fair and the sanguine.

Behind her back, the lock hissed shut. She looked

around, saw two black-and-reds at either side of it. Then she glanced at Softa, who was not looking at her, but met a stare from Marada Seleucus Kerrion filled with murder, a stare she had never dreamed his kind eyes could mount.

But then, she had never known him, but only known what she wished him to be, what she had fantasized him to be.

She sensed Chaeron's concern, his inspection, his approach. His voice whispered: "Be careful. Volunteer nothing. Let me help." His lips, as he spoke, did not move. He reached out a hand. It fell on her back, comforting. She fought the urge to turn in to his embrace.

Before Marada Kerrion, she could not. She shook Chaeron off and stood alone. He almost spoke again, but the words died on his lips and he wiped them away with his palm.

The gesture reminded her of Parma, and she squeezed her eyes shut that she might keep out the greater remonstrance which must be waiting for her on Draconis.

After that one interval in which Chaeron whispered, the silence grew long.

In it, Spry paled. In it, Shebat's calves began to tremble so that she fought to lock her knees.

Near his control console, Marada Kerrion touched a switch.

"If you choose, Spry, you can present your side of this." He stood at ease, weight on the balls of his feet, hands riding his hips: he had already won.

"For the record?" Spry spat bitterly.

"Of course."

"What are the charges against me?"

Marada chuckled. "I think it will be easier to have you read our indictment; speaking it will take too long." He slid his eyes leftward; a monitor jumped into life, filled with print.

Shebat would never forget his face, paled with fervor, or his eyes sliding over her, colder even than Chaeron's had been that first conjugal morning when she had spurned him and her own passion of the previous evening both with a slap and a snarl, sending him wordless from the room.

She could not deny, standing with them both and with Spry (who of all of them deserved her allegiance most), that it was to Marada her heart belonged. In the most unsuited of circumstances, she longed only to change his frown to a smile of tender welcome.

When Spry stepped back from the monitor, he said: "So?"

"So, my dear Master Pilot," Chaeron spoke first, "you are stripped of your license. You will never pilot another Consortium vehicle. Thus, since the space-enders no longer have possession of any stolen ones, you are effectively grounded. Your subversive ring is broken. Your friend, Baldwin, will be joining you here quite soon—"

"That will do, Chaeron," advised his older brother. "All he says is true. I am afraid you are here to a certain extent under false pretenses: I have no intention of negotiating with you. Wait—!

"Good. Now, though I have no jurisdiction here unless invited, your overture served as that invitation. As far as I am concerned, and as far as my superiors are concerned—" And here he reached behind him and without looking disengaged the arbitrational cube from its in-dash housing, hefting it in his hand. "—as far as cube arbitration is concerned, this matter is closed." The cube was fully colored: red, with stripes of orange. "The decision, as you can see, is not favorable to your endeavor on the whole." He tossed the cube to Spry, who caught it and held it as a man might hold a deadly viper.

"However, since you are already at space-end, since you have performed, however unintentionally, some few services for the Consortium, I am not going to take you back into Kerrion space. The necessary operation—"

"Marada, you cannot do this! Spry was trapped, unconscious, in *Bucephalus* until you attacked! He had nothing to do with this—"

"Young woman, keep silent. It does not matter whose hand was turned to this task, but whose thoughts precipitated it." So distant was Marada, as if she had never crept into his bed while he dreamed—but then, she reminded herself, he did not know. He did not know. . . .

"I will not keep silent! You promised me, should I ever desire it, no matter what the circumstance, that I had merely to call you, and you would deliver me home. Well, Marada, I am calling you. I have had enough of your

Consortium and enough of your tortuously conceived ethics, more decadent than the evils you seek to stave off thereby. I am calling you: Take me back to Earth!"

"Shebat!" Chaeron and Spry objected in chorus.

But Marada, nodding, said only: "I am relieved. It is the best choice for you. Should you stay, you would suffer more anguish than your primitive, reactionary behavior warrants. And yet—"

"You sanctimonious—"

"Now, Chaeron, do not try my patience. I have many things to sort out. I might get confused as to the magnitude of your own errors, or become convinced that they were not errors at all, but intentional malevolence."

"She is my wife!" Chaeron choked incredulously, as Spry tossed the cube onto *Hassid*'s console and took Shebat under his arm.

"Then go with her, little brother. We own Orrefors space, though it is troublous. Go with her, and good riddance. I care not one whit for your hide nor your plans nor even your propinquity to me. In fact, it would be a relief and a boon to the family."

"Kiss my ass," suggested Chaeron.

"Not very likely, considering that it is up to me whether you will still be able to call it your own tomorrow. Chaeron, for the last time: until we are back in Kerrion space, your words have no weight. I urge you to save them. They may fly back upon you, elsewise."

They all subsided, looking around at each other and at the two determinedly straight-faced black-and-reds whose chins were tucked into their chests, standing rod-straight by the portal.

"Gentlemen," said Marada Seleucus Kerrion, "escort Spry to our surgeon. Tell him to be gentle, the man has got to be fit to be shuttled down to his cohorts."

Shebat, finally uncaring that Marada watched, wriggled in Spry's loosening grasp:

"Softa, I am sorry. It is all my fault. . . . Forgive—"

"Ssh, ssh. Nothing is anyone's fault. Things just happen . . . men come to cross-purposes. He could have treated me less kindly. Let it go. I'll see you again, don't give me any long farewell. And don't be afraid. We have what we *have* had, each one of us. No more is allotted to any man than that." He kissed her, lightly, a dry kiss that made her forehead tingle.

She watched him ease his way out between the large guards, small and compact, bearing undaunted, as if he went to a new berth rather than sterilization and confinement away from all that he loved. Without a cruiser, what was Softa David? In point of fact, without a cruiser, what was any pilot?

She whirled, her pupils for the first time dilated with horror: "My cruiser, too, goes to Earth with me. Parma gave me the *Marada*. You cannot—" her voice seemed to lose its strength, grew tremulous—"take him from me." Then almost inaudible: "Please!"

But the arbiter was already shaking his head to and fro in negation. The corners of his mouth, within their fringe of beard, pulled in, making deeper shadows that reached up to either side of his nose. His limpid, poet's eyes seemed to soften, then glaze hard.

"I understand," he sighed. "Believe me, I do. But you have made it impossible for me to help you, other than fulfilling your request to go back whence you came. For all of us, it is best that you stay there."

Chaeron was sitting on the padded bumper of *Hassid*'s curved dash. His legs crossed, elbow balanced on knee and chin on fist, he watched his brother like a man viewing some distant holocaust. "Marada, leave off. I'll give her the damned cruiser if I like. There's nothing you can do about it."

"It is too bad for you both that what you say is not true. Chaeron, I am tired and, most especially, I am tired of you. Since we must finish this in Draconis, what say we put it aside until then?"

He reached over, stretching for the arbitrational cube Spry had tossed onto the console. Grasping it, he replaced it in its box.

"You do not mind," Marada said over his shoulder to Shebat with just a hint of a smile as if they discussed a pleasure outing, "stopping by Draconis on your way back to Earth?" He spoke in Shebat's language, suddenly, so that she had trouble making sense of his words, so that Chaeron could not understand at all. "It will be your last trip through spongespace; if it is longer, then there is no harm in that."

For a moment, she saw a flicker of hope. Then the hardness of his face extinguished even that.

Not knowing what else might serve, she appealed to Chaeron: "Please, don't let him take my cruiser away. Please." She found herself sinking down on the bulkhead, vanquished by tears. "Please, Chaeron, don't let him."

She did not see the hatred like weaponry flashing between the two brothers. She did not see anything but the bulkhead rippling through her tears, and then a hand that reached down to lift her up. The hand had auburn hairs fleecing it, and a strong arm attached to it on which she had to lean.

His nose brushed her hair, his voice wafted centimeters to her ear. "It is too early to give up hope. We will see what my father has to say."

Marada, to the accompaniment of the opening of the control room's doors, excused himself: "I must go see to my son."

When Shebat looked up, they were alone. So she said to the space where the doors had shut behind the arbiter: "I saved your son from years of unknowingness, brought him out of the well of dreams. Is this how you repay me?"

"Shebat, Shebat," soothed Chaeron, not listening, knowing only that he had her back again and he would not bow down to Marada's determination of her fate. Seeing that she yet wore the bracelet he had given her as a betrothal gift, he turned it.

She looked up at him through red-rimmed eyes, but what he longed to see in them, though he spied it, was not for him, but for Marada, who wanted no woman's love at all.

Some time later, when Chaeron judged Shebat sufficiently calmed, he raised her tearstained face to his. "There is something I must ask you, that Marada, my beloved brother, would not think to ask you, that I do not want to ask you. . . ."

"Ask, then."

"Where is my little brother, Julian?"

"Oh . . . Oh, Chaeron!" Then her eyes grew very wide and brightly shining in them he saw the answer he had hoped so not to hear. When she said: "He might have been transferred off *Bucephalus* before . . ." neither of them could pretend it might be true.

After a time, Chaeron said, "So that is that. Julian is gone. Marada will say that I killed him. Perhaps I did. . . . If not for my mother, Shebat, I think I would go with you."

"I am sorry," she said.

"He came with you willingly, did he not?"

"He insisted on coming."

"Then he chose it. But still, it hurts. I had a dream from which I woke up crying. . . . My mother was in it, and Parma, but I do not remember Julian being in it."

"Chaeron, I—" And then she could not finish it, but only stare into his battlefield of a face, where Kerrion composure sought to vanquish the assaulting tribes of grief.

So it came to pass that Julian Antigonus Kerrion was stricken from the Consortium census, though while Chaeron was first staggering under his burden of loss, a certain siren glided up to the *Hassid*'s midship port, drawn thither by a distant, compulsive need that had no words on it, and put his palms, then his blue, softly glowing lips against the glass.

But no one ever paid much attention to Julian, even when he was still a man.

Marada had much more to concern himself with than Julian: he must finish what he had started with Spry. It was this matter that took precedence over even his desire to see his son. He hurried.

As he entered the makeshift emergency hospital (which had once been his beloved Iltani's room and which, save for Spry, they had not needed), his steps slowed.

So consumed was he with the closing down of his investigation, he hardly noticed that the surgeon's assistant had nearly prepared Softa Spry:

His loins were lathered with foam and his knees drawn up.

"Doctor," called Marada, motioning the white-coat near. Then: "Don't sedate him, yet. Get everyone out of here."

The man had been ejecting a stubborn air bubble from a syringe. He lowered it, his mahogany face questioning, but obedient. "How long will you be, sir?"

Marada leaned near and whispered something in the

man's ear which sent him scurrying to gather up his cohorts.

Marada waited, arms crossed, until all had disappeared out the door. Then he asked *Hassid* to assure their privacy and slate the entire proceedings.

Then he approached David Spry, who watched him come without raising his head, accepting the inevitable like some animal run to ground.

"You don't mind if I don't rise?" The smile was wan.

Marada found his knuckles cracking behind his back. He pulled out his hands and spread them wide. "David, I could not succeed in wringing a confession out of you. Not even with that bloodchilling little scene, not even with this. You will negotiate a truce for the space-enders, you want me to believe, yet you are not one of them?"

"Don't tell me you're having second thoughts, hot stuff? Kerrions are constitutionally incapable of it."

"Are we? Don't let me stop you. . . . Go ahead, you're making me feel better about all this."

"Do you want something, Arbiter? I'd kind of like to put this whole thing behind me, since I can't avoid it."

"Embrace your fate, eh? You make a poor stoic, David. Your face is white as those sheets, and your eyes will haunt me forever."

"I know how sensitive you are, Marada. Forgive the imposition."

"There is a way out of this for both of us."

"I can't imagine what you're talking about."

"Tell me the truth."

"You mean who, what, where, when, and why? Sorry, I'm a rotten journalist." Spry's knees moved in the stirrups.

Marada pulled over a wheeled table, pushed instruments aside with a clatter, and hoisted himself up.

"David, let me help you." The desperation in Marada's voice brought Softa Spry up on one elbow.

"Go ahead." Cautiously.

"In the end, there can be no bargain. Your crimes are too grievous; there are too many of them, extending back to old Jebediah's murder.

"But that does not alter the fact that my brother's penchant for violence has given the space-enders, most especially you, since Valery can register no objection any longer, cause for complaint. It is true that no justice can be meted out before due process, and that Chaeron has acted unilaterally, from passion."

Spry sat up, in the process smearing the shaving cream over his belly.

"So," Marada continued, "I will offer you your potency in exchange for your agreement that no demand for redress be made, now or at any later date, by you or any space-ender against the house of Kerrion."

"That's all?"

"That's all. You have lost your citizenship, your pilot's license, your cruiser. It seems to me that is sufficient punishment, so far in advance of the determination of any crime."

"Put me out of your ship and out of your mind! I'm more than ready to go!" Spry grinned, grabbing up a towel and swiping at his foam-covered loins.

"End: *slate*," drawled Marada. "I'll arrange for your transportation to the reception platform. It's not working very well, so the space-enders say. From then on, you're on your own. I don't think enough damage was done here to endanger the colony's survival."

Spry snorted. "You'd have to kill them to the man to do that." Then his flat nose wrinkled up and his cheeks drew taut. "Marada, I've got to thank you."

"No, you do not. Chaeron's actions are categorically unacceptable to me. This state of war and piracy allows such students of despotism to come to the fore. Tell your space-enders that if they refrain from piracy, we will refrain from retribution."

And he got out of there, tasting the foulness of disgust—at Spry, at the Consortium and the space-enders alike, but mostly at himself. Must we play out the same parts, only the men behind the masks ever changing? Is eternity fixed, that man must judge his brother, and find him lacking, forever and ever? He wanted it not to be so. He wanted it so much that he forgot to tell the medical team of his decision, and had to retrace his steps to do it.

Then, finally, he could turn his attention to the thing most pressing. Hopefully, investigation would calm the storm riding just below the surface of his façade, that storm that had been roiling since those riding in the

Marada had been brought aboard—since he had heard the baby cry.

His steps quickened. Hopeless hope brought a slick film of perspiration to surface on his mil. His limbs trembled. He knew he had heard it. He wanted so to hear it. If only it could be true, if a miracle could come to him on gossamer wings . . .

When he held his flailing, red-faced screamer's damp bottom against his arm, the sun rose and shone, a soft breeze kissed him, he heard the worms moving in the bowels of the Earth and birds screech and insects hum happily, though his kind had been removed from the music of the fecund spheres thrice a hundred years.

It was not until much later that he thought to hole up in the *Marada* and see whether what the cruiser held in its silicon brain was as remarkable, as invaluable to his quest as he had long maintained that it was.

By that time Softa David Spry was among his brothers of the pirate's guild in their antiquated, barrel-like platform, staring out at the stars.

Everyone had been gentle, commiserating, even laudatory. No one had let even a single eye flicker to his ears, where empty holes lamented the loss of his pilotry rings.

Marada had taken them from him, just before he had been hustled off into exile.

"I must have those," Marada had said, holding out his hand.

It had been difficult to disengage them from his unwilling earlobes; he had never thought it would be so hard. He had had to say: "This clemency on your part changes nothing between us. I still spit upon your shadow."

"Good," had grunted Marada. "You had me worried."

And he had walked away, leaving Spry to be unceremoniously shuttled off into anonymity.

Yet, living was better than dying, Spry reminded himself, and set about finding some work with which to occupy his mind.

It was Harmony who suggested he take a command among the rescuers.

"I'm not much of a sailor," he demurred, envisioning the primitive sails unfurled to catch the light of Scrap's desultory sun.

"We have a few powerboats left," Harmony soothed. "And as for the solar schooners, I'm sure you'd excel at that, if you'd only try." The jelly of her flesh quivered, arms stretched wide to mother him.

Later, he thanked her. Then he had not been able, but had shrunk from her embrace.

It was no more than a week after the punitive expedition from Kerrion space had disappeared into sponge headed back the way it had come that a frigate dropped a passenger for him to rescue.

He had been in deep self-recrimination, reviewing endlessly his folly, that had brought him to such sad estate. He was uplifted, reborn upon hearing the scramble alarm: at least he had something to do.

The little rescue boat was adequate, chugging away under fusion power. He had explored its design, and come away nonplussed at the jury-rigged aggregation of scavenged parts. The helmsman, in answer to his questions, had offered wryly that he should not be uncertain of the ship: it ran not on proton pumps, but desperation and the power of prayer.

He found it simple to navigate, but lonely. He must perform every operation with his eyes and hands: the little rescue vehicle had no voice, no mind.

Ahead floated the helpless capsule, spinning slowly prow over stern. The frigate had merely dumped it, uncaring of its fate.

It seemed to him unnecessarily cruel, as he grappled the little egg-shape and drew it up into the rescue craft's receiving bay, that the new space-enders were from the outset helpless, at the mercy of their peers. But it was a lesson, and a situation that did not cease to obtain: they were all dependent upon one another, here; all equal, all equally guilty and equally punished.

As he secured the bay's lock and reestablished air pressure within it, he reaffirmed his determination that no one should know that he was not quite as equal as the others. No, none would hear from him that he had not given up fertility. The arbiter had done him a great service, the greater for its secrecy. He could not afford to be different from the space-enders in any particular at all.

He opened his intercom and read rote instructions to the unseen occupant of the capsule. When those had been followed, a grating sigh told him that the fish netted from the vast sea had arrived.

He swiveled his seat round, then rose, then sprinted half the cabin's length while Lauren's lips caressed his name. Then he held her, face buried in her golden hair, listening to her paean of joy and fortune.

When she had fallen silent, he arched back in her embrace, to see her. "Are you unharmed?"

Her lids fluttered. She pressed her lips tight and shook her head, unable to speak. Then she found the skill: "As much as any, here, are unharmed."

"I am sorry." And he was.

"It is nothing," she tossed back, a thin mask of bravery over her bitterness. "I am with you, when I thought to never be again. What of you?"

He laughed, praying it would not reveal how much the curious bark of man could hurt. "Happier than I thought I might ever be again."

Having said it, he realized that it was true.

Chapter Eighteen

The Kerrion convoy came out of sponge like diamonds falling from a velvet sack.

Ashera herself was informed, as she had demanded to be. With a swish of her azure gown, she settled behind Parma's desk, a bird of prey coming to nest.

To the tiny replica of Kerrion Authority's chief controller, she reiterated her orders: "Bring them in and bring them to me. And remember, not one word of what has happened, or the speaker will tell tales of my retribution henceforth!" She snapped the connection.

No use getting too explanatory with the help.

Then she set about ordering up amenities for her far-traveling sons, the sons of blood and the son of marriage.

She had need to make sure all things went as she had determined they must go, as she had made sure they would go by having Parma interred within a day of the announcement of his death, which she had held back twelve hours for safety's sake. There had been some risk: should the doctor she had been forced to call been capable of even counting on his fingers backward to the moment that her husband had died, she would have been in dire peril.

But she had kept him far too busy with a pyrotechnical display of hysterics and loudly screamed widow's demands. Those demands, coming from the throat of the consul general *pro tem*, were in the nature of unquestionable edicts. The possibility that the attending physician could himself become the subject of this bereaved woman's madness was one she was sure the physician was made to face. He was very careful, following her every instruction to the letter.

Parma was ash upon the solar wind so soon after being pronounced dead that Draconis had barely begun to mourn. Some had not even roused to the morning. Some had barely begun to enjoy the customary festivities hosted by the victorious house before those festivities took on the aspect of a wake.

But it had worked. It was done and done well. She had preserved the seat, as Parma would have wanted.

She would preserve more than that, if determination could sway the balance.

She punched up Parma's will once more, and frowned at the green letters glowing on the screen. The status of Shebat Alexandra Kerrion blinked angrily with two appended search codes, but she ignored it. The girl had defected, fled to space-end. Her citizenship was revoked: Ashera had made sure of it. Why had Parma struck her from the record so sloppily, in such a way that his action was negated by the method in which it had been performed? Procedure was something Parma understood too well to invalidate by such an error. Therefore, his declarations in regard to her were no error; his error was a protective shield behind which Shebat could maintain her claims while appearing to be no further threat.

Parma, thou art a snake! Notwithstanding Parma's ploys, nor her son's involvement, the girl had run off with Softa Spry to space-end. That gave an ending to the matter. Ashera, in her capacity as Parma's executor, had made sure that it did.

There remained Marada, of course, to be dealt with. But Marada would not be likely to trade his beloved arbitrational guild membership for a position whose very existence he decried. Marada, everyone knew, was sponge-struck, anyway. That his blood-tie to the mighty house of Kerrion was execrable to his refined sensibilities only proved it. And there was the matter of the condition Parma had appended to his place in the line of succession: all was void if it were demonstrated that the second son could produce no viable offspring. From what Ashera had heard, he had proved his unfitness to inherit more resoundingly than Ashera might have hoped possible. Everyone spoke of the reasons behind Parma's annexation of Labayan space. No problem there, then.

Third in line was Chaeron, and though Ashera would have some trouble controlling him, she was content not to contest his accession.

She pondered transiently the oligarchic reality behind the Consortium's façade of democratic referendum. On that familiar garden trail, she came quickly to the end-point she had visited often before: the stability of view-point necessary to sound government could be assured only by consistency in administration. Though favoritism and nepotism yet existed, they were as nothing compared to the corruption that would have gnawed away at the Consortium's effective strength if favors could be curried and bought of a ruler never sure of more than a provisional seat.

Yes, it would be Chaeron. Marada had disqualified himself in a host of ways. And Shebat . . . she was there as a monument to Parma's infinite despite. Yet, she was there, and none of Ashera's younger children even listed. Julian was not mentioned, thanks to Parma's installation of Shebat in the place of the first-born, which Marada's folly had made vacant so suddenly. When the news had come down of who had died on Earth, and for what disobedient whim, something had died in Parma—or hardened.

As she realized that Parma had not intended her son ever to become consul general, so she knew that old "Camel Lips" had never really wanted his first-born to don the dignity. That was why he had gone through so much with Selim Labaya to equalize Marada's claim. The Labayan alliance would have done it, but for the defective child.

But Fate loved Ashera, had always accepted her offerings and done her service. The Lords of Cosmic Jest were for men: they received no allegiance from her. They were not of her sort. Fate loved her daughter, and received oblations in return.

She snapped off the screen and leaned back in her husband's chair, waiting for the children to arrive.

When they came before her, Marada in shabby gray flight satins and Chaeron in rumpled black and red, they shared a subtler wrap, a pall she attributed to the length and strife of their journey.

She said, "Sit down, children." Firmly, gently, she waved her fingers at Marada, indicating that he pull up another chair.

Chaeron did not sit in the wing chair, but stood behind it, gripping it so that his knuckles were yellowish white.

Nor did Marada scurry to take the lesser seat she had ordained, but came right up to the desk, laying his palms on it and leaning forward: "Ashera, we have some bad news for you—"

"And I," she broke in, "have worse news for you than anything you could have to say about cruisers or platforms." Her eyes roved from Marada's hooded ones to Chaeron's beryl ones, so like, yet unlike her own. "Your father died in his sleep just after giving his acceptance speech."

Marada pushed away from the desk, strode to the closet wall, and leaned there, his back to the room.

Chaeron stood unmoving, his gaze a sapphire drill boring deep. His nostrils trembled, flared. His head lowered. A grunt came out of him. Then his whole body trembled, seemed to crouch inward, though his stance changed only by the raising of one hand to his head. Leaning with his elbows on the wing chair, he took several breaths, each less shuddering than the last. Parma had loved him cheaply, a thing of duty. Why should he feel so terribly lost?

He gazed at his mother, thinking horrid thoughts of the dissolution of the family. Almost, he asked her how they could go on without him.

She said, as if he had spoken aloud: "We will manage."

He hardly reacted, but Marada did:

"I am sure we will." He had turned to face them, still using the wall for support. His face was bloodless, his brown eyes wide and strange. "And you will manage, despite what I am going to tell you."

"I am sure I will. Do neither of you have a question to ask? No word for your father of love? No demands to see his remains?"

"If I were you, I would have had him long since incinerated," snapped Marada.

"Don't," choked Chaeron, imploring them both. "Cease this. . . ." Then:

"Mother, in the battle at space-end the *Bucephalus* was

totally destroyed. . . . My—Julian was on it when it ran straight up one of our beams. . . . It's my fault, my order. . . ."

Ashera shrieked: "My baby; my little one; my son!" A spew of negations came out of her; her agony filled the room so that both men wept and she herself doubled over in Parma's chair, her arms clutched to her belly, weeping, weeping. "You don't have to worry about him taking your honors anymore, Chaeron! You're safe now! Oh, it should have been you! My poor little Julian!"

It was Marada who went to her, intending to slap her. But he wrestled her hands to her side and held her instead, while looking at Chaeron over her shoulder with more empathy than he had ever thought he might have for his brother.

But Chaeron did not see him, or anything but his fingernails, swimming in his wavy field of view.

When he could, he took his weight off the old leather wing chair and half-ran from Parma's office.

In the secretary's antechamber he snarled at the girl, whose face held an offering of compassion which he could not bear to accept: "Out! Get out! Send someone with a sedative for my mother!"

Then he lay back his head in her chair and for the first time in much too long merged with the Kerrion data pool.

When he came out of there, back into the moment which he had fled, he knew that he had lost everything he had once considered important. He knew the order of Parma's succession and knew that the screaming, mysteriously healthy son Marada had named Parma had invalidated his claim.

He could probably remain as consul of Draconis, if he wished, under Marada, and bide his time until the pilots' madness in his brother forced his removal. Then he might regent, until the son reached legal age. Or act some way to change destiny. Chaeron looked at every specious, dastardly move that would resecure him the consul generalship, and put each one aside. Though he was the only member of his family qualified to succeed his father, not Parma, nor his mother, nor the old crone Chance wished it to be.

And because he was that man, he could not reach out for the seat of power with bloody hands.

No more could Marada refuse to sit in it.

He went after Chaeron, as soon as his stepmother was sedated, and extracted a promise from him not to mention Shebat to Ashera.

"Why? It does not matter. You yourself have ruled she goes back to rooting for grubs on her home planet."

"Because Ashera will come to her senses. When the curtain of suffering lifts, she will not fail to realize that as long as Shebat lives she is a threat to a child of hers who might seek to supplant me."

"Marada, leave off."

"Little brother, I must call it as I see it. We have lived with your mother long enough, both of us, to know that I speak the truth. Know also that I can deal with her, as Parma did: gently, without rancor. But keep in mind that though I come to this responsibility with mixed emotion, I intend to be an exacting, scrupulously fair and *long-lived* consul general. I would not want to disappoint Parma."

"Parma is dead."

"I meant, little Parma."

"Ah, I had forgotten."

"Not likely. Will you continue on as consul here? I need you more than I like to admit."

"I suppose, if only to ease your mind that I am not busily at work planning your assassination."

"Good. Then I can leave and fulfill my promise to Shebat."

"Orrefors space? *Now?* You are truly beyond redemption!"

"Most assuredly," Marada grinned. "I have you here to see about my interests. What fear could I have?"

"Do I get a grade?"

"What?"

"On this test of loyalty. Do I get a rating?"

"You get whatever you expect. But, speaking of ratings, you had better arrest old Baldy and take a hand in the choosing of his replacement. I'll give you some names, good and bad, so you'll know if we are being hoodwinked again."

So it begins, thought Chaeron, wryly.

Chapter Nineteen

Endings and beginnings have a certain thing in common, a thing that darts around in one's stomach whispering: the change is nigh.

It felt most like an ending to Shebat.

It felt unreal, and likewise supremely real, to be standing on grassy ground with the odor-laden air blowing dust and grit against her skin.

She looked up into the azure sky of earthly autumn dusk, trying to recall the glint of the little shuttle's mantis shape as it had climbed back toward the stars. The vault, that day, had been a deep, reproaching Kerrion blue. The shuttle, that day, had been *Hassid*'s: In *Hassid*, she had flown from Earth; in *Hassid*, she had returned.

Now the past seemed faded, dream-hazy, dream-distant, dream-lost, as if she tried to catch mist in her fist.

She was almost at the tumbled mounds of the city, that was no dream.

She clung the more tightly, the closer she came to there, to her memory of the little shuttle leaping heavenward on wings of flame.

She had been to Bolen's town. That had been no dream either, but a nightmare with a tinge of mercy: no one had forgotten the grubby waif who had been Bolen's drudge. She heard her name in connection with the fire-footed bird landed again just where it had landed once before—in the clearing, a hard ride through the trees.

Bolen was dead unmourned, and the whole of Bolen's

town rebuilt slightly southward of its original sight.

She had stood a time on a rise of grass burned sere in the drought, and then sauntered down the street so like the street of her indenture with every muscle of her body cringing and every hair aprickle.

Her enchanter's boots rang loudly on the planked porch of the new inn.

Within it, a dozen folk crowded about the windows watched without breathing as the tall woman in black blazoned with red approached the bar.

The sandy-haired barkeep made a warding sign and called her "Shebat of the Enchanters' Fire," and refused to take money for her drink.

Folk whispered like bees in the rafters; shoes shuffled behind her back. Her swallows seemed loud and uncouth as she drank the brown beer, while over the clay tankard's rim the barkeep's rheumy eyes weighed something more sinister against his fear.

In the hearth's shadows a soft noise, half like a mew and half like a groan, gave her an excuse to turn away. A bent-backed youth was the source of it, in rags as she had been, big-eyed as she had been—as one becomes when all the flesh of face is starved away.

She had walked over to him, hearing the rustle of her light satins and the whistle of the breath down his crusty nose, hearing her inner self counseling urgently that she must fly, flee the inn and its folk who knew her.

She knelt down on unbaked brick and the youth shrank back, eyes all pupil and mouth ajar. From out of that mouth came inarticulate sounds; she reached out and touched his throat, felt the skin tic beneath her palms.

He sighed, cringing like a love-starved cur, brown hock of hair as filthy, body odor as rank, as any poke-ribbed dog's.

She determined to take him with her when she left, paying in silver coin on which Parma's profile glittered. The coin said: step carefully. It had come from Marada Kerrion's pocket. Heeding its warning, she went so softly to the bar that her boot heels hardly clicked upon the planks. She lay the coin down there. The barkeep's pale brow rose.

In the corners, the ragged folk were unbending, easing

onto benches, returning to their drinks.

"I need a serf and a horse," she said clearly. "He will do for the serf—" She indicated the youth by the hearth. "Have you a horse to sell?"

"I've a horse, yes indeed. Come with me." He wiped his hands on his apron.

Out in the unrelenting sun, he introduced himself, and she gave her name.

"I know, we all know. Heard the roar, and the whine—" They went into dark, in the stable.

In her heart was a sick certainty that none of this would avail: she was neither one thing nor the other; not Kerrion, nor Earthly anymore.

She took a black horse and the mute youth and told the innkeep she would take up residence on yonder hill, in the old cave there, and that any could come to her for visions, for portents, for dreams.

But she found a way to heal the mute boy, and though the healing took one weight off her heart, it was soon replaced by another:

The enchanters got wind of her presence.

She came out of her cave one ruddy dawn, smelling an awful smell, and in the cauldron at its mouth a grisly stew bubbled, with yellow fat collecting on its surface and a face she knew staring up from within.

The horse was simply gone.

Her walk to the city had been a long one, fraught with difficulties she had almost forgotten how to surmount.

She had not cried: one does not cry in New York in droughty autumn, lest the moisture lost never be regained. She had walked blisters onto her booted feet before she came to the silted river in whose center precious trickle ran.

She laughed harshly, decrying the ease with which the old ways came back. The enchanter's boots had proved to hold an unsuspected magic: along with her fine flight satins, they had kept most men at a distance.

When they had not, she had employed the spell of "passing by unnoticed," or cast a hastily constructed dream over those whose eyes followed her too long.

Marada had offered her no weapon, and she had not asked for one.

When she ran into a real enchanter, he had warned, she was going to have a problem. The Orrefors yet deployed at Stump and below had not taken kindly to being ousted on account of so distant a change in the tide of power. They had refused to hand over their installations, seeking to hold out on their own.

Marada had thought it might take a year to claim what Kerrions already owned.

It seemed to her, trudging the treacherous riverbed too dry to stink, that it would take forever. The enchanters would not lightly loose their hold on Earth's grimy throat. She had not heeded his warning to stay away from them well enough, and a boy had died on that account. Should they come after her, no small spell would serve to cloak her in anonymity. Her thoughtless insistence on living her own life had seen to that. She was Kerrion, and the enchanters were Orrefors, and though she had been ousted from the bondkin, the taint was all over her: in her walk, in her clothes, in her memories. . . .

Kerrion concerns were no longer her concern. *He* had seen to that. He had turned her out without protection into a world to which she was no longer suited, because of him. . . .

Her decision, it had been. They had spoken of it, on the journey. He would not speak of other things: not of what he would do, or what the family would do. Mostly, he did not speak at all, but piloted *Hassid* in silence.

On the night before they came to the end of the journey, she had deemed it the end of all things. On that night, like every other night shipboard, she lay unmoving but wide awake, her limbs coursed with shivers, waiting for him to slip through the door and over the barrier he had made between them.

When it occurred to her, she could not remember. It was possible she had known she would do it all along. She hesitated, recollecting her clandestine tiptoeing down *Hassid*'s softly lit corridor, her agonizingly slow opening of his door. When she had stepped into his cabin, she had almost turned and run: *Hassid* would know; *Hassid* saw all. But she had had nothing to lose that was not lost: *She wanted one last dream to take with her into exile.*

She had been afraid that the spell would not be efficacious: most of hers, cast in the cruel light of Consortium logic, had not been. But she must try.

The blue tracings came streaming from her fingers into the air above his head. They danced there, illuminating his visage, less stern in sleep.

The crinkle of ozone fluttered his nostrils. He breathed it in, a soft blue ambiance and a deeper sleep therewith.

Then she lifted the cover from him, and slipped in beside him, to try a new thing: spellsleep mixed with dream dance. Deep where matters bow to mind, she made a peace with him, and a trysting.

The next morning she had hated them both, though Marada had betrayed no conscious inkling of what had transpired while he slept.

When the shuttle had landed in the clearing, she spat at him:

"What you did to Softa, for that I can never forgive you."

"His fate was one you would have shared, should my stepmother have laid eyes on you even one more time." But his gaze slid away from hers, and she knew a lie lay somewhere in what he had said.

"That is right, I had forgotten . . . I am a criminal."

"Shebat . . ."

"Will you tell me why it is that though I am a criminal, I am spared the Consortium's just punishment, as Softa could not be spared?"

"You *asked* to come here," he reminded her, his fists clenched and his eyes well-guarded. "You saved yourself, thereby. I would have suggested it, if you had not. This thing was ill-conceived from the outset. It has not been good for any of us. Having dragged you into peril to which you were not suited, it was up to me to see to the redress in a just fashion—"

"You mean, I am too much a savage to be punished as befits a Consortium citizen!" she accused.

He flinched. "Our lives are too different, too complex. I am sorry. I cannot risk what we have taken so long to build on a whim, an experiment—"

She snarled wordlessly, slammed memory's gate. She

quickened her pace over the riverbed, muttering that she must not think about him any more. Ever. Hurrying, in light ever more uncertain as the day waned, she twisted her ankle.

She sank down there, rubbing it. Then she pounded her fist into the crusty dirt. Words cannot be taken back, nor deeds. If she had hurt them, then they had hurt her, perhaps more so. She had lost everything, whether or not she herself had asked for this fate. . . . She *had* asked, seeing his face, his disappointment, his accusative eyes. She had asked, because of all the death and because of Chaeron and because Marada Seleucus Kerrion hardly saw her when he looked at her: yes, because of that, most of all.

The worst of it was that she was too changed to sink back into oblivion. The matters she had fled trailed her doggedly; her soul had turned Kerrion, somehow, when she had not been looking.

Marada had spoken to her of what she had cost the family. She had waited, wanting only to step into his embrace as the final increment of that sum.

But he had held her at arm's length when she went to him: "You are my brother's wife," he reminded her in a strained voice, so that she thought for a terrifying instant that he did remember the dream she had danced against him.

She had sneered: "Still?"

"No Kerrion gives up lightly what he has," he had said softly, taking his hands away. Bowing slightly, he had moved backward toward the little shuttle craft.

You are my brother's wife.

She shook her head, violently, cursing in Consulese. It mattered no more to her what Kerrions had and what they did not. It could have been said that she had owned, for a few unknowing moments, the very star around which her home planet revolved. When she had been Chaeron's wife in Draconis, she would have been able to lay claim to her own world, if she had chosen.

But she had not; now she could not. Even if she had, they would have taken it from her. No, that was not fair—this had been her choice.

But the choice had been no choice at all, the part of her which was frightened and horrified and mourned endlessly cried.

Usually, she shouted it down, but now she was tired and the day was failing, and she had nowhere to go, so she must go somewhere for the night.

It was as a monarch butterfly rushed by in search of a bed that she found her pallet in an old cellar half-filled with rubble in the middle of a wide court strewn with cyclopean stones.

Once Earth had been mighty, but never so mighty as the world Marada had boosted her into as offhandedly as he tossed her upon the tall horse that day it had all begun.

She wept without tears, a dry sniveling heave for what was over, and for what lay ahead. She had no idea what she could do to survive alone in the city. But she must try. There was a chance there. In the smaller towns, she had no chance at all of being more than a drudge-wife to some farmer. If that.

She must try. She had her dream dancer's skill, and even her old gifts of enchantment seemed to have wakened, no longer compromised by the Consortium's negation.

She sought peace early in the land of dreams.

But she could not stay in deep dreaming. Her mind kept bobbing to the surface like a dead fish.

"Marada," she whispered, finally in defeat, "I can do without it all, but for you." She envisioned the mighty cruiser in her mind, his lights lit in joyous welcome.

She dreamed of him, of surfing the choppy waves of gravity's sea in his care. And she dreamed of Chaeron, of those few nights they had been wed. But it was when she dreamed of the arbiter whom she had loved and who had decreed this as her fate, that she woke screaming in the night.

She had not been three days in the city when she realized that she was so lost as to never hope to stumble out by chance.

She had met no one with whom she would choose to join forces, though she had happened upon a few who looked at her with interest.

Was that what it would be: joining forces? When she had had better from which to choose, she had chosen wrongly. Marada Seleucus Kerrion was in love with *Hassid*, as she loved the cruiser *Marada* above all men.

It was late on a night whose heat she had thought to evade in dreams that a soft singing sound from under her head woke her, shivering.

It came again, from a spot by her ear.

Sitting up in a clatter of pebbles, she leaned against the brick of the corner she had chosen as her bed.

Dumbfounded, she raised her wrist to her ear.

Once more, the bracelet Chaeron had given her sang. A soft glow came from the middlemost of the large green stones.

Shebat bolted to her feet and began to run, her eyes returning to the bracelet which kept a beeping time while the glow coming from it grew brighter, then dimmed, then brightened again as she changed direction.

She refused to reason upon it, conjecture about it. She hardly watched where she sped in gibbous moonlight among the broken paving stones.

She forgot everything but how bright the bracelet glowed, how surely it sang.

From a shadowed shelter, a hand reached out, grabbing her around the neck, fumbling toward her mouth: "Don't scream. It's all right. It's all right now."

She went limp in his grasp. For an instant, he thought she had fainted. He took his hand away, to support her more surely.

She wriggled, turned round, peering up blinking into the gold moon's light.

"Chaeron?" she trembled.

"Who were you expecting?" he grinned, as if it were nothing.

"But—how? Why? I—"

"Sssh, we'll talk about it later, if we make it out of here. There's nothing less welcome on Orrefors Earth than a Kerrion. Come on, we must hurry!" Letting his grip slide to her hand, interlacing her fingers with his, he tugged her into motion.

"Twelve coils binding," she whispered into the wind. "Be it so then—bind and be bound; both ways."

Running slightly ahead of her, he did not hear.

They ran down dim city streets, dodging a groping blind man; a scatter of tumbled brick; a band of brigands chasing a shrieking quarry into an alley.

"Back! Hide!" she whispered urgently. They flattened themselves against rough brick.

Clop-clop, clop-*clop*, he heard, his cheek pressed to the abrasive wall, peering round the corner.

As the staccato clatter neared, silence fell: even the girl in the alley stopped shrieking. A cloaked enchanter on a magnificent, blue-eyed black horse ambled past unconcernedly.

He dared not breathe; he shifted from the strain of trying to keep perfectly still. A pebble shot out from under his foot to strike a piece of metal. The metal rang, hardly more than a click . . . But the enchanter pulled the frothmouthed black up on its haunches. It wheeled in place.

Facing them, its metal-shod hooves striking sparks as it pawed the pavement, it seemed to listen.

"Seek," said the enchanter, leaning forward to stroke its neck.

Dancing, snorting, its chin tucked in so that froth dribbled on its mighty chest, the blue-eyed steed headed directly toward them.

"Run," wailed Shebat.

Even as he ran, he knew it a hopeless defiance. Discovery had come too soon.

They ducked into an alley, bolted pall-mall through it, came out into an intersection. Around them burst a deep-throated growl. Shebat's bracelet began a high-pitched, steady keen.

"Keep running," Chaeron begged, as the intersection was limned in daybright floodlights and the enchanter's horse began to scream.

Out of the dark above the glare, the noise grew deafening. From the brightness something descended, writhing like a snake in death throes.

Chaeron and Shebat jumped as one for the emergency ladder dangling from the Marada's little black shuttle. The floodlights winked out.

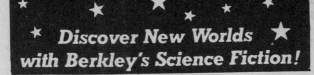